# Our Little Secret

I must have really shook him up a few weeks before that first anniversary. The wreck happened on the way to the airport en route to spending a week at Disney World, so when I saw an ad for Disney in the morning paper as the anniversary approached, it triggered a lot of sadness and memories. I started thinking about him and Mom fighting in the front seat, while they thought Winnie and I were napping in the back. He and I had never discussed the wreck, so I decided to ask him about it.

"Were you really pushing Mom out the car door?" I wrote on my slate and slid it across the breakfast table to him, too young to understand the threat such a question posed.

His eyes grew large and he took a single sharp breath before he hurriedly wiped away the chalk, looking over his shoulder to see if Juanita was still standing at the sink, intent on watering a cactus. Then he turned a glare on me that made me slink down in my chair in fear. Keeping my slate, he announced to Juanita that he would drop me off at day camp that morning.

# Our Little Secret

*by*

Edwina Dae

**Commonwealth
Publications**

A Commonwealth Publications Paperback
OUR LITTLE SECRET

This edition published 1996
by Commonwealth Publications
9764 - 45th Avenue,
Edmonton, AB, CANADA  T6E 5C5
All rights reserved
Copyright © 1995 by Edwina Dae

ISBN: 1-55197-183-6

This work is a novel and any similarity to actual persons or events
is purely coincidental.

Printed in Canada

*Dedicated to the women who had reason to but chose something better for themselves*

# Chapter One

I'm going through with it this time. Oh, I know. I've been writing the same thing for...is this really the tenth time? How embarrassing. Ten New Year's resolutions to kill him and it takes him dropping dead for me to decide to do it.

Do it. Do what? Kill a dead man? Sheesh. Listen to me. I sound like I've finally lost my mind.

Maybe that's it. Maybe that's exactly what this raw feeling—like I'm wearing my skin inside out—is all about. I'm whacko! Bonkers! Loop the fucking loop! Could be. All I know is that I've felt this way ever since the funeral a couple of weeks before Thanksgiving.

"There's just no justice," Mrs. Jenkins, an old family friend, said to me there. "Your dear father passing away in his sleep like that, still a young man. After all the good he's done, too."

I was stunned. Is that the right word? Maybe it was more like shattered. I just couldn't believe she said that to me. Not her. Not the one person who suspected, the one who made even Mom wonder about him. That woman was my lifeline. I wasn't alone with the secret. As long as Mrs. Jenkins was in the world, I wasn't alone. Ugh. The things kids tell themselves to make it through....

I feel like such a fool now. I bet Mrs. Jenkins never even gave me another thought after she asked Mom about what I said. Well, maybe that's not fair. It was probably only after the accident that Mrs. Jenkins dismissed how baths were done at our house. He wrote himself a pardon with the car wreck, the lucky bastard. After that, people looked at him in that wheelchair and never had a thought past "poor man."

I remember feeling so numb at the funeral until Mrs. Jenkins spoke to me. He was only forty-seven, so it didn't seem quite real that he was dead. At the funeral home I kept waiting for him to sit up in his top-of-the-line coffin and laugh at me for traveling all that way. "I always knew you cared," I imagined him purring through that twisted smile of his.

I hated his smile. Oh, he couldn't help it. His mouth had to be reconstructed after the wreck, leaving his lips looking flat, like they were pressed up against a pane of glass. When he smiled, the left corner of his mouth hitched unnaturally high and the right corner turned down instead of up. Somehow it still came across as a kind smile, but that just made me hate it all the more. It would have been so much easier to hate him, to kill him, if his smile looked as cruel as he was.

Of course, he didn't sit up in his coffin and laugh at me. Except in my dreams. He was really dead, his smile along with him. That must not have sunk in, though, until Mrs. Jenkins offered her words of comfort at the cemetery. As I stood looking down into the grave, my vertigo sent everything around me spinning out of control. I've had on-and-off problems with that dizziness since the accident. It's a good thing Mrs. Jenkins is a hoss of a woman like me. If she hadn't been stout enough to catch me, I would have fallen into the grave and stolen the show from him. He would have "loved" that.

My insides kept spinning long after the world around me fell back into place. I think I'm spinning still. I know I am. I have no idea what it will take to stop, either.

Unless maybe going through with it, like I say I'm going to. Whatever "it" is.

Oh, come on. Who am I fooling? I know exactly what "it" is.

I remember feeling something like this the time I was standing on the high dive looking down at the pool when I was eight. It was about a year after the accident and I was still having major problems with the dizziness. So much so that I'd missed an entire school year. He'd been on the diving team in college and he thought that teaching me to dive would help with my balance. So, there I was preparing for my next dive, wearing one of those practically see-through Speedo swimsuits that he always insisted I wear. He was sitting over on the side of the pool in his wheelchair with the clunky metal braces that he had to wear on his legs for so long.

"Now, I want to see a tighter tuck this time, Annie!" he shouted at me.

But I didn't dive. I just stood there still dripping from my last dive, teeth chattering from the air-chilled water on my skin. As I stood there looking down at the pool, my toes curled over the edge of the springboard, I knew I was going to do it. I was going to jump into the warmth of that heated pool and I was going to stay there.

I looked over at where he sat yelling at me to quit stalling and I just stepped off the board. I'd learned while playing underwater tea parties with my sister Winnie to blow the air out of my lungs, so I wouldn't float back up to the surface. That's what I did as I sank to the bottom of the pool. I hadn't planned to play tea party this time, but once my feet touched the bottom, I crossed my legs yoga-style and went through the motions of pouring myself a cup of tea. I poured one for Winnie, too.

As my lungs burned and my eyesight blurred, I

thought I saw her coming to join me and I remember being so glad to see her again. Even though that meant I was dead, I was still glad to see her. I opened my mouth to welcome her, to thank her for coming back for me, and words actually came out. I knew I was dead then. I hadn't spoken since the wreck, because of the injuries to my throat.

Then I heard the words I was saying:

"Annie! Can you hear me, Annie? Can you hear me?" And I could hear I was saying those words in his irritating, gravelly voice.

It's funny, but I didn't really know I was trying to commit suicide or that I was trying to get him to jump in after me so he'd drown, too. When I opened my eyes to see him sitting in his chair, though, his physical therapist bending over me with clothes dripping and face deathly white, I felt cheated.

Now he's dead and I guess I feel cheated again. How dare he die so peacefully! I know it's not what Mrs. Jenkins meant, but she's right that there's no justice in that. No justice at all! It's making me crazy thinking about it. And I do think about it. Every day since the funeral I've thought about it.

For all those years, I held onto the fantasy that I wasn't alone with the secret, because Mrs. Jenkins knew. Now I think the fantasy was the one holding onto me, keeping me from going through with any of my plans to stage his always excruciating death. As long as Mrs. Jenkins knew the truth about him, she'd know I had a motive, so I could never get away with it. The only thing I could get away with was making my murderous New Year's resolutions in the diaries that were his traditional Christmas gift to me after I lost my voice.

I started doing that when I was sixteen, after discovering why he gave me the diaries. He was so unnerved by my silence that he wanted some way of knowing what was going on inside my head. I never told him I caught him reading my diary the day I came home from school early with a sprained wrist. I'd hurt it when I fell off the elementary kids' swing set. If you call letting go falling off.

Anyway, the very next January I wrote my first resolution to kill him. That single entry was the only one I made in those yearly diaries after that. They always "mysteriously" disappeared from where I lay them on my bed for him to find. Besides stealing them, his only response to secretly reading those entries was to nonchalantly mention one day that he'd decided to leave his considerable wealth to charities instead of to me.

His money is what I've ended up with, though. I think that surprised me more than his death, until I discovered what was behind his decision to change his will last year: former Miss America Marilyn Van Derber Atler. It must have scared him shitless when she went public after her millionaire father's death, telling all about the years of sexual abuse. Of course, he left me the bulk of his estate after that. He was buying me off.

He always did have a flair for the dramatic, particularly the kind of cheesy drama one might find in a spy flick. So, as I sat there stunned after the reading of the will, his lawyer handed me a letter from him meant "for my eyes only." How James Bondish could the guy get?

As per his lawyer's instructions, I sat there and read the letter. Then the lawyer took the letter, doused it with lighter fluid and burned it on a silver platter while everyone present watched. How disappointing that he hadn't arranged for the letter to self-destruct.

As close as I can remember, the letter said:

Dearest Annie,

I thought it only fit to warn you, my sweet, that your estate is $250,000 poorer, because I've retained the services of a gentleman who is quite excellent at arranging tragic, untimely deaths. Should you ever slander me like that vixen Marilyn slandered my dear friend Francis—well, let's just say I paid an extra fee for the great pain you'll endure before you come join me on the other shore. What a pity you can't scream.

Love,
Dad

Who knows if he's bluffing or not. I don't even know if Marilyn's father was really a "dear friend" of his. I guess it doesn't really matter. I've never had the guts to call him on a bluff before now and I know I don't have the guts to call him on this one either. It's maddening that his power over me extends beyond the grave. I never expected that. Maybe if I'd made more than idle threats to kill him I'd be free. But I didn't kill him; I'm not free. I'm haunted more than ever. No amount of blood money is going to undo that.

The one thing I keep holding onto about his threat is how close to an admission it was. He never even acknowledged that our relationship was anything out of the ordinary, that I could even think of portraying him as less than an amazingly benevolent man. It was always important to him that he be seen that way. As the one who overcame the tragic loss of a wife and daughter; raised the surviving daughter by himself, despite his own crippling injuries; campaigned actively for increased rights for the disabled, playing an influential role in getting the Americans with Disabilities Act passed; and gave generously to almost every cause that crossed his path. He *was* all those things. Even I would agree with Mrs. Jenkins that he did a lot of good. There were times when I'd swear he was the kindest, gentlest, most generous man on the face of the earth. But his dark side, his secret self, was just as real, just as true.

I haven't always been as convinced of that as I am now. I used to wonder if he was right when he said brain damage from the wreck made me make things up.

I believe myself now. And when I think about the note he wrote, I know he believed me, too.

For so long I wanted that validation from him. I wanted him to say he was sorry, that he never meant to hurt me. I wanted him to say I wasn't crazy.

Last fall, when I was watching Anita Hill level charges of sexual harassment against Clarence Thomas during his Supreme Court confirmation hearings, I felt like a spectator to my own life. There I was saying, "This is the disgusting truth about him." And there he was saying, "It's all lies; she's a sick woman."

"The burden of proof lies with you," the men in suits on TV said to me.

"Why me? I'm not the one who did anything wrong."

"Because this is America," they said to me, "land of the innocent until proven guilty. May the stars and stripes ever wave."

"But how can I prove it unless he admits it? He is the only proof I have."

"Ah, you admit it, then. You can't prove a thing."

"Of course not. These things can rarely be proven."

"How brave you are to sound insane and have your character maligned in front of the whole country just to say something so clearly unfounded.

We admire that in you. It makes us proud to be in America, land of the brave women, home of the free men. Let us stand and salute the flag as we bring these hearings to a close. God bless America."

I watched Clarence Thomas confirmed to the highest court in the land, and I gave up on justice for women in this country. Our long-time housekeeper Juanita contacted me three weeks later. Dear ol' dad had died peacefully in his sleep. Then I learned that I would have to keep our little secret, and I gave up on justice for me. William Kennedy Smith was found not guilty of rape the next month and I thought *Of course he was. He's a Kennedy.* Now, heavyweight boxing champ Mike Tyson goes to trial for rape later this month and I think, *Why bother?*

Enough! I have had enough! And that terrifies me. I've never been quite to this point before. Sure, I've toyed with crossing the line for years, with all my resolutions to kill him. But that's never been serious. That's just been the one time of the year I let myself believe my truth, without letting his charisma and charm confuse me. This time it's different, though. This time I believe me when I say I'm going through with it. It's like I've already stepped off the high dive and I'm just waiting to hit the water. It's too late to stop. It's too late to change my mind. It's just a matter of when I pull the trigger. It's just a matter of who I kill.

I keep hearing this voice inside screaming, "No! You're wrong! It's not too late! It's not! You haven't even started." But I look around my apartment, packed boxes stacked in the corner, piles of miscellany strewn about still waiting to be packed and I know it's begun, all right. I've quit my job. I've forwarded my mail. By the end of the week I'll have moved back to his house.

Yes, I'm going through with it this time.

# Chapter Two

Saturday,
Jan. 4, 1992

It feels so weird to be back here. The movers left over an hour ago, but I still can't settle down, can't relax. I guess I'm waiting to hear the motorized hum of his wheelchair coming down the hallway.

"Where'd you get the key to Winnie's room?" I expect to hear him call out. "You know you're not allowed in there, Annie."

The keys came with the estate, big boy. I guess I can go anywhere in the house I want to go now. If I can just figure out which keys go to what. I don't have a clue about some of them.

I bet he never considered that I'd get the keys. Or maybe he did; maybe he knew I'd be haunted by him no matter what door I unlocked. No more wheelchair access problems for him. He must love ghostdom.

At least in this room he has to compete with Winnie's ghost for my attention. I think that's why I'm here sitting on her bed now, hugging her old Pooh bear while I devour a box of Twinkies instead of still tiptoeing around the rest of the house lest I wake the dead.

This is still very much the room of a seven-year-old. He insisted on leaving Winnie's and Mom's rooms intact after they died, perhaps as memorials, perhaps in denial of what he had done. Whatever his reasons, those rooms' doorways are the only ones in the house he didn't have widened for his wheelchair. That was wonderful for a while. Winnie's room and mine are joined by a bathroom, so whenever I'd hear his wheelchair coming, I'd scramble through the bathroom to her room and hide in the closet or under the bed.

I must have spent hours in her room, hands over my ears to shut him out, having make-believe conversations with Winnie to pass the time. He was utterly helpless; I was utterly safe. It was great.

I still don't know how he found out what I was doing. Maybe he just took a wild guess. But I still remember one day when I heard his wheelchair coming. I tried to slip through the bathroom, only to find the door sealed shut. Then I dashed down the hall to her bedroom door. A deadbolt had been installed. I looked up, my hand still on the door-knob, to see him coming down the hall. A hall just barely wide enough for his wheelchair to pass. I felt totally trapped. Even as a small child there was no way for me to slip past his chair and get away. The hall came to a dead end a few feet down at a linen closet.

It's funny, but I don't remember what—if any-thing—happened after that, but I never shook that image of him rolling toward me. I still wake up in cold sweats, trying to scream, when he comes to-ward me like that in my dreams.

I remember as a young teen, sprinting out of a movie theater, knocking other people's popcorn and sodas all over the place, just because a giant boulder was rolling toward Indiana Jones in *Raiders of the Lost Ark*. Not a cool thing for a teenager to do in front of her peers. Oh, well. Life with him was just like that.

It's strange that I sit here waiting to hear his wheelchair now. I mean, it's gone; the fold-up one out in the garage, too. They were the first things the movers loaded up for Goodwill. I cleared out his whole bedroom. I emptied my old bedroom too, for that matter. It reminded me of him as much as his room did. I kept the Annie Oakley poster that hangs on the far wall, but I got rid of everything else.

It's a great poster. An authentic Buffalo Bill's Wild West Show placard. That's why I left it in this house when I went away to school. He said it was too valuable for me to cart off someplace without his top-notch security system.

I never cared what it was worth. I just loved looking at it. Something about the way Annie Oakley looked back at me with her own steady gaze always calmed something that otherwise felt constantly at war inside me.

I still get a kick out of scenes of her in action. They encircle the drawing of her in her white sombrero, that trademark six-point silver star pinned to it, sporting shooting medals across her chest. Annie shooting on horseback. Annie shooting on a bicycle. Annie hurdling a table while she shoots. Annie hunting quail and deer. Annie shooting in a competition, then shooting six glass balls all thrown into the air at the same time, then shooting in the middle of a blizzard, then looking in a mirror while shooting a playing card held behind her in her husband's hand. There was nothing Annie Oakley couldn't do.

Did I mention Annie was my childhood hero? She was especially important to me after the wreck. Her father and a sister both died when she was a little kid. So, whenever I looked at that poster, I was convinced she felt exactly what I was feeling. As a kid, I pretended I was named after her, even though I was really named after my great-grandmother. Somehow being named after the Wild West's "peerless wing and rifle shot" seemed less depressing than having the name of someone who died during childbirth as a young bride.

I'm sure I'll need some Annie Oakley-style inspiration before long. Come to think of it, maybe that's why I didn't have the movers pack up his den. That's where he keeps his private gun collection and the china dolls he collected for me. I'll probably still get rid of the china dolls, but I may use one of those handguns. If I ever figure out who to kill. In fact, the more I think about it, using one of those guns seems more satisfying than my own high-powered rifle. A pistol will mean more close-up work than a rifle, so that will make things a little riskier for me, but the pistol idea is still appealing.

That whole collection was off-limits to me. For my own protection, of course. Everything was for my protection. Like all those deadbolts. After Winnie's and Mom's rooms were deadbolted, the den was next. He didn't stop deadbolting doors until all but mine had a lock. Then he just removed my door. That was all for my protection, too. Since I couldn't call out for help, he said he wanted to make sure I could always be found. He couldn't bear the thought of losing me too, after all. I guess he never considered giving me a whistle or something.

He and Juanita had the only sets of keys, so I couldn't so much as make myself a peanut butter and jelly sandwich without their presence. The crazy thing is everything was still locked up tight when I got here today, even though this is the first time in three years that I've been in this house.

It seems so absurd, all the ways he tried to "protect" me. I did need protection, but not the protection he offered. It reminds me of those nights when he'd go into his den after Juanita left, down too much scotch, and then call for me. He loved to play with those silencers on his pistols like they were toys, cap guns. Mostly he'd load blanks and wheel around with the gun pointed at me, trying to get me to call his bluff. Sometimes, though, he'd load a live clip and shoot out a window or two just to keep me guessing. I never called his bluff, so he could make me do whatever he wanted those nights.

Of course, he wasn't always like that. Far from it. Usually he was only violent after he had been drinking a lot. When he was sober, he could be fun. Likeable even.

Listen to me! That urge to protect him, to defend him. It's always there. It's like I'm obligated to use the good in him to cancel out the evil. As though the damage he did could really be canceled. Just look at me! Locked away in a dead girl's room, stuffing the gaping wound in my gut with Twinkies, terrified of an empty house, wanting desperately to kill a dead man. Who cares if he was usually a really swell guy? His occasional lapses were quite enough, thank you.

Right now, I want nothing more than to take those precious guns of his and kill someone. I don't even know who. But someone. Someone like him. I suppose the only thing stopping me is that the guns are locked away in his den. No way am I ready to go into that room yet.

I just can't seem to bring myself to go storming through this house, unlocking all the doors, flinging them open, declaring them conquered, claiming them as spoils of war. Juanita left his bedroom unlocked after she found his body, so unlocking that door wasn't an issue in moving everything out of his room. Winnie's room is the only one I've unlocked so far.

I don't know if that really counts, though, since the door is locked again. I guess it's all about keeping some ghosts locked in and others locked out.

It's creepy being back in this house. Especially alone. I don't recall ever being here alone before now. I find things I haven't thought about in years flashing through my mind like a ghostly slide show. Part of me welcomes these "willies." The part that moved back here with intent to kill. If I'm really going to hunt down someone like him, I know it's going to take the kind of constant reminder, constant haunting, that only this house could offer. Otherwise, it would be too easy to talk myself out of it, too easy to decide the past is finally over for me now that he's dead. As long as I'm in this house, I can't just go on with my life without ever looking back. As long as I'm in this house, I can't pretend that the past is finished business; I can't pretend it doesn't affect me now; I can't look the other way while others like him destroy others like me.

While others like him destroy others like me.... So, that's what I intend to do. I intend to put a stop to people like him. Not just a person like him, but *people* like him. I plan to be a goddamn vigilante, don't I? Sheesh.

I guess that makes sense, though. My whole life has been a training ground for a vigilante. It's the only thing I'm remotely well-equipped to do with my pain, especially since I have to continue protecting his precious reputation.

Even if he hadn't put a price on my head, I still have no voice. So, I can't go around like Marilyn, telling what he did to me and urging the powers that be to take the mistreatment of children seriously. I can't even be a Mrs. Jenkins and ask oblivious mothers things like, "Aren't the twins getting a little old now to be bathing with their daddy?"

The thing I can do is shoot. Better than anything else, I can shoot. When I took that firearms and marksmanship elective in college, it was mostly to spite him for making guns off limits to me, even though he knew how much I love Annie

Oakley. Before I knew it, the instructor had re-cruited me for the school's shooting team, and I'd been dubbed Annie Oakley Jr. by my teammates.

Everyone thought I was on my way to the Seoul Olympics, until I fired off some live rounds during an unexpected bout of dizziness when the coach was around. I didn't hurt anyone, but that pretty much ended my competitive shooting career all the same. Never mind that I'd only be using an air rifle in the actual competition. Now, I can use that skill again.

Even as I write that, though, I hear this voice in my head saying, "Excuse me, but we're talking about more than air rifles and paper targets here." I know that. On some level, I know that. But I'm so good at breaking myself down into little compartments just so I can function, just so I can survive, that I know I'll somehow turn a living target into something piece-of-paper-ish so I can pull the trigger.

You are living; you are breathing; you have intrinsic value apart from your deeds. That I will acknowledge about my target. Then I will put that acknowledgment behind a little door in my mind and I will lock that door. Then I will take aim at a target and I will shoot it.

Perhaps that need for locked doors in my mind is why I'm reluctant to unlock the doors of this house. Both sets of locks frighten me. The ones inside frighten me more.

I keep thinking of the Hannibal Lecter charac-ter in the movie *Silence of the Lambs*. He killed with such calm resolve, with such zest, even. He struggled with no moral dilemma. Is that what I'll become? Will I keep locking things away until I am as completely at ease with killing a person as I am with swatting a mosquito? Yes, I hear myself respond. Yes. I suspect I will.

I chose this, after all. Consciously. Deliberately. Mine won't be a crime of passion or self-defense. I believe I'll fit the category of cold-blooded killer. Unless I get some help before then. Unless I find someone to talk me out of it.

I'm waiting, Winnie. I'm waiting for you to talk to me. I'd listen if you'd only say something. Anything. Even if it were something I didn't want to hear, I'd listen.

"Don't do this, Annie. Let it go. It's not too late to put the pieces back together and have a decent life." Couldn't you just say something like that, Winnie?

Listen to me, trying to put such grown-up words in a seven-year-old's mouth. I guess I just can't imagine Winnie ever reaching this place, ever resolving to kill anyone. Even him.

I've often wondered about that, about what would have happened if I'd been the one lying on the back seat instead of the one lying on the floor board. Somehow I see Winnie making the best of it. Even if she lost her voice, she wouldn't kill just because she couldn't speak her horrors. She'd be a throat specialist, a mime. Something humane. Something to thumb her nose at his every effort to destroy her character. She always had more spunk, more courage, more resolve. I've been told that even as babies people told us apart by the sparkle in Winnie's eyes. The only real physical difference between us was a small birthmark on the inside of my left forearm.

She had always seemed more alive than me. After the wreck, he just assumed she was the survivor and identified her body as me. My left arm was in a cast for weeks, so he didn't acknowledge his mistake until seeing my birthmark again. I still remember the first time I visited the cemetery, only to find the headstone inscription hadn't been changed to read "Winnie" yet. I wasn't sure who I really was for a long while after that.

The thing that finally convinced me I was myself was when it came time to call his bluff on something. Winnie always called his bluff. I remember when we were little, we'd all three be in the bathtub between our bedrooms; a huge bathtub about the size of a wading pool, and he'd start his game.

"Come over here and sit on my lap, Winnie," he'd say.

"No way!" she'd say, giggling and splashing water on him. "You'll poke my pee-pee with your wee-wee."

He'd look at her with an exaggerated sad face, like he was about to cry.

"If you don't sit on my lap, I'll just go under water and stay there until you pull the plug. Then I'll go down the drain."

"Bye-bye," she'd say, shrugging her shoulders like it didn't matter to her.

"Okay, then," he'd say with a big sigh. "Here I go."

Then he'd slip under the bubbles without even taking a deep breath. Winnie would sit there laughing with delight, while I was scared to death he'd go down the drain. When I couldn't stand it anymore, I'd start feeling under the water for his head, so I could pull him back up for air.

"I'll sit on your lap! I'll sit on your lap!" I'd yell at the water, near tears as I tugged.

Finally, he'd come back up out of the water in a big whoosh, saying he was a sea monster and pulling me onto his lap.

"Aw, Annie," Winnie would say. "He was just playing."

She always knew. I never did. Even when he pulled the same trick again and again, I never knew for sure.

"If you don't sit on my lap, I'll just go back to the doctors and let them cut off my legs. Then I won't even have a lap anymore," he said to me several months after the accident.

A picture of him sitting in that wheelchair with bleeding stumps where his legs used to be flashed through my mind, and I scurried right over to his lap as fast as my vertigo would let me. I knew I was Annie, after that. Winnie would have just said, "No, way!" and skipped off to play.

I remember being so sad, knowing that I really was Annie. Like I'd just heard for the first time that Winnie was dead. And I remember starting to cry while I sat there in his lap, wanting him to put his arms around me and hold me tight. But he told me to hop down and go play. I remember.

Yes, I remember. That's the curse of being Annie. Part of it, anyway. Winnie always forgot. Even as things happened, she forgot them. She had the spunk; I had the memory. If only I didn't remember so much, didn't remember so vividly.

To one of my college friends, her childhood is almost a complete blank. I've often wondered if that's what Winnie would have been like if she'd lived. Kitty only remembers little pieces of things that get jumbled up into horrible nightmares. Everything else she knows about her childhood she's been told by someone else.

Her older sister and a cousin told her what her uncle did to them all. Her father told her about walking in on the uncle while he was molesting Kitty and about spending some time in jail for almost beating his brother-in-law to death. Plus, she's read the transcript of the uncle's trial. But she doesn't remember any of that herself.

Was she ever jealous of me? And me? I was jealous of her. I didn't want to remember that shit.

What a pair.

I cherish every little missing piece I have, like not knowing what happened after he came rolling down that hallway when he first deadbolted Winnie's room. I'm so grateful for those lapses. It's like having one less reason to kill.

I wish my memory had more gaps and that the memories I have seemed more surreal. Then maybe I could resist this murderous urge. Maybe the part of me that desperately wants to be a good girl would have a chance. As it is, that decent part is going to fight her little heart out, but I'll have a remember-when to counter her every blow, her every argument. The poor thing. She'll try so hard, but in the end I know I'll still be bad. It's just not considered nice to kill people in this society.

If only this country hadn't outgrown its Old West tradition of law and order. I suspect I wouldn't struggle so. I'd ride my Mustang across the plains, shooting the bad guys who prey on children, and I'd be a hero, a legend. Not vigilante scum.

That makes right and wrong seem awfully relative to me just now. Very relative, indeed.

# Chapter Three

I finally unlocked his den today. It was just as spooky as I thought it would be. The den is a huge, windowless, mahogany-paneled room near the center of the house; with little ventilation and sub-dued, cave-like lighting. Even Juanita didn't have a key to this room, so years of dust lay thick on books in the floor-to-ceiling shelves that line the far wall. Very little dust on the dog-eared spy novels piled helter-skelter on one of the shelves, though. He read them so much, he probably had them memorized. Cobwebs strung the diving trophies on the fireplace mantel together like paper dolls, and made the head of the twenty-one-point buck on the wall above them appear to wear a death shroud.

In comparison, the eighteen china dolls seemed particularly well kept. They're mounted on the re-volving panel that hides his gun collection on the flip side. The thin coat of dust on those dolls had obviously accumulated only in the couple of months since his death. It sent a chill through me, seeing the dolls as well-tended as his crystal decanters of liquor on the shelves to either side of the panel.

I'm not sure why it bothered me so much, see-ing the dolls like that, except that he called them mine. Never mind that I only saw them once a year. I guess it felt too much like I'd been on his mind, like he'd been invading me vicariously through the dolls. Or maybe the smashed faces made them feel like a whole collection of well-used voodoo dolls. Well-dusted, caved-in faces. That didn't seem natural, even for him.

He gave me the first doll on the first anniversary of the wreck, adding a new one every year thereafter. Even after I left home, he kept adding them. I had no idea he'd done that until I counted them today.

I must have really shook him up a few weeks before that first anniversary. The wreck happened on the way to the airport en route to spending a week at Disney World, so when I saw an ad for Disney in the morning paper as the anniversary approached, it triggered a lot of sadness and memories. I started thinking about him and Mom fighting in the front seat, while they thought Winnie and I were napping in the back. He and I had never discussed the wreck, so I decided to ask him about it.

"Were you really pushing Mom out the car door?" I wrote on my slate and slid it across the breakfast table to him, too young to understand the threat such a question posed.

His eyes grew large and he took a single sharp breath before he hurriedly wiped away the chalk, looking over his shoulder to see if Juanita was still standing at the sink, intent on watering a cactus. Then he turned a glare on me that made me slink down in my chair in fear. Keeping my slate, he announced to Juanita that he would drop me off at day camp that morning.

I was terrified. I kept picturing him pushing me out the door of his van, even though I wasn't really sure what I had done to deserve that. Then again, I wasn't sure what Mom had done to deserve that either, so that thought offered little comfort. When he made me work the wheelchair lift controls from outside the van, I was so nervous that I almost folded the platform up with him still sitting on it. He loved me for that one.

Once he got settled into the van, with doors

locked, he handed me my slate.

"What else do you think you remember about that day?" he asked, indicating for me to write.

I filled the slate again and again, obediently telling him all I knew: how we were on our way to the airport, and how Winnie and I were playing the quiet game, since Mom had promised the quietest one the window seat on the plane. We were so quiet that they started whispering so as not to wake us. We thought that was so funny, we both had to clamp hands over our mouths to stifle giggles. But then, Mom offhandedly mentioned what Mrs. Jenkins had said about our taking baths with him, and how Mom wondered if maybe it was time for that to stop, since we'd turn eight in a couple of months.

"Just what exactly are you accusing me of?" he asked, not whispering anymore.

"Accusing?" Mom asked, sounding both baffled and concerned by his reaction.

"I don't know how you could even think such a thing about me. I'm your husband, for Chrissake!"

"You're scaring me! I don't know what you're talking about. I don't understand why you're—"

"Fine! Why don't you just get out? Why don't you just get the fuck out of this car then?"

In the back, Winnie just stared down at me wide-eyed, mirroring the frightened face looking back up at her. The car swerved as we heard him try to force open her door.

"What are you doing? What are you doing?" Mom was screaming.

Then Winnie's face disappeared in the midst of a deafening noise, a sickening lurch.

"Don't try to talk, Winnie," some strange voice said. *Come on, Winnie, talk,* I thought to myself. I wanted that window seat. But she didn't say a word. Not ever.

I was crying by the time I finished writing for him. I held out my arms, hoping he'd hold me but he just handed the slate back to me.

"Do you remember how much your head hurt in the hospital?" he asked.

I nodded.

"That's because your brain got hurt. Hurt brains sometimes make things up that aren't real. They seem real, but they're not, kind of like when the tree outside your window seems like a monster.

"Now, my brain didn't get hurt in the wreck. Just my face and.... Just my face and legs did, so I know what really happened. Do you want me to tell you what happened?"

I nodded again.

"What really happened is a dog ran out in front of the car. You remember how much your mother loved animals. Well, before I could stop her, she reached over and yanked the steering wheel hard. The car lost control and—well, honey, you know the rest. At least your mother saved the dog. That was the important thing to her. You know how she loved animals."

What Mom loved was her dog, Caleb. A great big, gray and white Old English sheep dog that looked a lot like the dog in that old Disney movie, *The Shaggy Dog*. It was great having a mom with a dog like that. Caleb was why he and Mom had separate bedrooms. She always let Caleb sleep with her and he couldn't stand "the mutt."

After I came home from the hospital, Caleb started crawling into bed with me. Caleb was the only comfort I had during those long days when the dizziness was so bad. I could do little more than lie in bed with an arm around that dog and retch into my bedpan, while I waited for the merciless spinning to stop. Whenever I felt the rumbling of Caleb's deep-throated growl, I knew he had wheeled into the room. He never bothered me as long as Caleb was there.

Only, one day Caleb stopped coming. He never said what happened. I never asked.

"Don't you remember?" I can imagine him saying. "Caleb was with us in the car. I had the mutt buried in your mother's arms. That was just your hurt brain making you think Winnie's Pooh bear was a dog."

He dismissed so many things as "my hurt brain." I was such a confused little girl that of course I believed him. He was all that was left of my whole world. I had to believe him; I couldn't afford to lose him, too.

If only he had understood that, maybe he would have skipped the china dolls. But that wreck was his personal tragedy. The one he heroically overcame, becoming an inspiration to all who knew him and of him. I suppose it was all that was left of his whole world. He couldn't afford to lose that too.

So, when that first anniversary rolled around, he called me to his den and gave me the most beautiful doll I had ever seen. It had blonde hair and hazel eyes like me and was dressed in an adorable cowgirl outfit, complete with leather fringe and white boots. I hugged its soft, cloth body, holding that cool, smooth porcelain head against my cheek. I was surprised and delighted. I had no idea what day it was.

He reminded me. And after a lengthy discourse on how precious—yet fragile—I was, he smashed the doll's face against the arm of his wheelchair. He made me pick up the pieces that fell to the floor, and he stuffed them back inside that ugly, hair-ringed crater that had once been a daintily smiling face. Then he mounted it on that panel.

I know he meant for me to see my own face in that doll's, but for the rest of the day I kept watching Winnie's face disappear in my mind. Instead of just not being there anymore, though, I'd see her face smashed in like that china doll's face. It was horrible.

The next day I stepped off the diving board.

I left the dolls hidden today after turning the panel to expose the red velvet board serving as host to the four mounted handguns: a Browning, a Baretta, a SIG, and a gold-plated, .22 caliber Smith & Wesson single-shot target pistol. The room felt less haunted that way; he felt more thoroughly dead. I'd never been allowed to touch his guns. Today I touched them all. It felt somehow powerful to put the brokenness of those dolls away and to claim the power of those weapons as my own, as my birthright.

The gold-plated single-shot had belonged to Annie Oakley. It looked starkly out of place among the nine millimeters, with their air of espionage and intrigue. They even all have silencers. The SIG has a laser site, too. That must be new. I don't even know why he bought Annie's gun, unless it was just the sheer thrill it gave him to keep from me something I might enjoy.

I felt like a little kid who'd just gotten the best Christmas present in the whole world as I stood there cradling Annie's gun in my hands today. It made up for all the willies I'd felt earlier while looking at the china dolls.

It's funny how heroes work, how it can be so energizing just to think about them; so awe-inspiring to touch something they once touched. I felt a connection to Annie that I'd never felt before when I had that gun in my hands. Or maybe the connection I felt was with myself. Maybe adoring Annie Oakley from afar all these years has been me trying to adore the Annie I am.

Who knows? Whatever it was that happened when I held that gun, I liked it. I liked it so much, I considered using her gun for.... I don't know what to call it. For my murders? I think "pursuit of justice" is my preferred rationalization at the moment. I'm not sure I quite believe myself, though. At least I don't believe myself enough to use her gun to help me do it.

I did use her gun for some target practice while I was in the den. There's a wall near the door that's covered with a montage of framed photos of him and the various people who made him feel important by association. They're the only "family" photos in the house. If there were any photos before the wreck, he must have destroyed them. And he never wanted photos taken of either of us after the wreck. Except these. Him wearing Greg Louganis' Olympic gold medal for diving, as Greg kneels beside his chair. Him shaking hands with President Reagan. Him posing with President and Mrs. Bush, his hand resting on their dog Millie's head. Him with the major James Bond actors: Sean Connery, Roger Moore and Timothy Dalton. Him sitting in Franklin Roosevelt's wheelchair. Him at the grave of James Bond's creator, Ian Fleming, born May 28, 1908, died August 12, 1964.

I squeezed the trigger repeatedly, sending phantom bullets smashing with Annie Oakley precision into each gloating image of him. It felt somehow cleansing to use her gun on him. Even empty. I ran across some bullets for her pistol later, while scrounging through his desk. I was tempted to do some target practice on those pictures for real. But I didn't. Instead, I just slipped a single bullet into the pistol's chamber and put it back in its hiding place. That way it'll be ready when some special occasion comes along. Maybe I'll save her gun for some celebration of a victory over him. That'd be nice.

On others, I don't think it would feel so good, so pure, to use her gun. The part of me that knows I'm absolutely wrong in what I'm planning to do just can't use her gun to do it. His "007, license to kill" guns, on the other hand, will be a pleasure to use. It's just a matter of which one I'll use first.

The "when" of all this may be sooner than I envisioned. With his estate in probate until at least May, I'd planned to just wait until all of his funds were freed up to buy the computer equipment and pay for all the on-line database searches I expected to do in selecting and researching my targets. When I think about it, that seems like a pretty inane excuse, since I've already gotten a life insurance settlement that's ten times what my yearly salary used to be. Maybe that delay was just my unconscious way of putting this thing off a little longer. But when I inspected the huge, U-shaped desk at the center of his den today, with all of its high-tech gadgetry, I just thought, *so what am I waiting for?*

He must have added that whole set-up sometime in the few years since I've been in that room, but somehow finding the equipment there wasn't a surprise. That spy fixation he had was quite a consuming hobby, quite a fantasy life. I found myself feeling something akin to pity for him as I examined what seemed to be the best technology money could buy. Here were all these security monitors, a high-power computer with every peripheral imaginable, drawers packed with ammunition, bugging devices, miniature video cameras, night-vision goggles.

That whole conglomeration of power toys

struck me as the facade of a desperately powerless man. That surprised me. He was the most
powerful man I'd ever known. His power over me
was certainly without question. And his money
sure had power. Yet, something was lacking.

As I sat there, I felt his humanity. His vulnerability. His pain. I was looking through the play
things of a wounded little boy, and I felt nothing
but tenderness toward him.

I got over it.

It didn't take long, really. I started playing
around with his computer, amazed that even he
had somehow arranged access to things like law
enforcement networks and criminal records that
just aren't available to private citizens. He was
never the kind of computer genius who could break
into systems like that on his own, so he must have
paid someone handsomely. The question was why
he'd gone to the trouble.

I found the dossier on Juanita first. It was unfathomable—basically a blackmail file on the dearest woman I've ever known. He had documents with
photos of her as a young woman, indicating her
name wasn't Juanita at all and that she had immi-
grated here illegally. He had her bank records, credit
history, medical records, her son's criminal record.

He must have had files on every person he
knew; even his mail carrier was on file. I think the
only people who weren't on file must have been
his private investigators, his computer hackers,
his hit men, himself. Come to think of it, he didn't
have a file on Charlie, either. I guess Charlie was
the one person in all the world he trusted. That
struck me as somehow ironic. But then again,
Charlie never asked any questions when replac-
ing windows shot out in a drunken stupor. I guess
he proved his trustworthiness. Or maybe a

down-to-earth handyman like Charlie just doesn't have anything to put in a file.

What would it say? Something like, "Always wears red Marlboro baseball cap, even though never seen smoking or playing baseball. Awfully suspicious. Was paid enough to afford dentures but never wore any, even though constantly flashing toothless grins. Could mean something. Insists on hiding the fact that he drinks by dipping Skoal to mask his breath. What else is he hiding?" Please.

I joke about Charlie's "file," but I was anything but amused when I located my own file. It was such an invasion of privacy. He had photos of inside my apartment, which I'd purposely rented on the third floor of a building with absolutely no wheelchair access. I had blacked out every window with poster board, too. A lot of good that did. There were shots of me at my desk at work, at my laundromat, at my bus stop. He knew the last time I refilled my meclizine prescription for the vertigo; he knew my ATM pin number. It was creepy; it was infuriating. To make it worse, the computer has an audio card and the song "The Good Die Young" played continuously while my file was open. I never knew he thought of me as good—or as dying young because of it, for that matter. Then again, maybe he had Winnie in mind.

I deleted every one of those files. I just hope he didn't use any of that information to hurt anyone. I did keep Juanita's passport and immigration papers, which I found locked away in a filing cabinet. I thought about mailing them to her, but somehow I think hand delivering them to her someday will be more satisfying.

I worry about Juanita, especially now that I know how little he paid her all those years. He did leave her his Hawaii condo and a small pension in the will, but I think that was more about sending her away from me than being benevolent to her. I'll have to make sure she's particularly well cared for once the estate is finally settled.

As much as I hate that he used all that equipment to invade people's privacy, I know I'll find it useful as I make my plans, so I'm glad it's available. I think I want to eventually relocate this equipment to another room in the house, though. The den feels particularly haunted. I don't want any ghosts getting in the way of my work.

Speaking of work, I discovered he's already an on-line subscriber to the Crime News Network, probably just because he found out I worked there. I expect to select my targets from that database, so I'm glad I have easy access to it.

I went to work for Crime News right after college. I would have preferred to use my journalism degree as a newspaper columnist, but newspaper jobs are hard to get even with a voice. Without one, it was hard enough just to get my degree. I thought the database was a decent enough job at the time. I liked the idea of putting together information about all the crime that went on in this nation. When news and television crime shows used the database to research their stories, I felt I played a part in assuring that every breach of justice, every fugitive on the lam, was widely known.

After a while, though, I fell under the curse of this age of information. I knew of every atrocious crime committed, every inadequate criminal sentence passed, every case dismissed on a technicality. I knew too much.

I started clipping the headlines that felt like a kick in the gut, saving them in a box at my apartment: "Suspected Child Molester Wins Custody Battle," "5-Year-Old Raped in Crowded Park," "Boy Scout Leader's Molestation Sentence Commuted to Eight Days."

It's only now that I know what to do with them all. I'm using them for a little redecorating project in his bedroom.

I've had fun with that this week. I started out just planning to clean the room, mostly to get rid of the smell. Even two months after his death, the odor of lemons lingered in that room.

He always smelled of either lemons or booze. Or some nauseating combination of the two. Well, I take that back. He only smelled that way at home in the evenings after Juanita left, when just the two of us were there. Depending on his mood, he tended to either spend those evenings drinking in his den playing spy, or in his bedroom watching spy flicks and eating salted lemons. He took great pride in being able to eat lemons without making a face. It was some weird measure of his strength I think.

I remember those smells most from the middle of the night. He was a chronic insomniac—probably why he had high blood pressure—and he invariably found his way to my bedroom during those sleepless nights. I'd wake up to the smell and there he'd be, just sitting in his wheelchair, cradling one of his guns, moonlight glinting off the blue steel barrel; or cradling what was left of his mangled genitals, weeping in a drunken stupor; or leaning over me, probing me with his fingers.

I can't stand those smells now. The slightest whiff of either one sets off a panic attack. Hyperventilation, heart palpitations, tremors—the whole bit. I can't drink so much as a beer; I can't even dust with lemon-scented Pledge. How embarrassing.

I must have used a couple of gallons of Pine Sol this week, trying to get rid of that lemon smell in his room. When that was done, I painted his walls and ceiling blood red, and now I'm in the middle of pasting my collection of headlines to them. Well, actually I'm pasting up copies of them. I went to Kinko's yesterday, enlarged them all and made several copies. Then I started at the light fixture in the center of the ceiling, pasting the head-lines in a giant spiral pattern that covers the ceil-ing and spills over onto the top part of the walls to encircle the whole room.

On the walls, I'm grouping together little clus-ters of headlines and even some of the whole arti-cles on my potential targets. Until I started doing that, I didn't really have a concrete idea of who I planned to shoot. It's coming together for me now, in a particularly satisfying way, at that.

I've decided to give the justice system first dibs, give it ample opportunity to prosecute these peo-ple to the fullest extent of the law. Once the sys-tem fails, though, I'm stepping in. I'm putting a stop to them.

I know I can't stop every asshole who falls through the cracks. I'd need an army of vigilante types instead of this Lone Ranger. So I'm going to focus on the ones hurting kids. They're the ones who tap my rage most often, most intensely. Kill-ing them will be a pleasure. Killing them will feel like killing him. And that's what this is really all about, now, isn't it?

This new direction in my plans will no doubt make it incredibly easy to excuse what I'm doing. I like that. I won't pretend that I don't. I want this to be easy. I want every excuse I can find to justify it, so I can make it my life's work. So what if I'm not playing by the rules? Who the heck made the rules? People like him?

I'm twenty-five years old. My oldest living rela-tive just died at age forty-seven. Sounds to me like I'm more than halfway to the grave. So far, the bulk of what I've done with my life has been to struggle to survive, to keep my sanity. If I don't go through with this quest, this mission, I suspect I'll spend my final twenty or so years doing little more than struggling with the ghosts. Shooting people is a crappy legacy to leave, but at least I'll leave a legacy this way. At least I'll prevent some kids from being haunted by ghosts when they grow up. And they *will* grow up. With a little luck, they won't have to grow up polluting lives like he did or ending lives like I will.

I suspect that at some point he needed someone to stop whoever was hurting him. I know I needed someone to stop him from hurting me. Now I'm going to be that someone for some kids out there.

I can't be sorry about that. I won't be. At least not for now.

# Chapter Four

Sunday,
Feb. 2, 1992

I think I found him. He was paroled a year ago after serving only two years for kidnapping and raping an eight-year-old. He was found not guilty on charges of raping three other girls who were even younger. Here's what kills me: in the year since his parole, two of those girls have been kidnapped and raped again. They were both found wandering dazed and naked in the same field, only a few miles from his apartment. No doubt because those girls have been scared shitless by the bastard, they won't identify him as their attacker.

Gee, I wonder why? And after they were so well protected the last time they told, too. How's a justice system supposed to have half a chance when its victims won't even play fair and tattle on the baddies? Please.

*Annie, get your gun,* I thought to myself after printing out a copy of that article and pasting it to the wall. Then I went to his den and grabbed the Baretta. I drove his van over to the shooting range this afternoon and sent a few dozen rounds flying to their mark. I'm happy to report that I haven't lost my touch.

I drove to the mall afterwards. I'm sitting here in the food court, munching chips and salsa, enjoying the low buzz of so many people's collective conversations in the same way others might enjoy a symphony.

I'm fascinated with the human voice. Heck, I'm a junkie. I can rarely stand to be without a TV, a radio, a book on tape, something—anything—with words. While my friends in college wanted professors who were easy "A's," I wanted great lecturers. I couldn't care less about listening to music on the radio or going to concerts. Unless the music is acappella. Sometimes I watch that PBS kids' show *Where in the World is Carmen Sandiego?* just to hear Rockapella sing. Oh, and give me *The Radio Reader* or *All Things Considered* on NPR. Or *Car Talk*. Never mind that I don't even own a car. Tell me there's going to be a storytelling festival in town. Take me down to the comedy club and show me a comedian who can impersonate other people's voices. I'm in heaven.

My own voice, the one inside my head, never grew up. It drives me crazy sometimes when I hear this little girl thinking grown-up thoughts, using grown-up words. A few years ago I tried to change my "voice" to Candice Bergen's. I listened to her every chance I got. I lip-synched her lines on *Murphy Brown* and the whole bit. I think I wanted that Murphy Brown moxie as much as the voice. My timid seven-year-old voice just wouldn't go away, though. I finally gave up. Sort of. I still give in to that obsession whenever I catch Candice on a "Sprint" commercial.

Having a child's voice inside my head is getting hard to handle again. It unnerves me to hear a child thinking about murder. On some level I know that's appropriate. At least accurate. This is about the child's pain, after all. She's the one carrying the rage. Still, never getting to forget that, never getting to separate the adult I am from the child I was.... I don't know if it's more burden or more incentive. Whichever, it's maddening.

No doubt I've helped make it worse by isolating myself since moving back to his house, giving

me only my child voice and the ghosts to converse
with. This is the first time I've even hung out at
the mall. I don't know what's wrong with me. Gen-
erally, I like to at least get out and go to movies,
plays, ball games—something. Before today, about
all I'd done is drop by his attorney's office and
make a major trip to the grocery store after unlocking the kitchen. Otherwise, I've stayed barri-
caded in that house like some kind of prisoner to
his ghost. To my plans.

I think part of the problem is just how much I
hate to drive his van. The house is pretty isolated. A
fifteen-foot stone wall with razor wire coiled along
the top surrounds the ten-acre lot on the edge of
town, separating it from the nearest neighbors' respective walls. No public transportation services the
area, so I pretty much have to drive, unless I want to
mess with crappy taxi service. Or hire a chauffeur.

I don't have to use the hand controls to drive
his van, so the difficulty of driving the van isn't the
issue. I think it's just that the van used to serve as
an extension of his private domain, like having his
den on wheels. It has buttons that let him lock the
doors in such a way that only he could unlock them.
He could lock the seat belt around me the same
way by pushing some other buttons.

Even now, I'm terrified of accidentally locking
myself in. He left me in the van at times—doors
locked, seat belt locked—making me spend hours
sitting there alone in the silence. I taught myself
Morse Code just so I could tap out words on the
seat belt buckle. The Gettysburg Address, the preamble to the Constitution, the Bill of Rights—everything I ever had to memorize for school, I'd tap
out as I sat there. Four *di-di-di-di-dah* score *di-di-dit*
*dah-di-dah-dit dah-dah-dah di-dah-dit dit* and
*di-dah dah-dit dah-di-dit* seven *dah-dah-di-di-dit*

years *dah-di-dah-dah dit di-dah di-dah-dit di-di-dit* ago *di-dah dah-dah-dit dah-dah-dah....*

Sheesh. The more I think about it, I'm surprised I venture to drive the van at all. I'm usually more of a chicken liver than that. Maybe it's time I bought a car of my own. I've never had one. Doctors advised me against driving when I was a teen, since I'd likely wreck if the vertigo hit. And I couldn't afford one when I got older.

I have such rare problems with the dizziness now that I've stopped growing, though, I think the danger would be minimal. It's not like I'm legally restricted from driving or anything. I've had a driver's license since college, just for the identification. So, who knows? Maybe I'll start shopping around.

I'm not sure how much I want to break my isolation, though, beyond getting out among strangers more often. It seems my avocation requires a degree of isolation, invisibility. I mean, I can *never* let anyone enter his bedroom. Or his den, for that matter. Not as long as the guns and dolls are there. Even my old bedroom must look bizarre, since it's basically a storage room for boxes from my o[  ]apartment. I've unpacked little more than clo[  ]and house plants. I guess I feel like that st[  ]longs to someone else. That Annie is no [  ]

I can't afford people noticing my co[  ]goings, either. I need to be able to l[  ]stretches of time, without having to[  ]I've been or what I've been doing[  ]ally cease to exist as far as oth[  ]

Hmmm. I guess I might [  ]plants now. I hadn't thoug[  ]when I hauled them he[  ]can just see it now.

"Gee, those philode[  ]You must have forgotten [  ]

for weeks and weeks. Were you gone on an extended trip at the same time that maniac killer was crisscrossing the nation wreaking havoc and inspiring terror?"

"Uh. Uh. No, uh, I was here the whole time. Uh. My maid quit. Yeah, that's it. She quit. Just went off to start a new life in Hawaii without warning. She was the whiz with plants. They're all dying without her. I just don't have her green thumb."

I bet I couldn't even say that with a straight face. When I think of Juanita and house plants. Sheesh. The woman was a disaster. And he was just cruel enough to buy replacements for Juanita's every casualty. Oh, she hates plants....

Thinking about her reminds me how much I miss having Juanita around. I might not even take that final step over the edge if she were still here. I haven't seen her since the reading of the will. He made sure of that, giving her the pension and his Hawaii condo on the condition that she not step foot in his house again. Of course, he worded it in the will so it sounded like his main concern was that, after years of faithful service, she'd never have to work again. I knew it was really about distancing her from me. I think she knew it, too. She got one of those "for your eyes only" envelopes, anyway. From the files he kept on her, I can pretty much imagine what her note was about.

"I am sorry," she whispered in my ear, as she hugged me good-bye that day. "I want to stay, but he makes it so I cannot."

I nodded and signed that I would come visit.

"Good," she signed back.

We both smiled, enjoying the small act of defiance embodied in signing to each other. I was forced to learn sign language after the wreck. He wanted me to live as normally as possible and signing would prevent that.

When he hired Juanita, he didn't even tell her I couldn't speak. She told me years later that, for the first few weeks, she thought I was just an incredibly shy little girl who preferred writing things down to speaking. It was only after he started installing deadbolts everywhere that he mentioned they were for my protection, since I couldn't speak.

Months later, when he was out of town to receive some humanitarian award, Juanita showed up with sign language flash cards, and we secretly started learning it together. It was our single greatest coup.

"Tell me," I remember him saying, when interviewing her for the job. "I know you're new to this country. Can you read English very well yet?"

Crestfallen, she admitted she could not.

"Not to worry," he reassured her. "It won't affect whether you get the job. I was just curious."

"How will I talk to her?" I wrote on my slate and handed it to him.

"Annie was just letting me know how much she likes you," he said, reaching over and patting me on the arm. "I guess that settles it, doesn't it? When can you start?"

As it turned out, I did like her. Very much. Between sign language and Juanita's ever-improving English over the years, he didn't even succeed in keeping us from communicating. Except around him. Except about him. Come to think of it, "He makes it so I cannot" is the most she's ever said to me about what he must have put her through. I never even said that much about what he put me through.

I'm just glad he died while she's still a relatively young woman. I know she's still not free from him, but at least she doesn't have to waste any more of her life working for him.

For some reason all this reminds me of what Mrs. Jenkins said at the funeral. Maybe I'm jealous. That must be it. Jealous that I wasn't—that Juanita, Winnie and Mom weren't—among the many with cause to feel nothing but admiration for him. Oh, I know the old adage about the people we love the most being who we hurt the most. But good grief. If I were a stranger to him, I know he would have encouraged me to learn sign language or any other tool I needed. He certainly contributed regularly to a local fund to assist child victims of sexual abuse. He even got a plaque one year for his outstanding efforts in furthering the welfare of the community's children.

But me he loved? Love can sure be a screwed up, hurtful thing.

What drives me crazy is that I still love him. On some level. I think I prefer hate. Hate must have an honesty, a purity about it that love can't begin to touch. No strings. No mixed messages. No surprises.

Maybe that's what I'm feeling about that asshole who raped those girls. Hate. It must be. What else could it be?

What a great feeling! So energizing! There's a real decisiveness about it. A sense of clarity. I don't ever have to think he's adequately paid his debt to society. I don't struggle morally with whether his victims' safety or his right to life is more important. I hate him. So, of course his victims are more important than his potential for reform. His potential for causing more pain is all I'm concerned about. I hate him!

How freeing. Who knew?

# Chapter Five

Mike Tyson was found guilty of rape today. Isn't that amazing? I was so sure his moneyed maleness would get him off that I hadn't even been following the trial. Then the news came over the radio. I hopped right out of bed and broke out the gingerale to toast the highlight of my day.

His conviction really lifted my spirits. Not that I've been any more down than usual. Well, maybe I have. I wouldn't be me if I weren't at least somewhat in the dumps. Winnie was always the carefree one like Winnie the Pooh, and I was the despairing one like Eeyore. That's just me. But living alone with these ghosts.... I don't know. That's become a downer even for me. There's nothing much to distract me from the hopelessness that dwells in this house. Some days I don't even bother getting out of bed.

Today's conviction felt like a transfusion of hope. I needed some hope. I didn't realize how much until today. I thought hopelessness was the key to going through with my mission. Seal myself into this torture chamber of a house, and the hopelessness of it all would drive me to kill.

It drove me to paralysis.

*Why bother? Who cares?* That's all hopelessness has uttered this past week or so. But today a little hope reminded me that I care, reminded me that protecting four little girls is worth the bother. Today a little hope gave me a power plant of energy.

I finally moved all of his computer equipment and other gadgetry out of the den. I surprised myself some by moving it into his bedroom, but that seems to have become my mission command post. I moved all of the china dolls to his bedroom closet, too. I'm not sure what I plan to do with them yet. But something.

Today I even scrounged up the futon I slept on in my old apartment and drug it to a corner of his room. It feels like time to stop sleeping in Winnie's room. I find I have a hard time leaving that room once I start sleeping there. Bunking down here with my work may help me get on with it sooner. It's not as comfortable (or is it comforting?) as Winnie's bed. Those headlines staring down at me from the ceiling certainly inspire urgency.

This evening I even sat down with the classified ads and started looking for a car. The more I've thought about airport security and such, the better driving to target sites has sounded. I toyed with taking trains, since that's how Annie Oakley got around the country for her Wild West shows. But I think I'll need the flexibility of driving my own car. No way am I taking his van, though. I just wish I knew more about buying a car. Somehow none of the ads touted their cars as the perfect choice for a cross-country shooting spree. Guess I'll just have to keep looking.

# Chapter Six

I finally decided I need some help with this car search of mine. All it took was a couple of trips to car lots that had been hit hard by the recession. That hungry glint in the salespeople's eyes gave me the feeling that they weren't exactly being straight with me about the superior features of their automobiles. The scent of a sale worked one guy into such a frenzy that he even tried to sell me on the built-in cellular phone option.

"I can't speak," I reminded him.

He took the slip of paper I handed him, glanced at it, slipped it into the breast pocket of his jacket, and, without skipping a beat, said, "I could probably throw in the phone activation fee if that would help. That's fifty bucks, so I don't do that for just anyone. But for you, under the circumstances...."

Under the circumstances? If that would help? I just stood there for several seconds staring at him, mouth agape, as it slowly dawned on me that the recession had driven this poor man to temporary insanity. At least I hoped it was temporary.

I wasn't going to wait around to find out. I peeled out of that car lot and made a beeline for Charlie's house.

I almost didn't recognize the place. He's been restoring it for decades. It's a three-story, late 19th century, stone Victorian that was gutted by fire years ago. He picked it up at an auction for practically nothing right after Lilly got pregnant with their first kid. He's been rebuilding it around their heads ever since.

I'd never seen the outside of the house minus scaffolding, sheets of plastic and piles of building materials. If Charlie hadn't been sitting on the front porch enjoying the unseasonably warm day with a handful of his grandchildren, I think I would have driven right past.

The house is absolutely gorgeous: polished wood and antique fixtures inside, freshly sandblasted stone outside. Charlie beamed like a proud father as he gave me the grand tour. He still wants to remodel the carriage house out back for his old war buddy, Richard. But so far Richard won't hear of it. He'd rather keep his privacy. I know that feeling.

Turns out Richard came up with the money for Charlie to finish work on the house. Richard has this thing for antique cars. So, when he's not working for Charlie, Richard is forever traveling to vintage car shows and scouring the countryside for rusted-out junkers to restore. Wherever he goes, he plays the lottery. Always the same numbers—something to do with his and Charlie's regiment in Vietnam—and always the same number of tickets.

Well, he finally hit the jackpot somewhere out in the Mid-West. The lucky dog. Won a cool million about a year ago. Of course, taxes took a huge bite out if it, but still....

I was surprised by his generosity with Charlie. I have to admit I've never had a very high opinion of Richard. I always thought of him as a freeloader, who took advantage of Charlie's loyalty and good heart to bum a free place to live and a work-only-when-you-feel-like-it job for all these years.

I knew Richard couldn't be all bad. I mean, Charlie thinks the world of him and I've heard the stories of how Richard saved Charlie's life after an ambush killed everyone else in their platoon. Even though Richard was injured himself, he still

carried Charlie out of the jungle to safety. Richard wouldn't even accept medical attention for
himself until doctors convinced him that Charlie
would live. If Charlie wasn't going to make it, Richard didn't want to live, either.

"I can't live alone with this! I can't be the only
one who was there!" he kept screaming at the doctors, as he kept them at bay with his M-16.

Charlie still limps a bit and hides some jagged
bald spots under his Marlboro cap. Come to think
of it, he may have lost his front teeth in Vietnam,
too. Richard came away with a black patch over
his right eye. But overall, they healed amazingly
well. Physically, at least. Richard still seems
haunted in a way that sometimes makes him
spooky to be around. If Charlie hadn't taken Richard in, he'd probably be wandering the streets
somewhere. Or dead.

The money doesn't seem to have changed Richard. On the outside, anyway. He was still wearing
his usual black T-shirt—pack of unfiltered Camels
in the front pocket—camouflage fatigues and com-
bat boots. I half expected to at least find the win-
ning lottery ticket mounted on the wall or a picture
of a grinning him holding the oversized award check,
but I guess that's not his style. He'd clearly put some
money into the huge cranberry car he was tinker-
ing with, but otherwise Richard was still Richard.

The lower level of the carriage house was con-
verted long ago into a shop where Richard works on
his cars. When Charlie took me down there, Richard glanced up with his good eye, gave me a nod of
recognition, and went back to work on the massive
car's rear engine. He never was one to waste words.

"Oh, man. This is a beaut!" Charlie said, walking over to Richard, giving him a congratulatory
slap on the back.

The car really was nice. I'd never seen anything like it, with its long, rounded lines that tapered into a kind of duckbill look in the back. Besides, I thought only VWs had engines in the back. Shows how little I know about cars. At first, I thought maybe Richard had designed and built it himself, but Charlie later told me it's a 1948 Tucker Torpedo sedan. Only fifty-one were ever made.

"I think you've outdone yourself this time, buddy," Charlie said. "You're gonna win some prizes with this one for sure."

"Yup," Richard said, briefly flashing the warm smile he reserved only for Charlie. Then Richard went back to his work.

"Listen. Annie here is looking for a car," Charlie said, inspecting Richard's work. "She wants to putt around the country some, see the sights. Remember her dad died awhile back?"

"Yup."

"Well, she needs to get away, sort things out. I was thinking maybe a Volvo."

"Good car. Safe."

"Yeah, but she doesn't like 'em. Thinks they're snobby. I was hoping maybe you could look around some, see what else you could find."

"Done."

"Thanks, buddy." Charlie gave Richard another slap on the back.

Lilly had a plate of warm oatmeal cookies waiting for us when Charlie and I got back up to the house. We sat around the fireplace nibbling them while they filled me in on the latest about their kids and grandkids. They're a great family.

Charlie was left $50,000 in the will. Minus any "for your eyes only" notes, thank goodness. So, he showed me the brochures on the new truck he has custom ordered for his business. He's driven the same old sad-looking pickup for as long as I can remember. Richard had to work a few miracles just to keep it running all these years. So Charlie's pretty giddy at the prospect of his new toy.

Lilly, on the other hand, is more excited about the trip she and Charlie have planned. They were never able to afford a honeymoon or even a vacation, so they're making up for it with a month-long cruise. Just the two of them. The trip includes a stop in Honolulu, so they'll even get to see Juanita. I'm pretty jealous about that part.

Of course, Charlie and Lilly are eternally grateful for the generous bequest. And they hope I'll forgive their happiness in the midst of my grief. Needless to say, I reassured them that I'm happy for their good fortune.

Richard was kind enough to lend them the cash for the truck and cruise, so they don't have to wait for the estate to be settled. Between all he's done for Charlie and helping me find a car, I'm beginning to think I misjudged poor Richard. Oh, well. No real damage done, I guess.

Charlie walked me to the van as I left. "Come on back if you can't get the seat belt off," he said, with a mischievous wink before I drove away.

I forced a grin in response.

He found me trapped in the van once years ago. He got in to move the van so he could wash and wax it, and there I sat strapped in my seat. Just bawling my eyes out.

Somehow he managed to release the seat belt and held me for the longest time until I stopped crying. He even let me wear his Marlboro cap for a while and split the package of Twinkies in his lunch sack with me.

He's a good guy. No doubt about it. The only trouble is, he assumes everyone else is a good guy, too. If I'm stuck in the van, it must be a freak accident. If a window has been shattered by a bullet, I must have been pitching that baseball around again.

No wonder Charlie's inheritance didn't require a "for your eyes only" postscript. Having Charlie's blind faith in people sure has its benefits. Must be nice, trusting people that way.

# Chapter Seven

Thursday,
Feb. 27, 1992

I got a car! I never really thought I'd have one at all, much less one as perfect as this. Richard definitely came through. The car is a 1967 Ford Mustang in fantastic condition. It's black with tinted windows, red leather interior, and I fell in love with it as soon as I slid behind the wheel. Varoom! Varoom! This car was made for me. A wild mustang is the kind of horse I always fantasized about riding when I played cowboys. Now I can really ride across the country with my trusty steed, shooting the bad guys and saving the day.

Getting this car has given me an idea about how I'm going to dress for my little excursions in Old-West-style law and order. I'm going to put together an all-black western outfit. I already wear cowboy boots everywhere, but I'll need to buy a Stetson and a long, leather duster. I have a six-pointed silver star, like the one Annie Oakley always wore on her sombrero, that I can pin to my duster like a marshal's badge. I'll get a Lone Ranger mask to hide my face too, and a bandanna to tie around my neck and hide the scars on my throat. I think his shoulder holster makes more sense than a gun belt for my waist, since I won't be using a six-shooter, anyway. I'll skip the spurs, too.

It's not a very subtle outfit, I know. Neither is my car. But I expect to make my hits at night, so these clothes should work fine for helping me blend into the shadows. Besides, it'll be fun to have my own little Wild West persona. I might as well have a good time while I'm doing this, if I'm going to live out my days on death row once I'm done.

I've already started decking out Jurisprudence, as I've named my car. I put my rifle case in the trunk, should I ever need it instead of a handgun. The police scanner from his van is now mounted under my dashboard. I've got his miniature camcorder that can play back a tape on any TV, too. I figure I'll mount that to film through the passenger window, so I can scope out neighborhoods as I drive. His night-vision goggles are in the glove compartment, along with his pair of binoculars that are disguised as funky, wrap-around sunglasses.

I can't believe all the stuff he collected over the years. I guess for him they were just expensive toy props for the fantasy life he lived behind the locked doors of his den. For me, they may be much more useful. I picked out a nice collection that includes everything from high-tech listening devices to a simple glass cutter. I plan to keep all that stuff in a lock box in the trunk until needed.

I found the lock box while I was snooping around in the garage for a tool box or something to hold those gadgets. The box was just sitting there against the wall with a chamois cloth and turtle wax cans tossed on top of it. I'd been wondering what that little mystery key on his key ring opened. Now I know.

Inside the box was $250,000, all in non-sequential bills. I could hardly believe it. I was sick that I'd just withdrawn several thousand dollars from the bank to cover expenses. That was my first thought, anyway. My next thought? *What if he didn't get a chance to pay off his hit man before he died?* What if I can kill him—his reputation, his memory—and get away with it? Why do I need to go through with killing these others if I can have him, if I can take the one life I really want?

Those questions surprised me, maybe even disappointed me. I thought my mission had more depth, more purpose than just killing him again and again by proxy. I mean, deep down, I think it *is* about more than him. It's about a society that continues to let "hims" exist, thrive. A society that looks the other way while the unthinkable is done to its children, preferring not to believe that the normal-looking people sitting in our courtrooms are capable of doing what only monsters do in the movies. I hope that's what my new vocation is about, anyway.

Even if my motives are more base than that, I still can't risk taking shots at him posthumously, since there are no guarantees that the money I found was meant to secure my death sentence. Juanita got one of those secret envelopes, too. For all I know, that was the money to ensure her deportation. Or maybe it's just money he kept around for buying his spy toys. I can't begin to know for certain.

All I know for sure is the money's mine now, and it's going to go a long way in funding this little Wild West show I have planned. I've got the money stacked up on the shelf in his bedroom closet, along with what I withdrew from the bank myself. It seems utterly insane when I think about having all that money lying around. I guess it just doesn't seem like real money sitting there in the closet. I never even made it to $17,000 a year in my female-dominated field, so it's hard to really grasp how much money he had, how much money I'll have once the estate is settled.

I have no idea what I'll do with it all. I can't really seem to think beyond this work of mine. Even buying Jurisprudence was mostly about avoiding airport security.

The only thing I seem to want that money

can buy is the financial freedom to make killing these people my vocation. I think the money in the closet offers me that, so the rest of it seems pretty worthless to me.

I wonder if that's because, as a woman, I've had no training in harnessing money's power. I mean, I don't even know where to buy the kind of equipment and guns he bought. I don't know how to retain the services of a gentleman who excels in arranging tragic, untimely deaths. I don't know how to select the best lawyer, best doctor, even the best car that money can buy. I don't know a risky investment from a safe one, a good investment from a bad one. Even with his money, I don't have his power.

Maybe that's what happened to Mike Tyson. I had felt outraged earlier today, when I heard on the news about a group of black ministers in Indianapolis trying to get their "hero's" sentence reduced. He only got six years, after all. He could easily be out in three. As I think about not knowing how to harness money's power, though, I feel almost sorry for Tyson. Me, feeling sorry for a rapist? Sheesh.

I think what I'm feeling is really because of the ministers' involvement. I mean, throughout history black ministers have been the African American community's greatest source of strength and influence. I guess I just find it sad that a black man like Tyson, with all the trappings of a white man's power, in the end has nowhere to turn but to those ministers. The power of the powerless.

Oh, well. At least he has that. Where do I turn?

# Chapter Eight

Sunday,
Mar. 1, 1992

After I got my car, I realized I had no more excuses to wait. So, today I turned on all of his security systems, locked the house up tight and set off in pursuit of my first target. I just finished checking in at a Motel 6 on the outskirts of town.

So now I'm sitting around contemplating my target over carry-out Chinese. Right? Not! I'm too hyped about the first real road trip of my life. Short drives around town were the extent of my driving experience before today. Now I feel like I've completed some rite of passage. Just call me Annie: Road Warrior. No one need know I've only got 236 miles under my seat belt so far.

I can tell I'm going to enjoy the long drives on these missions of mine. The scenery, the speed, the rest stops, the sounds, the wind making a tangled mess out of my hair—I love it all. Hypnotic though the interstates may be. My brain felt like lukewarm oatmeal by the time I pulled into the motel tonight. Ick!

That mushy brain feeling is the one thing I'll have to better prepare for on future missions. Maybe I'll try some back-road routes sometime and see if they're any better. I was so brain dead today by the time I was filling out the motel registration that I actually started writing my real name. No kidding. I caught myself just as I wrote the "F" in my last name. I turned it into a middle initial, so that wasn't a disaster. I'll have to think of someone more imaginative than Annie F. Smith to be next time, though.

I didn't make any similar near slips on my address, thank goodness. And I didn't list having a car at all. I'll have to figure out someplace to park it tomorrow. I could just see some Lieutenant Columbo-type tracing all the shootings back to me through the car I listed on my motel registrations.

Sheesh. That's enough to spoil my good mood. Watching my every step until this target's disposal isn't going to be much fun. I'll just have to keep reminding myself that getting caught will be even less fun.

I do plan to be extremely careful with this target. The game plan at this point is to videotape his neighborhood and study it for patterns of activity, good places to make a hit, escape routes, the whole bit. I'm going to follow him around, too, and make note of his daily schedule, habits, hangouts. Then I'll decide the best time and place to make my move. Sounds pretty time consuming. But then again, life in prison sounds even more time consuming. I just don't want to go to prison over any stupid mistakes.

I feel like I'm doing everything right so far. Paying in cash, destroying all receipts, using an alias, staying low profile. This on-the-job training is still a little nerve-wracking, all the same. I'm not sure I even know what all the "mistakes" are. Is there something about these bullets or this Baretta that will leave a trail back to me? What about this china doll I plan to leave behind once the target has been exterminated? Were those dolls specially crafted just for him? Are they special editions for which someone keeps records? Is the cash I'm using all marked in some way?

Pretty scary. Maybe someone out there is trying to tell me something. Is it you, Winnie? Not telling, huh? Oh, well.

I guess I need to face that, if I go through with

this mission of mine, prison won't be an "if" I get caught but a "when." Too much about this line of work is beyond my control. Mistakes are too easy to make. I'm going to get caught.

Do you hear that, Annie? You're going to get caught. You are going to get caught.

Hmmm. That's a tough sell. I watched him not get caught for all those years, after all. I saw how little it cost this target when he did get caught. Why should I believe that one little pull of the trigger and I'm doomed?

Oh, I forgot. I won't be killing little kids. Damn. I guess I will get caught.

# Chapter Nine

Wednesday,
Mar. 25, 1992

I did it.

He left for his nightly stroll to the corner liquor store right on schedule, and when he came back, already swigging on the bottle in the brown paper sack, I just stepped from behind the shrubbery that blocks the view of the porch from the street. And I did it.

"Aw, man," he said when he saw me there in the shadows. "I ain't got the money yet. I told John I'd have it for him Thursday. This ain't Thursday, fool."

I hesitated for a moment, just from the shock that he didn't even know why I was there. It was only a moment. I spontaneously adjusted my aim to the outstretched hand in front of his face. He gripped the bottle with thumb and forefinger, as he nonchalantly took another swig. A final swig. I squeezed the trigger.

He crumpled heavily to the porch, the bottle shattering as it hit the cement. I was still calm until the smell of Jack Daniel's hit me. Then the conditioned heart-thumping, nauseating panic such smells trigger took over. I tossed the china doll onto his body and ran for the back alley.

I realized about an hour later that I was going some twenty miles an hour over the speed limit, still wearing the Lone Ranger mask, grasping the steering wheel with blood-specked pistol in hand and on some interstate driving west instead of north.

I pulled over at the next rest stop and just sat there in my car until I got my bearings.

I felt so stupid. Not only was it embarrassing,

it was awfully sloppy. I was practically asking to get caught. Come to think of it, maybe that's exactly what was going on. I'd killed him and I was ready to get punished for it. I must have changed my mind while I was sitting at that rest stop.

I changed out of my cowboy clothes like planned and I hid the gun in the trunk. But then I went to the vending machines to get a diet Sprite and ended up coming back with an armload of Twinkies, Hostess Cupcakes, SnoBalls, Zingers, Ho-Hos and Donut Gems. I sat right there in Jurisprudence and ate them all. Sheesh.

I couldn't bring myself to turn Jurisprudence around and drive back to the crime scene just to make my planned interstate connection. So, I just pulled out of that rest stop and kept going west. All night long I drove west.

I kept seeing signs for Ramada Inns, Best Westerns, Econo-Lodges. "Next exit," the billboards read. *This is the one,* I'd think to myself. *I'll stop at this one and get some rest, sort things out.* But I'd drive by those exits every time, telling myself I could hang on until the next one. I had quite a sugar buzz, after all.

When a police cruiser passed me around daybreak, it convinced me to get this car off the road for a while. And reminded me that I hadn't even turned on my police scanner all night. I ended up leaving the car in a downtown parking garage near a Holiday Inn.

I still haven't been able to rest, though. I took a long, hot shower. That helped some, but I find myself sitting here on the bed with the remote control in hand, switching compulsively from news channel to news channel.

"This special bulletin just in. Authorities are hot on the trail of a vigilante, reportedly driving west in a black 1967 Ford Mustang. At approximately 9:21 last evening, the suspect—who is described by a multitude of witnesses as a Caucasian woman with blondish hair and hazel eyes, approximately twenty-five years and seven months old, five feet seven and a quarter inches tall, weighing 188 pounds, unable to speak and believed to be the youngest of a set of twins—gunned down an innocent child molester in cold blood, while he enjoyed a nightcap on his porch. The perpetrator was reportedly dressed in black and wearing a cowboy hat, leather duster, a Lone Ranger mask and a bandanna around her neck that is believed to be concealing scars on her throat. Her hair is cropped close around the face and long and wavy in the back, in the same style Wild West star Annie Oakley wore her hair at the height of her career. She is considered armed and dangerous and is wanted by authorities dead or alive. Preferably dead. A 1-800 hotline number has been established and operators are standing by now for your tips in this nationwide woman hunt."

I guess that's what I'm waiting to see, ridiculous as it sounds. I know good and well this is not the makings of a national news story. It's just a local murder with no witnesses, set apart only by my "brilliant" idea to leave behind a china doll signature. And maybe shooting him through the hand.

That was purely spontaneous, yet it appeals to me as a signature. The image that keeps coming to mind is the huge, bronze hand mounted on top of his tombstone at the cemetery. No, monument. The hand reaches skyward in an open gesture that pays tribute to his benevolence and generosity. The things he did to me with those "benevolent" hands.... Maybe I'll put a bullet through all my targets' hands.

But enough about that. Back to this first target. It was a clean hit and a clean getaway. In a few days I'll search the databases on the computer back at the house and I'll find a little blurb buried deep in the metro section, probably among the obits. And that'll be it.

I've probably still got a good two or three targets to go before someone starts noticing a pattern, before I'll have to do more than just pull the trigger and leave town.

It's funny how rational thought can seem so meaningless sometimes. Saying all that to myself doesn't help at all. I'm still just as wired as I can be. It's as if I refuse to let it be this easy. I keep thinking about the movie *Thelma & Louise*. After Louise shot that guy, they got chased all over the place; they had to always be on their guard; they were always running scared. I guess I expect the same for me. Maybe I even *want* the same; maybe I think I deserve that. Only, this isn't a movie.

I keep hearing this little voice saying, "Okay, it's time to feel guilty now." And I do feel guilty. But not in the way that little voice means. It wants me to feel guilty for shooting him, for running away instead of turning myself in, for, having every intention of shooting again. I don't. I can't.

I've tried to feel guilty about all that crap, but the truth is, I'm glad he's dead. Now, I'm sorry I was here stalking him yesterday when Christie's Auction House sold one of Annie Oakley's rifles. Tremendously sorry. It's really a shotgun disguised as a rifle that is fitted with five cartridges filled with fine shot instead of bullets. And it could have been mine, if it weren't for this creep.

Even that doesn't make me regret shooting him, though. It just makes me regret that I didn't shoot him sooner. I'm glad he can't hurt any more little kids and that he can never again hurt the girls he's already hurt. I'm glad I'm not sitting in jail, so I'm free to kill again. And I hope I don't get caught anytime soon.

Ah, but do I feel overwhelmingly guilty for having all those guilt-free feelings? Absolutely. I guess I'm disappointed that I'm so lacking in moral fortitude. I feel like shaking myself and screaming, "You just killed a man, Annie! Can't you at least show some remorse?" Of course, I can't really do any screaming, so I just sit here with the volume turned up high on the TV, letting it scream for me. At me.

I have to admit, the words on news channels are all wrong for inspiring remorse, though. A high school teacher who stands accused of being in a sexual relationship with a student for three years is trying to get his case thrown out today on the basis that the law he's being charged under—felony assault on a child by a person in a position of trust—wasn't on the books in Colorado when he seduced her. A man convicted of vehicular manslaughter was released yesterday after serving only thirty-one days in jail. Another man ran down his wife in the family car, pushing her through an office building wall. I wonder how many days he'll serve. The Supreme Court has refused to reinstate the conviction of a man's 1980 murder of a prosecutor, so he has to either be retried or set free. Only, he can't be retried. The Texas Court of Criminal Appeals doesn't allow the retrial for a negligent homicide conviction that's been overturned. So, never mind if he did it. He's free.

On top of all that, a study just came out showing a national pattern of child neglect. Child poverty rates, teenage violence, infant mortality, violent deaths—they're all climbing for kids. North Dakota is the only state in the whole country that demonstrated the slightest glimmer of hope. And even it had large increases in juvenile offenders.

These things are supposed to make me feel bad about inventing my own little justice system, for carrying out my own criminal sentences? I can see that feeling bad for not feeling bad is going to be about as remorseful as I get today.

I'm even starting to relax some now, not feeling nearly so much on edge. I think I'm going to try to get some sleep. I wonder how guilty I'll feel when it turns out to be an exquisitely restful sleep.

# Chapter Ten

Thursday,
Mar. 26, 1992

As I slept soundly yesterday, the US Supreme Court threw out a suit filed on behalf of a group of abused children to force Illinois to respond faster to troubled family situations. The ruling effectively bars children from filing civil rights lawsuits against state agencies that fail to protect them properly and makes federal judges powerless to force states to improve their care of abused and neglected children.

I ceremoniously replaced the single missing cartridge in my clip after reading that article in the morning paper, feeling a fresh sense of resolve, a fresh absence of guilt.

This is America's version of a highest court? A highest law? This country can't be the final word on all that is just, all that is right or wrong. There must be a higher law somewhere.

Until I find it, I'm sticking to the higher law within me. And I'll be damned if I'm going to feel bad about that.

# Chapter Eleven

Wednesday,
Apr. 8, 1992

He's not dead. I left him there on the porch with nine rounds still in the magazine and he wasn't even dead. Shooting him through the hand must have done something to the force of the bullet, so it just ended up lodging in his brain. That's all I can figure, anyway. I was so sure that single shot would kill him instantly. I was so sure.

Of course, it was the certainty of one accustomed to killing only paper targets. But I shot him in the head, for Chrissake. What else could I have done? Shot him twice? Duh. Of course I should have shot him twice. I should have emptied my clip.

He may be dead now. This stupid database took all this time just to get the story about the shooting on-line. Who knows what's happened since then. I've been going nuts waiting to find out something, and now I'm going nuts over what little I know. It's not like I can call up the hospital as a "concerned relative" and ask for an update. I could get a TDD operator to call for me, but that would be too conspicuous. I guess all I can do is wait for follow-up stories. If there even are any.

At least the article reported no witnesses and at least he hadn't regained consciousness when the paper went to press. But I am still sick about the whole situation. A slow, lingering death wasn't in the plans. Neither was a potential recovery, for that matter. I meant simply to remove a threat. Not injure. Not torture. This is not about inflicting pain to exact revenge. It's about a society failing to protect its children;

it's about taking extreme steps in response to an extreme problem.

Even if he dies, though, I've still failed in my quest to protect the children. One of the kids living in the upstairs apartment found him after the shooting. So once again a child has gone unprotected from undeserved trauma. And it's my fault. That's what bothers me most. I keep playing the surveillance tapes, watching those kids playing in the front yard, wondering which one she is, wondering how haunted she'll be by the image of him lying there bleeding, dying.

I was supposed to protect kids from him; I was supposed to help them. What a joke. What a lousy joke.

This is the first time I've felt any remorse, had any second thoughts, since I pulled the trigger. Until now, I've felt refreshed, energized even, by a new sense of purpose. I had at last found a use for my pain that was going to make a real difference, provide a needed service. I had finally found my niche in a society that had always left me feeling like an outsider, a misfit.

I drove back here after that initial night of panic, glorying in how vibrant the spring landscape seemed. The world around me was so alive. As if for the first time to me, the world was alive. When I saw little kids at fast-food restaurants, in cars, at rest stops along the way, instead of my usual twinge of pain, wondering what horror life held for them, I actually felt a soaring sense of hope for them, for their futures. I was proud that I was making this country a little safer for them. I felt like a superhero, hiding behind a mild-mannered Annie disguise.

Since I've been back here, I've been strutting around like the reincarnation of Winnie, feeling strong, courageous, indestructible and oh, so full of life. So very full of life. The past couple of weeks have been the absolute highlight of my life.

That's gone now. All that remains is vintage Annie misery. And I'm not really sure where to go from here.

To make it worse, I ran across an article on Marilyn, touting her as a role model for survivors of incest. She did it right; I did it wrong. Now when I get caught, I'll taint the image of incest survivors everywhere.

Between my blunder with this target and Marilyn's glaring reminder of all that I'm not, I feel like a pretty despicable person right now.

After reading all that, I logged off the computer and walked out of his bedroom, locking the door behind me. I don't think I ever intend to go back in there. I even threw away the key after going outside to sit on the old swing set. As I watched the key arc through the air and disappear into the overgrown lawn, I knew it was over. I'm finished. I've barely begun, and I'm already finished. Oh, well. Who cares?

All I really care about is punishing myself. That's why I went to the swing set. After the wreck, I'd go there whenever I wanted to hurt myself. Back then, it was usually after he'd been particularly slimy to me. I knew somebody needed to be punished. Might as well be me.

The swinging motion was always enough to bring on the vertigo as a kid. Even after the dizziness started, I'd keep swinging, swinging, swinging, in the midst of the spinning vortex I'd created. Finally, I'd lose my grip on the chains and go crashing to the ground, picking up some nasty bump, scrape, cut or break. I'd want to scream in pain, to jump up and go running to Mom for a

Band-Aid and a kiss. But I couldn't scream. I couldn't even get up off the ground until the dizziness went away. And Mom was dead.

Strangely enough, I usually felt better after all that. I'd paid for my wrong. I guess that's what I was seeking for myself on the swing set today, too. It was harder this time, though. Harder to summon the dizziness and harder to gain any pardon for my guilt. I even shook and hit myself on the head as I swung but I still couldn't get a full-blown spin. Just a little nausea.

I finally just let go of the chains anyway, only to have my fall cushioned by a mud puddle left by last night's rain. What a mess.

I guess it's just been one of those days. Thank goodness I have a couple of boxes of Little Debbies in the house.

# Chapter Twelve

I'm back in his room. Oh, I didn't break down the door or anything. I just dug Juanita's old set of keys out of a junk drawer and took her copy of his bedroom key.

I noticed for the first time today that there's another key in his set that isn't in hers. I find myself wondering if it's to another lock box somewhere. Maybe even another undelivered hit man payment. *The* other payment. Not that it would ease my paranoia about his reach beyond the grave. Still, I wonder.

If for no other reason, I think I wonder about the mystery key so as not to wonder why I'm back in his room. Technically there's nothing to wonder about. I read an article a few days ago that continues to bother me, so I'm in his room to search databases for more information. That's it. Technically.

But deep down I know something else is going on. I worked in the information industry long enough to know what freebasing "more information" does to me. It fans my rage; it confirms my paranoia; it drains my hope. It stirs my most base instincts. Soon I won't be able to resist the urgings of what I have learned. That knowledge will feel bigger than me. A threat. Fight or flight? That's what I'll be forced to choose. Technically.

Only, flight was already chosen when I left this room. Now that I'm back, I wonder if I'm back to fight.

Maybe not. Maybe it's pure curiosity that wants to know more about Robert Alton Harris. He's supposed to be executed within the week for the 1978 murders of two teenage boys. Only, all kinds of people are rallying to his support trying to stop the execution.

Apparently life began for him when his drunken father kicked his alcoholic mother in the gut, sending her into labor two months early. Things went downhill for him from there. That's why people want to save him. He had a crappy childhood.

No kidding. They wait until he grows up and kills two kids and now they want to save little Bobby. I just can't get over that. Is the concept "It's too late" that hard to grasp? Robert Alton Harris was a grown man in 1978. Individuals, society, institutions, government—anyone could have rallied to his support at any time during his childhood years, his teenage years, his young adult years. But in 1978, it was too late. They'd waited too long. I'd waited too long. We all did.

But have we who are troubled by the things little Bobby endured learned from him? Are people out there crusading, intervening, legislating to put a stop to the mistreatment of kids like Bobby? Oh, no. They're trying to put a stop to an execution that's too late to stop. They'd rather have pity on the adult than take responsibility for helping the child.

I don't want any part of that!

Whoa, partner! That makes me cringe inside. Those definitely sound like fighting words to me. So much for the "just curious" theory. I can't believe this. I really did come into this room looking for a fight. I sure am getting good at fooling myself. Guess I have to be in my line of work.

Wait. What line of work? I thought you were through. Finished. Kaput. Remember your bungled mission? Remember the terror you caused the kid who found him? You blew it! Remember?

Aw, give it up. It's too late, Annie. You had your chance to walk away from all this but you came back. So stop using your guilt to weenie out of your responsibility now. You don't want any part of that. Remember?

Yeah, yeah, yeah. The fighting words. I remember.... I just wish there was a way to exterminate a target without hurting others along the way. Oh, I know, surely this is the worst blunder I'll make. But blunders aside, some son or daughter or mother or uncle or neighbor is going to be impacted when every target falls.

Just look at what it did to me when he died. Look at what his death cost some of the causes he supported. Not to mention the unexpected nose-dive in the lemon, china doll and spy gadget industries.

I'm not used to thinking about my work in terms of its cost to innocent bystanders. I've assessed the cost to the targets and have found it reasonable. I've assessed the cost to myself and have found it no great loss. But to others....

I don't know how to deal with that yet. Well, outside of not shooting anyone else. As great a cost to others as it is to exterminate the targets, the cost of not exterminating them is greater. Period. So, I'm going to continue. I'm going to execute some more of this country's Robert Alton Harrises before it's too late for their victims.

I'll just have to accept the unintended fallout as my responsibility and find some way to ease the impact.

It's the best I can do.

# Chapter Thirteen

Saturday,
Apr. 18, 1992

I can't believe this. The nightmare just keeps getting worse. Now the father of one of the little girls who were raped has been charged with the shooting. Of all people to have no alibi that night. The newspaper said that after his daughter was raped again, this father went storming into the body shop where the target worked, carrying a Louisville Slugger and threatening to "bust his balls." Almost a dozen people witnessed the whole thing. This father is sunk. He makes me think of Kitty's dad, which just makes me feel worse.

All kinds of solutions have been flying through my mind: turning myself in, mailing a letter to the cops, killing myself and leaving a suicide note confession. The thing I keep going back to, though, is striking again. Establishing a series of these shootings, while the innocent suspect is tucked safely in jail unable to make bail. I can keep doing the bullet-through-the-hand and leaving china dolls to tie all the hits together. It seems perfect.

I've been looking over my wall of possible targets and two live within a four-hour drive of each other and less than a day's drive northeast of here. I don't have as much background information as I'd like. I don't know what one of them even looks like. I still think I could knock them both off within a month, though. I'd really like to get that man out of jail as soon as possible.

# Chapter Fourteen

Thursday,
Apr. 23, 1992

I felt a little more at ease as I gave my fake name and wrote down my fake address at the Knights Inn today. This time I'm Louise L'Amour of Truth or Consequences, New Mexico. I've put together a whole list of fun aliases from which to choose. Benita Cartwright, Lona Ranger and Jane Grey are among my favorites. It helped keep the stress down to know ahead of time who I planned to be. Still, it was hard to keep a poker face when the guy behind the counter, assuming I was deaf, slid me a piece of paper asking if I was related to the writer. I just nodded and took the key.

This motel is great. My room has bright red carpet and a deep purple, fake velvet bedspread with matching drapes. The colors of royalty. A couple of stone-framed castle windows have been stenciled onto the walls, so I can pretend I'm looking out over my kingdom. A few fake wooden beams grace the ceiling to cap off that castle ambiance.

I would have loved staying here as a kid. Winnie would have, too. But, alas, he always booked us in five-star hotels where all a kid could do was try real hard not to break anything. Oh, well.

I made a pass through my target's neighborhood and video-taped it before hunting down this motel. It was already dark when I hit town, so the video isn't that detailed, but I still got a pretty good feel for the cul-de-sac, with its pristine lawns, well-lighted streets, security system signs in most front yards.

I won't be shooting him on his front porch, that's

for sure. I won't even be able to park a car across the street and make note of his comings and goings. This neighborhood is too Leave-it-to-Beaver-ish. They'd notice an outsider right away.

I guess I'll have to stake out his dental practice. I hope it's not in some high-rise somewhere, or he may be a lot harder to kill than I'd hoped.

This one's a kids' dentist who was charged with molesting his son and daughter. His lawyers characterized the charges as fabricated by his wife as part of a messy divorce, the impressionable children having been coached in what to say and brainwashed into believing it themselves. Not only was he found not guilty, in a custody battle he was awarded unsupervised weekend visits with his children. Now he's remarried to a woman with three small children of her own.

He's got to go. There's too much legally sanctioned opportunity to hurt too many kids.

I guess following him to work in the morning will be the easiest place to start the extermination process. I'll just park near the entrance to the cul-de-sac before dawn and see what happens. I don't know if dentists even work on Fridays. Oh, well. I knew this wasn't going to be a well-oiled operation when I started it, so I'll just have to keep all my gear handy for whatever opportunity I get.

For now, I'd better get some rest. This may be an exhausting one.

# Chapter Fifteen

I've been having a hard time staying focused on my task today. It started this afternoon. I followed him to his ex-wife's house and watched him pick up his kids, presumably for the weekend. Ever since then I've wanted to rush in and empty a clip into the bastard. There I was watching through binoculars what the legal system never seems to see, never seems to consider, when it declares the innocence of these men of such fine character: a little boy crying, screaming, clinging to his mother's jeans, begging her to let him stay; a girl a little older, standing stiffly to the side, watching with no emotion, numbly waiting to be led away.

Finally, he pried his son away from the mother, carried him to the car and strapped him into the car seat. The girl just followed along, head down and climbed into the back seat behind her father, kind of like Robert Alton Harris climbed into California's gas chamber a few days ago. Only, she's going to her living death because of someone else's guilt instead of her own.

As he drove away, the mother just collapsed onto the steps with her head in her hands. With good reason, I'd say. He didn't even take the kids back to his house. I followed them to a motel on the outskirts of town. I've been sitting out here in the car for five hours, working my way through a box of honey buns, watching the door, wondering what's going on behind it. A Domino's guy delivered pizza about an hour ago, but other than that, the door has just stayed closed. No trips to the motel playground or the park down the street. Just a closed door with drawn curtains.

I find myself methodically loading and unloading the Browning's thirteen rounds, as I sit here fighting the urge to charge up to room 218 and take him out. Empty the clip. Make thirteen his unlucky number.

The only thing stopping me is knowing I can't shoot him in front of his kids. The boy looked like he's maybe four or five; the girl can't be more than eight. After what they've been through already, they don't need to witness his death, too.

I've got to kill him soon, though. This has got to be the last weekend he has them by himself. Even if he's doing nothing to those kids right now, he's free to hurt them behind a locked door with no witnesses, with no way for those kids to get help.

What is wrong with this country? Not only does it let people hurt its children without real penalty, but it actually court orders that people like this guy be given opportunity to hurt them. It wouldn't do to offend him just to make sure that a couple of kids are safe. Oh, no, his civil rights are at stake, after all. It just wouldn't be right.

What is right? Does anyone even know anymore? Does it even exist anymore? Maybe it doesn't. Maybe right and wrong have been reduced to just wrongs, and it's a matter of choosing between the lesser wrong and the greater wrong.

Only, we don't know that's what we're doing yet, so we're still trying to decide if abortion is right or wrong, if capital punishment is right or wrong. If what I'm doing is right or wrong. Okay, so it's all wrong. So what? It may be wrong to kill an unwanted, developing fetus, but it's a greater wrong to force a woman to let that fetus develop into an unwanted child. It may be wrong to execute a human being as punishment for murder, but it's more wrong to kill innocent victims; it's more wrong to risk a parole or escape that threatens the lives of other innocents.

Of course what I'm doing is wrong, taking the law into my own hands, passing capital sentences on non-capital crimes, behaving as though I'm above the law myself. I know all that. I'm willing to pay for my wrongs. They'll have to catch me first, but once I'm caught, I'm willing to pay. In the meantime, I'll keep reacting to the greater wrongs of betraying children's hope in the justice system, of leaving them unprotected, unbelieved, unavenged, of giving perpetrators no reason to stop or get help for themselves.

What reason does that creep have to stop messing with his kids? He's been exonerated. He's been legally empowered to do even more to them if he wants. That's wrong. And since there are no "right" means available to fix that wrong, I've got to fight wrong with wrong, like fighting fire with fire. It's destructive as hell, but it works. I'll have him snuffed out within a week.

Searching for some "right" way to deal with him might take years, decades, if ever. By then those kids will be adults. And they might just be adults like me or like Robert Alton Harris or like their father. What a waste.

I hate sitting here tonight feeling so helpless to stop him. I don't even know why I'm still here. I've got to pee so bad I'll have to reupholster Jurisprudence if I so much as sneeze. But I can't bear the thought of leaving them alone with him. As if I'm really making a difference by being here. What a joke.

Hey, what do you know? I'm not the only one feeling helpless tonight. Mom just tip-toed over to the door and has an ear pressed up against it. I wonder how she found him. She's trying to peek in through a crack in the curtains, now. Oh, crud, someone opened a door a few rooms down. Good. She moved down one door and is acting like she's unlocking it. Smart move. Wait. She's not acting. She's really in the room next to her kids. I guess she doesn't want them to be alone with him either. No doubt she's flouting a restraining order to be here tonight. It's pitiful that wanting to protect kids has to mean breaking the law.

I keep thinking about a listening device I've got in the trunk. It has a microphone that looks kind of like a stethoscope, so it works through walls. It even connects to a miniature tape recorder. I'm tempted to get that out of the trunk and leave it outside her door with a note to let her know she's not alone in this.

That's how totally lacking in caution this is making me. Not only could I jeopardize myself by doing that, but if she made tapes of what's going on in that other room, they might later be used to implicate her in his death.

Probably the best thing I can do tonight is just leave. Then I'll stop being tempted to do such stupid things. I'm not going to make a move on him as long as he has the kids, so I'll just resume stalking him Monday at work. Mom can take over here.

# Chapter Sixteen

Saturday,
Apr. 25, 1992

While I was watching the news this evening, I saw a clip of Afghan rebels sporting their rifles and ammunition. They looked so proud of their weapons, so eager to use them. It's a scene I must have seen hundreds of times in the news, but this time I felt a great sense of jealousy. Men going off to war, like they have for centuries. Men free to kill for a cause they think is just.

When will women ever have sanction to kill?

Oh, America will let me in the military, but it will keep me off the front lines. Never mind that I'm one heck of a shot. Only men get to fight for their causes, for freedom from their oppressors. They're the only ones who don't get charged with murder for it, anyway.

Me? I'm stuck with my enemy, my terrorist. I can't hobble him. I can't kill him. The only power society has bestowed upon me is the right to tattle. I am woman. Hear me whine.

"Mr. Policeman, he's being mean to me."

"Well, we can't have that, now can we little lady?"

"You'll protect me, then?"

"Oh no, we can't do that ma'am. He has rights, you know. We can offer you male sensitivity training, though. It will help you identify what you do that makes him so mean."

"Like what?"

"Well, like telling me about this, for example. Once he finds out you're nothing but a little snitch, that's going to make him mean to you. Heck, he might even kill you. But don't you worry yourself.

If he kills you, we'll lock him right up. He's not allowed to kill civilians, you know. We'll put your story all over the news, too, so other ladies won't make the same tattletale mistake you just made."

So much for the power to tell....

I don't know why I'm complaining, really. It seems almost rhetorical, considering I've sanctioned myself to kill. I guess it just annoys me that I'm not supposed to kill. Ever. I am woman. Even abortion is considered murder for me.

It makes me wonder if I'm what the oppression of women is all about. Oh, not me personally, but the fear that deep down every woman has someone like me waiting to take over. Let women have unlimited access to abortion and we'll slaughter all the babies. Take marital rape seriously and we'll never have sex with our husbands again. Expect women to physically protect ourselves and our children and we'll kill as a first resort. Believe little girls who say men are hurting them and we'll start making up tales out of spite. Pay us what men are paid and we'll break up families at the first sign of trouble.

It's so absurd, so insulting, this notion that society must legislate and regulate the female, since she's incapable of making sound choices for herself and those her life touches. Just look at me. No, not as the example, silly. The exception. I'm not what women are waiting for the chance to become. I'm not even what *I* was waiting for the chance to become. It took a lot to transform an intense, trusting, affectionate little girl into this grown-up monster. I'm no naturally occurring phenomenon. I'm America's own Frankenstein. Not that anyone's scared of me. Yet.

Anyway, enough of my soapbox. After I left the motel last night, I decided to take advantage of Mom's stakeout to nose around her house some. I thought it would be a breeze to get in, with the help of his nifty, battery-operated lock picker. I'd come and go without anyone ever knowing I'd been there. Not!

See, I didn't exactly take the time to learn how it works first. So, I found myself at her back door last night with only a pen flashlight to help me see, trying to make this lock-picking contraption work. It always looks so easy in the movies, too. Oh, well. I did finally get it to work. Sort of. It broke out that window just fine, anyway.

I feel bad about that, since I know she's going to feel invaded when she returns. I debated whether to steal some valuables to make it look like a theft, but I decided to just make it look like I'd broken in because I was hungry. I made a sandwich, drank a glass of milk, heated up a can of soup—and left the mess. I was pretty proud of myself for thinking of that.

On a notepad I scribbled, "Sorry. Hungrey. Thancks," using the handwriting of an old gardener who worked for him after the wreck for a few years. I guess he didn't want the outdoor plants to suffer Juanita's touch of death. Poor old guy fell off a ladder while tending the ivy that covers the face of the house. Broke his neck.

Anyway, imitating other people's handwriting, like Rich Little imitates other people's voices, is a little trick I picked up as a kid. I mostly just did it for fun back then, except for faking an occasional note from him to get me out of school on depressing gray days. It may be quite a useful little tool of the trade now.

I found a row of coffee cans in the cupboard while I was searching for soup. They had varying amounts of cash in them, so I guess that's how she budgets things. I felt like some kind of Robin Hood as I added a few $20 bills to each can. That way I covered the broken window and then some. I figured out while poking around the rest of the house that she works as a secretary, so I know money's got to be tight, even if he's paying child support. I noticed some college info lying around too, so she may be planning to go to school. That's going to be rough with two kids.

She'll be out of town for some kind of secretary's conference on Tuesday and Wednesday. The calendar says the kids will be at grandma's. That gives Mom a solid alibi, so I'll try to make my first attempt on him Tuesday night.

His work schedule by the phone shows evening hours on Tuesdays, so I might manage to get him as he leaves the office. I sat in the parking lot outside his office for a while tonight, trying to get a feel for the activity in the area at that hour. It's pretty dead. But then again, it's a Saturday night. I'll come back Monday night to make sure.

His office is set in a mixed residential and commercial area. In fact, the office building looks like it used to be a house. It's set off from the main two-lane road by a small pharmacy that virtually hides all but the rear third of the building from the road. All parking for his office is behind the pharmacy, which closes at 5 p.m. How convenient.

There's a street light behind the pharmacy near the dumpster and another at the far corner of his office building. Those light the area well, so I'll have to shoot them both out sometime Monday night. I've already taken the light bulb from the office porch light. It wasn't on, so I assume they only use it Tuesday nights. With any luck, no one will notice it's gone.

His looks like a solo practice, so I won't have to worry about any other dentists being around that night. There's still the problem of any dental assistants or secretaries who might be working that night, though. That's the main factor I won't be able to control for.

Depending on where he parks that night, I'll have good hiding places behind the pharmacy dumpster or lying against the building behind the hedges that line the front. If I have to abort at the last moment, either way I'll go undetected.

Sounds like a pretty solid plan to me. If I can just keep from panicking this time, it should work out fine.

# Chapter Seventeen

Tuesday,
Apr. 28, 1992

Rain. I didn't allow for April showers, or how people dash to their cars when they're caught without their umbrellas. I knew his female employees would move quickly to their cars, keys in hand, heads up looking around, aware of their surroundings. That's everyday life for women in this country. But I expected him to stroll to his BMW, fish in his pocket for his keys, click off his car alarm, maybe polish a smear on the hood with his shirt sleeve. Then as he stood there, I would step out from behind the dumpster, kick over a Pepsi can to get his attention and shoot as soon as he felt a flash of fear.

But it rained. So, after spending over an hour crouched down behind the dumpster waiting for him, thinking about how miserable cowboys must have been on rainy cattle drives, he came dashing out of the building with key in hand and had hopped into his car by the time I wrestled the gun out from under my slicker. On impulse, I shot out his front left tire as he backed out his car. Engine still running, windshield wipers still going, he stopped and got out of his car to inspect the tire. A soft, incessant pinging sound reminded him he'd left the keys in the ignition.

"Goddammit!" he muttered, giving the flat tire a kick. He got back into his car and slowly drove it closer to his office. The porch light had been replaced after all, so he had more light there for changing the tire. With two other cars still on the lot, I knew he wasn't the last one out of the office. That left me stuck behind the dumpster. Oh, joy.

I toyed with taking a shot at him from there, but a moving head shot while he changed the tire would have been extremely difficult at that distance, even for me. It was just too dark to get a fix on him. Guess I should have picked the SIG with its laser sight instead of the Browning. I finally just put the pistol away,

resigned to try again sometime tomorrow.

"I thought you were already gone," one of the two women called out to him from the porch, when they came out of the office several minutes later.

"Can you believe it?" he asked. "I'm backing out of my parking space, and the tire just blows. Of course it'd be on a dark and stormy night when the street lamps aren't working."

"We'll leave the porch light on for you, and I'll pull my car around to give you some more light," the woman in red said.

"No, you girls have put in a long day already. I'll have this wrapped up in another ten minutes. Go ahead and leave."

*That's right. Go ahead and leave,* I thought.

"Nonsense," the one in red said. "Holly, I know you've got to pick up your kids, but I can stay with him."

"Okay," Holly replied. "But I'll leave my umbrella for you."

So, one left and one stayed, and I just sat there wishing they'd hurry so I could get back to the Knights Inn, take a hot bath and maybe gaze out of my painted castle windows for a while.

Finally, he lowered the jack and put it away.

"Thanks for hanging around, Penny," he said as he closed the trunk. "I'm going to go in, wash my hands and turn off the porch light. I better give Carrie a call and let her know why I'm late, too."

"Okay," Penny called out, as she got into her Hyundai to drive away. "See you tomorrow."

This was it! This was my chance. I could hardly believe it.

He left his headlights on and car running while he went inside. Kitty was forever doing stuff like that. It drove me crazy when we were in college. I just knew someone was going to steal her jeep someday. Or worse.

Well, Mister here was about to find out just how right I was. Too bad Kitty wasn't around to see and learn.

Once the parking lot was empty, I went over to his car, shot out the left headlight and crouched down on the other side of his car.

"What the fuck!" he exclaimed, when he came back out a few minutes later. "This is not my friggin' night."

He walked over to inspect the light, like I hoped he would. When he bent over to put his hand to it, I quietly moved behind him.

"Hey! This thing's busted!" he yelled above the thunder. Then sensing my presence, he whirled around.

"Look," he said, holding a dripping hand out in front of him in response to my gun. "I've had a really crappy night and I just want to go home and get out of these wet clothes. So just name what you want and it's yours. Take the car, for all I care. I won't even call the police. I swear."

Of course, I couldn't say, "What I want is your kids' lives back; what I want is to make sure you never hurt your step kids or any of your patients." So, I shot him instead.

One bullet through the outstretched hand. He looked surprised. A second bullet through the head knocked him onto the hood of his car, splattering blood onto his illuminated windshield. Ugh. I hate being able to see the blood. Thank goodness it was raining hard enough to wash the blood away by the time I leaned inside to switch off his car and lights. Then I went back to where he lay and felt for a pulse. Nothing. So, I wrapped his arm around a soggy china doll. Mission accomplished.

It was so dark and deserted, I just strolled down the alley to my car.

Now, I'm back at the motel, feeling much better than I did right after shooting the first one. I've had the motel send my soggy clothes to the cleaners. I've had a hot shower. Now I'm lounging around watching David Letterman, sipping vending machine hot cocoa, and eating a fresh box of Hostess Cupcakes

I pulled out my file on the next target, but I haven't even opened it yet. I guess I just want to bask a while in the satisfaction of having done this one the way I wanted. Besides, a marathon of Clint Eastwood westerns starts at midnight and I want to watch him mete out some Wild West justice.

I'll have plenty of time tomorrow to plan for the next target. After all, it may be several hours before the body is discovered. I doubt it will even make the morning paper.

# Chapter Eighteen

Even I'm shocked this time. I mean, I knew the justice system didn't work, but the videotape of those cops beating Rodney King made the whole nation witnesses to that crime last year. And it *was* a crime. I don't care what the jury's reasons were for acquitting those police officers today; it was still a crime. I saw it. Over and over I saw it. Now a jury tells me—tells the whole country—that we didn't really see what we thought we saw?

Of course there is rioting in the streets of Los Angeles tonight. Of course there is. Take all hope for justice from a people and what recourse is left but lawlessness?

Such an unchecked outpouring of rage is frightening to watch, even from the antiseptic distance of a television set. I can only imagine what it must be like in the midst of it all. Or to be a Los Angeles cop, knowing that this rage is all about you. I find that power to invoke such terror enviable.

Black males seem to have so little power in this country as it is, having to beat the odds just to live to adulthood, then having to beat the odds just to stay out of jail, then having to beat the odds not to drop dead at middle age from a heart attack or stroke. They still have the power to utterly terrify their oppressors, though.

You don't see police officers swinging their sticks, trying to stop these rampaging men in Los Angeles tonight. The burning police car being flipped over onto its side by a frenzied mob—that's the image playing again and again in my mind. No one's going to challenge those men tonight. The powers that be will have to wait until they have a legally sanctioned mob of their own to gang up on these rioters. For tonight, terror reigns. Tonight the powerless have power, have control. Tonight the voiceless have all of America's ear.

I covet that kind of power for America's women. We've never struck such terror in the hearts of our oppressors as has been registered in Los Angeles tonight. It's little wonder. Women have been so thoroughly socialized to play by the rules, to be nice, that it's hard to envision a female uprising.

When Clarence Thomas was confirmed, we didn't spill out onto the streets and rough up wolf-whistling assholes en masse. We didn't run trucks off the road for sporting buxom women on their tire flaps. We didn't burn bars named after various parts of the female anatomy. We didn't start sporting baseball bats and stun guns at work with every intention of ending sleazy treatment on the job.

Those of us who believed Anita Hill did let loose a collective "That sucks!" It was noisy, but it accomplished little. Some of us kept making noise, are still making noise. Some of us voiced resolve to gain more political power for women by running for political office. Some of us risked filing sexual harassment charges of our own. All of us played by the rules, just like we were supposed to.

It makes me think of kindergarten and learning to color inside the lines. Color the hair purple if you want, color the fire truck blue, but never, never, never, never color outside the lines. What's the name of that book? I think it's *Everything I Ever Needed to Know I Learned in Kindergarten*. Let's see, what did I learn in kindergarten about purple hair and blue fire trucks that are colored inside the lines? It's okay to distort reality, just don't cross the lines. Yes, I suppose that about sums it up.

It's okay for defense lawyers to trash the character of victims and witnesses, to have truth stricken from the record, to twist evidence to their guilty clients' advantage. That, after all, is just distorting reality. But I'm not to kill those who were unjustly set free because of that distorted reality, and people in Los Angeles tonight aren't to resort to violence. Doing those things is crossing the line. It's bad to cross the line. Bad! Bad! Bad!

"I'm sorry." Sniff, sniff. Droopy face. Teary eyes. "I didn't mean to be a bad girl.... But I want my fire trucks RED!" Down on the floor. Kicking. Screaming. Tantrum extraordinaire.

I don't think a red fire truck is so much to ask. If cops beat the crap out of someone, it should be called "beating the crap out of someone," not "using necessary force" or "doing one's job." And it should be dealt with justly for what it is. Then people wouldn't need to respond lawlessly to a ridiculous miscarriage of justice.

As soon as the justice system—this whole society—stops calling child abuse the product of overactive, young imaginations or spiteful lies, when it stops calling rape something women ask for or secretly desire, I'll stop killing. I'll stay inside the lines.

What reason would I have to kill if those things were called by their true names? That would mean dealing with sex offenders' actions in a way befitting the crime. There'd be no more of this getting off just because they're rich or because they've been such good people otherwise or because their victims are sexually active or too young to bear facing the accused in court.

I would stop the killing then. I would never cross the line again.

As it is, though, I don't know that I'll ever stop. Not on my own, anyway. With any luck, I'll inspire some fear along the way. Fear of not taking these cases seriously; fear of pronouncing a death sentence in every not-guilty verdict handed down, in every early probation granted. Maybe that fear will make a difference, make my efforts less necessary. But mine is a small war and will probably make only a small difference as such.

It will certainly never have the impact in this country that the Rodney King verdict is having on Los Angeles this evening.

I'm committed to doing what I can, though. Any questions I had about all this a few weeks ago seem distant, irrelevant. Certainly I want to avoid the mistakes I made during the first shooting, but I don't want to stop doing this. Especially not tonight.

# Chapter Nineteen

I've moved on to the next town, the next target, but I've been so distracted by the violence in
Los Angeles that I've spent the past couple of days
in my room at the Red Carpet Inn doing little more
than watching news coverage. I haven't even
videotaped this target's neighborhood or taken a
serious look at the information I have on him.

I understood my interest in the initial riots to
protest the Rodney King verdict, but I'm not sure
what my continuing obsession is about. I see the
raging fires, the looting, the profiles of innocent victims, and I know it's out of control. I know it's gone
too far. I've lost a degree of sympathy with the rioters, shifting my support to Rodney King in his pleas
for it to stop, for everyone to please just get along.

Even so, I still watch. It's not because I want
to watch anymore. It's that I can't stop watching.
Like I've sentenced myself to seeing it all from inspiring beginning to wretched end.

Maybe that's exactly it. Maybe I'm forcing myself to watch how easily the understandable, the
justifiable, can become the very monster it seeks
to destroy. Maybe I'm looking for myself in those
televised scenes of devastation, inhumanity, grief.

It's a difficult mirror in which to peer. Mirror,
mirror on the screen, what am I seeing? What does
it mean? The mirror's voices talk and talk, but
somehow they never quite answer me. How rude.

I think I'm afraid. Afraid of stepping off some
tightrope I've stretched out for myself. Afraid of
crossing some internal boundary, past which I will

have officially gone too far, will have officially become like him.

That sounds totally absurd when I read it. I mean, I killed a man a few days ago. The only reason I'm here now is to kill again. How much farther can I go?

Yet, I feel as if I could, indeed, go farther. I feel as if I could commit a greater wrong than the ones I'm stamping out. I desperately want to avoid that. Whatever "that" would be for me. It would really have to be something, wouldn't it?

Well, maybe not. When the first one didn't die, when he was found by that little kid, it felt like one of those greater wrongs to me. It's unnerving that I crossed that line so easily, so unwittingly. Now I'm hoping that these two targets will make up for another greater wrong with the first target by getting that innocent man out of jail. So far it's working. At least inside myself. But what if next time the wrong is so great I can find no penance?

Good grief. Listen to me. Leave it to a woman to be a killer with a conscience....

I know I need to take heed of what's happened in Los Angeles, since my violence, too, is in response to and in protest of injustice. But there's no mob mentality for me to get caught up with, since I'm acting alone. So, I'm probably over-identifying with the stuff in LA just a tad.

I guess it's just such a glaring reminder of how badly things can go, if I ever lose sight of what I'm doing and why I'm doing it. It's frightening, especially since I've put myself in a position that's particularly vulnerable to lost bearings.

I'm putting a stop to these targets for a reason, and I want to keep it within the bounds of that purpose. Or maybe I should say, within the bounds of that "self-deception." Whatever I call it,

I want to be able to feel good about it when I'm done. Like I did with this last guy. He died quickly; police found his body. It was a squeaky clean operation and I felt proud to have orchestrated it.

When the article came out, I clipped and mailed it to the police in the first target's city, taking such care that I didn't so much as lick the envelope. After being force-fed so many spy flicks while growing up around him, I guess it's left me paranoid that technology can always track me down if I leave behind even the slightest trace of myself. Who can tell what's fiction and what's real these days? I guess I'd rather err on the side of caution.

Speaking of caution, I really need to get off my butt and start scraping up more info on this next target. I still haven't got so much as a mug shot of him. I've got an address. I know he's got graying hair and I know he's got an American flag tattooed on the back of his right hand and a bald eagle on the back of his left. That's about it. The tattoos are how the little boy he attacked identified him as being the guy who lived down the street.

This one confessed on tape after he was arrested, waiving his right to have a lawyer present. He said he was glad he'd finally been caught, that someone was finally going to make him stop. But someone didn't make him stop. The idiots. He got a five-year probated sentence, no therapy required. He's right back in the neighborhood.

# Chapter Twenty

I'm getting frustrated—not to mention bored—stalking this target. I'm pretty sure from the name on the mailbox that I've got the right house. I've been watching it four nights, though, and I still don't have a clue what he looks like or if he's even still living there.

This is a rural area, houses spread out at least a mile apart along a two-lane highway. I can't exactly park along the road and stake out his house under these conditions. I've been driving out to the area after dark and leaving my car behind an abandoned house that I found on a nearby dirt road. Then I've been putting on those night-vision goggles and hiking over to the house armed with a little periscope-like thing to peer through windows, my most sensitive listening device and a couple of boxes of doggie treats to keep their dogs happy to see me.

So far, all I know is that no one has come to visit; the phone hasn't rung; and the only sign of life has been one frazzled-looking middle-aged woman shuffling around the house. The only clue I have that he might be there is that I've seen her carry a plate of food into a mystery room every night before she goes and sits in front of the TV in the living room with another plate of food.

I can't see into the mystery room. Cardboard has been taped to the inside of the windows. Alas, I have no gadget that lets me see through walls. I can't hear anything in there either, except for the TV that's always playing. So, I don't know if this target goes in there every evening—just like Father

Dearest used to lock himself in the den every evening—or if this woman is caring for some invalid in that room.

I think I have a lingering fear. Is that the right word? It's a lingering something that makes me wonder if this target is a total bust. He may have gotten a divorce after his confession and be long gone. Yet, there's a "for sale" sign in the front yard where I think his victim lives, so he may still be in the area. It's a confusing situation.

The only clear thing is that my nightly stakeouts aren't getting me anywhere. I hope this area is sparsely populated enough to allow me to go undetected if I switch to days. Well, I say "days," but really I'm only willing to risk one daytime operation. If I can't find out something about him after that, I'll just call it quits.

There's a propane tank sitting in a field behind the house. I'll move into place behind that before dawn and see who comes and goes—or maybe even try to go inside the house and snoop around.

I think my biggest concern about going there during the day is the dogs. I can just see them gathering near the propane tank wagging their tails, wanting doggie treats or wanting to play. Then, before I know it, I'm caught. And all because of some stupid scenario that should never happen outside of a bad sitcom.

I guess that's the down side of having made pals with the pups. I've enjoyed their company these past few nights. One of them in particular has won my affections. He must be part sheep dog because he reminds me a lot of Mom's dog, Caleb. Only, he's smaller. That one has been unshakable. While the other two only stick around for the snacks, Caleb Jr. has stayed right with me every night, as I've crawled around the house, trying to see or hear something useful.

Last night he even got me out of a tight spot. Someone had put a Weedeater up against the house. Well, I wasn't paying attention to what I was doing, since I pretty much knew my way around the house by then. Bam! I walked right into it, knocking it over onto an aluminum trash can that sits beside the kitchen door. What a racket!

I ducked back around the corner of the house as the porch light came on, but Caleb Jr. walked toward the door, wagging his tail when the woman looked out the screen door.

"Get away from there, you stupid dog!" she snapped, clapping her hands. "Go on home! Shoo! You scared me to death."

I breathed a little easier once she closed the door and turned off the porch light, but I didn't snoop around anymore after that. I just sat there petting Caleb Jr. for a while, looking up at the stars, listening to the crickets.

Besides the general frustration I was feeling at my lack of progress toward getting rid of this guy, I felt weighted down with utter hopelessness as I sat there in that peaceful setting. I know that sounds insane. But if there's no safety for kids in an area like that, so far removed from all those urban-associated social ills, where in this whole country can a child grow up in relative safety anymore? This is the kind of place where families move to get away from crime, to give their children wide-open spaces to play, unpolluted air to breathe. Yet even here the perps lurk, waiting for a chance to prey on the children. The only real difference is that here there are no witnesses.

Here, I can sit beside a house all night—listening, spying—without anyone knowing. Here, strange noises in the night get blamed on stray dogs. A scream, a cry for help, could get swallowed by the sheer distance to the closest available ear.

It's discouraging to think about. I have the sensation of shrinking to insignificance in my efforts to give some safety to the children. Even if I give the rest of my life to the elimination of known threats, I'll have accomplished depressingly little by the time I'm done. When I ride in to save the day, the damage has already been done. And even if I get rid of a threat to other kids, there are plenty of other perps out there to fill the void.

It's like living in one of those horror movies where the monster refuses to die. Every time the hero thinks the monster has breathed its last, it comes roaring back to life just as frightening, just as vicious as ever.

This monster is too much for me. I'll never win. How discouraging. But I know it's true, especially at the rate I'm going. It's been more than four months since I resolved to do this, and all I've managed to do is incapacitate one and kill another. I can't even find this third one. I may never find him.

*"Sorry kid. I meant to take the jerk out, but I was busy making friends with his dogs, so I never got around to it. You understand, don't you, kid? I'm sure you'll get over what he did to you. Time heals everything. Right? My pop did that stuff to me, too. But I grew up, and just look at how I turned out. You'll be just fine, kid. Just like me.*

Yeah, right.

I guess I've got to do the little piddly bit that I do, if only for that one kid out there somewhere whose childhood won't have to hurt so much if I remove the threat. I just wish it didn't feel like such a hollow victory to save one kid. I have this image in my head of me dashing out of a burning building with a kid tucked under my arm like a football. Passersby cheer; the kid's parents weep with joy as I give them back their child. But as I turn to go back inside for another, the building collapses in on the millions of screaming children still inside. I'm glad I saved one, but I'll forever be haunted by the chorus of screaming kids who didn't have a chance.

That haunting makes my blundering efforts with this target even more frustrating. It makes it harder to just give up on this one like I want to.

Then there's Marilyn. She was in the news again this week. The article credits her with sparking a national movement of incest survivors who now realize they are not alone. They're drawing strength from their new-found community and finding validation for their pain.

The article holds such hope that I want nothing more than to walk away from this target. I want to take my own place among the ranks of the healing and help show the wounded children that there's a way past the pain.

I guess the question becomes, "Can I stand by and let the burning building collapse on the children, and then poke through the ashes for survivors?" I don't know if that's enough for me right now. All I know is, I've been up all night and I need to stop thinking so much so I can get some sleep. I don't have any business making plans or decisions while I'm this exhausted.

# Chapter Twenty-One

Thursday,
May 7, 1992

I pitched a tent out behind that abandoned house last night. I was getting sick of motel rooms, so it was a nice change, except for the few annoying mosquitoes and a little bit of campfire smoke blowing in my face. Besides, it gave me a chance to rest until the pre-dawn hike to his house. It's almost an hour's drive from the motel, on top of an hour's walk to his house.

Winnie and I used to camp out on warm summer nights. We'd build blanket tents on the swing set in the back yard, and spend the evening holding flashlights under our chins, trying to outdo each other's horror stories. Somehow those stories were always about nice daddies who got turned into monsters that ate up little girls. That seems sad now, but it was great fun then.

We always fruitlessly begged to have a campfire to roast hot dogs and marshmallows. Well, last night I finally did it! It was a pitiful little fire, since I wanted it to go unnoticed. Not to mention that I know nothing about building fires. It was enough for charring my hot dogs and marshmallows, though. That's all I cared about. It made me miss Winnie, so I was glad for the company when Caleb Jr. came ambling into camp about the time I usually arrive here for my nightly trek.

I treated him to leftover hot dogs and let him crawl into the tent with me while I took a nap, never mind that he was in desperate need of a bath.

I felt bad about chaining Caleb Jr. to a tree before I left, but it was the only solution I had to keep him from underfoot. I lured the other two dogs into the woods behind the house with their beloved boxes of doggie treats and chained them a little closer together. They barked like crazy, but they were so far away they sounded like they might just be off chasing rabbits.

I took my place behind the propane tank just before dawn and waited. The waiting was hard for me. I usually keep a Walkman and book on tape with me. But this time I needed my ears to hear the comings and goings at the house, so I had nothing to artificially break the silence except Morse Code tappings on the propane tank. Only, I can't even remember much of the Gettysburg Address or the preamble to the Constitution anymore.

I found myself searching so hard for every bird chirp, every rustle of wind through the trees, every distant hint of a car coming down the highway, that I almost jumped out of my skin at the sharp report of a car door slamming. It's embarrassing to be so terrified of silence, to literally be terrified of nothing. Sheesh.

I peeked around the tank and watched the woman pull out of the driveway alone in the car. It was a little after 8:00 when she left; I hoped that meant she was on her way to work and not just making a short trip to pick up groceries or something.

I really hate doing this kind of work during the day. I hope it's the last time I have to. It was nerve-wracking wondering who could see me, wondering how to make a getaway if something went wrong. My car was at least three miles away. I couldn't jog the distance, since anything more than a brief dash leaves me laid out on the ground with dizziness. I didn't want to leave the dogs chained up, either.

I figured it was either going to work out without a hitch, or it was going to be a total disaster. I prefer my odds to be a little better than fifty-fifty, thank you, but it was the best I had at the moment. So, I just took a deep, steadying breath and went for it.

I dashed from propane tank to maple tree to holly bush, feeling incredibly silly that I lacked the courage to just walk up to that house with the cool confidence of the fully armed person that I was. Once I reached the house, I walked around the outside to the mystery room's window. The TV was still playing, so I had to assume someone was in the house. If it was him, I'd simply kill him; if it was someone else, I wasn't sure how I'd handle it. The unknown was the worst part as I entered the house.

Of course, the screen door screeched as I opened it; of course, I fumbled noisily with the lock pick—which I'd finally figured out how to use—only to discover the door was already unlocked; of course, the wooden floors creaked and my boots clunked with every step. The mystery door still stayed closed as I looked around. I kept the SIG drawn, finger on the trigger, all the same.

Two sets of dirty dishes sat in the kitchen sink. Over the fireplace in the living room sat photos of grown children and grandchildren, him with arms around his wife, American flag forever waving on his hand. In every picture, on every face, was the same plastic smile, on the same stiff bodies that looked like wind-up toys keyed too tight. At least I knew what he looked like now. At least I knew I had the right house.

A stack of unpaid bills sat on the coffee table, all in his name. Dirty boxer shorts were in the clothes hamper. So, I was pretty sure he lived there, that he was holed up in the mystery room. What I didn't know was if he was sitting in there with a shotgun pointed toward the door waiting for me to walk in uninvited.

I tipped over a lamp to see if the crash would draw him out. When it didn't, I pressed my back up against the wall next to the door, like the cops always do on TV, adjusted my Lone Ranger mask and threw the door open. Nothing. I took off my cowboy hat and cautiously held it out in the doorway on the barrel of the SIG, like the cowboys in the movies always do. Well, you know, except for the SIG part. Still nothing. So, I put the hat back on and edged into the room, gun up, the red dot from the laser sight tracing my movements along the ceiling.

The room was dark, except for the blue flicker from the television, quiet except for Joan Lunden talking on *Good Morning America.* Ah, another voice I wouldn't mind having. The stale air reeked of body odor, undaunted by the multiple air fresheners scattered on every flat surface.

It took me a moment to realize that the crumpled spot on the bed was a person. He was lying perfectly still, eyes open, staring at the ceiling, oblivious to my presence. Only after the red dot from the laser sight moved into his line of vision did he turn his head toward me.

I didn't recognize him at first. His face was more gaunt, his hair longer, grayer, his beard untrimmed. I thought he must be the woman's invalid father and I was embarrassed to be standing there holding a loaded gun in front of a shell of a man who didn't even seem to know where he was. I lowered the gun and moved closer to pat the back of his hand in a gesture of apology.

I stopped short when I saw the bald eagle etched in that basic tattoo blue-green. Stepping back, I raised the gun and let the red dot rest on his forehead.

As if he suddenly understood why I was there,

his eyes lost their glazed look and he stretched his arms out wide, palms up, as if in surrender.

"Go ahead," he croaked in a voice hoarse from not being used. "Go ahead."

I didn't know what to do. I realized I was standing inside a man's prison cell, self-made though it was. The judge had set him free, but he was still in jail.

I don't know how long I stood there, flexing my trigger finger, readjusting my grip. I knew I could walk out of that room without him ever mentioning I was there, without him ever giving my description to the police. Besides, he had created a prison for himself, a sentence for himself, far worse than the judicial system could have imposed. Frankly, I didn't want to offer him the bullet that would set him free from that hell. Yet, I needed to establish a series of shootings to get that innocent man out of jail. And there was always the chance he'd snap out of this blue funk and prey again.

The self-made-hell sentence finally won out over my death sentence. So, I swung the red dot to the palm of his right hand and pulled the trigger. He didn't even whimper. I targeted the left palm and fired again, hoping that would be enough to tie all the shootings together.

When I glanced up from pulling the china doll from my shoulder bag, I realized I had made a horrible mistake. One look at that once-tortured face and I knew immediately that he was free. I had redeemed him, like hurting myself on the swing set used to redeem me.

"Thank you," he whispered, still lying there with arms spread wide. It didn't look like surrender anymore. Now it looked like he wanted to give me a big, bloody, bear hug.

In a flash of rage, I threw the china doll at his feet and whipped the gun up, sending a bullet smashing through his head.

I stood there trembling, the red dot still resting on its mark, feeling the blood still running hot in my veins. I think I was in shock. I was standing there with the gun in my hand, my finger around the trigger, but I was surprised that he was lying there dead. I actually looked around to see who had shot him.

It finally sunk in that I had pulled the trigger. I lowered my gun and reached over to press a gloved hand to his bloody wrist. He was dead. So, I just left and set the dogs free.

I was still feeling a little shaky, so I was glad Caleb Jr. was there as I packed up my tent to leave. I really wanted to take that dog with me when I left. He climbed inside Jurisprudence like he wanted me to take him, too. But I couldn't. It ripped my guts out to leave him behind, but I just couldn't take him. Not while I'm living like this. It would be unfair to him, being left in kennels for weeks at a time while I'm out target shooting.

I almost wished I could just stop. But I couldn't. Not yet. Maybe never. So, I shooed him out of my car, gave him a hug and drove away.

I was in a pretty bad mood after all that, so I really wasn't up to anymore blows. I just wanted to relax at the motel and maybe catch up on the news, eat some Twinkies. Only, when I was reading the newspaper, I found a follow-up story on my second target that called it a copycat shooting, because I used a different gun, fired two bullets instead of one and left a brunette china doll instead of a blonde. So, even though his ex-wife had a solid alibi that night, she has been called in for questioning on suspicion of hiring a hit man. Sure. On a secretary's salary, she hired a hit man.

Now, I've killed target number three with a different gun, and I used three shots to do it. On the same day that a story about a copycat came out in the paper. Great. At least I'm back to a blonde china doll. Oh, but the newspaper told me to do that. Damn.

How could I have been so stupid? Of course the same gun would be the key thing to tie them all together. I was so eager to use all of his guns that I didn't even think about that. Stupid, stupid, stupid! I just assumed the china doll, bullet through the hand and child molester threads would be enough. And here I was starting to think I had a knack for this.

Some knack. So far, I've got one innocent man still behind bars and an innocent woman being accused of all sorts of stuff. I wonder which innocent will be harassed for number three? I'll have to think of some way to tie the three together in a nice, indisputable package before any more innocents are hurt.

# Chapter Twenty-Two

I'm rich. It's official now. A message was on the answering machine from his lawyers when I got back in town this weekend, notifying me that the estate is out of probate. So, when I went over to the office today, they outlined what is mine after estate taxes and their fees. I'm still nauseated. Oh, not at the taxes and stuff. At what's left. No one should have that much money. But he did. And now I do.

Why does this Ross Perot character suddenly come to mind? Because I hear he's worth even more than me? Who knows. I've been keeping an eye on him in the news. He's gathering petitions across the country to put himself on the ballot for president. An intriguing fellow to say the least. I think his irreverence for the establishment and his kick-butt, who-cares-about-checks-and-balances solutions for the nation's ills have made him feel like a kindred spirit. Except for his wealth. That made me a tad suspicious. Until today. Now that I'm wealthy myself, I'm not sure what to make of Perot's billions.

I've always thought of money as an evil thing. Maybe I even believed that he wouldn't have treated me so badly if he hadn't been "corrupted" by money. But maybe money is more neutral than that. Maybe it's neither good nor bad. Maybe it's just a tool. A tool he used to harm me. A tool Ross Perot may use to get the country back on track.

What will I use it for? I have no idea. I'm still in shock at how much is at my disposal. It sure puts all his years of charitable giving into perspective. Generous my ass. He barely dipped into his pocket change.

I don't want to just sit on this money and watch it grow like he apparently did. But that's the extent of my clarity.

I keep thinking, *I need to go see Kitty. I need to go see Kitty.* She's the only one I ever told about him. It was my first and her last year of college. The dorms were so crowded that year, she got stuck sharing her room with me, even though she was a resident assistant who was supposed to get a room to herself. I guess it's amazing he never found out I told her. Too bad for him.

Kitty went on to law school after college. She wants to work on fixing the justice system from within. I haven't so much as sent a Christmas card to her in the past couple of years, but I suddenly feel like I might explode if I don't see her soon. I don't even know why, unless I just need to tell someone about all the money. Of course, I might just be wanting some companionship via a safe, distant friendship. She lives at the far end of the state. Leaving Caleb Jr. behind seems to have awakened a sense of loneliness that I can usually ignore if I keep myself immersed in enough noise.

It would also be nice to get some financial advice from someone other than his lawyers or his accountants. I feel like I almost know what to do with the money, but not quite. It's like having a word on the tip of my tongue but not being able to spit it out. I must think Kitty can help me reach that thought. I hope so.

Enough about that. I clipped the article on the third target the day after I killed him and mailed it in another attempt to get that father released from jail. I also wrote "NOT!!!" across the copycat article, using his "N," Charlie's "O" and Juanita's "T". I wonder what the handwriting experts will make of that. I don't know if those articles will get the guy out of jail, but I'm not going to wait around until some article is loaded on a database to find out. Yesterday afternoon I fired a round from each of the three pistols into the huge oak tree by the swing set. I dug the bullets out and put them together in a small pack to mail to the police, each bullet taped to a copy of the article reporting that gun's respective shooting. I plan to fly to Canada later this week just to mail it. Surely that will be enough to convince the police they've got a vigilante on their hands and they'll let that guy go.

Just in case they're still determined to take the other man to trial, I'll use the Baretta again for my next target: a guy all the way on the West Coast. He served his full term for child molestation and upon his release went straight to the nearest playground. He was behind some bushes showing a kid his dick when the police pounced on him. But did he go straight back to prison? Oh, no. A judge ruled the police violated this man's civil rights by following him from prison in an unmarked patrol car. This man had paid his debt to society, after all. Never mind the rights of the kids the police protected by following him. So, he's still out there, no doubt still roaming the playgrounds and the school yards and the malls.

But not for long.

I want to spend some time searching databases before I go after him. I'm hoping there are some others I can put a stop to during the same trip, since it will be such a long drive. I don't want to wait too long, though. It's pretty obvious that he's a true-blue pedophile who's making up for a lot of lost time.

# Chapter Twenty-Three

Saturday,
June 20, 1992

The past six weeks have felt really productive. After that quick trip to Canada, I mapped out a nifty little cross-country shooting spree that let me visit for a few days with Kitty on the way to tracking down five more targets.

After stopping my second target, I drove through L.A. to check out the riot damage. What a mess. It felt a bit like a déjà vu encounter with that image of the burning building collapsing in on the kids. I even got out of the car and poked around through some of the rubble. I think I was looking for survivors. Didn't find any. But I seemed to find some inspiration to loop down through the western states and put a stop to three more creeps.

The drive reminded me of the scenery in *Thelma & Louise*. Those incredible rock formations that seem to shoot up at random from the desert floor. The colors at the red end of the spectrum which virtually explode at sunset. Ah, the advantages of not taking the interstates anymore.

The only hitch in the whole trip was when poor Jurisprudence tuckered out and broke down a few days ago, leaving me stranded waiting for car parts. I guess this is the thanks I get for buying American.

It's actually been kind of nice to pause after such a non-stop whirlwind operation. Things went beautifully. I think I'm getting better with practice. I'm tired, though. So, I may hang around here for a few more days, even though Jurisprudence is chomping at the bit, rearing to go again.

I have to admit that it's more than just R&R

keeping me here. I've been sitting in on some trials down at the local courthouse to pass the time while waiting for my car. I started doing that because of Kitty.

It was good to see her again. I've done such a Dr. Jekyll and Mr. Hyde number since I saw her last that I halfway expected to find she had changed a lot, too. Her unruly red hair has been tamed to a shorter, more lawyerly look. But other than that, she seems to be pretty much the same ol' Kitty. Still athletic. Still drives that canary-yellow jeep. Still hates cats because of her name.

A flattened rubber cat with a tire tread running its length is stuck to the picture window in her living room. She has a complete collection of those uses-for-dead-cats books gracing her coffee table, too. Oh, and she has a goldfish and a canary now to save them from the cats of the world.

I couldn't believe she still collects refrigerator magnets. The gaudier the better. I ran across a couple during my trip to add to her collection: a "Miss Kitty" magnet from *Gunsmoke* that I'm sure she'll hate, and a refrigerator that sports a refrigerator magnet that sports a refrigerator magnet that sports a refrigerator magnet.

But how did I get off on Kitty? Oh, yeah. The trials.

"Watch some trials, Annie," she suggested during the visit when I noted that what I really wanted to buy with all that money was something I couldn't buy: a little justice for people. "Maybe you'll find some way to do that. People purchase injustice all the time, in ways you've never imagined. I don't see why someone of means can't turn the tables and buy some justice for a change. Why not?"

I don't think I've gone to enough trials yet, because I haven't quite grasped what she was trying to tell me. But I have found a trial that I'm watching closely, waiting for the outcome. He's a Persian Gulf veteran who lost his job while he was in Saudi Arabia. He's accused of supplementing his family's income by taking nude photos and videos of his five stepchildren and selling them to an underground porno ring. The kids say the mother knew nothing about it, because she was at work. She says nothing like that could have happened without her knowledge, never mind the photos presented as evidence.

She also says the kids, the oldest of whom is nine, took the photos themselves. Their biological father was killed in a construction accident a few years ago and the mother claims they're trying to frame their stepfather because they're so angry with him for not being their real dad.

It's mind boggling watching this woman proclaim her husband's innocence. I'm just glad that, as witnesses themselves, those kids haven't been forced to listen to her abandon them in court. Of course, if she succeeds in getting him off, I'll kill him, so she's not going to keep him either way. She might as well give her kids the support they need.

I'm a little intrigued by this woman. I can tell from the sheer passion of her testimony that she believes herself. I also know she's dead wrong. Those kids risked everything, including her love, to tell. There's no way they're making this up. Since when do kids lie about things that will get them in trouble with their folks? That's totally lost on her, though. I get the feeling that, even if her husband confessed, she'd argue for his innocence, saying that he confessed just to protect the kids from further trauma.

"That's just the kind of man he is," I can imagine her saying.

From what Kitty's told me, her mother made

the same choice as this woman. She just couldn't believe that her brother was capable of doing those things. So, she walked away. Left her husband and kids to their "sick delusions" and walked away. She won't speak to Kitty to this day.

Before watching this woman in court, I just dismissed Kitty's mom as a fruitcake. An anomaly. But suddenly I find myself seeing glimpses of my own mother in what Kitty's mom did then, what this woman does now. Mom was oblivious to what was going on, too. Even when she brought up what Mrs. Jenkins said about baths, it wasn't because she suspected anything. She just wanted to avoid the appearance of anything going on; she was just worried about what this neighbor seemed to think. It was his own guilt that made him lose control of his cover—and the car. She didn't want to hear; she didn't want to know.

Sheesh. Writing that makes me feel so disloyal to her. But I just can't stop thinking about it. I've always known that she didn't know the truth until the very end. Even though I went through a stage of being furious at her for dying and leaving me all alone with him, I never wanted to ask her why she didn't know. Until now.

Why Mom? Why didn't you know? He took baths with us almost every night he was home. He took us skinny-dipping in the pool. We were constantly jumping into bed with you and Caleb in the middle of the night. Didn't you wonder why we had so many bad dreams? Didn't you wonder why we didn't go jump into bed with him? Did all those vaginal infections happen by themselves? Why didn't you know, Mom? Why?

No answer. Not even a peep. Dead people can be so stuck up sometimes. But maybe I'll get some answers—or at least some more questions—watching this wife of the accused.

Thank goodness Marilyn is still out there making it harder for mothers not to know. All across the country I bump into stories about her efforts. No wonder he was so concerned about what would happen to his reputation if I followed in Marilyn's footsteps.

I heard that she and her husband received the Anti-Defamation League's Distinguished Community Service Award early this month. I was impressed, especially when I heard that their fellow honorees were Holocaust survivors. It felt incredibly validating that an incest survivor was included in the company of survivors of such horrors. At last! Someone gets it! Someone understands!

Why does that make me think of the guy who recently set out walking across America to prove that most people are good? Maybe because he didn't get it. Even when he got mugged last month he probably didn't understand. It doesn't matter if most people in this country are good, any more than it mattered that most people in Germany were good in the Second World War.

All the "good" factor does is make it harder for the most to believe the horrors committed by the few.

Maybe that's what happened with Mom. She couldn't fathom anyone treating her children the way he treated us, since she would never treat us that way herself. Hmmm. It's a thought.

# Chapter Twenty-Four

Wednesday,
June 24, 1992

They convicted him! Isn't that something? I could hardly believe it. I felt like jumping up and letting loose a victorious war whoop. Oh, well. At least I whooped it up inside my head. I plan to go out and celebrate later this evening.

His wife didn't share my joy. She almost collapsed when the jury foreman read the verdict.

"What am I supposed to do now? What am I supposed to do now?" she screamed over and over at the jury as the judge pounded his gavel demanding order, threatening contempt charges.

I expected someone to take her to the doctor for a sedative or to get her in touch with a crisis counselor. No one did. There was no one to do that—or anything else—for her. She was completely on her own. Totally alone. I'd somehow never noticed that before then.

That concerned me, especially as I watched her herd the children out of the courtroom and into her car while she was in such an agitated state. I thought they'd be in foster care or something.

She didn't bother with car seats or seat belts. She just opened the doors and ordered the five of them to get in. Then she slid behind the wheel and sat there for a while as she slowly, methodically banged her forehead against the steering wheel.

Seeing her in that state gave me a sinking feeling. I kept flashing back to the wreck, as I rushed to get Jurisprudence so I could follow her. I was just glad my car was running again.

I don't know what I thought I'd accomplish by

following her. I guess I'd at least be on the crash scene to give immediate first aid. I'm told that's what saved me in the wreck. Someone came by who knew enough to open my trachea with a ball-point pen, while he basically strangled me to keep me from bleeding to dead. I guess I was going to return the favor for one of those kids. I just hoped I wouldn't have to pick which one to save, like the guy who picked me.

She went straight to a pawn shop and must have sold something, since she came out counting cash. I don't think it was enough, though, because once she got back into the car, she beat her fists against the steering wheel, still gripping the money.

She went to the bank after that, cash still in hand. Before going inside she tried to comb her hair and put on fresh lipstick, but it must have gone badly in there, too. She looked disheveled again when she came back out some thirty minutes later, staggering across the parking lot like she was drunk. Actually, she was crying. Heavy, body wracking sobs. She walked right past her car. The oldest child jumped out of the car and ran after her mother, helping her find the way back.

I couldn't let her drive those kids anywhere else in that condition, so I drove Jurisprudence over in front of the car, blocking her in. I could see her hunched over the steering wheel sobbing, car running, hand on the gear shift. I sure hoped she wouldn't try to drive right through my car.

"Can I help?" I quickly scribbled on the notepad I always carry with me. My porta-voice I call it. I went over to the car and handed the paper to the oldest child through a crack in the window.

She looked at it, at me, at her mother, at me. Wide eyes, but she said nothing.

"Never talk to strangers. Right?" I wrote, holding it up against the window for her to read.

She gave me a hint of a smile and nodded.

"That's okay," I mouthed to her, returning her smile. Walking around the back of the car, I went up to the driver's window.

"Do you need me to do something? Drive? Take the kids somewhere?" I wrote. Holding the paper against her window, I tapped to get her attention.

She looked up, tears still streaming down her face. She seemed to look right through me. I tapped on the window again. She gave her head a shake like a wet dog. That seemed to help her focus.

"No, I'm fine," she croaked through the glass, waving me away. "I'm just having a really bad day."

I looked at the kids. Two of them were quietly crying; one was patting her mother's arm, trying to comfort her; the other two seemed shrunken, as if they were trying desperately to be invisible. This guilty verdict was no victory for them. At least not today.

"Isn't there anything I can do?" I tried again. "I'll do anything you need. I really don't mind."

She wiped the tears from her eyes, then gripped the steering wheel tight until her knuckles stood out like a snowcapped mountain ridge across her hands. She took a few deep, settling breaths.

"I'm fine now. Really," she at last said. "I just needed to get my bearings. Thanks for the offer, but there's just nothing you can do. There's nothing anyone can do."

She did seem calmer (or was it just numb?) so I nodded and waved good-bye. But I stopped short and turned around.

"I'm going to follow you as far as your house, just to make sure you make it home safe. Okay?" I wrote.

She nodded her permission, then warned that she had to make a stop on the way. She went back to the pawn shop. I guess she bought back the thing she had hocked. Must have been a wedding ring or something. She drove straight home after that. I don't know if she felt better once they were all safely home, but I was certainly relieved.

I think about that woman's duress, and it seems to be about so much more than her husband's guilt or innocence. It seems to be about being left all alone with five kids to raise, about being abandoned by him, by the courts. And it was about money. Definitely about money. Her job must not pay very well. Surprise, surprise. I guess she has daycare expenses, too, now that he's not taking care of the kids while she works. If you want to call what he did "taking care of the kids." No wonder whatever happened in that bank left her a wreck.

It's almost as if she needed her husband to be found innocent, if for no other reason than to keep the checks coming from...what? More porno pics? More than an innocent verdict, she needed the abuse to have never been discovered at all. If only she made decent wages herself, maybe she could have afforded to want safety and justice for her children. As it is, she may not be able to afford food and shelter for them.

It makes me think of that dentist's ex-wife. She was some gutsy woman, leaving her husband and pushing for a molestation conviction, even though that meant raising two kids on a secretary's wages. I don't think Mom would have been willing to do that for us.

She got pregnant in college and dropped out of school to marry him and raise us. I remember once hearing some people call her a gold digger who got pregnant on purpose just to get at his money. Who knows? Maybe it's true. The only trouble with that theory is it wrongly presumes that he was an extraordinary catch.

In any case, they didn't have much of a marriage. If she'd acknowledged the abuse and left him, though, she would have had a hard time supporting twins without her degree. Heck, she would have had a hard time even if she had a degree. Just look at the big bucks my degree earned me. And hers wasn't even as marketable as mine. She was studying fine arts.

Earning higher wages sure gives men a hell of a lot of power. I wonder if money is the very essence of male power in a country that so values that resource. Oh dear, I'm forgetting my sophomore economics. Money isn't a resource is it? It's a means of accessing resources. Picky, picky. The bottom line's still the same: men have more access, so men have more power.

I guess I've theoretically got the same power now. Many times over. It's a shame I don't fully grasp how to use it. At this point it mostly feels a bit slimy to think that he bequeathed his power to me. Well, all but $250,000 of his power, anyway. It's like he gave me a house full of electricity but he gave the fuse box to someone else who's free to turn my lights out anytime. He certainly bought some injustice there.

I wonder if Kitty was right that I can turn the tables now and use this money power to buy justice for some others. Or even to see that others' reputations aren't unjustly kept intact. Now, that would be a blast.

I don't know where I'm going with all these thoughts yet. I guess it's just dawning on me that I really can use his money to do more than just fund my extermination work. Once I learn to tap the power, maybe I can even share the power.

I don't have a whole lot of cash with me right now, because of this unscheduled layover on top of car repairs, but I can still leave what I have in that woman's mailbox. That'll give her a little power. Hey, but why stop there? When I get back home, I can mail her a letter, asking what she needs help with—mortgage payments, child care, utilities, whatever—and make arrangements to pay those things for her. Hopefully, she won't take so much frustration out on her kids that way.

Only I won't send that letter from me. I'll get Kitty to advise me on setting up some fund. The WJF Memorial Fund—that's what I'll call it. No hit man could find fault with me for using his initials on a memorial fund that will only enhance his reputation. Privately, though, WJF will stand for "When Justice Fails." Ah, the joys of being secretly devious. It's like mixing some spit into his scotch and getting to watch him drink it.

This could be fun. I'm going to have to think some more about it all, but it feels like a start. I may beat that asshole at his own game yet. But first, I'm going to go to a baseball game and buy me some peanuts and Cracker Jacks and not care if I ever get back, because today justice didn't fail. That's something to celebrate.

# Chapter Twenty-Five

Thursday,
June 25, 1992

I often sleep with the TV playing. It's that same old embarrassing avoid-silence-at-all-costs thing. Anyway, because of that, I'm used to things on TV getting mixed up in my dreams. Like when the space shuttle Challenger exploded. I was asleep when that report came on TV and I dreamed I was riding on the shuttle as it plunged to earth. Everyone was trying to jump out and grab tree branches on the way down, so we wouldn't hit the ground and die. It was a scary dream. It was even creepier when I woke up to see a replay of the shuttle actually exploding.

Then this morning I dreamed those kids' mother was pointing the Baretta at them, crying hysterically and screaming, "What am I supposed to do now?"

"I'll help. See, I have money. I can help," I was calling out to her. I often dream that I can talk. Today I had Maya Angelou's incredibly powerful and soothing voice. I liked that.

"No, I'm fine. Really," the mother said, pulling the trigger. I woke up as the gun fired.

"That was the scene at 554 Maple Drive late last night after police investigated what they thought was just a prank call," the news anchor said, smiling one of those perpetual TV journalist smiles that so often seem inappropriate. I hate how their voices all sound the same, too. "In other news, the Los Angeles City Council is reportedly moving toward proposing a five to eight million dollar settlement of a lawsuit filed by Rodney King...."

I lay there wide awake, heart pounding, as the

TV droned on. Intellectually, I knew it was just a dream. Something on TV was just mixing with the guilt I felt for not dropping that money off at her house last night after the ball game.

The game went into extra innings, so by the time I fought my way out of the post-game traffic it was after midnight and I was exhausted. I'm usually just getting cranked up by that time; I've become quite the night person since entering this line of work. But with the long days I've been spending at the courthouse, I was wiped out last night, so I just made a beeline for the motel.

I had a private chuckle at myself this morning for being overly dramatic about everything, even in my dreams. Then I got up and took a shower, vowing to get that money to the woman today on my way out of town. It was a leisurely morning of packing and mapping out a route home that would let me drop in on Kitty again. I hope I can bribe her with those magnets to help me establish my WJF Memorial Fund.

Once I checked out of the motel, I stopped by Waffle House for a grilled cheese and an order of hash browns scattered, smothered, covered and chunked. I enjoyed listening to the waitresses call out orders to the cook in that funky little code of theirs.

I made plans for my cash drop while I ate. I figured I'd drive by her house and either pop the package in the mailbox or stick it inside the screen door, depending on how many neighbors were around. Hopefully, she wouldn't see who left it, but even if she did, what's the crime in dumping cash? Besides, I hadn't even killed anyone at this stop, so nothing was really at risk.

Once I was back in Jurisprudence, I reached into the glove compartment for the little notepad where I'd jotted down directions to her house.

"Maple Drive, third house on the left," jumped off the page, and I jumped out of the car. I ran so hard back inside Waffle House that my head was starting to spin by the time I reached the stack of morning papers others had left behind on the counter. I snatched them all up and made for the nearest booth, not caring that I was making a scene.

I didn't have to look long. It was the banner headline on page one. "What Else Could I Do?" it asked in bold, 72-point type.

"Something! You could have done *something* else," I wanted to scream back at the headline. I wanted to scream at her. I was so tired of wanting to scream at dead people: at Winnie, at Mom, at him, at everyone I'd shot. I finally just rested my spinning head on the newsprint and cried.

The what-else-can-I-do feeling is a horrible thing. I know that. It's why I do the work I do. Yet, as much as I understand that sense of hopelessness, helplessness—that rage—right now all I feel is the familiar black hole in my gut that might collapse in on itself at any moment. This woman's expression of hopelessness has left me utterly grief-stricken.

"What else could I do?" I can almost hear her ask it, scream it. She wrote those words before hanging herself in the garage with her husband's camera strap.

I don't know whether she formed the question before or after shooting all five of her kids. Probably before. She bought her pistol at that pawn shop yesterday. As I followed her home, she did this. I could just die. When is that damn Brady Bill going to pass?

Now, I keep wanting to throw up, to purge myself of something. I don't even know what. I've checked back into a motel and have been lying here for hours with a trash can at the ready. In silence I've been lying here. Even the constant chatter in my head has been mostly quiet.

The sound of my pen scratching against this paper actually seems invasive just now, maybe even obscene. The silence feels that sacred to me at the moment. I don't have a clue what this sudden immersion in silence means. If anything. Maybe for me the world has just stopped. I've pushed the pause button and the mute button, and that's just the way it's going to stay until I'm ready to let the world start spinning on its axis again. Or maybe this woman's last bit of rhetoric has been one sound too many. I've had my fill and I just don't care to hear anything more.

She really blindsided me with this. I think I'm disappointed in her in the same way I heard a black woman in Los Angeles express her shame in her race during the riots as she watched people looting stores. I was disappointed like that on a smaller scale when I heard a woman who had been raped herself accusing Mike Tyson's rape victim of making the whole thing up. There was no physical evidence of Desiree putting up a fight, after all. Like that tiny woman was supposed to whoop up on a man who only a few, extremely well-paid, comparably sized men would venture to fight.

My disappointment in this mother is on an even deeper level.

I know there's something ironic—hypocritical even—about the feelings this woman has stirred. I'm not exactly a pristine example of womanhood myself. Other women will no doubt feel someday that I have shamed or set back the cause of women by what I've done. Plenty of them have been handed the same flavor of shit that I have without resorting to murder. Plenty of them have grown up to become women of outstanding character and integrity. It's like something Kitty said to me once: "I'm using the shit life handed me as fertilizer to grow one helluva garden. That's my revenge. Instead of getting buried under the crap, I'm growing my life into something more than it was going to be. Something a lot better than him."

I've always admired Kitty for that, especially as I've watched her really do it. I imagine that's how Winnie would have been, too. The two of them seemed to share that same eternal flame within, that nothing or no one could douse.

Hmmm. That sounds unfair to them now that I've written it. It sounds like I'm negating the struggle that people like Kitty go through to take the broken pieces of their lives and put them into something like a kaleidoscope where the very brokenness makes such magic, such beauty possible. That takes a lot of effort, a lot of deliberateness. It's not going to just happen.

It's much easier to be like me, to scatter those jagged, broken pieces about where they'll cut anyone who comes near. I send shards of myself flying out of those pistols every time I put a stop to someone. It's been much easier to pull the trigger during the past few months than it was to refrain from pulling the trigger all these years. Much, much easier.

The hurt kids who grow up to be adults like Kitty are miracles of personal fortitude. Yet, no one seems to know that. It's expected, taken for granted. Like with me. It's just assumed that no matter what he did to me, I won't grow up and kill other men like him to save other little kids like me. I'll be strong and noble. Above all else, I'll be law abiding.

It seems pretty natural to me that I do what I

do, like this is the kind of equal and opposite reaction one might expect in a world that made sense.
Only, the world—or at least this country—doesn't
make sense anymore, so neither does its expectations, its assumptions.

I assumed this woman would cope. Maybe it
wasn't a fair assumption. I don't know. Now, no
doubt, it's assumed that the one child who survived the bullet through her throat will get past
this trauma and go on to lead a productive life.

No, I'm wrong. That's not the assumption at
all, is it? It's assumed she'll never lead a "normal"
life after going through all this. She's expected to
live out her days in a psych ward.

I don't know which assumption is worse. Probably the latter, since it pretends that society at
large won't ever have to deal with her wounds.
We're great pretenders. I guess that's why the cy-
cle of wounded people wounding other people goes
on and on, generation after generation, growing
ever larger, like the concentric circles of a tree.
Until someone like me comes along and chops
down a tree.

That mother certainly gave her family tree a
good chopping. Surely there's some other way,
some better way, to get out of that loop.

Listen to me. Ms. Shoot-'Em-Up herself saying there's got to be a better way. But.... Of course
there'd be a "but." But I think that what I'm doing
is a little different. A lot different. Well, okay, I don't
know if in reality it's all that different—whatever
reality is—but it feels different to kill the wounded
who are busily creating new wounded. The children still embody hope, wounded though they may
be. The oldest child who survived her mother's
massacre doesn't have to grow up and be like me,
or like her mom or stepdad. She could grow up

like Kitty or Marilyn—or like Oprah Winfrey. That's her choice.

As a fellow killer, I guess that's where I take issue with this girl's mom snatching that choice from four innocents. I'm trying to protect kids, avenge kids, so they can choose something better for themselves than what I've chosen for myself. She never even gave her kids the option of aspiring to a life better than her own. It pisses me off!

I'm really worried about the kid who lived. Her mom has bequeathed her one hell of a guilt trip. She's the one who turned in her stepdad during a sexual abuse prevention program at school.

Then on the evening of his conviction, the paper says, she awoke to gun shots and ran out of her bedroom into the hall to see her mom coming out of her brothers' room with a gun. When the girl called out, her mother turned and yelled, "This is all your fault!" Firing twice, the mom shot the girl once in the neck. The girl stayed on the floor where she'd fallen, feigning death when her mother walked over and prodded her with the pistol. Smart kid.

Moments later the girl heard the shot that killed her sister and heard her mother go out to the garage. The girl made her way to the telephone in the living room and dialed 911, only to discover she couldn't talk. So, she tapped SOS repeatedly onto the mouthpiece until she passed out.

Her youngest brother was still alive when the police arrived but he later died at the hospital. The girl is out of danger, though. The doctors expect a full recovery. She'll even get her voice back. But it's going to be hard to get past "This was all your fault."

I suspect she would have felt that way without her mother ever verbalizing it for her. I know I felt like the wreck was all my fault and all I'd done was ask Mrs. Jenkins why Mr. Jenkins wasn't taking a bath with her daughter Sally and me. Sally was my best friend, next to Winnie, and I was spending the night at the Jenkins' house for Sally's birthday. Winnie and Sally were so much alike they never really got along.

I wonder if that's what it was like for this girl. She asks some innocent question or makes some innocent comment about having to pose for photos. The next thing she knows, her world has turned upside down. Her stepfather is arrested; strangers are prodding her for details; lawyers are wanting to know about every fib she's ever told and wanting her to confess that she lied about her stepdad, too. Her mother doesn't believe her, either. Kids at school are pointing at her and whispering. Then when it finally ends, her mother goes off the deep end. And all because she opened her big mouth at school. I wonder if that's what it's been like for her. I wonder if that's what it's like for her right now, as she lies in the hospital with nothing else to do but think. In silence.

She may blame herself, but I blame her stepdad. He's the one who started it, who tipped the first domino that sent the whole line crashing down. He's the one who betrayed his wife in the process of betraying those kids, leaving her to clean up his mess without giving her so much as a rag to make the job easier.

An editorial noted that over $1000 in cash was confiscated by the police as evidence in the case, even though the mother had insisted it was money she was putting away from her own paycheck. The bank was about to foreclose on her house. The shoe factory where she worked had notified workers the week before to expect a couple of hundred layoffs by the end of the month.

"What else could she do?" the editorial joined

her in asking. I thought that strange. A more fit-
ting question would seem, "What else could we
have done?" But maybe questions like that died
with President Kennedy long before I was even
born.

"Ask not what you can do for your country,
but what your fellow Americans should have done
for themselves." Is that how it goes today?

I know what I could have done. I could have
dumped a pile of cash in her lap before I went to
the ball game. I could have offered to take a couple of her kids with me to the game just to give her
a break, or I could have stayed with the kids and
sent her out for an evening on the town. Maybe
she wouldn't have accepted any such offers from
a total stranger, but then again....

I know what I can do now, too, besides contributing to the fund set up for the girl. He's going
to be allowed to attend the mass funeral two days
from now and I can execute him as an accomplice
to murder. That will put an end to this nightmare
once and for all.

# Chapter Twenty-Six

Saturday,
June 27, 1992

Trying to shoot this guy at the cemetery was going to be risky. I knew that. The graveside service was scheduled for 10 a.m. He'd be escorted by police. Even though I was going to use my rifle for this one, I'd still likely get caught before I could get out of the cemetery. Shooting from that distance, with that many people around, meant I risked hitting the wrong person. But none of that seemed to bother me. Not enough, anyway. I was still at the cemetery before dawn, sloshing through a heavy dew, feeling my way among headstones, unassembled rifle in a case under my arm. I guess killing purely for revenge makes one reckless that way.

At least I went to the cemetery the day before, scoping out the area for the best spot to play sniper. With five graves being dug, it was easy to find where the funeral would be. I chose a grassy knoll off to the east of that spot so the sun would be at my back, and hopefully in the cops' eyes. Near a tree there's a headstone with a cross tacked on at just the right height to support the barrel of the rifle as I kneel on the ground. "Here Lies Whitney Buchanan. Taken Too Soon," the epitaph reads. "Born 1912. Died 1918." It seemed an appropriate place from which to shoot him. Besides, all the headstones are so old in that section of the cemetery it seemed unlikely that there would be any visitors.

All I did in the pre-dawn hours this morning was assemble my rifle and run it up the tree on a rope, like a flag on a flagpole. Only, this flag did not so proudly wave. Even though I was determined to shoot him, my motives felt too base to evoke any pride. This was a killing for something more personal than justice.

I returned to the cemetery shortly before the graveside service was to begin, wearing inconspicuous clothing and carrying a single red rose, as though visiting the grave of a loved one. Before driving my car to the cemetery, I emptied it of all guns, gadgets and my shooting-routes road atlas, putting them in a locker at the bus terminal. So, I'd taken about as many precautions as I could by the time I was in position. I'd take my shot, put the rifle back up in the tree, go put my rose on somebody's grave and maybe even "witness" someone fleeing with a rifle in hand. When it was safe, I'd go back for the gun and leave town.

I hadn't anticipated the massive crowd of people who turned out for the funeral. I expected the publicity to draw some curious onlookers, but as isolated as the woman seemed, I didn't expect hundreds to show. As it was, even though I saw him arrive via police cruiser, I couldn't begin to get a clear shot at him until the end, after the curious, the guilt-ridden, the media, all began filtering away.

As the crowd thinned, I caught a glimpse through my scope of the other thing I hadn't anticipated: the girl. I assumed she'd still be in the hospital, but there she was, throat bandaged, holding one of her stepfather's handcuffed hands, as they stood together beside the row of coffins.

My scope suddenly blurred, so I pulled my eye away, only to discover that everything else around me had blurred, too. I was crying. I hadn't even known.

I lowered my rifle. I couldn't shoot him. Not now. I didn't even need to shoot him anymore. I just sat there, leaning against Whitney's tombstone, crying, crying. Not for their loss. For my own.

When I saw the two of them standing there hand in hand beside the caskets, I knew I'd missed something by still being in the hospital when Winnie and Mom were buried. More than just the chance to say good-bye, I'd missed the chance to share the pain. If only to share it with the enemy. Neither he nor the girl looked like they were trying to speak as they stood there. Silence. The silence of one has such vast capacity for pain; yet shared silence seemed a comfort to them both.

No wonder I've distanced myself from silence. I've never had anyone to go there with me, to hold my hand for that first frightening plunge into the abyss. I'm glad that girl had someone, even if only him. I hope it helped.

I'm glad I didn't kill him. I know now I was trying to kill some ghost, some demon, of my own at the funeral today. I wouldn't have done the girl any favor by exacting my own revenge from her stepdad. Not after everything else she's gone through, slime though he may be. At least he's safe slime while he's behind bars.

After I finally stopped crying, I put the rifle back up in the tree; I'll go back sometime tonight to retrieve it on my way out of town. I had parked Jurisprudence way over near the entrance of the cemetery, planning to meander about the grounds on my way back there. But since I hadn't shot anyone, I just laid my rose on Whitney's grave and slowly walked down the knoll past the mass grave site, pretty much lost in my pain.

As I made my way through the handful of people still milling around after the funeral, I felt a tug on my shirt. I turned around and my red, puffy eyes met the girl's red, puffy eyes. For a brief moment, I almost felt like a twin again. Except her eyes are blue.

She opened her mouth to say something. When nothing came out, she raised a hand to her throat and dropped her head. I knelt down on the grass in front of her, lifted her chin and brushed blonde curls aside until our eyes met again.

"I can't talk either," I mouthed, untying the scarf from around my neck and showing her the scars on my throat.

She nodded and smiled a little sheepishly, like she had already figured that one out. Opening the little black purse she carried, she pulled out a crumpled piece of paper.

"Can I help?" it read. She still had my note.

I was taken aback. Letting out a deep breath to express some of the feelings I had just then, I took the note and pointed to each word to let her know I was asking again.

She dropped her head again, shaking it no. I felt so asinine, like a firefighter arriving after a home has been reduced to smoldering ashes and asking if I can put out the fire. I reached out and lifted her head again.

"I'm sorry," I mouthed.

She nodded.

"Heidi, we need to get you back to the hospital," a woman called out.

So, her name is Heidi. She has a bit of that Shirley Temple look about her, so it sort of fits. Still, the sweet little baby names we females get burdened with sometimes....

The woman started walking in our direction, looking a tad suspicious of me. I wasn't exactly decked out in my finest funeral attire.

Heidi started to leave, but I touched her on the arm and indicated for her to wait while I pulled the pen and paper from my pocket. I quickly wrote down my name and address, adding at the bottom. "I can help."

"Okay?" I mouthed after she saw what I'd written. She nodded and mouthed "okay" back.

I stood, waved good-bye to Heidi and nodded at the woman to acknowledge her presence. Heidi grabbed me around the waist, giving me a quick good-bye squeeze and went with the woman.

"Do you know her?" I overheard the woman asking Heidi as they walked away. Heidi nodded and looked back at me for a final good-bye wave.

I believe I've found the first beneficiary of the WJF Memorial Fund.

# Chapter Twenty-Seven

The house looked as haunted as it really is when I got back home yesterday afternoon. The lawn was looking pretty bad when I left in May, but it's a virtual jungle now. There must have been some kind of storm while I was away as well. Some shingles had blown off the roof and I had to move a tree branch from the driveway just so I could make it to the garage. I later found that lightning had split the old oak tree in back, smashing the swing set and some patio furniture when it fell. It's probably just as well that I lost a tree with three bullet holes in it.

The swing set is the only real loss. We've been through a lot together, that swing and I. Even so, I'm not sure whether to replace it. I keep wondering if maybe it's time I find another way to deal with my shame and guilt. It sure would be nice if I could do that and have a swing set, too.

Charlie and Richard are out there now mowing and chain sawing the whole mess into oblivion, so things are nice and noisy around here this afternoon. Ah, the joys of home ownership. And to think I spent so much time pouting in my former life because I had to rent. Oh, well. Live and learn.

I started out this morning chasing down all the cobwebs and dust bunnies in the house because it was so embarrassing that people were just a trip to the bathroom away from seeing what a mess things are inside. But I figured anybody cleaning up out there wouldn't be surprised by any mess inside either, so I gave up—even though

I'm sure I heard Mom's ghost wail.

She was always a stickler for a clean house, but wouldn't hire a maid for anything, never mind that the house has some forty-seven rooms. Or is it fifty-seven? I can never remember. What the four of us needed with a house that size I'll never know. I guess he just wanted to keep it in the family. He was like the fourth generation to live here. I guess that makes me number five. I sure as heck don't know what little ol' me needs with it, except to commune with its ghosts.

Once I gave up this morning on my noble pursuit of a dust-free living environment, I spent some time just wandering around the house, unlocking doors I hadn't stepped beyond in years. It's kind of wild to think about, but in all the months since I moved back here, I've stayed pretty much on the first floor in his bedroom and den. I did venture briefly to my old room and Winnie's room, but these days I sleep on my old futon in his room. I guess the house feels more like a headquarters or a home base for my operations than a home.

I think I was looking for a place to call home as I wandered about the house today. That surprised me. I don't know which surprised me most: wanting to find a place for myself here or wanting a place apart from my work. Either way, I figure what the heck? It won't hurt anything and it might even be fun.

I guess this latest mission has left me feeling kind of upbeat. Come to think of it, I don't recall the last time I felt so...alive? That seems a strange word to use having returned from shooting five and watching five others buried. I don't know. Maybe encountering Heidi at the funeral or outlining plans for the WJF Fund with Kitty a couple of days later left me feeling this way. Whatever did it, I like it.

I enjoyed walking through the house today, unlocking doors, flinging them open, leaving them open. Most of the rooms' furniture is covered with sheets, so it looks like great, hulking ghosts sitting in the rooms. That didn't dissuade me in the least. I think it even added to the fun.

None of those rooms whispered "welcome home" to me, though. So, I went looking for the doors leading to the twin attics. Only they weren't there. It freaked me out. I mean, my memory is great, so I didn't think I had just imagined them. Mom had an art studio in one. Winnie and I weren't allowed in there, but the other attic was our fortress, our desert island, our cabin in the wilderness. He never went to the attics for some reason.

"Bad memories," he muttered once to Mom in refusing to go see some painting she'd done in her studio. Who knows what happened in the attic when he was growing up in this house. Whatever haunted him made it a safe haven for us.

I never went back up there after the wreck. I don't really know why, unless when the deadbolts started appearing I didn't bother venturing outside my room. Today I was ready to go back again, so it bugged the heck out of me not having a way in.

I went outside and looked up at the roof just to reassure myself that I hadn't imagined it all and sure enough those twin peaks were really there. I scurried up the ladder Charlie had propped up against the house to inspect the roof and gingerly made my way across the sloping eaves to the closest attic window. Mom's studio. The window was locked, so I went over the ridge of the roof where she'd had skylight windows installed on the north face. I couldn't get in there either, but at least I could see inside, where her cobweb covered easel stood, bearing some unfinished canvas. Her painting smock was tossed carelessly across a table scattered with tubes of oils, brushes, loose sketches.

I could almost smell the linseed and turpentine she seemed to wear like perfume, as I lay there peering headlong into her private domain. I was surprised by the lack of order, by the clutter. It was hard picturing her so at ease somewhere. She cleaned the rest of the house almost compulsively. It seemed the vacuum cleaner was always roaring, freshly mopped floors were always drying, dust was never appearing. The studio was a side of Mom I didn't know. I guess there was a lot I didn't know.

The window to the other attic was locked too, but by then I remembered that this is my house. So, I kicked out that pane of glass that belongs to me and crawled in.

It was exactly how Winnie and I left it nineteen years ago, except for a layer of grime so thick I left footprints, like I was walking in snow. I had to use the scarf around my neck as a dust mask so I could breathe as I walked around pushing cobwebs aside. I felt like I had passed through a time warp. No kidding.

It was like I had been there just the day before playing dress up in some of Grandma's and Grandpa's old clothes that Winnie had dug out of an old trunk. The trunk was still standing open. The freakiest thing I found was a box of Twinkies that I don't remember which of us swiped.

Wait. I do remember. Charlie slipped those to us. He always was the devious grandfatherly type.

Those Twinkies didn't look any worse for wear. I was almost tempted to try one. Almost. I kept thinking what a great commercial it would make. "I was given a box of Twinkies when I was just a little tyke, and nineteen years later when it was finally safe to eat them, since my parents weren't around anymore, those Twinkies were still as fresh and delicious as could be." I could sell my story to Hostess and get rich. Wait, I'm already rich. I keep forgetting.

Anyway, I solved the mystery of the missing door while I was up there. At the bottom of the stairs, studs have been put up across the door-way and they're covered with dry wall. Whatever ghost was haunting him got sealed alive in these attic tombs. I guess he had Charlie do it when he was making the rest of the house wheelchair-accessible. It's pretty wild that he didn't even care what he was boarding up inside. But I can understand it. I think I feel about the rest of the house what he must have felt about the attics. I'm just surprised he didn't have the attics closed off sooner.

He inherited the house—and the money—when Winnie and I were two, after his mom and dad died together. Some snowmobile accident, I think. They went over a cliff or something scary. I can't remember exactly. I guess grandparents didn't come up all that much, since there weren't any by the time Winnie and I were old enough to be aware of that kind of stuff. Mom's dad ran off after her mother died when Mom was a little kid. Charlie was really the closest thing to a grandparent we had. I don't think he was even old enough to be a grandparent stand-in. I guess the toothless look just gave him that grandpa feel.

Grandparent stuff aside, I like the idea of the attic being separate from the rest of the house now. It makes it even more of a sanctuary than it was when I played there as a child. I think it'll make a great place to call my own.

While Charlie was around today, I had him crawl into the attic to lay out an apartment up there. Of course, he wanted to reopen the doorway and turn the area into a loft with finished walls and ceilings like he'd done with Mom's studio. But I want to keep the rafters and sloping walls. I want it all just like it is, except for adding a bathroom and a kitchen. The fewer changes the better.

He agreed to do it like I want it, but since the window is too small to move materials in and out, I had to compromise and let him take the whole front off the dormer. As if I even know what that is. Guess I'll find out. He's going to replace the window with the equivalent of a small glass door and then do the same to Mom's studio so they'll match.

I agreed to let him reopen the doorway to Mom's studio. He'll also install a fire escape of sorts at the back of the house. That way, I can either get to my place by walking across the roof from the studio or climbing the fire escape stairs. The house sprawls out so much that the roof isn't steep at all, so as long as the vertigo doesn't act up there's little danger of me falling off and breaking my neck.

I know Charlie thinks I'm batty all the same. He kept readjusting his Marlboro cap and spitting tobacco juice into an empty Coke can to keep from laughing out loud at my plans. He used to do that to keep from laughing at Juanita every time she killed another house plant.

Oh, well. Let him laugh. He can't be too surprised at my borderline insanity, considering who he used to work for.

# Chapter Twenty-Eight

Well, it's been nineteen years since the wreck. I almost missed the anniversary. That's so unlike me. I haven't forgotten since the first year. Usually, the wreck is all I think about from Memorial Day on. I struggle with flashbacks and dreams, feel a sense of impending doom. I never expect to make it to the Fourth of July alive. It's just a crappy time of year. A time when I question my sanity most.

I skipped all that this year. If Charlie hadn't stopped by this morning to take some more measurements of the attic, I wouldn't have even remembered what day it was. When he mentioned he was going to spend this Fourth of July camping at the lake with his grandkids, I felt like he'd hit me with a two-by-four. How could I have forgotten? I'd been in Winnie's and Mom's rooms just yesterday as I went through the house unlocking doors. I'd peered down into Mom's studio for the first time yesterday, too. But nothing clicked. Nothing reminded me that today's the day.

I don't know what to make of that. I feel terribly disloyal to them, like I should guard their memory more carefully than that. Of course, after nineteen years, it's probably about time I almost missed an anniversary. It probably should have happened sooner than it did. All the same, I feel bad about forgetting.

I'm at the cemetery now, sitting here at the foot of the four headstones. The fourth is mine. Instead of having the stone removed after learning Winnie died instead of me, he just had the date of death sandblasted off. He took a year or two to do that much.

"It's just a matter of time anyway," he explained keeping my headstone. No wonder that stone always felt like a death threat.

I guess the joke's on him, since he needed a tombstone first. Of course, his wasn't already in place like mine. So, everyone thinks I was being the eternally grateful, loving daughter when I selected the majestic granite monument with the giant, open, bronze hand on top, reaching skyward. "Open Always. Giving Always. Missed Always," the inscription on the base reads.

Needless to say, I didn't so honor him. That was a prearranged honor he gave himself. He knew better than to have a flower vase installed as part of that grand monument to his false sainthood, though. Its perpetual emptiness would have told too much truth. I certainly brought him no flowers today.

I brought armloads for Winnie and Mom. I always bring daisies for Winnie, tiger lilies for Mom. Those were their favorites. He'd always send roses, just because they were expensive and made him look good. He never visited the graves himself. Because of his wheelchair, he always said. I never saw him let that wheelchair stop him from doing anything else, even if he had to pay people to carry him. He made it to Ian Fleming's grave just fine for that photograph.

I usually don't bring as many flowers as I did today. I guess the guilt of almost forgetting got the best of me at the florist. Oh, well. At least I didn't go seek out the nearest swing set. Different is good, right? The flowers do look nice en masse against the black marble stone.

I don't know why I did it, but I bought a single Easter lily for my grave. I'm not sure if I'm paying homage to the bulk of me that's truly dead or the sliver that's felt almost alive for the past several days.

I often lie on the plot beneath my tombstone during these visits with Mom and Winnie. I guess it makes me feel closer to death, which makes me feel closer to them. That sort of thing. I don't feel like doing that today. I'll just let the Easter lily stretch out there beside them instead.

I guess a lot feels different about sitting here today. I feel different. This time last year I was sneaking into town on a bus and taking a taxi out here so I could visit Mom and Winnie without him knowing I was even in town. I was my usual miserable self, as unchanging as this graveyard, desperately wanting to hurt him for what he'd done to them, to us, yet poisoning myself instead.

This year I sit looking down the hill at the pond in the valley, where ducks and swans gather around a handful of people offering stale bread and crackers. A little stream off to the left runs down from the pond and disappears into a grove of Buckeye trees. As I watch that stream skim water off the pond, I feel like I'm watching the poison inside me slowly, steadily, trickling away. It's been bottled up, completely contained for all these years, but I'm finally doing something about it, doing something with it. And it's going away.

I didn't plan that when I started putting a stop to people. It just happened. I like it, but it makes me wonder if any action on my part would have let that poison escape—if I really needed to shoot anyone at all. I know it's a moot issue at this point, since I have, indeed, shot. And shot and shot. Still, I wonder. I suspect the shooting wasn't necessary. I suspect that's why a huge chunk of the female population isn't out there stalking perps. Just me.

America's been lucky so far that so many of its

hurt little girls have grown into women of character who wouldn't dream of stooping to the level of
those who hurt us; who are determined to model
a higher standard of humanity. If this nation got
what it deserved for just giving lip service to the
well-being of its children, there'd be a whole underground network of women like me, operating
our own alternative justice system.

I guess that's why I'll keep putting a stop to
people. For now. I think this country deserves me,
just like it deserved the Los Angeles riots. It's not
enough for me that my own abscessed wounds are
draining some, are healing some. It's not enough
that I know now I didn't have to do what I've done.
There's more to this than my singularly insignifi-
cant pain. There's a collective pain out there that
I have felt, a collective scream that I have heard. I
cannot pretend now that I didn't feel it, didn't hear
it, just because my own pain has eased. I'm still
wild with the children's pain; I'm still crazed by
their screams. I can't respond "politely" in that
state. I won't.

It's funny, but when I first started getting serious about this extermination thing, I imagined visiting the graveyard like a puppy with its tail tucked
between its legs for letting Winnie and Mom down
by doing something they never would have done
had they survived in my stead. I still don't think
they would have stooped to my level, but I don't
feel ashamed to visit them today. If anything, it's
easier to be here than it's ever been before. For
the first time in nineteen years, I don't regret that
I survived. I regret that they didn't, but I'm not
sorry I lived.

I'm making a difference with my life now. I'm
starting awfully late and who knows how much
longer I can go without getting caught. But my

survival doesn't feel like a total waste anymore. With one perpetrator incapacitated and seven others dead, the country is that much safer for some kids out there. That makes me feel proud.

I wouldn't really expect Winnie or Mom to share my pride. I know it's the same brand of sicko pride the neo-Nazis and religious fanatics have for their own tunnel-vision views of the world. I hate to admit it, but it's probably even the kind of pride he had in pulling off such a finely tuned double life, knowing he could maintain the facade even beyond the grave.

Oh, well. I guess lowering myself to his level was a predictable trade-off in choosing this work. It's unfortunate, but I knew this was a costly path when I chose it. So, until I choose something else, I'll just have to pay up....

The way I feel about myself isn't the only thing that's different this anniversary. I notice that I feel differently about Mom, too. I guess I just wonder where she was. It's not like I have no memories of her or even unhappy memories. She was the kind of mom who thought rain puddles were meant for splashing, straws were meant for blowing bubbles in drinks, spaghetti was meant for slurping. She was a blast. Come to think of it, her cluttered studio was not so much out of character as her incessant house cleaning was.

Hmmm. Now that I think about it, she only cleaned house so feverishly when he was home. He was home a lot, since he wasn't under any nine-to-five job constraints, so of course the house was spotless.

I've often thought I have holes in my memory when it comes to times when the whole family was together. I mean, I have lots of memories of Winnie and me with just him and with just Mom. Except for family vacations, though, I don't remember us all being together much. I'm not sure we were really together even then.

Maybe I don't have memory lapses. Maybe there's just nothing to remember.

Good grief, Mom. What were you thinking? He was so oppressive, so disgusting, that you went on a cleaning frenzy anytime he was around. Either that or you escaped to your art studio. You couldn't even stand to share the same bedroom with him. But still you left Winnie, you left me, to deal with him day after day? You couldn't deal with him but you thought a couple of little kids could? Come on. Oh, and let me guess. You stayed with him, miserable though you were, for our sakes, didn't you? Why? Because he could offer money and you couldn't? Because you'd rather us come from a secretly shattered home than an openly broken one?

Tell me, Mom. If you'd lived, would you have walked out on the bastard, would you have rescued me from him? I wish you could answer. I want to believe that you would have saved me. As hard as you worked at not knowing what was going on, I want to believe that once it became impossible to deny anymore, you would have done something about it. Something better than the mother who shot her kids.

The woman I hope you were would have come to my aid. I guess the good thing about you being dead is, I don't ever have to let go of that hope. You'll never prove me wrong. I'll never have to ignore you like I'll ignore him during these graveside visits forevermore. I'm glad. I like having a mother who cares about me, who I care about. Even a dead one who's mostly whatever I imagine you to be. I'd hate to find out you were like Heidi's mom all along.

# Chapter Twenty-Nine

Sunday,
July 5, 1992

I'm going to keep his room locked for the next couple of weeks while Charlie and crew are here working on my attic. I guess I'm feeling a tad paranoid about keeping that one room secure, since it contains such damning evidence. While I've still had the house to myself this weekend, I've spent most of my time in his room glued to the computer terminal. Mostly I've been browsing databases, searching for articles on past targets to add to my walls and to keep abreast of the investigations.

Apparently, the three bullets I mailed finally opened some eyes and the authorities dropped the attempted murder charges against the girl's father. The first target is still alive. He hasn't regained consciousness yet, but it's still a little worrisome knowing there's someone out there who might be able to ID me. Someday.

Right now, no one has a clue. I'm presumed to be a white male with a daughter or some other relative who was raped and possibly murdered by someone who wasn't brought to justice. I'm believed to have a military background. I probably spend a lot of time in public libraries browsing newspapers for potential victims. I do this browsing as I drift back and forth across the country, picking up odd jobs along the way to buy china dolls, gas for my late-model car and camping supplies. And I may be traveling with a dog.

All this they think they've figured out, even though the only clues they seem to have are from that one hit in the rural area. They got a good boot print, found my little camp with the remains of a fire and made a plaster cast of a tire tread there. I couldn't have planted better false clues if I'd tried. I don't typically camp out; the late-model car they've tied to the tire tread isn't the junk heap they're on the lookout for; and I wear a common, national brand of men's boots, since I inherited his wide, square feet. Women's shoes never quite fit.

I guess I'll keep wearing the boots, but I'll go out this week while Charlie's here making me nervous and get new tires—new wheels if I have to—to change that tread. I guess I better not camp anymore, either, and I should stop staying at economy motels.

I'm disappointed about the camping. I enjoyed that night under the stars, sitting beside my little campfire with Caleb Jr., and I've been thinking about making campouts a more regular part of my trips. Oh, well. It's definitely not worth risking a prison cell suite for a few blissful summer nights in the great outdoors. Besides, hotel life might not be so bad if I start staying at places with a few more amenities than basic cable and an ice machine.

Even though the traces I've left behind thus far seem to have helped me out, I'm still concerned that I slipped up so easily. It's not like I've got this extermination business out of my system. I can't simply walk away, never worrying another day about getting caught now that the authorities are hot on the trail of the wrong "man." And the more I do this, the more pieces the cops may put together. I guess it's the cumulative effect of a boot print here, a tire tread there, that worries me. I'll have to be exquisitely careful to keep my tracks covered from this point.

Being a woman is probably my best cover for now. Part of me is relieved by that, but another part is angry. Angry that, man's boot print or not, no one has considered that I might be a woman. Why a man who knows someone who's been raped? Why not a woman who's been raped herself? Why the heck not? What's so far-fetched about a woman getting fed up and fighting back? The same mentality that denies that so many kids are being treated badly in this country also seems to deny that a woman would have any cause to murder. Men have every motive in the world to resort to vigilantism, but women don't. A man whose little girl is raped can be envisioned as a murder suspect but it's unfathomable for that same little girl to grow up and become an avenger herself. Whose pain are we talking about here, anyway? Her pain doesn't exist except in how it affects a man? She has a lot more reason to turn vigilante than him. *I* have more reason.

Heck, there may be more of us out there than anyone imagines. This insistent pretense that we don't exist doesn't make me or any of my other invisible colleagues go away. It just means we don't get caught. Ha! The joke's on you, America. Go ahead and pretend I'm not here. See if I care. But all you who dare harm a child better hope Lady Justice makes you pay, or you may just have to tangle with one ferocious invisible woman someday.

Goddamn that feels good! Speaking of God, I've officially been nicknamed. I'm now "The Crucifier." I can't believe it. Mrs. Jenkins always insisted that I go to Sunday School with them if I slept over with Sally on a Saturday night, but those were the only times I ever went to church. Of course, Juanita is a devout Catholic, so I sometimes heard her talk about church stuff. But that's it for me on the religious front. Yet, now I'm "The Crucifier," all because I'm fond of putting a bullet through the palm of each target's hand.

Actually, I was dubbed that after I shot the one who was holed up in his bedroom. The paper said that when they found him lying there with arms outstretched and a hole through each hand, he looked like he'd been crucified.

I don't really like the label, especially the association between these creeps and that always-did-the-right-thing Jesus guy. It implies a sense of innocence that isn't true, except in the sense that the justice system failed to prescribe adequate guilt. Hmmm. I guess that means these men I've killed really are innocent in some screwed up legal sense. Great. I guess I truly am a crucifier, then. Only, I'm a savior who crucifies, instead of a crucified savior. Figure that one out. Sheesh. It's beyond me.

Anyway, after I'd finished plowing through all those articles and printing up copies to paste on the wall, I browsed briefly for prospective targets. I even found a couple of possibilities. But mostly I worked on designing a letterhead for my WJF Fund. I rented a post office box, set up a bank account and ordered checks a few days ago. I'd like to start mailing out letters as soon as the checks arrive.

Unlike Mom, I've never been very good at drawing things, so I didn't have much luck in coming up with a distinctive design for the fund, even with the help of his computer graphics program. I finally gave up and started browsing the software's clip-art file for something remotely appealing. When I ran across Lady Justice, I knew I had something. I repositioned the two scales that usually hang below her outstretched arm so that they're hanging upside down above her arm. That way, even the most basic law of gravity has been defied. With the scales in that position, I stretched the center point of the scale until it looked like Lady Justice had a "W" at the end of her arm. Then I stacked a "J" and an "F" under the "W." Voila! I had my own trademark. I'll take it to the printer tomorrow.

# Chapter Thirty

Friday,
July 10, 1992

Last night I dreamed he was chasing me around the house in his wheelchair, firing his pistol at me like he used to. Only the bullets weren't blanks. I wasn't a kid, either, and his wheelchair wasn't hindered by the furniture I kept knocking over to block its path.

Somehow I ended up in his bedroom—like it used to be, not like it is now—and Juanita was refilling his lemon bowl.

"You've got to help me! He's trying to kill me!" I called out in Sigourney Weaver's voice.

She gave me a puzzled look and went back to putting lemons into the bowl beside his bed. I knocked over the big screen TV and tried to hide behind it as the bullets whizzed by.

Suddenly my skin started splitting, falling away, and I realized I was becoming some kind of alien-style monster. *I've got to be stopped*, I thought to myself, so I got up from behind the TV and just stood there facing him, waiting for him to shoot me, waiting for him to kill me. I woke up in a cold sweat just before he did.

I couldn't go back to sleep after that. I was too unnerved. Since then, I've just kept asking those obvious questions: Am I a monster? Is that what I've become? Do I need to be stopped?

No easy answers.

Part of me says that all the dream really means is, I've seen one too many ads for Sigourney Weaver's *Alien 3* movie this summer. But another part thinks dreams hold a lot of truth, that there's an honesty about them. No doubt I'll ponder that dream for a long time to come.

It seems a bit ironic that I dreamed this now, when behaving monsterly is the farthest thing from my mind. Sure I had the tires changed on Jurisprudence so I wouldn't get caught. But mostly I've been composing letters and writing checks, trying to help people in a law abiding sort of way. It doesn't seem quite fair to get a nightmare slap on the wrist for that.

Of course, I did read an article in *USA Today* a couple of days ago about those four teenage girls in Indiana. That's enough to inspire nightmares. They molested, beat and burned a twelve-year-old girl to death last winter. Definitely monsterly.

I haven't been able to get that story out of my mind. I think I've felt as sad as I've felt horrified by what those girls did. I'm not sure why really. I guess the idea of girls hurting each other like that just strikes me as a mutated version of how females have been trained for so long to turn our pain in on ourselves. Just look at me. Swing sets, Twinkie binges.

It's almost as if the growing societal shift to not hurt ourselves anymore has taken away young girls' only outlet for the pain. Without giving us a new one. We can't hurt ourselves anymore when we're in pain but we can't hurt those who caused our pain, either. What's left but hurting each other? How depressing.

I think I'm definitely ready to move on to a lighter topic.

I'm having a good time with this philanthropy thing. The checks arrived yesterday. Since I'd already finished writing the letters, I put in the checks and mailed them this morning.

I was still too paranoid to unlock his room to do the letters on the computer, with Charlie in and out of the house so much. I guess the room just feels like a Pandora's box when others are around, so I haven't wanted to open the door so much as a crack. Even after Charlie and crew are gone for the evening. I know it's irrational but it's how it is. So, when I was ready to type the letters, I resorted to digging out my clunky typewriter from among the boxes still stored in my old bedroom.

I sent letters to the man who was falsely arrested, the dentist's ex-wife, the fund that was set up for Heidi and the family of a man I put a stop to during that trip to the West Coast.

My basic strategy is enclosing an initial check, along with a letter that requests a more detailed outline of any money needed because of what has happened to them. Like with the guy who was arrested. I'm offering to compensate him for things like lost wages and legal fees. I can pay for counseling or whatever his little girl needs, too. I hope he'll even give the other three families involved the fund's address.

With the dentist's ex-wife, I can make up for lost child support and pay for college or something. I can pay funeral expenses for other families and take care of other assorted bills to get them back on their feet. I don't know what I can do for Heidi, except try to make sure she's well cared for. Oh, and I want to give her a wish. I requested that each of the kids write to the fund with a wish for something they'd like to have or do. I always liked organizations that did that for terminally ill kids.

The make-a-wish part was still a little scary for me. I guess I'm scared they'll wish for something like, "I want you to make things like they were before he did stuff to me" or "I want my daddy back" or "I wish they'd catch the guy who shot him." I'll just have to cope when such impossibles or uncomfortables come up. I mostly just want to give them each a good memory, so their whole childhoods can't be summed up by what one creep—or one misguided vigilante—did to them. And I want to use his money to do that. It seems a particularly satisfying in-your-face, spit-on-your-grave way to spend it.

I guess now it's just a matter of waiting to hear back from them all. Between waiting for replies and waiting for Charlie to wrap things up with my apartment so I can plan my next hit; I'm feeling kind of restless. I'm thinking about contacting Juanita and taking a trip to Hawaii for the next week or so. I let Charlie know what I'm thinking of doing and he said he'll keep an eye on things if I go. He even volunteered to make phone calls to Juanita and a travel agency for me later this afternoon. So, maybe I just will.

# Chapter Thirty-One

I'm on my way! I'd forgotten how much I like to fly when I've got a window seat. Now if only I could get my ears to pop. Picky, picky. The clouds are gorgeous. As a kid I always wanted to get out of the plane with Winnie and romp around on them. Especially towering thunderheads like the ones out there today. No way could they be wispy nothingness. They looked as solid as we were.

Ouch. It's funny how even pleasant memories can ache sometimes. I guess I'm just reminded of how Winnie and I both wanted that window seat the day of the wreck. This is the first time I've had the window seat on a flight since then. Guess I won the quiet game....

Winnie would have been some kind of jealous that I got the window seat all the way to Hawaii. He made trips there two or three times a year to stay in his condo, but he never took anyone with him. Not even Mom. That was Winnie's big dream, that he would take her to Hawaii on one of his trips and let her sit by the window the whole way.

I'm just glad I'll be spending this trip with Juanita instead of with him. Charlie put her on the speaker phone when he called and she kept lapsing into Spanish with that staccato rhythm I love. That's a sure sign she's excited about my trip. That made me feel good. I think she was glad to hear Charlie's voice, too. Having both worked for him, I guess they share something like Charlie and Richard share. A bond that can't be broken.

Juanita and Charlie reminisced about their

visit during his and Lilly's cruise. But mostly they talked about me, with Charlie warning her that I'd gone a little loony since she saw me last. He told her in comedic detail about my tendency to suddenly disappear on long road trips and let the house fall into disrepair. My latest harebrained scheme of moving into the attic was, of course, the grand finale of his tale.

Juanita laughed a lot but otherwise didn't seem concerned—or surprised—by my eccentricity. She was just glad I'd thought to include her in my travels.

I was so excited about seeing Juanita again that I forgot all about packing her immigration papers and passport. I so wanted to hand those to her in person. I imagined us going out to the beach one night and having a ceremonial burning of those papers. Oh, well. I'll tell her that I have them and ask her what she'd like me to do with them. I can always mail them to her or bring them with me on my next visit.

My next visit.... That sounds so good. Like another victory over him. Like another shovel of dirt on his grave. Maybe he could send her far away but his money makes that distance irrelevant. I can always hop on a plane to see her. Heck, I could buy a place of my own in Hawaii if I wanted to.

Well, I could unless that wouldn't be safe for Juanita. Maybe we'll get a chance to discuss that stuff. I guess that will be the true measure of how dead he is: what we do and don't talk about while I'm there.

Speaking of hopelessness, I was reading a newspaper earlier in the flight and ran across an article about that Perot fellow. I was quite taken by something he said in a speech to the NAACP yesterday: "Hungry people steal. Hopeless people kill."

This guy gets it! He understands what despair and powerlessness do to people. Do to this country. Do to me.

I'm so encouraged that this guy is making a run for the presidency. He sounds like he could really shake things up.

# Chapter Thirty-Two

Friday,
July 17, 1992

I'm enjoying my visit with Juanita. The Hawaiian clime seems to agree with her, as does freedom from him. She looks happier than I've ever seen her. Even the clothes she wears are brighter colors. She's started her own cleaning service in the high-rise near Waikiki that houses her condo and is doing quite well for herself, with the added boost from the pension he left her.

I've been tagging along with her on her cleaning jobs for the past few days, visiting with her as she works, helping out when she lets me. It's been like the old days—I hesitate to call them "good"—when I followed her around as she cleaned the house just so I could spend time in rooms other than my own. She's been prattling on and I've been signing when she lets me get a word in edgewise. It's been fun.

I'm happy to report that Juanita is no longer a homicidal maniac when it comes to house plants, so Hawaii is safe as a tropical paradise. That reminds me of a time several years ago when he saw an ad for a Hawaiian something or other, which was touted as the plant anyone could grow. Well, anyone but Juanita, as it turned out. Now, she just tells customers up front that she'll do just about anything—even windows—but she doesn't do plants. So there.

I'm not making rounds with her today. She says I'm too pale these days and need to get myself a good Hawaiian suntan while I'm here. I guess she hasn't heard about ozone depletion and skin cancer. Oh, well. I agreed to spend the day on the beach, enjoying sand, sea and surf. But I'm joining the Japanese tourists in enjoying it from the nice shade of a palm tree.

It's a gorgeous day. Blue sky, cool breeze, sunlight adding just the right sparkle to sand and ocean. It's the kind of day travel posters use to lure drooling tourists here. Even so, I still prefer the evening strolls on the beach with Juanita.

That's when she's spoken most freely with me during this visit. I think it's when she feels most safe. She doesn't talk to me at all when we're at her place. It's strictly sign language—rusty though we both are—and passing paper back and forth. She showed me a bugging device that she found soon after moving into the condo. She was changing a light fixture when it fell out, so she's still a tad worried that there may be others. I think she worries more since I'm here.

I got a hotel room after she showed me the bug, so we've been having slumber parties away from those electronic ears. We hope. I still don't think she's completely at ease even in the hotel or when she's cleaning the condos. Only when we're on the beach do conversations move away from surface chitchat.

During those walks, she's talked much about her life before coming to America. I suppose that's because I told her early in our visit about destroying the file he kept on her and about the papers I still have.

"Did you read them?" she asked.

I indicated that I'd read enough.

"I have no shame," she said, lifting her head and straightening her shoulders.

"I'm not ashamed of you," I wrote. "I'm ashamed of him."

"Yes," she said and started to say more, but we were at the hotel room at the time, so "another time" was all she said.

She'd never mentioned her husband to me before those evening walks on the beach, much less that he'd been assassinated for his political views. He believed in democracy and wanted such a government for his own country. A dangerous thing to want in a place where death squads and disappearances in the night were the norm. And for lesser evils than he espoused. She was as involved in the movement as he; it was how they met, why they married.

"Between us, we broke every law in the land. The surprise was never that he died but that he lived so long, and that our son and I live still," she said. "I have no shame for what we did. Only, having seen democracy, I regret we suffered so much for so little.

"I mean no disrespect to you, Annie, by what I must say about your father, but he stole from me something more beloved than my husband when he dirtied democracy. It was my hope. I believed in democracy more than I believed in the Virgin Mary. But your father showed me that evil men reign whether there is democracy or dictatorship.

"In my country, at least evil is where all can see. It is easier to fight an enemy that calls itself by that name. With democracy, who can tell friend from foe? The power is scattered and hidden. How can the people fight a snake with so many heads?

"It was a dark day when your father showed that my America dreamland is a breeding place for such beasts as he. I hope you take no offense, but the day your father died was as glorious as the day I first touched free American soil. The first freedom I lost to him. This second freedom I will let nothing take from me, not even burning letters or listening walls."

I signed that I could cut my visit short if my presence threatened her freedom.

"No!" she insisted, pushing me playfully toward the waves. "You are my hope for America! From the loins of a monster, yet no beast yourself. You remind me that all is not lost. It is good you have come."

*If only you knew,* I thought to myself. *The monster beget a monster, after all. Perhaps all* **is** *lost.*

It was an embarrassing moment knowing my secret self would disappoint her so. As I've thought about it since, though, I'm not so sure she would be disappointed. She said that she and her husband broke a lot of laws in their push for democracy. That didn't really register at the time, since I'm so accustomed to the American way of thinking that laws standing in the way of democracy aren't as valid as laws made within a democracy. And here I thought my "higher law" approach to knocking off perps was so shockingly original.

I don't think I'm ready for any true confessions to Juanita, as one law breaker to another, but I might ask her what she thinks about this Crucifier I've "read" about. She's a wise lady. Besides, she knows a monster when she sees one, so I'd have to take her opinions seriously. It would be nice to get a reality check from someone I trust before I get in any deeper than I am.

She thinks a lot of my WJF Memorial Fund. That feels good. Of course, I had to let her know what the WJF really stood for before she fully appreciated it.

"You beat him! How wonderful! You have won!" she shouted in her native tongue, as she laughed so hard she wet her pants and fell to her knees in the sand.

I got so tickled watching her, I had to drop to the sand myself to keep from soiling my own pants. Afterwards, Juanita decided she'd rather be known as eccentric than incontinent, so we waded into the ocean fully clothed, rolled a bit in the sand and continued our stroll. She's something else.

When I mentioned wanting to give her some more money, since I knew her pension didn't begin to compensate for years of ridiculous wages, she insisted that I put that money toward WJF.

"Use that money to help the people be free from monsters," she said.

I haven't quite figured out how to do that, outside of using it to fund the extermination process. I'd rather her money go toward something a little more constructive than that. I'll have to give her instructions some thought to make sure I do something worthy of Juanita.

Of course, I wish she'd accept the money, even though I know she declined because her business is booming, never mind the recession. Her son and two other women are all working for her.

Roberto is kind of an on-and-off worker for his mom now that he's in college. I've enjoyed seeing him again, too. He looks great. I can't believe how much he's grown since I saw him last. He's gone from pimply faced, insecure brat to bronze Aztec warrior. Juanita says he looks a lot like his dad now.

She says he's really taken to island life, too. I'm glad he's doing well. Back a few years ago when Roberto first got his driver's license, the man we all love to hate let Roberto take the van out for a spin and then called the police, reporting it stolen.

I was away at college at the time, so I never found out all the gory details. I know Roberto had to spend some time at a juvenile detention center before the charges were graciously reduced by the magnanimous victim who didn't want to see a young man's life ruined by one foolish mistake. I suspect that what really happened was Juanita agreed to some god-awful terms to save her son.

I found out about the incident during a trip home over the holidays. He was bragging to me about teaching Juanita and Roberto a lesson and something just snapped inside. I went and found Juanita in the kitchen and asked her to call me a taxi. I remember sitting there at the kitchen table crying as I waited for the taxi to come, signing my profuse apologies for what he had done. When the taxi came, I gave Juanita a hug and left without so much as a good-bye to him. I didn't go back to that house again until after the funeral.

Of course, the downside to that was I didn't see Juanita or Roberto again, either. We've had a lot of lost time to make up for during this visit. It's funny how not being around Juanita for a while made me forget just how much she means to me. I'm going to have to make these visits much more often. I may even extend this one a little longer than the one week planned. Who knows? I'll talk to her about it at lunch. If she ever shows up. She was supposed to meet me by this very palm tree over an hour ago. Oh, well. I guess successful businesswomen are just going to run late sometimes.

* * * *

Juanita's dead. I just found out. If there's life after death, I hope she's somewhere beating the crap out of him right now.

# Chapter Thirty-Three

Monday,
July 20, 1992

I still can't believe Juanita is dead. It happened while I was on the beach that day. The official police report says it was an accident. She fell over a balcony railing several floors up when a stool tipped over while she was standing on it watering some-one's plants. Yeah, right.

Roberto and I tried to tell the police that Juanita never watered plants.

"Well, this time she did," the police officer replied. "A water can went over the side with her, and her fingerprints were all over it." So, that was the end of that. Whatever happened to "Hawaii 5-O"?

We scattered her ashes over the ocean yester-day as the tide went out. Roberto wanted her final resting place to be away from this country's shore.

He's an angry young man right now. Most of that anger is directed at me and I can't blame him for that. I think Roberto is right that Juanita's death has something to do with me being here. I don't understand what, but I can't help but feel that if I hadn't come, she'd still be alive.

Roberto is determined to find out who killed her, and what I had to do with that. I've tried to tell him how much I loved Juanita, how she was like a mother to me, how I would never have come here if I thought she'd be harmed. But he has just turned away from everything I've written, refusing to read.

He did let me pay for the cremation and the private investigator he wanted to hire. The P.I. is no Thomas Magnum, but he managed to find six other bugs in the condo right after Juanita accidentally found the first, so maybe he can scrounge up some answers. I'd take just about anything right now.

This whole thing has been as terrifying as it's been heart wrenching. I'm keenly aware of the price on my own head, the "accident" waiting somewhere for me. His warning was obviously no bluff. There's always the chance that the money I found in the garage really was the undelivered retainer for offing me, especially since he changed his will just in the months before his death. Maybe he never got around to finalizing the arrangement. "Maybes" aren't exactly comforting just now.

I never dreamed an "accident" would be arranged for Juanita at all. All he had to do was fix things so the authorities would deport her. No doubt her own country would severely punish her for crimes against the state. They'd do the dirty work for him. Having her killed makes no sense. Unless the private investigator digs up something, I'll probably never understand. But then, when did I ever understand him?

I feel so crappy. The sense that it's somehow my fault makes it even worse. It's like Mom and Winnie all over again. If only I hadn't said anything to Mrs. Jenkins, they'd still be alive. Now, if only I hadn't come to Hawaii, Juanita would still be enjoying her second chance at freedom. Knowing me does horrible things to people.

I hope Kitty is safe knowing me. Probably the best thing she has going for her is that he never met her. Or heard of her. When I think about the dirt she knows on him, though, I feel frightened for her. It's something I plan to discuss with her tomorrow. Sort of.

I'm in flight from Hawaii to Los Angeles now. Roberto asked me to leave after he'd scattered Juanita's ashes. I took the first flight out of Honolulu this morning.

I've got the window seat again, but the clouds hold no wonder for me this trip. They just remind me of high ledges and long plunges to death. Hopelessness definitely has me in its grip just now.

Do you know that even Ross Perot is a bust? He pulled out of the presidential race the same day Juanita died. No, was murdered. I couldn't believe Perot quit. For someone who seemed to understand what hopelessness does to people, he sure was quick to yank the plug on our hope.

Losing the hope embodied in Juanita and Perot all at once, has left me feeling like I'm collapsing in on myself. Again. This portable black hole of mine is getting old.

If the window suddenly popped out and I got sucked through the opening, I don't think I would register the slightest surprise. That would slip naturally into my realm of expectations just now. I couldn't imagine hoping for anything more.

Well, that's not quite true. I do hope to at least live long enough to see Kitty. I sent a fax to Kitty, telling her I needed to see her on business, so I'm going to stop off there instead of flying straight home. I want to get some kind of will in order right away, before I encounter an accident of my own. I want to see that Roberto continues getting the monthly payments that Juanita would have received and I want the WJF Fund to get the rest, with Kitty overseeing its administration. If she agrees. She may not, especially since her safety may be jeopardized just by being associated with me. Not that I can fully explain the danger.

As I think about all this, someone else I want to provide for in my will is Heidi. That seems kind of weird, since I don't even know her, but what the heck. She could use a lucky break. If I'm going to take my leave of this world, I might as well help a kid on my way out.

Of course, I'm probably just a tad paranoid about all this right now. I haven't even broken any of his terms yet. I guess it's just that Juanita didn't seem to do anything to cross his ghost, either. With her death feeling almost random, it's hard to guess what might happen next.

Oh, well. As long as I live long enough to get that will written up, I'll be satisfied that he didn't completely triumph over the grave. I'm just keeping my fingers crossed until then.

I'm so sorry, Juanita.

# Chapter Thirty-Four

Wednesday,
July 22, 1992

I'm still alive. I'm even starting to feel less paranoid. All the same, I'm glad I have a will in hand. It'll come in handy when I make the gas chamber scene, if nothing else.

I'm as bummed about Juanita as ever. I feel like I'm walking around in a black cloud, like I've taken a step back from myself, so everything's a bit fuzzy and out of synch. It's pretty miserable.

Being back at this house just makes it worse, since it holds most of my memories of her. The haunted house adds a ghost. What joy.

I was hoping Charlie would have my attic finished by the time I got back today, but he had a bout of food poisoning while I was gone and Richard had some car show, so the attic is behind schedule. I've warned Charlie about eating sushi this time of year. Of course, for all I know the "food poisoning" was really somebody trying to kill him for associating with me. I have such a charming effect on people.

I had imagined coming back here after my trip to Hawaii and going through all the old trunks and boxes stored in the attic, getting rid of some stuff, moving in some things of my own. It was going to be fun. Oh, well. I probably wouldn't have felt up to working on the apartment even if he had finished. Grief sucks.

Charlie was really torn up about Juanita. He and Richard were in the attic when I told him. Almost in a single movement, he dropped the piece of paper I handed him, buried his face in his hands and sat down on the sawdust-covered floor in tears.

I'd never seen Charlie cry. He had always been one of those perpetually cheerful kind of people. Richard must not have ever seen Charlie cry, either. Richard acted pretty uncomfortable about it, anyway. He picked up the message Charlie had dropped, read it, reached out as though to touch Charlie on the shoulder but then stopped himself mid-air. Stuffing his hands in his pockets, he turned and walked away. By the time I sat down beside Charlie in tears myself, Richard was leaning against a sawhorse on the opposite side of the attic, fumbling with his pack of Camels. Once it was clear that Charlie and I weren't going to stop crying anytime soon, Richard clumsily lit a cigarette, mumbled something about needing some air and quickly exited.

I don't know how long Charlie and I sat there quietly crying together. Long enough for me to remember Heidi and her stepfather standing hand in hand in front of those five graves. Long enough to feel the surprising comfort of shared grief.

It's a relief that losing Juanita doesn't mean losing Charlie, too. Or Kitty.

I keep hanging onto something Kitty said yesterday when I was telling her about Juanita: "Annie, knowing you isn't what keeps getting people killed; it's knowing him." That made me feel a little less guilty about Juanita and a lot better about Kitty's safety. When I've let myself believe it, that is. I think I believe it more when it comes to Kitty than Juanita. Kitty never so much as met him. He never even knew she was my friend. Surely she's safe. His powers don't extend that far beyond the grave.

Besides, I can't lose Kitty. Who else would I give that god-awful hula dancer magnet I picked up in Hawaii? It plays "Tiny Bubbles" and she swings her grass skirt every time you pat her on the head. Seriously though, I need at least some-body out there to help keep me in touch with the real world. Otherwise, I think I'd get lost in this vigilante persona.

Kitty's a particularly valuable voice to keep. She's not always a goof ball, after all. In some of her more serious moments, she's expressed deep conviction that true change can only come about by playing according to the rules.

"Once you break the rules, society can dismiss you and your cause along with you. Who cares if what you were trying to do was right? Breaking the rules was wrong, and that's all they'll remember."

That's her philosophy, anyway. I know there's some truth in what she says, just like there's some truth to my screw-the-rules philosophy. I guess hearing from Kitty from time to time keeps me from mistaking my own version of truth as the absolute, the one and only. Of course, she thinks her own truth is absolute, so I never completely trust it. Or her. But still, I'm willing to hear her truth. I need to hear it to temper my own narrow tendencies.

I know without even asking that Kitty could never approve of things I've done. But that's not enough to make me stop. I was prepared to put away my guns forever if Juanita thought "The Crucifier" was out of line. Of course, I never got a chance to ask. Still, that's a very different response than I'd ever give Kitty. I guess knowing Juanita had pursued her own higher law at such cost, I'd trust her hindsight.

So far, Kitty hasn't got much hindsight to of-fer. She's only been out of law school about a year. In a job market already glutted with lawyers, she had to settle for work with a firm that mostly does bankruptcies and other financial stuff. That's a far cry from the prosecuting attorney she aspires to be, but she's sure been handy in setting up the fund and stuff. Whatever she ends up doing, she'll make a difference. And she'll do it without ever compromising the law, without ever resorting to sleazy lawyer tactics. It's just going to take her longer than it took me.

I wonder if, once she gains her own years of hindsight, she'll see a place for the likes of me, doing my own rogue style of shoveling the justice system's manure. I'd like to hear from her after she's had a few years in the business, after she's seen a few guilty's set free to prey on more innocents. I suspect she'll still say I'm absolutely wrong, but I also suspect I'll trust her opinion more then. Of course, it's presumptuous to think I'll still be hard at work on the vigilante scene by then. With any luck I'll at least still be waiting on death row so I can ask her—if she ever visits.

Listen to me going on and on. Sometimes I bore myself. This journaling business was so much simpler when I was a kid. "I went to school today. When I got home I found out Juanita killed another plant. Isn't that funny? He's out of town until tomorrow, so Juanita and Bobby are spending the night with me. I'm glad. Maybe we'll play hide-and-seek. It's Bobby's favorite." Of course, that was pretty boring drivel, too but at least I didn't take myself so seriously back then. Maybe I'll hunt down all those old diaries of mine sometime. I haven't seen them in years.

I'm not in any rush, though. I don't really want to stick around here right now, with the house feeling so freshly haunted. I figure I'll just stay long enough to rustle up a fresh batch of targets. Forget waiting for Charlie to finish his construction work before I unlock the bedroom. I'll just go in there late at night when no one else is around and hope for the best. I'll pick some targets. Then I'll get out of here for a good long while.

Oh, I almost forgot my fund. I haven't even checked the post office box to see if I've gotten any replies. I guess I'll take care of that before I go, too. And a letter to Roberto. Maybe he'll listen to me if I write him a letter. I hope so.

# Chapter Thirty-Five

Saturday,
July 25, 1992

Jurisprudence is packed; checks are in the mail. I'm all set to hop in the saddle again. The only thing left is to lie here on a mat in his gym and try to rest until dark. I'm having a hard time getting my body clock switched back over to the night life, especially with Charlie and Richard still working on my attic during the day. The gym is as far away from that power-tool racket as I can get in this house.

I'm a regular vampire-type on these shooting sprees, preferring to rise at dusk and return to my hotel coffin by dawn. I even prefer making my drives at night now. I guess I feel less vulnerable, more invisible at night, since Jurisprudence is such a striking steed.

I'm heading east on this trip for the first couple of hits. Then I'll turn south along the coast and maybe pick off a few more. I'm not sure if I'll shoot this trip's sixth target. Something about the case just doesn't sit right with me, but it won't hurt to go down there and take a closer look. I packed six dolls just in case.

It was really weird—but nice—to take those six dolls and realize I only have four left. I like it when they disappear in such huge chunks like this. It makes me feel like I'm sloughing off something dead and scaly every time I leave one of those dolls behind. It'd be great if I could eventually get rid of them all.

With one more major trip like this, I'm sure I could do just that. Barring my capture or "accidental" death. But part of me thinks this will be my last extended target shooting trip. Now that I'm trying to dole out money from this fund, I don't think it will work well to be absent for extended periods anymore. If I weren't so grief-motivated to stay away from the house these days, I wouldn't even make this trip.

The fund only got two replies while I was in Hawaii: a family out west and the guy who was in jail for so long.

The woman out west sent me copies of some funeral bills. She enclosed a note admitting that she'd gotten enough insurance money to cover those things, but expressed hope that this wouldn't disqualify her.

"Even with the insurance money, I'm having to work two jobs just to get by. If I could just get caught up enough to afford a move, I know somewhere my son and I could go to get back on our feet."

So I sent her the money for the funeral and a little extra to help her move. Her son asked for either a pair of Air Jordan sneakers or a portable CD player with a set of Garth Brook disks. It sounded just like a teenager. I sent both.

The request from the other family's little girl for an extended family vacation to the mountains rang a little hollow, especially in grown-up hand-writing. After all that family's been through, I'm sure they do need to get out of town for a while and regroup, but it pissed me off that they'd use their daughter's wish to do that. I sent the money for a vacation anyway, but I enclosed a note to the girl, asking that she write back with a wish for something just for herself.

I can tell that administering the fund is not going to be the feely-fuzzy experience I had envi-sioned. Oh, well.

Heidi and the dentist's ex-wife are the two I

had most hoped to hear from. Now it could be weeks or even months before I get back with them. It was a hard choice between waiting around for their replies and leaving on yet another round of killings. But I just can't stand to stay here twiddling my thumbs right now. I desperately want to keep busy so I'm not thinking about Juanita's death every waking moment. It hurts too much.

I've routed my drive through Greenville, Ohio. That's Annie Oakley's hometown and she has a park there. I'd like to stop by and maybe let my hand rest on the bronze sculpture of her. I guess I need her to ease my pain. She's the only dead person I know who still feels alive enough to do that.

# Chapter Thirty-Six

Monday,
Aug. 17, 1992

This shooting business is becoming almost routine. Men make such easy targets, especially the white ones. It never seems to occur to them that anyone would stalk them in the same way they might stalk their own victims. They walk around day or night. It's all the same to them. No thoughts of lurking danger in the shadows.

I don't know if beating the justice system increases that sense of being untouchable, invincible. Whatever it is about these guys, there's rarely any challenge to shooting them anymore. I've stopped videotaping and studying neighborhoods or following them to work in the mornings or making detailed notes of their daily schedules. I just show up at night, either on foot or in car, depending on what's less conspicuous. Then I just wait for an invitation to shoot them. It always comes. I just have to be patient.

With the first target on this trip, I only had to wait four nights before he left his garage door open and lights off while he made a quick drive to the grocery store for some milk. When he got back, I was waiting for him. Before the garage door even had a chance to close me in, I'd shot him, dropped a doll and slid under the descending door for my getaway.

His conviction was overturned on appeal because the majority of jurors in his trial were women. I couldn't believe it. Of course, I guess that means that all the laws passed by the Senate should be nullified, since all but two senators are men.

"Of course not. Don't be absurd. That's not the

issue," the white men in black robes say.

Fine. But the issue is, a poor sap's dead when he could have just been jailed. Perhaps an "oops" is in order, your honors.

The second target took a little longer, since he worked nights. He finally had a night off and went to a bar to drink himself into a stupor. That was on the thirteenth, so I guess he was celebrating Annie Oakley's birthday. How sweet. The bar was country-western, so my cowboy get-up wasn't even out of place in the parking lot. I took advantage of that to approach him as he fumbled with the keys to his pickup. No way was I going to let him drive away in that condition and he was too soused to protest.

I helped him get his door unlocked and helped him get behind the wheel. Of course, I had to keep holding my breath during all that so the smell of too many beers wouldn't trigger a panic attack.

It was a hot night, so I even rolled down his windows for him. How thoughtful I've become. Okay, so I didn't want a bullet to smash noisily through anything. It worked. I put his cowboy hat over his head where he'd fallen over onto the seat. That way, he just looked like he was sleeping one off. Then I turned on his radio for an added touch, only to have Patsy Cline croon "Crazy" at me as I went on my way. No one in the parking lot gave me so much as a second glance.

The third target was let out on shock probation after only a few months in prison, even though he'd been found guilty of over fifty counts of child molestation. He was an otherwise upstanding member of the community, after all.

I shot him in a deserted post office parking lot a couple of nights after target number two. After shooting him, I realized he'd just picked up some child porn from a P.O. box under an assumed name. How nice of him to remind me why I do what I do.

Now, I'm waiting for contestant number four. He really must die. As a "man of God," he's got too much of an airtight front for his secret self. Besides, it really pisses me off when trials for people like him become contests of character between the victim and the accused. Does that happen so much because of TV, movies, books? Is it because this nation so believes in fiction, where the evil protagonist is evil to the core, where a kind gesture or pure thought would be considered so grossly out of character, critics would tear it apart? Only the stupid bad guys and hard-core bullies go the pure evil route in real life. It's too easy to get caught.

Look at me. I'm a serial killer, for Chrissake. But I don't drink or smoke or do drugs. I've never even had a parking ticket or bounced a check. Even before I was rich, I vote on election day. I love baseball and apple pie. My clothes and my car are made in the USA. I'm unethically rich, but I'm doing my darndest to give that money away. Oh, and let's not forget I'm disabled. That's always good for a few sympathy points. Everyone who knows me thinks I'm swell. Well, except for Roberto these days, but even he used to like me. I'm a friend to children and stray dogs. I recycle. I don't eat tuna that got dolphins killed and I support the United Way, despite indiscretions at the highest administrative level.

What can I say? I'm just one heck of a straight-laced, clean cut, all-American gal. Oh, except for that one little flaw I mentioned earlier. But look at how wonderful I am otherwise. That's what really matters. Isn't it? Why would you want to put me in jail just because of a little shooting problem? Putting a stop to scum should be applauded, not punished. Don't you think? Just look at them. Just look at what they did. They don't even recycle like I do. I saw their garbage cans while waiting to kill them, so I know. How can you put me in jail? I only shoot people worse than me.

How absurd. Yet that defense argument mysteriously works for men accused of sex crimes all the time.

"She asked for it, your honor. She was dressed like a girl. She's had sex before, too. How can someone who's had sex before possibly be raped? You know she secretly enjoyed it. She wanted me to do it. She said 'no,' after all, and you know girls only say that when they really want you."

I'll never understand why those arguments are so effective.

This godly man went the slightly different route of, "I didn't do it. Oh, they wanted me to, but I cared about them too much to do that. Now they've filed charges out of anger at me for spurning their advances."

Yeah, right. This guy spends a lot of time counseling young, troubled teens at his church. Yes, I do mean to use present tense. I think he's in the church counseling someone even as I write. Another car is in the parking lot tonight, anyway.

He's got a great scam going. After all, in a contest of character, who is the jury going to believe? Kids who have been in trouble before, who have no doubt lied before, or the guy who has devoted his life to helping them? As long as such trials remain contests of character, a goody two-shoes who only does evil deeds on the side will win every time. I guess no one warned those kids about that before they reported him. They were duped by that American penchant for fiction, too: Truth prevails; bad guys get what they deserve; justice is served. What bunk.

I'll be glad when I finally get a chance to get rid

of this holy jerk. I'm thoroughly sick of waiting around for him to screw up. I'm still hoping tonight's the night. That mystery car is the one variable unaccounted for. It was parked here when I arrived, so I'm not sure if someone's with him inside the church or not.

Whoa! Stop the presses! A teenager just came flying out of the church. Oh, man. That fuckwad better not have hurt her. I'm not waiting for him to come out. I'm going in.

# Chapter Thirty-Seven

Tuesday,
Aug. 18, 1992

I've been driving pretty hard for the past several hours. It's approaching four in the morning and I'm just now feeling far enough away from the last hit to pause here at a truck stop for a breather. And a dozen donuts. And an ugly little, red-haired troll magnet.

After the girl ran out of the church, I went flying inside like some kind of crazed comic book hero, ignoring how dizzy that made me. The church was deserted and mostly dark, except for the hallway leading to his office. The office door was closed, but I could see light coming from under it. I threw the door open and barreled in with gun up, ready to fire.

I smelled the gunpowder first. Then I heard him. Then I saw him. He was curled up on the floor with his back to me in a growing pool of blood. I felt vomit rise to the back of my throat and my knees buckled, dropping me to the floor as the room started to spin. So, this is what I put people through, leaving all these bodies for them to find. I know I deserved coming across something like that, but it was still a bitch.

I sat there a long while just fighting gag reflexes. Even after I'd somewhat regained my composure, my skin felt cold, clammy, and my knees kept threatening to fail me as I tried to walk over to where he lay.

His pants and underwear were down around his ankles and he had both hands cupped over what was left of his genitals. He was still conscious, but I doubt he knew I was even there.

"Forgive me, forgive me, forgive me," he was moaning almost chant-like. I wasn't sure if he was talking to the girl who'd shot him or to God, but he wasn't going to be talking to either one much longer. That was clear. No matter what I did.

The girl had dropped the revolver on the floor after shooting him. I fished it out of the blood. Yuck. It was empty, which was just as well. Without thinking, I probably would have used it to finish him off. If I wanted to salvage the girl's life, I really needed to use the SIG to tie this mess to me. I put the first bullet through the back of his cupped hands, the second through his head.

I was glad I had the SIG for this one so I could focus on that red dot instead of the gore. The tinny smell of all that blood made me nauseous enough without the visual aids.

I dropped the doll beside him and deliberately stepped into the sticky blood to leave the positive ID of my boot prints. Then I got the hell out of Dodge.

Not knowing if the gun could be traced back to the girl if I got caught with it later, I tossed it off a bridge into a river about three hours down the road.

I hope I did the right thing. I know the two-gun factor is going to cause major confusion whether she goes to the police or not. Hopefully, the cops will still figure out I came in after her and finished him off. The autopsy will show that the bullet to the head finally killed him, so maybe blowing his balls off will only get her charged for assault with a deadly weapon. Even that should be ruled self-defense.

If she went in intending to shoot him, making him drop his pants before she did, she probably hasn't gone to the cops yet and now she won't ever have to. Unless her conscience gets the better of her.

I just don't want to see her mess up her life

over this. She's too young. Mine's already a done deal. What's one more life sentence or death sentence tacked on to all the others I've earned? But she's still got a chance to make it. I hope she takes the bit of grace I've handed her and makes good on her second chance.

This country has got to stop driving its kids to ruin their lives like this. It's absurd what she had to do to get something so basic as safety.

This whole thing has really wiped me out. I think I'm going to find a hotel somewhere nearby and stop for at least a day before I continue on toward the next target. A nice hotel. Covers turned down, mint on the pillow, fresh flowers when my breakfast and morning paper are wheeled into the room. The next one feels personal, so I want to go into it in top form.

He's a rich guy who only got off because he was able to afford a bang-up defense team. He has a penchant for raping his baby-sitters and turning their names over to the police as young prostitutes who unsuccessfully attempted solicitation. If they got roughed up, it must have been some john, not him. He's a happily married man, after all. Unfortunately, he is also rich and is often the target of unfounded claims by people hoping to pick up some fast cash.

I dare say his money won't buy him sufficient defense against me.

# Chapter Thirty-Eight

Sunday,
Aug. 23, 1992

I may have been wrong. This target's money may buy him a defense against me after all. I've seen enough security systems in my day to tell he's living in a virtual fortress. He's even got a little guardhouse outside the main gate that's always manned. I'll never get within so much as rifle range of him there. He's not exactly the type to run to the corner grocery when he's running low on caviar, either. I don't know if the guy so much as takes a piss by himself. It's pretty frustrating.

The only place I've seen him go alone so far is the marina. He took a boat out by himself for a couple of hours last Friday. After I watched the boat pull away, I took a casual stroll to see how easy it'd be to wander among the piers. Not! Even feigning deafness didn't get me anywhere.

"Miss! Miss! You can't go in there. Miss!" His voice had all the authority of a drill sergeant.

I just kept walking, looking around at all the boats like some awestruck tourist might.

"Miss! I'm warning you. Miss!"

I heard feet pounding the boardwalk coming up fast behind me. I prepared to turn on the sign language routine as soon as "Sarge" grabbed me. The next thing I knew I was eating splinters and seeing stars. A knee pinned my arms behind my back. So much for that swell idea.

"I'm deaf. I'm deaf," I mouthed until I finally got his attention.

"Oh, shit!" he said, releasing his hold on me. I was amused to discover that "Sarge" even sported a military-style crew cut.

I signed some gobbledygook just to drive home the deaf thing. And to give me time to think. Then I reached into my pocket for pen and paper.

"My cousin Dixie said I should come here to rent a boat," I wrote.

"Dumb broad," he mumbled under his breath as he scribbled a reply. I read his note and smiled sweetly as I returned the compliment by signing something obscene to this walking dick.

"Come back in the morning," the note said.

It was a surprise, maybe the only break I'll get with this target. What I rented when I came back the next morning was a houseboat. It's not exactly something I can trail him with the next time he takes out his yacht, but at least it gets me inside the marina. Besides, it gives me a break from hotel life.

I was a little woozy at first when I got settled in here yesterday, but I guess I'm getting my sea legs now. I hardly notice the gentle rocking, anymore. We'll see if I feel the same at the first sign of choppy waters.

I think the boat will give me my best chance of hitting this target, so I'm glad I stumbled—or rather got tackled—into it. I had to rent the boat for a whole month, whether I use it that long or not. So this will definitely be the last hit on this trip. I'm starting to run low on cash.

I left Jurisprudence in a parking garage in another town along with my cowboy attire and other damning evidence just in case my added visibility in the marina backfires on me. Besides, I don't want it to get back to the FBI later that I was seen driving a black Mustang. I'm dependent on taxis until I'm finished here.

The plan at this point is to assume that he's

the creature of habit that he appears to be and likes to take his yacht out on Friday evenings for some end-of-the-week solitude. I boarded his boat without any problem during the wee hours this morning. Security concentrates on the outer fringes of the marina, not within. The boat is large enough for me to stow away undetected in a storage area down below, so I'll board again early Friday evening and wait. I hope he comes.

I feel a little naked without my cowboy getup, so I picked up a red-haired man's wig, fake mustache and a nylon stocking to pull over it all. I got some men's clothing, too. Corny, I know, but most security-blanket-type things are. Besides, since the FBI is looking for a male anyway, I might as well try to look like one for the benefit of any witnesses. If only I could get rid of these monster boobs....

Just in case anyone ever searches the houseboat, I pulled a few strands of hair out of a blonde wig at a shop that boasted all their products were real hair. I plan to scatter them around the houseboat before I leave just in case. I bought a Dustbuster too, so I can make sure I don't leave any hairs of my own.

I found an inflatable dinghy on board his boat with a tiny outboard motor. If everything goes right, I'll shoot him, leave his boat adrift and use the dinghy to get back to shore.

If he comes to the marina another night, I'll just follow him back to his car and look for an opportunity to shoot him in the parking lot. I figure if I don't get him one of those two ways, I won't be able to get him at all this trip. My cash is running too low to stay any longer. No way am I going to risk using a credit card.

It's raining this evening, so I'm pretty sure tonight is a scratch, but weather reports are good for the coming week. Maybe I'll get lucky. I sure hope so. It'll be hard to walk away from this one. His wealth makes him a very attractive target. That's probably why I find myself nearing stupidity in straying from my tried-and-true routine.

I hope I keep my wits about me enough to know when to bail out on this target. It will probably help that I'm feeling a little anxious to get back and check the mail. Besides, I can always come back here and try again.

I don't know if wanting to go back means I'm getting past Juanita's murder or not. I still find my thoughts drifting her way quite a bit, especially during these long waits in-between shootings. At least the memories feel more comforting and nostalgic now, so it's less like I'm walking around with my own pet poltergeist.

I've been thinking quite a bit about how much like a mother Juanita was to me. I've often thought of Juanita that way in terms of my affection for her. So, on one level my thoughts are nothing new. As I think of the way I've chosen to pursue justice, though, it occurs to me that growing up with Juanita's influence helped me choose this. Until now, I've credited him with driving me to kill. Yet, when I think about what I'm doing, it has very few parallels with him.

I mean, I didn't take him to court. I never even told anyone but Kitty about what he did and I didn't tell her everything. The justice system never even got a chance to fail me. Except in the sense that I watched it fail for so many others that I never had reason to trust it for help.

If this were just about him, though, I'd be out stalking the invisible perps in the homes, the churches, the schools. The ones who never get caught, who are too good at intimidating their victims into lifetimes of silence. I'd be killing the ones like him.

Instead, I find myself reacting against the failures of a system I never used. Juanita must have had something to do with that. Even though I only recently found out about her political dissidence, it was no surprise. It just made everything else that I already knew about her make sense.

She always spoke in terms of systems: the immigration and naturalization system, the political system, the family system. To her, nothing happened in isolation. Everything happened in the context of some system; every effort at change needed to focus on the system that birthed the problem. It's no wonder she took on the political system when she saw a need for change in her country.

Having spent most of my life under her tutelage, no wonder I've framed my anger in terms of the justice system's failure. What I'm doing with that anger isn't exactly changing the system, though. It's more like I've staged twelve mini L.A. riots across the country. It may be an effective way to register my protest at some really bad calls by the courts, since my work is messy and impossible to ignore. And it may have prevented a handful of kids from being hurt further. Other than that, though, the state of things is pretty much like they were when I started. That's why I never run out of targets. The system is intact. It hasn't been so much as nicked by my volley of well-placed bullets.

I think this tells me how Juanita would have answered my questions about The Crucifier. While I know she would have understood following a higher law, I think she would have taken issue with such a wasteful use of that principle, since I'm not changing anything. What was it she said about her own efforts? "I only regret that I gained so little at such cost." But at least looking at her country years later some changes can be seen. That may not be specifically because of Juanita and her husband, but at least she made a contribution. I'll not contribute toward one changed verdict, one denied parole, one legal reform.

So, do I stop because of that? Do I rethink this whole thing just because I'm not changing anything? I don't know. I mean, if Juanita had lived long enough to tell me any of this, I would have stopped right then. I would have gone straight home and concentrated on making the WJF Memorial Fund an instrument of social change instead of the Band-Aid service it is now. I would have changed the whole direction of my life. If only Juanita had said the word.

Now that I'm saying the word for her, though, I have questions. I knew I wasn't making a huge difference when I started this, so why should that stop me now? And even if I wanted to take on changing the system, how the heck would I do that? Where would I even start?

Changing the system feels so abstract. It would be hard for me to trade the concrete tasks of stalking and shooting an immediate threat, with the instant result of one less perp in the world, for the abstract process of changing a system that took a couple of centuries to screw up and will probably take as long to straighten out.

I'm an American, after all. I like my potatoes instant, my dry cleaning in an hour, lines at the grocery store short and my gasoline cheap. I'm willing to pollute the world and squander its resources so I can live a life of comfort and convenience. In the context of that, my shortsightedness on this vigilante issue shouldn't surprise me terribly. Maybe if I had come from another culture like Juanita did, it would be easier to choose some long-term solution over my knee-jerk, quick-fix response.

Oh, well. I can tell I need to think through all this some more. But not until I'm finished here. This one's too personal.

# Chapter Thirty-Nine

Friday,
Aug. 28, 1992

Today's the day. I hope. I'm sick to death of waiting around. There's too much noise and activity around the marina during the day—imagine me complaining about noise—so I'm back to an awake-days/sleep-nights schedule. Since I can't shoot him during the day, I've tried to stay away from here as much as possible to help pass the time. I've seen every summer movie in town, from *Batman Returns* to *Buffy the Vampire Slayer*. I even saw *Unforgiven* and *A League of Their Own* twice. Cut me and I'd bleed popcorn.

I've looked all over town for refrigerator magnets, too. I think Kitty will love the one that's an oversized gold fish standing outside a little fish bowl and swatting at a cat inside.

In my spare time I hit a used book store, picking up some of Louis L'Amour's and Zane Grey's tales of the Old West. I haven't read a novel in years. Not since audio books hit the market. Now that I'm "deaf," I guess it's back to basics. At least I'm catching up on lots of westerns that never made it to tape. Somehow, sitting on the beach with sea gulls screaming and waves lapping against the shore makes it hard to feel transported to some Old West desert scene, though. Oh, well. Life should always be so "hard."

I also started reading Maya Angelou's *I Know Why the Caged Bird Sings*. I'd listened to it on tape years ago, but I'd never actually read it. Well, a funny thing happened to that book. I left it behind in a taxi or something right after I read the part

about her uncle raping her. Just lost that book.
Poof! It's gone.

I got to thinking about that later and realized I
was almost to the part where her uncle is beaten
to death after being let out of jail. Sounds like something I'd do. Give that sucker what he deserved.
Only, I don't think I wanted to be reminded that it
wasn't the rape that made Maya stop talking for
all those years. It was her uncle's murder at the
hands of someone like me. Ouch.

Anyway, back to planning for tonight, I found
a great fake tattoo to cover that birthmark on my
arm. It's of a six-shooter that's just been fired, so
the bullet flies down the back of my hand. It's big
and gaudy, so it'll surely catch the eye of anyone I
might need to see it. When I'm finished, I can wash
it right off with water.

My disguise for the evening feels awfully juvenile. I'll be glad when this job is done, so I can go
back to my cowboy-in-black look. Which, of course,
isn't juvenile at all.

Kiddy suit or no, I feel better when I'm in my
usual costume. It gives me the delusion of invincibility, feeling more like Batman's armor than the
mere cloth and leather it is. In this line of work,
such delusions are about as important to me as
Linus' blanket is to him. I guess the bottom line is
I'm going to feel pretty vulnerable tonight, make-
shift disguise or not.

I figure I'll board his boat in another hour or
so. The tattoo is on. I'll drape a beach towel over
it, with the wig, gloves, etc. pinned to the under-
side. I'll carry the doll under the towel, too. The
Baretta is strapped under my jeans to my leg. I've
got cash in my pocket in case something goes
wrong. I'm all set. Now, it's just a matter of whether
he'll come. Alone....

Despite all my movie watching, book reading and disguise making, I've still thought some more about my work. The purpose of staying so busy the past couple of days was to keep me from thinking so much about that issue. But, alas, it slipped into my head, anyway.

What did I expect, reading something like Maya's book and watching something like *Unforgiven*? Twice. *Unforgiven* is Clint Eastwood's latest western. Only it's different. No one's all bad. No one's all good. Guilt and innocence keep getting blurred. The movie debunks the romantic view of killing another person, too. It doesn't pretend that killing is easy to do. It doesn't pretend that the killer isn't affected.

How could I not think about the things I've done watching a movie like that? The impact on me, that's what I've thought about most. I don't call what I do "killing." But it's what it is. And it has taken a toll on me. Down deep. I can feel a growing deadness there. In the midst of all the newfound life I've experienced since starting this work, I'm dying. It seems so strange that both can be true. I'm not even sure what part of myself is dying. It feels like an important part, though....

I'm a little surprised to admit this, but I think I'm ready to stop after this one. For a while, anyway.

When I think of planning future hits, I feel really tired. Like it's more of a chore than a mission. Maybe I'm just burned out. Maybe I just need a break to re-evaluate, to remember why I'm doing this at all. Or maybe I just need to do something else for a while.

If this target didn't feel so much like a chance to kill part of his ghost, I probably would have driven Jurisprudence off into the sunset by now. Guys like him use their money to make themselves so untouchable, though. In their own minds at least. Just once I'd like to prove him and everyone else like him wrong. I'd like to show his ghost that if I'd ever decided to go through with my resolutions before he died, he would have been powerless to stop me. Just like Juanita, Winnie, Mom and I were powerless to stop him from what he did to us.

It gets dangerous when it gets this personal. I know that. Even so, I can't bear the thought of leaving without trying.

\* \* \* \*

He didn't show. I'll try one more time tomorrow.

# Chapter Forty

Sunday,
Aug. 30, 1992

He took the boat out last night. I almost missed him, he came so late. I'd decided to call it a night and had come up out of the cabin for a peek to see if it was safe for me to leave. That's when I saw him coming down the pier. He was talking to someone, but I didn't really give that person a second look. I was too busy scrambling back down to my hiding place.

Only after I heard them come aboard did it dawn on me that the person he'd been talking to was coming along for the ride. It sounded like a female voice, so for all I knew it was his wife or a mistress. I could have kicked myself for not paying attention. Not that it would have made that much difference, except in terms of predicting the emotional state of the witness I'd leave behind. I didn't know whether to chance being seen or not, so I just stayed put.

He took the boat only fifteen or twenty minutes off shore before he cut the engines. The two of them stayed up on deck where it was hard for me to hear what was going on. It sounded briefly like they were having a disagreement, scuffling even, but that was punctuated by intermittent belly laughs. So I wasn't sure. I stopped hearing much from her, but I heard enough grunting from him to assume they'd gotten past any arguments to proceed with their tryst under the stars.

The thought of rudely interrupting appealed to me, but the witness thing made me hesitate. When I later heard retching and moaning I was tempted again, since it sounded like my witness might be conveniently seasick or maybe even drunk. But I couldn't decide if I was hearing him throwing up or her, so I didn't budge. It was the same thing when I thought I heard crying. I almost went, but stayed put. Is this why women get stereotyped as indecisive? How embarrassing.

I finally made my move, but only after I heard him come down into the cabin alone.

"How absurd, officer. No. How about 'How ludicrous, officer'?" he was rehearsing out loud in a strong, steady voice, as he banged around the cabin doing who knows what. "Yeah, that's better. How ludicrous, officer. The guard at the marina can testify that I was alone when I boarded my boat on the night in question. No, he'd cost too much. Hmmm. Maybe 'My wife can testify that I was at home with her at the time,' would be better. That's it. How ludicrous officer. My wife can—"

# Chapter Forty-One

Monday,
Aug. 31, 1992

It's a little scary to still be here. I've never stuck around this close to the crime scene before. The police are still here and will no doubt try to question me when I finally venture out. I just hope they haven't brought in an officer who knows sign language. I'll be sunk. I don't really know that much of the official language. Juanita and I made a lot of stuff up.

I'm worried about all the things I left behind, too. The beach towel is still in that closet on the boat, along with the china doll. The nylon stocking is on the boat, too. Then there's the wig, mustache and Lone Ranger mask I left in the water. I hope they sank.

As if that weren't enough, this stupid, wash-off tattoo hasn't washed off. It's merely faded a bit. After all that time in the water, after the scrubbing I gave it in the shower, it's just faded. I doubt the girl even saw it, but now I'm stuck with something that is noticeably out of place on a sweet little deaf woman's arm. I don't even have a long-sleeve shirt to wear over it. Sheesh. When I slip up, I go all out.

I've been all over this houseboat this morning, wiping away fingerprints, sweeping, Dustbusting, packing up every last trace of myself, dropping those wig hairs. Now, it's just a matter of getting up the guts to walk out of this houseboat, with my beach bag in tow, just like I have every day since I got here. I know it's important that I not change that routine. Especially not today. But I think it'll be the hardest thing I've ever done.

* * * *

I waited as long as I could. Then I casually left the houseboat, with beach bag slung in such a way that it hid my tattoo. In the performance of a lifetime, I joined other curious onlookers near the boat for a while, jotting down questions on my notepad. Then I marched straight to the marina office and asked them to call me a taxi. It wasn't a safe place to stay anymore, so I was leaving.

They tried to reassure me that I was perfectly safe, since what I'd seen was the work of a serial killer who was probably long gone and who only killed men, anyway. But I pushed away everything they wrote. Roberto trained me well for that one. Then I went back to the houseboat, got my other bag, and came back to the marina office to wait. I just sat there in the office hugging my bags and shaking all over until the taxi came.

The shaking was real. This one had been too risky. I was just lucky the police ignored me.

I heard about myself on and off on the radio after I picked up Jurisprudence. The revelation that The Crucifier was apparently a woman and that I'd almost gotten caught helping a teen who'd just been raped by my thirteenth target, struck a nerve with the news media if no one else. I checked into the Hilton in plenty of time to watch the local news, only to find that I'd made national news as well. That was threatening and encouraging at the same time.

I didn't like having that much scrutiny, especially with it being broadcast across the nation. Fortunately, the girl was in no state to remember anything significant about my appearance, beyond the fact that I was a woman wearing a black mask. She hadn't even noticed that I never spoke to her.

I don't think that means I'm home free. Not by any means. But I do feel confident that I'll at least make it back home. I'm definitely going to lay low for a while. Definitely.

I may talk big about being willing to pay for my deeds, but when it comes down to it, I'm like every other criminal out there. I want to keep my freedom. Oh, I'll be deeply remorseful once I get caught. But not for what I've done. I'll just be remorseful that I got caught. That's the only thing I'll regret. What a petty little criminal I turned out to be.

On the news tonight I was characterized as a vigilante who kills men who have gotten off easy for the sexual abuse of children. The guys at the marina had called me a man killer, too. Hearing that twice in one day has really made me think. I've never thought of myself as a man killer. I consider myself a vigilante who shoots people who slip through the cracks of the justice system and thus pose a continuing threat to children. Sure, they've all been men so far, but it's not my fault that most perps are men. That's what I tell myself, anyway.

The truth is, though, I think I am a man killer. Only one woman has even made my target list. She was to have been contestant number six on this trip; yet, looking back, I've been trying to take her off the list from the beginning. I was saving her for last, because I wanted to do some investigating of my own. I never quite believed she was guilty of molesting her older daughter. So, I wasn't that concerned that the courts had given her daughter back to her or that they had never even taken away her younger daughter. It was enough that her boyfriend had been found guilty and sent to jail.

Was this because there was more evidence of her innocence than of the others I've killed? No. The only difference was her gender. Then I conveniently ran out of money just before I'd have to kill her. Not to mention my sudden burnout. After killing over a dozen men in rapid succession, I suddenly felt a need to re-evaluate before continuing? Oh, please. I just didn't want to kill a woman.

It's embarrassing. Embarrassing that I'm just like the predominantly male lawyers and male judges and male juries who can't bring themselves to believe that one of their own kind could treat children so badly. Now that the accused is a woman, I want her guilt proven to me beyond a doubt. I want there to be no question, no chance that she was railroaded, framed. I basically want to see her hurt her daughter with my own eyes before I'm willing to pull the trigger.

Good grief, Annie. Does your bias run so deep? What? Kids don't deserve protection from women? Didn't you learn anything from Heidi's mom?

I'm disappointed in myself. Disappointed that my own enlightenment has left me so blind. I may need to go through with killing that woman before I'm through. I'm not going to do it now, though. Now, I'm going to work real hard at saving my own ass. I burst from my hiding place to find him standing naked, his penis coated, his pubic hair matted with still drying blood. He was so stunned by my presence that he froze in mid-wipe on a huge screwdriver. Other blood-covered tools were on the counter.

"It's not what you think, officer," he finally said to me, holding out his hands in front of him as he took a step backward toward the steps. How he mistook me for a cop in my Lone Ranger and pantyhose masks, I'll never know.

I didn't know which hand I most wanted to shoot, since in one he was holding that bloody screwdriver between forefinger and thumb, and in the other he was holding that bloody rag. I finally shrugged to myself and shot them both in

nally shrugged to myself and shot them both in quick succession.

"The Crucifier!" he gasped, pitifully raising his arms to cover his head, hands dangling like they were broken at the wrists.

I was so taken aback that he'd heard of me that I lowered my gun for an instant. He took advantage of that to barrel back up the stairs to the deck screaming, "No! No! No!"

I followed right behind him, noticing for the first time the bloody footprints he'd made coming down the stairs. He was panicked and in shock, so he wasn't very good at getting away.

"No! No!" he kept screaming, as he stumbled away from me. "Somebody make him stop."

Stupidly, he ran toward the nude woman who was curled up in a fetal position. Not a smart move if one is trying to save one's ass from someone like me. Even with only the light of the moon I could tell he'd hurt her badly. I think he realized his mistake when he passed close enough to slip on her blood.

"It's not what you think," he said, forcing a chuckle. His voice didn't sound so strong and steady anymore. "Her period started. She gets really bad cramps. Isn't that it, hon? Tell him. Tell him!"

When he reached the railing his knees almost buckled in horror. I knew that feeling.

"Look. I have money. I can pay. Just name your price."

Talk about some poorly chosen last words.

The force of the bullet sent him tumbling over the railing. So, now he's cheap fish food. It seems appropriate.

When I turned around, gun still in hand, I saw that the woman was sitting up. Only, she wasn't a woman. She was in her mid-teens, max. I started quickly walking toward her, utterly relieved that she was still alive. She started scooting away from me just as fast, breaking into hysterical sobs. I thought she was going to keep scooting until she was over the side of the boat. She must have thought I was going to shoot her.

I stopped dead in my tracks, wishing I could tell her I wouldn't hurt her. I didn't even have my usual paper and pen. Not knowing what else to do, I held out the Baretta so she could see it. Then I flung it overboard as hard as I could.

I could tell she was still terrified, so I stopped trying to approach her. I went over to where he'd thrown her clothes, instead. They were torn, but they were better than nothing. I tied them together in a little bundle and gently tossed them in her direction, hoping to lure her away from the railing.

I went below after that to scrounge up a blanket and a first-aid kit. I happened to walk past a mirror while I was down there and realized how ghoulish I looked with the stocking pulled over my face and the Lone Ranger mask on top of that. I decided to take the pantyhose off, so I wouldn't look quite so frightening to the girl. I kept the wig, mustache and Lone Ranger mask on, though, so I wouldn't frighten myself.

The first-aid kit I found was designed more for the sunburned and the seasick than the brutally raped. It did have a roll of bandages that I thought might help stanch the bleeding. It looked like he'd raped her with those tools, so she needed something like that.

When I went back up, she had the dry heaves and was shivering, holding her clothes to herself like a teddy bear instead of wearing them. I hoped that giving her a first-aid kit would clue her in that I wanted to help, so I slid it across the deck. Then I tossed her the blanket and sat down about twelve feet away.

She just looked at the first-aid kit. I'm not sure she even knew she was bleeding. She seemed too stunned. Besides, it's hard to see blood in the dark. I think that's why I like shooting my targets in the dark. She took the blanket, though, and wrapped it around herself.

"Are you like Bat Girl?" she asked several minutes later. Her voice was hoarse and without inflection.

So much for the mustache disguise. I smiled at her and shrugged.

She didn't respond. Several minutes passed in silence, broken only by an occasional round of dry heaves. I felt so helpless. I wanted to do something. Anything. Without an invitation to help her, though, I was afraid she'd slip through the rails and into the ocean trying to save herself from me. She didn't look good. She kept shivering and she was having a hard time sitting up, even with the rail supporting her.

"I'm cold," she finally said, just before passing out.

I rushed over and grabbed her as she started to slip through the railing and pulled her into the light of the cabin door. Her skin was ice cold and without color, except for splotchy bruises and scratches and smears of dried blood. I got the first-aid kit and packed a wad of bandages in her crotch, where blood still oozed. Then I wrapped her back up in the blanket.

I went back down in the cabin and found a sleeping bag and a pillow. I even found a little stuffed dolphin that must belong to one of his kids. Once I had the dolphin in her arms and the sleeping bag tucked around her for added warmth, I just sat there for a while holding her and rocking her, all the while wondering what the heck I was going to do next.

The dinghy escape was out since I now had her to consider. That left this boat. Kitty loves to water ski so I'd driven a boat with her before, just not one this size. I'd never tried to dock any boat. That made me nervous.

I could see lights on the shore. Whether they were the marina's lights was anyone's guess. I knew I needed to get her some help, but I didn't know how to do that without getting caught myself. I didn't even have a gun anymore to help me out.

I finally just decided to go for it. I'd known all along that I might get caught, that I might have to pay. And if this were the night, so be it. Besides, after sitting in that closet letting him do this to her while I played it safe, it seemed only right that I use a little reckless abandon to get her to safety. I wasn't going to walk up to anyone and suggest they put handcuffs on me and haul me to jail. Not by any means. But I was going to do whatever it took to get her to shore.

She was still out cold. That was probably best, since I didn't have to worry about her wandering too close to the railing again. I went down below one last time and got a flare gun and air horn I'd seen earlier. Then I went up to start the boat and turn it back to shore.

It wasn't that difficult to navigate with the shore lights to guide me in. My one lucky break of the whole night was that he'd taken a bee-line route from the marina, so the lights turned out to be home sweet home.

I knew that, even as late as it was, I'd never manage to dock the boat without drawing attention. All I could remember about Kitty docking her dad's ski boat was that she threw the engine in reverse to brake as she entered the boathouse. That was hardly enough boating knowledge to make for a flawless first-ever try. I had visions of me plowing into the dock, boards buckling, piers collapsing, boats sinking.

Since creating a ruckus felt so inevitable anyway, I decided to make it something that no one could ignore—except maybe a certain deaf tourist I knew. As I entered the marina, I fired the flare gun and started belting out SOS calls with the air horn. I looked for an empty slot in the general area of my houseboat. Docking in the one I finally spotted was going to be like playing a hole of golf with a softball, but I went for it anyway, making toothpicks of the dock in the process.

That got people running in my direction, headed by my ol' tackle pal, "Sarge." So I switched off the engines and made for the other end of the boat as fast as I could without getting dizzy. I paused before diving over the railing to look back at the girl—and the crowd running toward me. She was sitting up again, watching me. I raised my hand in a farewell gesture. Then I took advantage of every diving and swimming lesson he'd ever forced upon me to make my getaway. Swimming underwater, feeling my way among the pilings and under the boat hulls, I slowly made my way to the houseboat where I'd left the ladder over the side for my dinghy escape plan.

It wasn't a piece of cake. I must have been in the water for a couple of hours, dodging search lights sweeping the area for me, hiding in every available shadow as I went from boat to boat. All of this I did fully clothed, except for the wig and mustache I lost when I dove in and the Lone Ranger mask I ripped off soon afterward.

The girl must not have been in any condition to tell them much before the paramedics whisked her away to the hospital because everyone was running around looking for the man who had hurt her. It was quite a circus. One I wanted to stay out of. I didn't climb aboard the boat until I was sure no one would notice.

It was a major relief when I finally crawled safely on board. With the ladder to hang onto I hadn't had to tread water the whole time, but I was still exhausted. I didn't even have the energy to peel off my wet clothes and crawl into bed. I just lay there in my own puddle on the floor and fell asleep.

Bang! Bang! Bang! I awoke to hours later. I guess it was hours. My hair and clothes were stiff with dried salt, anyway.

"Open up! This is the police!" I didn't move; I didn't breathe. I just lay there, my eyes following the flashlight beam along the pulled curtains.

"That one can't hear you. She's deaf," I heard "Sarge" call out. My buddy. "She didn't see nothin'. Probably slept through the whole friggin' thing."

The police moved on. I got up and peeked out of a window to see what was going on. It looked like the authorities were going around gathering statements from everyone who'd been in the marina at the time. His boat had been cordoned off with yellow police-line tape. Some officers were still aboard taking photos, gathering evidence. Several news teams were on the scene. I wasn't going anywhere soon, so I got out of my clothes and took a shower. And now I'm going back to bed. I'm pooped.

# Chapter Forty-Two

I was actually glad to see this place when I rolled through the front gates yesterday. It didn't even have that haunted house look about it, since Charlie had arranged to have the lawn mowed while I was gone.

My attic was all finished and the key waiting for me on the hall table. A dusty, old metal lock box a little smaller than a briefcase was on the table, too. A note from Charlie said he'd found it under the floorboards in the attic when installing the kitchen sink. He thought it might have belonged to me or Winnie, since we used to play in the attic so much. I'd never seen the box before in my life.

I thought immediately of the one remaining mystery key. But it didn't fit. Curiosity wouldn't let me just walk away without knowing the contents, so I finally took the box out to the garage and used a tire iron to beat and pry it open. Needless to say, I was underwhelmed to find an old spy novel inside.

As I looked at it more closely though, I realized it was an autographed first edition of Ian Fleming's first James Bond novel *Casino Royale*, published in 1953. What a treasure that must have been. I think it would have meant to him as a kid what Annie Oakley's pistol meant to me. And he didn't have a key....

Sure makes me wonder if that novel had something to do with him buying Annie's gun and then keeping it from me all those years. Guess I'll never know. I put the novel with Annie's gun behind the revolving panel. I figure they belong together.

But back to the attic. It was nice to climb right

up to my little hideaway. I've even started rearranging some things and opening old boxes and trunks. I'm almost ready to move in and make the attic my own. I'm wanting to enjoy the attic while I still can. There's nothing like a close call to inspire me to enjoy the moments of freedom I have left.

I don't know if it's possible to administer a charitable fund from behind prison walls and I can't exactly ask Kitty about that fine legal point, so I'm anxious to respond to all the letters I have as soon as possible. Besides, some of them have been languishing in the mailbox for over a month. I almost wish I had a secretary who could call these people for me and make sure their needs haven't changed. Who knows, maybe I'll visit a temp agency or something.

The dentist's ex-wife, Edie, is the one I'm most worried about. I caused her some major problems. I hadn't been established as a serial killer when I killed her ex and when she got called in repeatedly for questioning by police she lost her job, supposedly for absenteeism. Without child support, she had to sell her house and has been living out of state with her parents all summer.

She'd already been planning to go to college part-time this fall. Now that she's unemployed, she plans to go full-time on student loans instead. Since she was a secretary, I had just assumed she didn't have her bachelor's but it turns out she's going for her Ph.D. She's wanting to research incest families and develop a prevention model aimed at adult family members. She says she's annoyed at current prevention efforts because they expect kids to recognize, stop and then report sexual abuse to skeptical adults. She thinks this type of prevention is based on a false premise that sexual abuse strikes mysteriously at random. So only children are in a position to stop it.

Edie is convinced from her own experience that incest in particular is just one of many symptoms of a family in trouble, so there are always loud and clear warning signs that a child is at risk. She'd like to research and compile these warning signs.

Her plan is to interview survivors of incest about the non-verbal ways they tried to communicate their distress, non-offending parents about what they did notice and how they misinterpreted what they saw, and offenders about steps they took to make the incest possible and how they kept it from being detected for so long. She hopes what she learns will help de-mystify incest once and for all.

But that's not all. She's an ambitious one. Once that's done, she wants to work on setting up programs for incest offenders that would bypass the criminal justice system. She's particularly interested in a treatment program for sex offenders within the Vermont prison system, in which only seven percent of child molesters reoffended during an eight-year period.

"The economic impact on the family of a key breadwinner's imprisonment, coupled with the actual costs for the state, are an absurd waste, when the perpetrator will come out of prison with the same emotional problems that caused him to molest in the first place," she writes in her letter.

Despite her persuasive passion for this, it all sounds like la-la land to me. Especially when I think about how slick he was and how oblivious Mom was. Edie seriously lost me with her "treat them, don't punish them" ideas for perps. He would never admit that the things he did to me were because of some problem of his, much less seek help for it. Her husband didn't sound any better. But I can't knock her ideas too hard. At least she suggested some solutions. That's more than I seem to do. All I do is play shoot-em-up.

I guess that stems from a premise of my own that these creeps are criminals and it's about time they're called by their true name and punished accordingly. I'm sick of babying them, of giving them the benefit of the doubt, of looking for their potential as valuable human beings. What about my potential? As a blank-slate little kid, I had a lot more potential as a human being than his cluttered psyche had by the time he was doing that shit to me and Winnie.

It gives me the creeps to think of lollygagging around trying to fix these assholes, while in the meantime they're free to hurt other kids.

"You did all that to your daughters? Oh, you poor man. You must be carrying around a lot of pain inside to have done things like that. Now, tell me where it hurts so I can kiss it and make it all better."

Sheesh. I want them punished. I want them to hurt. I want them sent so far away that they'll forget what a kid even looks like. And I want everyone in that prison to know why they're there, so they'll get treated just as badly as they deserve. Eye for an eye; tooth for a tooth; rape for a rape. Let the punishment fit the crime.

Unfortunately, none of what I want solves anything. I seem to have a knack for things that smack of vengeance and little else. I guess I'm just like a kid with a sweet tooth who can't get enough revenge candy. How embarrassing.

If Edie wants to look for solutions, though, even solutions that taste foul to me personally, I want to use his money to fully fund her research and pay for her schooling. For all I know she's right. If she is, at least I can be part of the solution vicariously. I just hope I'm not too late to help her this semester. I think school started this week; I really need to get someone to call her for me.

She must have told her ex-husband's new wife about the fund, because I got a letter from that Carrie woman, too. I wasn't thrilled to hear from her. It was like getting yet another mirror to take one more hard look at myself. As if the man-killer mirror and revenge mirror weren't enough. Since she married him after he'd been accused of molesting his kids, I really didn't care what his death might do to her. I wanted to punish her, too, since she put her own kids in danger by marrying him. She deserved financial disaster, emotional trauma, for selling out her children. That sounds pretty callous. Probably because that's what it is. I just don't have any patience these days with women like Mom who are determined to pretend it all away, to believe the man they love, no matter what the cost to their children.

It turns out Carrie's loving husband was messing with her kids after all and now the kids are guilt ridden because they'd started asking God to kill him a few weeks before I came along. The things kids blame themselves for.

That reminds me, I heard from Heidi, too. It's funny how that slipped my mind. I guess that's what I do with things I don't have a clue how to handle. It's that wish thing. I knew it would come back and haunt me. Sure enough....

Heidi enclosed the "I can help" note that I wrote my name and address on that day at the cemetery. Her wish? "I wish I could live with that lady and she could be my family." No kidding. Cross my heart and hope to die. The kid actually wrote that.

I don't know what to do. I mean, I care about that kid. No question about it. But I cared about Caleb Jr. too. I didn't load him up and take him along for the police chase, though. That wouldn't have been fair to him. I don't think it would be fair to Heidi, either.

Still.... I have a voice in there reminding me that I'm at a different place now. I may be finished with target shooting. Well, except for that one woman out there, I may be finished. If I had encountered Caleb Jr. at the marina instead of months ago, I don't think I would have shooed him out of my car. I would have been thrilled to have him around for my last few days, weeks, months of freedom. I'd love to be around Heidi, too.

If my days as a free woman are really numbered, though, how can I even consider uprooting Heidi? She's a child. She doesn't know what she's wishing for. The end. Case closed.

So, why haven't I simply composed a letter expressing the fund's regrets that it is unable to fulfill her wish? Who knows? Maybe I'm just immoral to the core. Maybe I get a perverse kick out of considering things that shouldn't be considered. I can sure be a creep sometimes.

I think I'll write a letter to Kitty about Heidi just to pull another voice into the dialogue inside my head.

# Chapter Forty-Three

Friday,
Sept. 4, 1992

Happy birthday to me. Well, not too happy. I almost missed it. No kidding. I usually at least acknowledge it, but this morning I got so caught up in working on my attic that I didn't even think about the date. If I hadn't gone out to pick up a shower curtain and some ice trays for my new place, I might not have ever remembered. While I was driving to the mall, the radio announcer reminded me with one of those today-in-history things.

At first I thought I'd go ahead and just get my shower curtain and ice trays, since my new attic apartment was a fine birthday present in and of itself. But then it occurred to me that this could very well be the last birthday I spend outside of prison. Is that a nasty thought or what? Shower curtains and ice trays certainly wouldn't do after thinking that. I knew immediately what I wanted for my twenty-sixth birthday. I wanted to spend my twenty-seventh birthday out from behind bars.

So, that's what I gave me. I gave me my best chance, anyway. I went and got my hair cut short, permed and darkened. Then I went to one of those one-hour eyeglass places and got myself fitted for some John Lennon frames. Never mind that I don't need glasses and don't care for the Beatles. The eyeglass people didn't care if the lenses were prescription or not. While I was waiting on the glasses to be made, I got my ears pierced. One ear twice. But I drew the line at getting my nose pierced. I think I'd rather get caught.

I started to shop for a whole new look in clothes,

too. But it occurred to me that people at the marina never saw me in anything but high-necked T-shirts and shorts. So, I just bought a floppy leather hat. Sort of like a cowboy hat, sort of not. I decided it was time to forgo wearing cowboy boots all the time, too. Hiking boots seemed like a good transition. They feel a little clunky right now, but I think they'll grow on me.

Oh, and I got the brand new Annie Oakley biography by Shirl Kasper. I was walking past the bookstore when I saw my Annie Oakley poster out of the corner of my eye. It's on the cover of the book! I haven't started reading the book yet. Just thumbed through looking at the pictures.

Of course, it made me miss my hair to see those pictures of Annie in her prime. At least I don't look like the same person. I'm taking comfort in that. Now, if only I could get rid of that birthmark on my arm.... Thank goodness it'll be sweater weather soon.

Now I'm sitting in the mall food court enjoying a happy birthday frozen yogurt. I—hey, that's Sally Jenkins. I can't believe it. Haven't seen her in years. I'm going to go over and say hello and try out my new look on her.

\* \* \* \*

Sally definitely had to do a double-take when I walked over to her table. That made me like my new look a lot. I may make that next birthday as a free woman yet.

It felt weird seeing Sally after all these years. We lost touch after she went east to college while I was finishing up high school. That year of school I lost after the wreck really messed things up that way. Anyway, it turns out that instead of getting her MBA like her family wanted, she got her masters in administrative social work.

It sounds like the perfect field for her. I remember when we were kids we had these ongoing Monopoly games. She always used the top-hat game piece because she was the boss and she always gave me the wheelbarrow because I secretly worked for her.

The game went beyond the usual rules. Together we'd buy up the utilities and decree that no one's electricity or water could ever be cut off. We'd buy up the railroads and only let people who couldn't afford a car ride them. Her favorite thing of all was to buy Boardwalk and Park Place and let homeless people live there for free.

Now she has started an agency in town that offers vocational training to single mothers and battered women. None of this training is in the pay-nothing fields women usually get stuck with. This is in construction, electronics, plumbing. All good-paying, male-dominated fields. She said the only problem they're having is keeping the battered women safe long enough to complete the training and find a job. One of the women was killed by her husband just two weeks ago. I was out of town when it happened, so I didn't even hear about it.

Sally said the violence invariably escalates when the men realize they'll lose economic leverage over their women. But there aren't any long-term safe houses in the area where these women can go. And her grant writer can't scrounge up enough funding to establish any. Ah, the legacy of the Reagan years continues.

Of course, my first response was that money is no object. I could buy some property and have a building constructed with the best security systems money could buy.

But then another thought occurred to me. His

house is already built. It already has the best security systems money can buy. It already exceeds the *Americans with Disabilities Act* standards. The bedrooms already have their own locks and are already furnished. And now that I have my own attic apartment, I don't even use it, except for the garage and his bedroom. And I could always move my command post. His van might even be useful.

I might have to install a sprinkler system or make some other changes to use the house as a shelter. And I'll need a new swing and other playground equipment for the wee ones. But otherwise, it's perfect. I could even use the money I planned to give to Juanita to get this going. A shelter for battered women. What better way to "help the people be free from monsters." I could even name the shelter after her.

Of course, Sally almost fell out of her chair when I suggested all this.

"You're serious?" she gasped.

"I always 'worked for you' when we were kids. It'll be just like old times," I wrote.

She couldn't argue with that, so we scheduled a time to get together and talk more. She wants me to come to a board meeting at her agency next month, too. All this because I needed a shower curtain and some ice trays. Who knew? Quite a productive little trip to the mall, I'd say.

When I got back home to attic-sweet-attic and saw something in the news about Marilyn, I didn't even feel like the black sheep survivor hiding in her shadow. I could just be glad she was in the news again, keeping the facts about child sexual abuse straight. This time she was refuting some gay-bashers' assertions that fifty percent of child molestations are committed by homosexuals. Yeah, right. America would love that. Let's pretend that incest right away, shall we? Go get those idiots, Marilyn.

All that reminds me of something else Sally told me today. Well, actually several "something elses."

I was inquiring about her mother, since I hadn't seen Mrs. Jenkins since his funeral. It turns out Sally's family won't have anything to do with her. They don't even know she's back in town. No kidding.

At the funeral, Mrs. Jenkins acted like she had it on good authority that Sally had never been better. What an act.

Sally's dad is this big-shot tax lawyer and it seems tax season really stresses him out. Well, instead of taking up jogging or finger painting to help manage the stress, his hobby was crawling into bed with the kids that time of year and jacking off. And his wife was worried about bath times at our house. Sheesh.

Once Sally escaped to college, she took care of tax season by refusing to go home over spring break. She's the baby of the family, so that was quite a loss for dear ol' Dad. He kept pressuring her to spend spring break at home until she finally told both her parents exactly why she wasn't coming home. Aren't speaker phones wonderful?

Anyway, that little bombshell went over well. The whole family got together and reached a consensus that Sally is crazy. How convenient.

She had told them a few months earlier that she's a lesbian, so they used her orientation to support their position that she's a depraved lunatic. Sally's "sinful" lifestyle had warped her mind.

It was hilarious to hear her tell it. I love how her voice has developed over the years. I could listen to her for hours. She can convey so much with these subtle changes in pitch and tone. Quite the storyteller. But I could tell there was pain beneath the mirth in today's story. Speaking the family secret had been costly. I guess it always is.

# Chapter Forty-Four

It's hard to believe he's been dead a year. I haven't felt an urge to visit his grave today, but I did consider making a trip earlier in the week to visit Annie Oakley's grave. She died November 3, 1926, and her ashes are buried in a little cemetery off Highway 127 in Ohio. I wanted to go lay a spent cartridge and one of my shooting medals on her grave. But I decided I was wanting to go there this year more to avoid the anniversary of his death than to observe hers.

So, I stayed home. I've found myself sitting here in his room today, scanning the new black paneling, the X-ray vision of my mind's eye seeing the red, news-plastered wall beneath. The headline spiral on the red ceiling remains, only the spiral has been expanded with headlines about wives being killed by estranged husbands, women being raped, children being beaten to death. The old light fixture at the center of the spiral has been replaced by a tear-shaped glass fixture, which now hangs over a tear-shaped, black mahogany conference table.

Sally's partner, Libby, handmade the table for me. She's some kind of talented. When Sally first told me about Libby, it was in the context of her running the family construction business that is helping Sally's agency with the vocational training. Apparently, Sally and Libby met in college and then moved back here to take over the construction business after Libby's dad died. Anyway, with all that talk of construction work, I imagined this big, hulking, don't-mess-with-me, spits-nails kind of woman.

Not even close. She's this slender, petite, intensely private woman. I've yet to hear her voice rise above a whisper. She studied art in college and thinks of herself more as a furniture artisan than as a carpenter. Oh, she can build anything with a blueprint, all right. From start to finish. But furniture is her passion. Sit in a chair at their house and it's like participating in an art exhibit.

Needless to say, the table is gorgeous. A life-size Lady Justice, her scales hanging upside down, has been etched in glass that lays over the wood. It adds just the right touch. That was Libby's idea, too.

This barely feels like his room at all, much less the place he so often killed me, the place he died a year ago. It's a welcome change, like a ghost has been exorcised—or is it a demon that gets exorcised? Oh, well. That fits, too. So, whichever.

I'm glad I decided to go the conference-room route. I started paneling the room more out of necessity than anything else. After seeing Sally at the mall that day, I knew I wanted to help women get themselves and their kids away from abusive husbands and boyfriends. Using his bedroom for my own version of a Bat Cave got in the way of that, though.

So, I moved the computer equipment to another room, disconnected the on-line connections to criminal records and cleared the closet of cash, dolls and guns. Then I hunted down some do-it-yourself videos and paneled over the evidence myself. It looks sharp, especially with the paintings I've hung.

One depicts a muscular construction worker, jeans unzipped, hands gripping the jack hammer that protrudes from his groin in his penis' stead. Where the jack hammer pounds the pavement, a crack has formed, outlining a woman—the jack hammer point at her crotch. Another painting is a family portrait. The mother and father figures aren't human, though. They're a tangle of thorns. Each holds a young child, torn and bleeding from those thorns. Yet, the whole family is smiling. I can almost hear them saying "cheese" for the camera.

The other one is, at first-glance, the face of a lovely, smiling woman—radiant even. If you look closely, though, each of her teeth is a skeletal face that's twisted in anguish; her hair is really chains; her eyes are deep, empty pits; the hooded figure of death resides in the shadows of her face; the background is that of a prison cell's bars.

No, Libby doesn't paint. I found all three in Mom's studio. No kidding. There were more. Lots more. Those were just among the most striking.

I had no idea that those were the kinds of things she painted. I expected to find bowls of fruit and flower arrangements, so it was pretty draining to stumble across her pain. No wonder she never hung any of her work outside the studio. It would have given too revealing a glimpse behind the facade of order and cheer. That's probably why none of the paintings are signed.

I've respected her anonymity since hanging them in the new conference room. I'm good at secrets. But others have certainly seen the paintings during the many meetings to discuss making use of this house. The paintings add something to the atmosphere, so much so that this has become my favorite room in the house. I find myself drawn here at odd hours, sitting in silence even, studying the paintings, reading the spiral on the ceiling. What a switch. His bedroom has gone from dungeon to sanctuary. Who would have thought? It's amazing what can change in a year.

It's hard to believe that four women and their

children live here now. I know that's nothing compared to the number who still have no place to go, but I always was a small-scale operator, so four sounds great to me. I'm hiring them as "live-in help" while they train for their new careers. That's to get around any zoning spats with the neighbors over having a shelter for these "awful women" in their ritzy backyards. Never mind that they were perfectly content to live next door to him all those years.

The live-in-help route was Kitty's idea, along with advice that I retain my own residence here instead of just signing the house over to Sally's agency. At least until Kitty has a chance to work out more permanent arrangements. It's crazy how victims are considered undesirable neighbors. I guess it's victim blaming at its pinnacle. Sheesh.

It's a good thing that Kitty works for me now, though not as a live-in herself. She's got a tiny little apartment on the other side of town. I tease her that it's barely big enough for her magnet collection. But she says the only things that matter are that she's got a great view, an ideal place for her morning runs and only a thirty-minute drive to her dad's place. She always did know what she likes.

I'm glad she's here. Not just as a friend. I need someone who knows how to play by the rules, to make the system work for her. My own tendency to just shoot my way past the system wouldn't have been very effective in helping these women. She's not just giving legal advice to me, either. She's helping these women work through the legal system. It's much closer to the kind of law she wanted to practice, so she seems happy.

It's funny how it happened. I wrote her a note to tell her about my plans for turning the house into a high-security shelter and a couple of days later she left a message on the answering machine.

"Your idea's great, Annie, but you're going to need a lawyer. I gave two-weeks' notice as soon as I read your letter, so I'd better be the lawyer you hire. I'm coming down this weekend to discuss the terms of my employment."

That pretty much settled that.

She's been looking into fulfilling Heidi's wish, too. Kitty says it's difficult to get foster kids transferred out of state, so she's trying to get Heidi's stepfather to let me adopt her. Imagine that. I flew down and interviewed with the adoption folks a few weekends ago. I visited Heidi too, so she'd know I was trying to give her that wish and to make sure she really wanted that. I think she does.

Heidi still isn't talking, even though the doctors say the bullet wound has healed and there is no permanent damage to her vocal chords. The thought of her coming to live here worries me some because of that, especially since that mutual loss seems to be a big part of the connection between us. I guess I just don't want to hold her back from finding her own voice again.

At least with lots of noisy little munchkins running up and down the halls of the house, she won't be completely surrounded by silence here. I've decided that if the adoption goes through, I'm going to fix up Mom's studio for her bedroom. I've already had Charlie build a railed walkway from the studio to my attic, so it'll be safer to go back and forth between the two. That way Heidi can come to the attic with ease when she wants to be with me, but she'll still be connected to the people in the main house, too. I hope it works out.

Of course, I kind of hate to dismantle Mom's studio now. I never knew the woman who painted those pictures. Every time I go in there to look through paintings and drawings, I feel like I'm meeting Mom for the first time. Mostly I feel nostalgic and closer to her than I've ever felt, but I also feel flashes of anger from time to time that she didn't heed her pain and get away from him—and save Winnie and me. I don't understand the generation she came from, a generation of women who seem to have lost themselves to a husband, a society—something. I'm not sure what.

One thing I found in the studio utterly blew me away. It was a page ripped out of a diary from the day she found out she was pregnant.

"I went to the doctor for the stomach flu and found out I'm going to die. Just kidding. Since Momma's in her grave and Daddy's long gone, there's no one left to kill me for getting pregnant. I tried to get the doctor to give me an abortion, as awful as that is, but when I told him the father is my boyfriend, the doctor didn't believe I'd been forced. 'You go marry that boy,' he told me. 'It's the only decent thing for a girl like you to do.' I guess he's right."

I had to sit down after reading that. I had no idea he'd raped her. And to think people had the gall to call her a gold digger. So, that was life before Roe v. Wade, huh?

No wonder they slept in separate bedrooms.

I think Mom was painting that diary entry when she was killed. She must have painted her words a lot, because I found a metal pan with the ashes of burned pages. I think it was some kind of cathartic ritual for her.

I looked through the old roll-top desk up there, but I couldn't find the diary the page had been ripped from, so I don't know what happened to it. I found some interesting "secret" compartments in that old desk but they were all empty. Maybe the diary is hidden in one I haven't discovered yet.

Maybe she only saved certain pages. Maybe the diary was lost in the wreck. I have no idea. I just know this page was lying among some sketches of what she was painting when she died. She was almost finished.

It depicts a headstone with her name, birth date and a death date corresponding to the diary entry. The grass over the grave isn't flat, it's more like a death shroud that clings to the form of a pregnant woman, holding a bridal bouquet where her hands are folded across her chest in death. Caleb sits at the figure's feet. From the grass that covers her womb grows two white lilies, with mine and Winnie's faces painted in the blooms. She had yet to finish painting him standing beside the grave in his bridegroom tuxedo. So, he looks like a ghost. Seems appropriate.

I've got that one hanging in my attic now. When I look at it, I have hope for her memory. Hope that she was gathering strength within herself to leave him. I can't imagine painting images like that without some self-awareness. She was trying to work through stuff. I think. I want to believe so, anyway.

I stumbled across some of his past, too. While I was going through the trunks in the attic, I found several pairs of blood-stained boy's underwear, with WJF embroidered on the waistband. They were all wadded up and stuffed in a locked trunk packed with a toy fingerprint dusting kit, decoder ring, spy comic books, how-to detective books and such. I guess his spy fixation started earlier than I'd imagined.

I can't help but wonder if that James Bond novel Charlie found ties in somehow to what was done to him in the attic. The underwear was different sizes, so whatever happened went on for a long time.

Finding the underwear wasn't the surprise to

me that finding Mom's paintings and the diary entry were. I'd always suspected he'd been through something horrible as a boy, since I can't believe monsters like him happen on their own. I guess that's why I didn't feel any more endeared to him after seeing those remnants of his pain. I hate to think of a little boy being hurt that badly, but that doesn't excuse him for what he did to me and Winnie—and Mom. He betrayed that little boy's pain by inflicting it on others. That sucks.

Listen to me. You'd almost think I was doing something different with my pain. The recipients of my pain are different than his, but I've still grown up to be just like him. I wonder if that would make him feel proud. I've always heard we humans tend to hate most passionately the faults in other people that we don't want to face within ourselves. Maybe I hate him so thoroughly because I'm so thoroughly like him. Yuck.

I tossed the underwear, but I'm using the trunk where he stashed them. The last of his mystery keys fits the trunk lock. It amazes me that he carried that key around with him for all those years. Now the trunk holds my secrets: the cash, the five remaining dolls, the two remaining guns. Everything I'd kept in his bedroom closet. It's nice knowing what all the keys fit now.

It's been nice giving some of the keys away as people start living here, too. When they arrive, I let them walk through the house and pick out a bedroom or two. Then I give them the keys, so it's their own private space for as long as they choose to stay.

The key to Winnie's room was the only one I hated to part with. I have her Pooh bear in the attic, now, so that helps. I guess. Turning over that key felt too much like letting her go. I felt like my guts had been ripped out. So, I climbed up to my attic after that to hold Pooh, fill in the pothole in my gut with a box of Twinkie Lights and have a long cry.

The flip side to giving Winnie's key away was having a door and lock installed on my old room, so the woman could have both bedrooms, adjoined by the bathroom. It was so satisfying to have a door on that room again. It felt like getting dressed after walking around naked in the house for years. I wish I'd thought of doing that sooner. I moved my Annie Oakley poster up to the attic. A lot of the other stuff I was storing in there I gave to Goodwill. Except for my shooting trophies and medals. I moved them up to my attic, too. They look nice arranged on a shelf beneath the poster.

Doors on community rooms like the kitchen and living room are gone. Locks and all. I had fun with those keys, standing on the roof one night and flinging them far into the darkness. The only house keys I still carry around are to his den, the conference room, Mom's studio, the trunk and the security door on my fire escape. I guess they represent the secrets I still hold.

I can deal with that. It feels much lighter than anything I carried this time last year. In fact, I think I'm at the opposite end of the spectrum this year. I feel better than I ever have. Working with Sally over the past couple of months toward opening this shelter and becoming friends again has been absolutely life-giving. I think it's even reviving the part of me that was dying.

That dying part seems to be about relating to people. That was a little scary to realize. What's a woman minus her most basic orientation?

I should have known. I mean, turning a dozen or so people into mere targets was bound to affect how I relate to other people, too. I've noticed with Sally that it's hard for me to relate to people on anything more than a functional level.

Well, actually she noticed. I relate to her fine as far as setting up the shelter goes. Just like I can relate to Kitty in legal matters and Charlie in construction matters. But when it comes to connecting on an emotional plane of any depth or revealing anything remotely intimate about my person, forget it.

"I miss you, Annie," Sally said out of the blue a few weeks ago. "Is it really that uncomfortable for you that I'm gay?"

That one threw me. I must have looked as puzzled as I felt, because she went on to explain that she found a lot of her female friends became distant once she came out to them.

"They forget I'm still a woman. Relationship is what matters to me, not sexual conquest. It's not like I'm on the prowl."

I used his and Juanita's deaths to explain away any strange vibes she might be getting from me. But the more she talked about relationships, the more I knew my shootings were killing off the very essence of the woman I am. I can only wonder if killing is as costly for men.

I still feel a sense of relationship with things like Jurisprudence, my attic, Mom's paintings. And with myself. The points of disconnection seem to be with other people and with America.

*I've broken all of its rules. Of course I feel disconnected from this nation.* That was my first thought. But then I thought about Sally. Her whole person resides where she is at any given moment. She doesn't worry that the deployment of peace keepers to war-torn Bosnia has been thwarted today. She doesn't want to be bothered by an in-depth analysis of why Clinton won and Bush lost the presidential election. If it isn't in the local newspaper, she doesn't want to know. It drives me crazy.

In setting up this shelter, I poured over databases, trying to get a feel for the impact of domestic violence on this nation's women and children. So many battered women have been driven to kill and so many child witnesses have grown up to be batterers themselves that I felt a definite kinship. I also felt overwhelmed. The problem seemed too big to fix. When I expressed that sense of hopelessness to Sally, though....

"Look around you, Annie," she said, waving toward the bustle of activity as the house was being transformed into a shelter. "Here is where we are. And here we're doing something about it. Here there is hope."

At the time, I thought hers was a conveniently narrow view. But I'm beginning to realize she may be on to something. My relationship with this country for the past year or so has definitely been one of hopelessness, as I've tried to live everywhere at once via the media. No wonder this nation's ills feel so overwhelming. No wonder it feels like there's no justice anymore. No wonder I had to disconnect emotionally.

I guess that's why I decided to disconnect the databases when I moved his computer equipment. I can't bring myself to turn off National Public Radio or the evening news, but no more freebasing on-line information for Bonzo. At least for now. For now, I'm subscribing to the local newspaper for the first time in my life. I want to see what America is like here where I live. I don't really know.

I'm working on the people part, too. I'm spending more time with Sally and getting to know Libby. Having Kitty close by again has helped me with the people part, too. Not to mention the women and children living here. I usually join them for a meal at least once a day. I've never had so many people in my life all at once.

I hope I'm not overdoing it. But probably I am. I do believe a tendency toward extremes would qualify as one of my dominant personality traits. Oh, well. I'm having a good time, and I'm definitely in a good mood these days.

Of course, some of my good cheer right now may be leftovers from Tuesday's elections. See Sally, all news isn't bad. Forty-eight of one hundred and six women who ran for the House were elected and four more women were elected to the Senate. I know that's still just a drop in the bucket, but it sure feels like a start. And I used his money to help. That felt so good, giving money to some of these women's campaigns and seeing them elected.

I even have hope for president-elect Clinton. I didn't contribute to his campaign. Or vote for him, for that matter. Perot re-entered the race about a month before the election, so I went ahead and voted for him. I was annoyed at him for yo-yoing in and out of the race, so I was really voting more against this nation's complacency than for him. He got about 19 percent of the vote in the end. It was good to know I'm not alone in being fed up with the direction this country is going.

Anyway, back to Clinton. I think what I find hopeful about him is that he likes women. And he doesn't seem afraid to express the warmth and caring that most men ridicule as weak, feminine qualities. I like Hillary, too. A strong, capable woman. An advocate for children at that. Maybe all is not lost for this country after all.

I hear Clinton even drives a 1967 Mustang.

# Chapter Forty-Five

Friday,
Nov. 13, 1992

*America's Most Wanted* aired a show tonight focusing on serial killers still at large, and lucky me was one of the featured bad guys. Is this a Friday the 13th kind of thing to happen or what? I swear. They focused primarily on the boat fiasco, of course, since that's the only one with any witnesses. I also found out my first target finally died a couple of months ago. He never regained consciousness. That's a relief.

The girl who was brutalized on the boat talked some about that night, without even a blue dot to cover her face or a fake name to hide her identity. I was glad to get Tammy's name. Now the fund can make contact and do something to help. It made me feel good to see her talking without hiding, without shame. Maybe rape is finally losing its stigma in this country. I hope so.

The hard part about tonight was hearing Tammy frame what he did to her in terms of what I let him do to her. She thinks I purposely waited to shoot him, so it would be considered justifiable homicide if I got caught.

"Maybe she was right to kill him," Tammy said, "but I don't see why she had to use me to make it okay. He hurt me really bad."

That stung. I wish I could let her know that I had no idea what he was doing to her, that I hate knowing I could have stopped him before he even touched her. I'm not sure she'd believe me even if I told her, though. I think I've hurt her too badly to warrant any trust.

I've hurt so many innocents in the process of stopping these targets. I keep trying to make up for that by giving them money, but it's probably as much blood money when I give it to them as it was when he gave it to me. I'm never going to buy off their pain; I'm never going to make up for what I've done to their lives. Sure, the money might be helpful, but no doubt it goes further in easing my conscience than in erasing their horrors.

Putting a stop to these assholes has turned out so much more complicated than I expected. I was prepared for the heavy guilt scene over my evil deeds, but that never really materialized. I'm at ease with the elimination of these threats. I don't feel tainted as a human being by what I've done. Pulling a trigger is just something I do, like I used to pound a keyboard. When I'm finished, I go home, watch TV, visit with friends, do laundry, take out the trash. Just normal people stuff. What's to sit around and feel guilty about? I'm just doing my job.

These fringe people who keep getting caught in the ripples as each target falls, though. That wasn't supposed to happen. I guess vigilante justice isn't the simple, straightforward solution it masquerades to be.

I wish it were. The whole point has been to stop these creeps before they get a chance to hurt anyone else. Sure enough, I've done that. But look at the "anyone elses" I've hurt in my targets' stead: the kid who found the first guy I shot, the man who was thrown into jail, the woman who lost her job, the girl who thinks someone with the power to stop him sat by and let him torture her.

And what about the girl who shot that dear "man of God"? I don't know that I did her any favors by finishing him off Crucifier-style. Secrets can tear people up inside. I should know that. Now I suspect she'll never tell. She may have been acting in self-defense. She may have nothing to hide. But she's hiding it anyway. Who knows what I've done to her? Who knows what I've done to others I've never even considered?

Ah, that reminds me. On *America's Most Wanted* tonight, my so-called latest victim isn't even mine. In early September, a teacher in Texas who had been fired by one school and basically run out of town amid reports that he molested several students, was killed Crucifier-style as he prepared for the first day of school at his newest job. An aide who apparently walked in on the shooting was killed, too. So, now an innocent person has actually been killed because of me. I may not have literally pulled the trigger on this one, but the blood is on my hands all the same.

Needless to say, I'm a regular "hero" in America tonight. Between that aide's death and Tammy's feelings of being used by me, the program presented a pretty good case against vigilantes in general and sounded a war cry for bringing this particular vigilante to justice. It was a pretty grim commentary on me.

I don't think it will help anyone catch me, but that's more out of sheer luck than anything else. It sounded like the FBI suspects that The Crucifier is the woman who rented the houseboat, since the name and address I used didn't pan out. Not to mention that the houseboat was wiped clean of fingerprints and such. So, tonight all of America is looking for a tall, heavyset, deaf woman with longish blonde hair, whose composite drawing face is unfamiliar even to me. Now that I've changed my hair and started wearing these glasses, I don't even remotely resemble the face broadcast into homes across America this evening. I've even dropped some weight in the past couple of months, now that I'm not subsisting on McDonald's and Little Debbies anymore. They didn't mention my birthmark at all. For the first time since that night on the boat, I feel like I made a successful getaway.

Now that I feel invisible again (or is it invincible?) I'm tempted to venture out on a little trip to take care of that woman I chickened out of shooting earlier. Wanting to play vigilante again is a little embarrassing to admit, considering all the soul searching I've been doing about the impact of my work on so many innocents. On my person. The problem is, it always feels like such a fluke when someone gets caught in the crossfire that I expect each time to be the last. So, while I regret the pain I've caused, that's no real deterrent to killing. And even though I'm no longer searching databases for new targets, I can't seem to get this old one out of my mind. Whether I shoot her or not, I need to go find her, if only to look this "man-killer" thing in the eye.

Besides, it goes back to my greater wrong premise. It's wrong for me to keep killing, knowing full well that some innocents could be hurt in the process, but it seems a greater wrong to let the people keep hurting the children. It's a nice rationalization anyway, since it lets me do what I want.

Things are going pretty smoothly here, so it would probably be a good time to disappear for a week or two. I can always use the anniversary of his death as an excuse for needing to get away from the house. So, if I'm going to kill her, I might as well get it over with.

# Chapter Forty-Six

Sunday,
Nov. 22, 1992

This woman is hard to kill. Mary stays holed up in the house with her daughters most evenings. So far, the only place they've gone at night is church, both Wednesday and tonight. I don't know if this church is taking Mary and her daughters under their wing in the wake of the trial's publicity, or if the church is putting on its blinders and pretending nothing is wrong. In either case, a church bus has stopped by to pick them up both evenings. She doesn't have a car.

I know. Without a car, no wonder she hasn't gone anywhere else at night. But have I switched to a day schedule to better my odds at getting a shot at her? No. *I've already been seen once, so I can't risk having that happen again,* I say to myself. But when I hear those words in my head, I feel like I'm in grade school fibbing to the teacher that Caleb ate my homework. Deep down I know the only reason I haven't tried a daytime stakeout is because I'm hoping the day will come when I'll shrug my shoulders and say to myself, *Oh, well. I tried to kill her, but I can't stay here forever. I have other work to do.* Then I'll pack up and go home, satisfied that I've conquered my prejudice and demonstrated my willingness to kill female threats.

I won't hold it against me that I never actually leveled a loaded pistol at her. I would have shot her if I could. So, I'll have proven to myself that those who would dismiss me as a mere man hater are narrow-minded idiots, projecting their own hate of women onto me in a twisted sort of way.

The truth is, I don't really want to have to test my willingness to squeeze the trigger with Mary. The truth is, I'm afraid I'll find I can't do it, so I'm glad I've had no opportunity to try.

I'm sitting in the church parking lot now, going through all the motions of making a serious attempt. I'm in uniform; the Browning in my shoulder holster has a full clip; the china doll is lying on the seat beside me. So, if she comes out of that church alone and is the first to board the bus, I'm all set to make a quickie hit and getaway.

Only, I know full well that she's not going to walk out of that church alone and head straight for the bus. She's going to come out with other people and she's going to stand around and visit until it's time for the bus to depart. I'm not about to kill her tonight under those conditions and it's absurd that I've gone to such lengths to play make believe with myself, as if I fully expect to get my chance to shoot her tonight. I don't want a chance tonight. Maybe not ever.

The only thing I've proven to myself so far on this trip is that I really do prefer to kill men. Listen to me. I make it sound like picking chocolate ice cream over vanilla. I think I'm just more clear about his dark side than my own. I have no problem believing that any seemingly upstanding man is capable of horrific deeds. After all, I know what Mr. Inspiration himself was capable of doing to me after a full day of charming others and promoting human welfare.

But me? I shoot more than a dozen people in the midst of turning philanthropist and social activist, yet I fail to grasp just how similar that makes the two of us. He was evil! I'm just rebelling against society's ridiculous mores. Men like him must die! America would be a better place with a few more women like me. Men have no right to treat kids that way! I'd hardly call what I do murder, considering the slime quality of my targets.

Yes, I'd say I have a few teeny-tiny blind spots when it comes to looking at myself. I seem to see just as dimly when I look at Mary. All I see is a person struggling to take care of her daughters all by herself, without even a social life beyond a couple of trips a week to church. She has no car in a town with no public transportation, so no doubt she doesn't have a job. That puts her on the bottom rung of the economic ladder, just one precarious step from homelessness. No one has visited her all week, the publicity of such an ugly trial no doubt leaving her ostracized from any friends she might have had before. Mary has been through hell, and it's far from being over.

If she were a man, though, I know I'd be outraged that she'd regained custody of her daughter. I'd consider her isolation an opportunity to do whatever the heck she wanted to do with her children, her church attendance a what-a-swell-gal smoke screen. No matter what it took, I'd have blown her brains out days ago. If she were a man.

So, do I take pity on her gender or do I take pity on her daughters and any other children she might encounter? I guess that's the choice it's going to come down to. It's not a choice I'll make tonight, though, so I might as well give myself the night off and go back to the hotel.

The church has a sign out front advertising a mother's day out program on Tuesdays. I'll hang around her place that day and see if she gets a break from her kids.

# Chapter Forty-Seven

Tuesday,
Nov. 24, 1992

I struggle with some bizarre moral dilemmas. I mean, who else would consider it a severe breach of ethics, a character flaw even, to decide against murdering someone? Good grief. I am such a mess.

I'm exhausted, too. This whole day I've felt like I've had a team of horses hitched to each arm, pulling me in opposite directions, ripping me in half. It's taken all my strength just to survive the day in one piece. If I've even done that.

I reluctantly drove to her neighborhood as planned this morning, decked out in a new dress, narrow flats that were killing my feet, and dainty white gloves, hoping I'd never have cause to get out of the car and show off my outfit. But around eight o'clock, a car drove up, giving a couple of quick toots on the horn. The daughters scurried out and got into the car.

If only Mary had come out and helped put the seat belt around her daughters or even waved good-bye. That would have made it so much easier to justify going back home. I could have told myself, *See, she's not like him; she's not like any of the others. She cares about her daughters. She was just a victim of circumstance.* Never mind that he was prone to buckling me in after the wreck and giving me good-bye waves for show. I still would have reined Jurisprudence around and headed for home without so much as dismounting.

As it was, I drove Jurisprudence around to the alley, grabbed the Gideon Bible I'd borrowed from the hotel and walked up to the back door of her duplex. The Browning and the china doll were safely tucked in a shoulder bag. Smiling ever so sweetly, I knocked on the door and flashed the Bible like some kind of press pass when she opened the chained door a crack to peep out.

"Oh, are you from the church?" she asked, undoing the chain before I even had a chance to nod in reply. Her voice practically dripped of Southern hospitality. "Well, come on in. 'Scuse the mess. I don't usually have folk come 'round to the kitchen door. Go on into the livin' room and make yourself at home; it's just down the hall there. Want some coffee? Just made a fresh pot."

I shook my head no and wandered on into the living room, wishing she'd just snarled something like "Whatcha want?" or "I already go to church," leaving me with no other option but to force my way in before she got the door closed again and shoot her before she had a chance to scream. Alas.

I noticed the cutest little magnet on her refrigerator as I walked by. It was Tweety Bird holding a big-game rifle and posing as if for a photo beside its trophy: Sylvester the Cat. A woman after Kitty's own heart. How much harder was this going to get?

While Mary was in the kitchen pouring a cup of coffee for herself, I sat on the couch, positioned the pistol on my lap and put the Bible on top. I pulled the china doll out, too, putting it beside me with a throw pillow on top. So, I was all set by the time she came in, switched off *Sesame Street* and sat down at the other end of the couch.

"Oh my, that Polly is forever leavin' toys all over the place," she said, noticing the china doll's leg protruding from under the pillow. "Let me get that out of your way. You know, I don't remember seein' you at church before. Are you from First Baptist?"

She reached over and grasped the doll's shoe as she spoke, pulling it toward her with an apologetic smile. That smile quickly turned into a look of horror when she glanced down at the broken face. Taking a sharp breath, she let go of the doll and scooted back against the far corner of the sofa. Her mouth open in a silent scream. I pulled out the pistol.

"He-he's not here. He's in jail," she finally whispered, eyes glued to the gun. "You're the one that killed them men, aren't you?"

I resisted the urge to nod, since that might be about to change. It was too soon to tell.

"Sweet Jesus. I forgot she's deaf," she said, reaching over and grabbing a blue crayon and a Big Chief pad off the coffee table. Too unnerved to look for a clean sheet, she wrote on a page of jagged red and black scribbles. "He's in jail."

I nodded my acknowledgment, but didn't lower the gun. I wanted to. Each time I looked at her eyes—so frightened, vulnerable—I wanted to lower the gun. But then I'd glance at those angry crayon strokes, and I couldn't quite do it.

"Dear God, help me," she whispered as she flipped to the next page in the sketch book. "You want me?" she wrote, this time on a picture of a woman stick figure with her hand on the crotch of a girl stick figure, while a man stick figure looked on.

I gave a light nod.

She raised a trembling hand to her mouth. "Help! Help me!" she yelled from behind her hand, no doubt hoping I wouldn't notice if she kept her mouth covered. She still thought I was deaf, after all. I adjusted my aim to her hand, just to remind her why I was called The Crucifier. She seemed to get the message, quickly dropping the hand back onto her lap.

"I didn't want to do those things. They just happened," she wrote on a picture of a bedroom full of monsters, tornadoes, and lightning bolts.

I believed her. I believed she believed herself, anyway. I believed she felt helpless, trapped. I believed she felt as much the victim as her daughters. Believing her saddened me. So much so that tears welled up in my eyes and one by one trickled down my cheeks.

"Oh, thank you. Thank you," she said, breaking down in tears herself. But she misunderstood my tears. I wept because I knew I had to be true to my own skewed sense of ethics. I couldn't leave her daughters in the care of someone like this who so easily dismissed her responsibility as things that "just happened." Her daughters needed more than "I'll try to do better next time."

I lowered the gun for a moment. I'm not sure why, unless it was just that Mary had become more than a paper target to me by then. I guess it's harder to shoot someone who feels like a real person. When I lowered the gun to my lap, I could visibly see her body relax. She closed her eyes and let out a sigh of relief.

Before she could open her eyes, before her sense of peace could return to terror, I fired a bullet through her forehead. Only then did I shoot the hand that held the crayon.

Not wanting her children to come home to this, I dialed 911 and tried Heidi's trick of tapping SOS until a voice on the other end promised, "Someone's on the way."

I patted Mary on the shoulder before I left, Bible tucked under my arm. As an afterthought, I swiped the Tweety Bird refrigerator magnet for Kitty.

I was embarrassed afterwards. No, not because of the magnet. Because I had feelings for this target. How could I feel any tenderness toward someone who'd put her child through such hell? I've always been sickened by that love-the-person-hate-the-deed crap, yet here I was, sad that killing this woman was the resolution of my struggle.

*At least you didn't compromise your integrity*, I tell myself in reassurance that pulling the trigger was the "right thing to do." Why is it that I feel like an oatmeal commercial every time I say that to myself? I think I need a little more than a sales pitch here. Oh, well.

I'm not sure how many more times I can do this. Killing her has left me feeling that same kind of inside-out rawness that I felt at his funeral last year. It's like I've come full circle since then, having traveled absolutely nowhere.

Maybe if I felt this bad after every target, I could have made it back to start with a smaller loop. As it is, it's taken fourteen hits to knock me on my butt—literally. I'm sitting here on the bathroom floor while I write because killing this woman has left me so nauseous I fear I may puke up my toe-nails at any moment. No way would I have spent fourteen nights like this. I develop my aversions much more rapidly than that, thank you.

# Chapter Forty-Eight

Thursday,
Nov. 26, 1992

When I got back home yesterday, I found a message from Sally on the answering machine inviting me to pop over for a little Thanksgiving get together she and Libby were having today. Since I was still feeling a tad shaken from my latest hit, I thought it might help to be around people. If nothing else, it would help to be surrounded by Libby's handiwork for a couple of hours. I stayed ten.

Sally had invited me because she knows my whole family is dead. But the other four women and two men there were from a support group Sally belongs to for adults molested as children. A group he had given seed money to help start several years ago, I was "thrilled" to learn. Talking about their abuse had cost them their families in one way or another, but as I watched them all today, I knew they'd found a new family—a nurturing family—among each other. I envy them that. What a difference it must make for the secret not to be a secret anymore.

Before today, I thought that robbing me of the satisfaction of telling was the highest cost of his posthumous death threat. But I realized today he cost me my chance to belong somewhere, to find community with others who had survived the same. I mean, I spent all day with people just like me but I couldn't let them know I've been there too. I couldn't say "I'm one of you."

Thank goodness Kitty was over at her dad's today. It's dangerous enough that Kitty lives in town knowing about Daddy-o. I couldn't tell these people too, especially not after Sally introduced me to them as his daughter who was carrying on the family's philanthropic heritage.

"I always thought a lot of your father, from reading about him in the paper," one of the women said to me. "He gave me hope for the male species."

*You might as well give up then,* I wanted to reply, but I just smiled sweetly and nodded. The things I do to stay alive. I wonder if I'll ever decide it's not worth it?

I didn't decide that today. Today I enjoyed even secretly being a part of that group of young victims who somehow managed to become grown-up survivors.

I got the sense that they're doing more than just surviving, though. They seem to work hard at overcoming their childhoods, refusing to let their ghosts rule. In that sense, I knew I didn't belong at all today. My whole life is driven by what he did to me. He's rotting in the ground, but still I let him call the shots. I haven't overcome anything. At the rate I'm going, I never will.

Those people today are just as angry as me. I know, I know. Duh, of course they're as angry as I am. But that honestly never clicked with me before today. It was pompous of me, but I think I thought Kitty became a lawyer and Sally a social worker because their rage was more manageable than mine. I thought that if they shared my fury, they'd kill, too. Period. I never allowed for little things like integrity and strength of character.

The people I was with today fantasize about the kinds of things I do. It seemed devilish fun for them, a healthy release, when they swapped favorite imaginings for their perpetrators' demise. They described doing everything from slicing up the offending organ, frying it and making its original owner eat it—without even a dash of salt for flavor—to tattooing an illustrated account of the perp's acts all over his face. Told with such flair, such enthusiasm, it was hilarious to watch, to listen. I've always heard the best comedy comes from pain. There was so much pain in Sally's apartment today that people were rolling on the floor, laughing themselves to tears.

After that, I knew I had nothing on their anger. It's funny how my anger is fueled by the monstrosity of child sexual abuse, yet I have felt alone with my rage. Like I was the only one mad enough to finally do something about it. Instead, I'm just one of the ones who doesn't know how to enjoy the empowerment of a good balls-busting fantasy, who doesn't know it can stop at make-believe, so real life can start.

I felt I was among people today who do live real lives. Having passed through a kind of death, they seem clear about how best to be alive. They have an aura of deliberateness, strength, courage, that thumbs their noses at those who once tried to destroy them. I have no doubt that their lives are better than the lives of those who hurt them.

That seems the sweetest victory of all to me, since it was always such a sore point for me to think of him with all of his wealth, all of his success, all of his respect, while I had nothing but my anger and agony. I would have loved to live more at peace than him. But I never did. Never will.

Being with these people today gave me a glimpse of what might have been, what kind of life I could have built from the rubble he left me. But I'm not Scrooge being whisked through time by ghosts who would give me one last chance. Somewhere back there I flubbed my chance and I can't go back now and undo it.

I felt connected to Sally's friends-turned-family because I'd been a victim, too. But I've gone a step further than they have. I've crossed that line from victim to perpetrator. What a betrayal. I had no right to turn an innocent girl into a guilty woman. I had a responsibility as an adult to finally get some help for that wounded little kid inside. Instead, I just let her suffer, let her die, while I went around exploiting her pain for my own self-righteous, murderous indulgence.

I did myself a disservice. I know that now. But it's a little late for knowing. I needed to know that before I shot my first target, not after shooting number fourteen. Even if I turned myself in or simply vowed to never kill again, it wouldn't reverse the damage done to myself. And frankly, that's the only damage with which I'm concerned. I could care less about the other lives I've taken. They deserved more gruesome death sentences than I carried out. They deserved the stuff of today's torture fantasies. I just regret that I took my own chance for life in the process. I think little Annie deserved more than that. Her hero was Annie Oakley, after all, not Jesse James. I seem to have gotten mixed up on that somewhere along the way.

So, where am I going with all this? Out of the killing business? Again? I wonder how many times it takes. Maybe this really is quits. But then again, at the back of my mind I keep mulling over the story one of the women told about being molested by a brother ten years her senior. He has children of his own now, plus nieces and nephews, and he and his wife run a day care. His sister filed charges against him as an adult in hopes that he'd be forced into counseling but instead he was completely exonerated a few months ago and has since filed a counter lawsuit against his sister and her therapist that is still pending. The defense used something I've never heard of, false memory syndrome, to say she made everything up. What an insult.

She said she wishes he'd drop dead now that all of her other efforts have failed. Her fantasy for his demise made that quite clear. She even joked about wishing she knew The Crucifier, so she could suggest him as a target.

I wrote her a note suggesting that she contact the WJF Fund for help with her legal expenses or to discuss the case with Kitty if she was in need of a lawyer. But I have every intention of ensuring that she'll have no need of either form of help. I know the name of his day care and I know it's in a town only a couple of hours from here. It will be no problem at all to pop over there and put a stop to him.

I guess that's the advantage of having already lost hope for salvaging my own life. It's like already being sentenced to life imprisonment or being given the death penalty. There's nothing else to lose when all is already lost. So, why not kill one more? Or twenty more, for that matter? I can't do much more damage to my future than I've already done.

That woman, on the other hand, has everything to lose by carrying out her death wish. Besides, I suspect she's come too far in her own recovery to choose a path like mine. She's gone beyond merely growing up, so society won't ever have to look over its shoulder keeping an eye out for her. She's not the raging, wounded child disguised in a grown-up body like I am. She's put some salve on those wounds and is tending to them with the gentleness they deserve.

That's taken a lot of effort on her part. I know, because becoming me took no effort at all. I'm the natural by-product of the brutality I've known. It doesn't surprise me at all that I kill. The only thing that surprises me is that more women don't.

Have I mentioned how lucky this country is that so many women have decided to overcome their abuse, their oppression, instead of lashing out in response to it like I have? Of course, lots of other women like Mom and Mrs. Jenkins have kept the whole unsightly mess tidily swept under family rugs where the rest of the country doesn't have to see. I guess America considers that part lucky, too.

Well, its luck ran out with me. And as I look at the growing number of women prisoners in this country, the rising incidence of juvenile delinquency among young girls, I know I'm not the only one out there putting cracks in that lucky streak. I don't know whether to regret that so many females are compromising our own lives, or to celebrate that we're finally sending out a long-deserved wake-up call to this country. Probably I regret more than I celebrate, since our own lives are a high price to pay, considering there's so little evidence that America is even listening.

Whether this country listens to me or not, I'm going to put a stop to that man. Someone's got to.

# Chapter Forty-Nine

Friday,
Nov. 27, 1992

I woke up this morning to the sound of the security system going off. Talk about unnerving. I didn't even know what I was hearing at first. Was this what it sounded like when the FBI came to cart someone away? Was the house on fire?

Then it hit me. One of the women's husbands must be on the grounds. I jumped out of bed, threw on some clothes and got the Browning out of the trunk. After making sure I had a full clip, I went out to the roof and scanned the grounds. No one was charging the main house with an assault rifle. That was a good sign.

Unless he was already inside.

I made my way to Mom's studio as fast as I could without getting dizzy. I had such a sinking feeling that I was too late. It didn't help that the alarm had fallen silent. When I heard screams of terror once I reached the main house, I almost couldn't go on. I was too late. I was sure of it. My knees kept giving out on me; my hands were shaking too much to even flip off the gun's safety.

I took a few deep breaths to pull myself together and started working my way toward the screams. I'd seen enough bullet wounds of late to know what kind of scene might be awaiting me. All I could hope was that no one had been shot yet. That he was still down there just waving his gun like a madman. That he was on too much of an adrenaline rush to notice me quietly coming up behind him.

I could drop him with a single shot. I knew I

could. If only I could get my hands to stop shaking. If only I wasn't too late.

Before I could get there, I heard footsteps coming in my direction. Someone was making a run for it. I didn't know what else to do, so I just dropped to the floor, took aim and waited for them to turn the corner.

A clearly shaken Misty herded her two children into my line of fire. She looked more surprised that I had a gun than relieved that the cavalry had arrived. She didn't miss a step in hurrying toward her room, though. I was amazed at how fast she could move, considering she's eight months pregnant.

"Everything's okay," she called out as she went past. "Some guy has climbed a tree just inside the wall. The police are on their way."

No wonder she was in such a hurry. Misty's husband is a cop, so she couldn't afford to be seen. But what was this about a guy in a tree? He sure had the women scared, whoever he was.

I hid my gun on top of the first available shelf, and went to find out more. Bonnie, who had just moved into the shelter yesterday, was sitting on a couch in absolute hysterics. Several of the children were crying, too. Ruby was doing her best to comfort them all. Haley and Trudy stood huddled around the security monitors.

"Someone's husband?" I wrote.

"We don't know who the hell he is," Trudy said. "I don't think he even knows we can see him with the cameras. He got a real smart-ass look on his face when we turned off the alarm. Like he thinks he got away with something."

I motioned for them to let me have a look.

"I know him," I wrote in a rush, slamming down the pad in my anger. I turned to go straight to that tree but realized I might have a thing or two to say to Roberto. So I needed my voice.

"Call off the police," I wrote after retrieving the pad. "This guy's stupid but harmless. No need to put Misty at risk."

If I hadn't put the gun on top of a shelf I might have walked right out to that tree and shot Roberto. I was that angry. I felt like I might explode by the time I was standing at the foot of the old magnolia tree just inside the fence. It had been his favorite spot when we played hide-and-seek as kids. I didn't even look up into the tree to find him. I just stood there, arms crossed, waiting for him to climb down.

"Aw, Annie, don't be mad," he said as he made his way down. "I didn't mean to trip the alarm. I was just trying to make a surprise entrance. Thought you'd be impressed when I came knocking on your door in broad daylight."

What I would have given for a voice just then.

"Impressed that you know how to scare people to death?" I wrote, thrusting the note into his hands angrily. I hadn't noticed until then that he was dressed to blend in with the bleak, pre-winter landscape. He'd improved at hide-and-seek over the years. He also had what looked like a small pair of binoculars and a miniature camera clipped to his belt. A leather-bound notepad was tucked in his shirt pocket. What was he up to?

His almost sheepish expression at being caught quickly twisted into a smirk as he read my note. "And who would you be afraid of coming over the wall? The FBI perhaps?"

"What do you want, Roberto?" I wrote, hoping my face wouldn't betray me just then.

"What do I want?" he asked, with a nasty little chuckle that didn't suit him. He pulled the notepad from his pocket, licked the tips of his fingers and started leafing through it. "What do I want? Let's see, I want to know if you happened to watch *America's Most Wanted* a couple of weeks ago. I want to know if you have an alibi for the evening of August 30th, oh heavyset blonde woman who knows just enough sign language to play deaf. While you're at it, tell me where you were March 24th and April 28th and May 6th and...."

He was getting more and more agitated as he listed the dates of the Crucifier hits, pacing back and forth in front of me, smacking the notepad with the back of his hand to punctuate each date. Suddenly stopping, he turned to me with tear-filled eyes.

"I want to know who witnessed you sitting on the beach the morning of July 16th!" His voice cracked. "I want to know if you told my mom what you'd been doing. I want to know if you had to kill her to keep her from going to the police."

Here he was, accusing me of killing Juanita, tears reluctantly streaming down his face. Here he was, correctly identifying me as The Crucifier. But the only thought going through my head was, *It's November. Why isn't he in school?* No kidding. Never mind that it was Thanksgiving weekend, so there was a perfectly good reason for him not to be in school. That's all I could think.

"Why aren't you in school, Roberto?" I wrote.

He looked at me like I was insane after reading that note. He stood there speechless for several seconds.

"School?" he finally sputtered. "What does this...who cares about...have you heard anything I've said? I'm a P.I. now. I'm investigating you!"

The sheepish look returned. Like he had said more than he meant to.

Like he had laid out his whole hand in front of me,

and he hoped I hadn't noticed he held nothing but suspicions. But there was more to the look than that.

"I...I could use some money." He was looking down at the ground, toeing a leather brown leaf with his boot.

Ah, so that's why he'd been hoping to impress me with his stealth. He hadn't planned to confront me at all. He'd planned a slick entrance, a suave announcement that he was now in the private investigating business and an exit with a fat check to help him get his venture off the ground. Oops. I don't think he planned to tell me just yet that I'd be financing my own demise. That was going to be part of the legend. Not only had he single-handedly brought The Crucifier to justice. He'd gotten me to pay him to do it.

"My checkbook's inside," I wrote. I'm not sure which of us was more surprised by that. I guess I would have done about anything to get rid of him just then. Besides, if I'm going to get caught, why not by him? I'd rather that someone I care about benefit from such notoriety. I owe Juanita a secure future for her son.

I took him up the fire escape to my attic, so as to avoid upsetting the others any further. Imagine my chagrin when I stepped inside to find that I'd left the lid up on my Crucifier trunk after getting the gun. Smashed doll faces and the barrel of the SIG peeked out from under my Stetson. I casually scooped up pajamas and a few other stray clothes, tossing them into the trunk before closing it with an apologetic shrug for the mess. I motioned for him to have a seat. I could tell he was scanning the attic, making a mental note of anything that looked like a clue. His eyes never rested on the trunk, though, so I don't think he saw anything important. Still, I felt better once I'd escorted him out and on his merry way. I just hope he takes his little P.I. game to some of my crime scenes instead of hanging around here. I sure gave him enough money to go far, far away.

I did show him the bronze plaque on the front of the house before he left. It dedicates the shelter to Juanita's memory. "Helping the people be free." Roberto wasn't in the mood for that, though.

He read the plaque, folded the check I'd given him, slipped it into his front pocket and strode off down the driveway without a word.

One of the women had called Sally about the intruder and she drove past him as he was walking down the driveway. I knew he'd stalked off for my benefit, so I got ticked at him when he wasn't able to keep up the act when Sally drove by. He couldn't resist eyeballing her van with slack jaw amazement. I've yet to meet the person who can.

Sally drives this old, sad looking white mini-van. But you'd have to look really close to know what color it's painted. She has that thing *covered* with bumper stickers. I've yet to read them all. They say things like, "Bush Is Pro-Life Until Birth," "Behind Every Successful Woman Is Herself," "Better Gay Than Grumpy," "I'm for Hillary's Husband," "Hate Is Not a Family Value." That sort of thing. The van embarrasses poor Libby to death, but Sally loves that van and wouldn't part with it for the world.

I get a kick out of it myself. I was needing something to lift my spirits after that insane start to my day, so I was glad to see her arrive. Today I noticed a sticker that reads, "It Shouldn't Hurt to Be a Child." I thought it a nice sentiment.

Unfortunately, the good mood didn't last long. Sally was concerned about Roberto getting onto the grounds.

"I heard he stole your dad's van once," she said. "Are you sure it was wise to call off the police?"

Poor Roberto. No wonder he's grown up to be such an ass.

# Chapter Fifty

I meant to put a little time between that Thanksgiving discussion of Sissy's brother and the actual hit. Not to mention Roberto's little surprise visit. I thought it would be a little suspicious if Sissy's brother died too soon after her Crucifier wish. I was thinking maybe after Christmas or the New Year even. But today Kitty came bursting into the conference room where I sat studying one of Mom's paintings.

"We did it! We did it! You're going to be a mommie. God, I'm good. You've got yourself one helluva lawyer, Annie."

I was so stunned I could barely move. I finally managed to motion for her to tell me more.

"Okay, okay. The adoption is basically final. The foster family she's with will keep her until she finishes out this semester of school, so she'll be here by Christmas. Isn't this great, Annie? So, how does it feel to be a mom?"

I just gave Kitty a wide-eyed, white-faced shrug.

"It'll be great, Annie. But you better get hopping. There's not that much time to get ready for her."

That's for sure. I haven't even started fixing up Mom's studio yet and I sure haven't done any Christmas shopping. Then there's this target to put a stop to. How am I going to do that once I have a little girl to take care of? And what's this "mommie" thing? Somehow that concept never occurred to me before Kitty voiced it. I think I've thought of being more of a big sister to Heidi than someone ultimately responsible for her care and well-being.

As the reality of my impending "motherhood" sunk in, minus the usual nine months' advance warning, it finally clicked why women didn't spill into the streets after the Anita Hill fiasco. They had to go pick up their kids at day care and from school; they had to see that their children were fed and bathed and tucked into bed; they had to help with homework and scraped knees and broken hearts. They couldn't spontaneously ride off to war with the men in suits, not without abandoning their children to the care of other men in suits who might or might not assume responsibility for the children's care.

Things are going to change in a big way once Heidi is here. I may be done with my work whether I'm ready or not. At least for a few years until having a "mother" is more of a bother than a benefit. Or maybe I can still put a stop to targets occasionally. I don't know. I haven't really had enough time to work through it all.

The one thing I'm clear about is that I want to rework my will now. I want to give Kitty power of attorney, too, and take other steps to safeguard the shelter's financing in the event of my demise. Or arrest.

Actually, I've been thinking about this a lot in the past couple of weeks since Roberto's visit. I keep telling myself that there's no real evidence out there for him to dig up. And I'm confident he won't tip the police, since he'll want to take credit for bringing me in. I might as well prepare for the worst, all the same. No need to be stupid about it.

Now that Heidi's about to enter the picture, I've got an excuse to approach Kitty about making the changes I want. Not to mention a responsibility.

But first I want to get rid of Sissy's brother. While I still can. No one like him should be allowed to work so closely with little kids. It's absurd. So I'm leaving tomorrow and hoping for a quick hit, so I can come back and concentrate on Heidi's arrival.

Sheesh. Is this as crazy as it sounds?

# Chapter Fifty-One

Monday,
Dec. 14, 1992

Killing him was no problem at all. He carried the trash out to the curb tonight without bothering with a porch light and he was dead before he realized he hadn't just impaled his hand on something in the trash. Since it's only a two-hour drive home, I decided to go ahead and drive back tonight. Only, I stopped for a late supper first.

Thirty minutes tops. That's all I took. But when I got back to the parking lot, Jurisprudence was gone. I'm not making this up. The Browning under the seat. A glove compartment full of cash, and my name and address on the car registration. A road atlas with *all* my travel routes marked. The lock box with his gadgetry and the rifle in the trunk. If I hadn't taken my shoulder bag in, I would have lost this journal, too. I'm just glad I didn't mess with my cowboy attire this trip.

Now, I don't know what to do. I'm sitting here in a bathroom stall so I don't draw attention to myself in this panic. My mind is racing, considering all options, all consequences. I mean, do I report my car stolen and have on police record that I was in town tonight? Or do I just go to a hotel and have on credit record that I was in town tonight? What if I don't report my car stolen and it's used in some liquor store heist? What if it's found abandoned after a joyride with all my evidence intact? How will I get back home? Does anyone rent cars this late at night?

I'm in trouble. No matter what I decide, no matter what I do, I'm in trouble. Short of hitching a ride with a truck driver, there are no clean escape routes for me tonight. If I had the Browning in my bag, maybe I'd try the truck driver route. But I don't. So, I won't. I'd rather risk prison than rape.

Well, at least that much is decided.

# Chapter Fifty-Two

Tuesday,
Dec. 15, 1992

Someday I'm going back to that truck stop and leaving a waitress named Bunny one heck of a tip. I'll mail it to her from prison if I have to. She saved my hide last night.

After resigning myself to disaster, I wrote her a note telling her my ride had apparently stood me up and asking if she knew any place that would rent a car this late at night.

"Honey, I can do you one better than that," she said, chewing the heck out of a piece of bubble gum. "My baby sister drives a cab. She'll take you anyplace you wanna go."

Well, where I wanted to go was the ATM across the street from a movie complex back home. I withdrew enough money to handsomely pay Bunny's sister, a woman as tough as I had imagined Libby would be. Then I bought a ticket for the late night showing of *Malcolm X*. Never mind that Malcolm was already making his pilgrimage to Egypt by the time I found a seat. I'd seen the movie just last week, so I didn't care. I just needed some place to say I'd been for a few hours.

After the credits rolled, I roamed through the parking lot for a while and went back inside the theater to get someone to call the police. Yegads! My car had been stolen!

Now that the saving-my-ass part is over, I really do miss Jurisprudence. Kitty is throwing a small wake of sorts at her place tonight to mark the car's passing. The invitation says we're going to quaff rootbeer and sing "Danny Boy" as we cry in our pizza and watch cartoons. Sally and Libby are coming, too. Should be fun.

Of course, the whole reason Kitty is doing this is to gloat in the fact that she, who is forever leaving her keys in the ignition, has never had her jeep stolen. The twerp. Me? I'm forever locking things up. Especially Jurisprudence. A lot of good it did me.

It's hard to imagine target hunting without my trusty steed, my partner in crime. It's hard to imagine being stranded in this house again, too. Oh, I know I can get a lift from Sally or Kitty, but it's just not the same.

As much as I miss Jurisprudence right now, I have to admit I hope I never see that car again. I hope it's in another state by now, sporting a fresh coat of hot pink paint and a new zebra-striped interior so the cops will never know it's mine. I sure gave the thieves as much of a head start from the law as I could.

I guess I'll go rent a car later today so I can wait a respectable time before buying a replacement. Have I mentioned grief sucks?

# Chapter Fifty-Three

Thursday,
Dec. 24, 1992

Heidi will arrive at the airport in just a few hours. I don't know if I'm ready for this or not. Oh, Mom's studio has been transformed into a nifty loft bedroom that any kid would die for. Except for Mom's big roll-top desk the room is still unfurnished, but that's just because Heidi is scheduled for the biggest Christmas of her life—a few days after the fact—when we go shopping for her room.

I've got a Christmas tree set up in the loft that's decorated with miniature wrapped boxes. Each one has a gift tag specifying something she can pick out for herself. There's a box for everything from the bed of her choice to the desk lamp of her choice.

I figure I'll just take her up to my attic today and then tomorrow morning we'll take a stroll across the roof walkway—barring any ice storms—for a little Christmas extravaganza. I went ahead and got her a few things so she'd have some actual gifts under the tree. But it was really hard to know what to buy. That's when I started getting seriously anxious about her arrival. This is a kid I do not know. I don't know what kind of music she likes, if any; I don't know if she likes to read or watch movies or play Nintendo; I don't know her favorite colors or if she'd be more thrilled with a new dress or a new baseball cap.

I've only seen her three times. We've only exchanged four sets of letters. Now suddenly she's moving into my life to stay and I don't even know what to buy her for Christmas. Sheesh. Have I mentioned that I'm not sure I'm ready for this?

I was embarrassed when I realized the first gift I'd bought her was a bound sketchbook like this so she could have a journal. After all those Christmases when he gave me a diary, it felt like a creepy thing to do to her. But if he hadn't turned those diaries into a sleazy way to get inside my head, it could have been the nicest gift he ever gave me. I didn't stop having things to say just because I lost my voice. I suspect the same is true of Heidi. I guess I'll go ahead and give the journal to her, even though he makes it feel so slimy.

I got her a telescope that she can set up under Mom's northern skylight windows. I hope she's not too young for that sort of thing. I got her a teddy bear, too. I hope she's not too old for that. Did I get her anything that I feel completely at ease about? Not! Oh, well. Them's the breaks.

The truth is I've secretly enjoyed all my fretting about Heidi's impending arrival. It's kept me from obsessing about Jurisprudence too much. I always did prefer stuffing things and letting emotions build up until there's an ugly explosion that transforms me into a serial killer or something. There's got to be a better way to deal with things, but I don't seem terribly anxious to find out what those better ways are.

Speaking of Jurisprudence, I have a new steed: Gypsy. I was reading in the Annie Oakley biography I got for my birthday that Gypsy was the name of one of her favorite horses. It seemed like a nice name. I toyed with naming the car Silver since it's white like the Lone Ranger's stallion. But it doesn't rear up on hind wheels or anything. It's not even as sleek looking as the Lone Ranger's horse, since it's a Volvo. I know, I know. I couldn't believe I got one, either. But what was left for me out there in the world of cars? A Ford Pinto? Please. So, I went for maximum safety, instead. I'll be driving Heidi around, after all. I don't want her dying in a car wreck or anything.

Good grief. Am I going to be one of those over-protective, mother hen types? I get no protection when growing up, so I react by protecting Heidi to death? What was that child thinking when she asked to live with me? What was I thinking when I commissioned Kitty to find a way to give Heidi her wish?

I may be doing Heidi a real injustice, dragging her so far from everything familiar, secure. To give her what? Me? What does a serial killer on the lam have to offer a child who's already known far too much tragedy? What will it do to her if I get caught?

Then there's always the hit man possibility. The stakes on that one jumped a little higher a few days ago. Sally, Kitty and I were discussing families one afternoon after a board meeting and Sally's Thanksgiving with fellow survivors came up. When Kitty heard I had been there she assumed I had told Sally about him. Kitty said something about being glad I wasn't keeping all that to myself anymore now that he's dead.

"Why didn't you ever tell me about your dad, Annie?" Sally asked.

Visions of brakes failing on Gypsy and me plunging off a cliff to my death flashed through my mind. I hope the air bags work.

"I know that kind of stuff's hard to talk about," Sally went on, "but after me telling you about Dad and all that stuff you heard at Thanksgiving. It just doesn't make sense, Annie. 'Me too.' That wouldn't have taken so much effort to write. It helps to tell people, Annie. It really does. Besides, he's been dead more than a year. Don't you think it's time you stopped protecting him. He can't hurt you anymore."

I thought of the money I found in the garage and hoped she was right. I hoped he'd never gotten around to arranging my death. But I sure wasn't about to start blabbing about him to test that out. Juanita was enough of a test for me.

"I told Kitty about him years ago in college," I wrote. "Some things I can't tell you about have changed since then. Please don't ever breathe a word of this to anyone. *Please.*"

She read what I wrote and passed the piece of paper to Kitty.

"I'm sorry, Annie. I just assumed she knew," Kitty said.

Sally sat there for a moment studying me, forehead furrowed, eyes narrowed, clearly puzzled.

"You sold out to him, didn't you," she finally asked. No, stated.

"No! It's not true! I don't give a shit about the money, Sally. He'll have me killed if I say anything." That's what I wrote. I can't believe I actually wrote that down. But I wadded it up before I showed it to her. I sighed and nodded that she was right. I'd sold out.

"Okay," she finally said. "I don't.... I don't understand that. But okay."

Now it was Kitty's turn to look puzzled. She knew me too well to believe I'd sold out to him. Not for money. She reached for the wadded paper in my hand, but I slipped it into my pocket.

"It doesn't matter," I mouthed to her.

"I've got to be going," Sally said, getting up. "Libby will be home from work soon and it's my week to cook."

I knew there was more to her leaving than that. She was disappointed in me, disgusted even. By refusing to keep silent, she had sacrificed all the wealth I still have, after all. I hoped that disgust

271 OUR LITTLE SECRET  271

would pass. I didn't want to lose her friendship. Again. Not after just getting it back after all these years. But I didn't want to die, either.

"Oh, do you remember Sissy from Thanksgiving?" Sally asked at the door.

I gave her a vacant look, like I couldn't quite remember which one she was.

"The one being sued by her brother. The one you suggested the fund or Kitty could help."

Ah, yes. I knew the one now.

"Well, remember how she said she wished she could get The Crucifier to knock him off? It actually happened a week or two ago. The night your car was stolen, I think. I heard about the murder the day after we had that wake over at Kitty's."

"Wow!" I mouthed, motioning for her to tell me more.

"Yeah, well, anyway, it's strange because her brother's trial never even made the paper or anything, but somehow The Crucifier got wind of it. So, that's the end of him."

*Oh, shit!* I thought, giving a little shiver at my unwitting slip.

"Yeah, it is a little creepy," she said, responding to my shudder. Her voice was strangely quiet, as though part of her had already walked out the door. "They buried him last week. Sissy is taking it pretty hard."

Sally suspects? I have no idea. She's very close to suspecting in any event. And now she knows about Daddy Dearest, too.

To think this is the kind of "security" I'll offer Heidi. I really don't know what's going to happen. Apparently Sally hasn't taken any suspicions to the police or anything, since no one has come knocking on my door, flashing an FBI badge. With any luck she's slipped into that lifelong training as a female to mistrust her reality. So, maybe things aren't as shaky as they seem.

Heidi is coming regardless of what might happen to me, though, so it's all pretty irrelevant at this point. If I was going to protect Heidi from me, I needed to have done that long before now. It's a whole lot late for cold feet and hindsight. I guess we'll just have to make the best of the time we do have together. I hope I haven't really screwed things up for her. It's pitiful how I can't seem to consider consequences until it's too late to change anything, too late to choose something different.

I guess the concept of consequences is just beyond my realm of experience. I'm American, after all. Through and through.

# Chapter Fifty-Four

Friday,
Jan. 1, 1993

It's resolution time again. That feels strange this year. I mean here I am, twenty-six years old and for the first time in a decade I don't feel like resolving to kill anyone. I don't know that it's accurate to say my anger has burned itself out. It's more like the wind has shifted, fanning the flames in another direction.

In any event, I feel like I'm finished with the killing. Whether it's finished with me is a whole different matter. Sally's out there, and Roberto, Kitty and the people at the marina. They all have pieces that could come back to haunt me if they ever get put together. I could get arrested at any time. Or killed. That was the chance I took when I opted to be less isolated. A killer like me just shouldn't have friends, just shouldn't invest in people at all. That'll put you out of business fast.

I guess that's what I've basically done, isn't it? I've surrounded myself with people and now I'm packing the guns away. Oh, well. It's not such a great loss.

Don't get me wrong. I'm glad America has fifteen fewer sex offenders walking the streets than it had last year. I'm proud, even. But when I see that accomplishment as the drop in the bucket that it is, I doubt that I'll be sorely missed on the child abuse prevention scene. I haven't really changed anything. I may have raised some public awareness but public awareness doesn't do much. So I haven't exactly gotten a good return on the effort I invested, on the chances I took, on the cost to my own well-being. I feel a lot better about what I'm doing with the fund, with this house, with Heidi.

It felt like progress when I made contributions to the campaign funds of women and men who consider the welfare of the children a priority and they were elected to office in November. It feels the same way when I help women get the education or vocational training they need to be less financially dependent on an abusive partner, and when I can make sure that funds are available to the kids for therapy so they have a chance to grow up and be someone better than I have been. Options. That's what feels good. Giving them options.

I like that this house can be a safe haven for women and their children, a place where they can live and work for a while in relative safety and comfort while they train for something better. The men whose abuse they're trying to escape can't even drive down the road in front of the house gates without being videotaped by the security cameras. Kitty has a real knack for talking these women into exercising their legal rights, so once those men are stupid enough to come around here, Kitty takes advantage of anti-stalking laws to file additional charges against them.

Ten women and their kids are living here right now, doing everything from secretarial work for the fund to child care to cooking to lawn care to security system monitoring. Of course, while they're here they're well paid for their work and the hours they put into training. Then when they're ready to leave they get a lump sum severance pay equal to the wages they've already earned. Seven women have left so far and seem to be doing okay.

That makes seventeen women and their children who have lived here. More than the targets I've hit. Helping these families has been just as satisfying. Maybe even more.

There's such a hopeless, last-resort aspect to killing. It's like shoveling dog poop at the vet or smelling arm pits at a deodorant factory for a living. A real downer at times. But being around these women, seeing their spirit, their courage, their determination to make it—that's a whole different experience. A better experience. I enjoy helping them get the one lucky break they need to make better lives for themselves and their kids.

I hope I can be a lucky break for Heidi, too. This first week has been quite an adjustment. I think Heidi and I both still feel a tad awkward. Me treating her too much like a guest who requires constant entertainment, her trying to figure out where she fits in this house teeming with women and young children.

She finally asked me about it yesterday while we watched movers put together her new bunk beds.

"Did the people before me take everything with them when they went away?" she wrote.

"There wasn't anyone here before you. My mother used to paint in here with the stuff I gave you, but that was a long time ago," I replied. I'd given Mom's paint supplies and easel to Heidi after she gave me a painting she'd done in therapy. It's a picture of me hugging her at the graveyard. Neither of us has mouths. I've got it hanging next to Mom's graveyard painting in my attic.

"That lady left with those two kids yesterday," she wrote.

I wasn't sure what she was getting at, so I just nodded and handed her back the slate. She erased it and wrote again.

"What about me? When do I get took away?"

"You don't," I wrote, hoping I was being truthful. "This is your house, now. This is your room.

The others are just visiting."

She nodded a bit tentatively.

"We're a team. You always stay with me," I wrote, giving her a reassuring wink and a hug. I think I was trying to reassure myself as much as her. I really like this kid and care about her.

I don't want her getting hurt by my sordid past, yet I can't undo what I've done. I'll just have to keep my fingers crossed and hope it's enough that I'm putting my guns away.

# Chapter Fifty-Five

Monday,
Jan. 4, 1993

Roberto showed up again this morning. I wasn't home, since today was Heidi's first day of school here. I was giving her the grand tour when Roberto showed up at the front gate of the house. I'll have to remember to thank him for not scaling the wall this time and scaring those women half to death with his junior private investigator shenanigans.

He had something for me from Juanita's estate that she'd requested he hand deliver to no one but me. How do you like that? I still don't know what it is. He told Sherry, who was monitoring the security system at the time, that he'd call tomorrow to arrange a meeting time and place because he had "things to do today."

I know he grew up around here and has friends to see, but I'm still nervous that he's in town. I guess I have visions of him snooping around, trying to avenge his mother's death by uncovering dirt on me. I might not mind if there weren't so much dirt to be had. I've been wearing sunglasses and a toboggan ever since I heard he's around, just in case he's perched somewhere with a high-powered camera—that I bought for him—trying to get a decent photo of me. I can see the headlines now: "The Crucifier Nailed by Teenage Private Eye." Oh, wait. I think he turned twenty a couple of months ago. I guess I should have sent him a birthday card and tried to get chummy with him again to get him off my case.

It's funny, but I'm so preoccupied with Roberto being in town that it's completely overshadowed the reason he's come. I can't imagine what Juanita would have so wanted me to have that she'd insist Roberto bring it to me himself. It must have been in a safety deposit box or something for it not to have been released from her estate until now. Of course, this whole thing may just be an excuse he made for coming to town again. Yeah, that's probably it. Not that I'm a tad on the paranoid side or anything.

Heck, I'm so paranoid I had one of the women here call Kitty and invite her over for dinner and a game of Pictionary with Heidi and me this evening. It's not that I wanted some legal advice on protecting myself from Roberto's inquiries. It's just that I wanted Kitty to spend some more time with Heidi, so they could get to know one another, grow attached to each other, just in case something happens to me.

That's horrible, I know. But it pretty much reflects how scared I am that Roberto may be on to something, that I may have set Heidi up for some major chaos. I was so relieved Kitty accepted the invitation.

The two of them hit it right off. It turns out Heidi hates her sweet little baby name as much as Kitty hates hers. They teased each other mercilessly about their names tonight. Before the evening was over they'd dubbed each other Cat Woman and Swiss Miss. What a pair.

In the midst of the evening's playfulness, Kitty still sensed my anxiety. Only, she assumed it had to do with Heidi. After we put Heidi to bed, she suggested I might need some therapy to help with this adjustment.

"It's got to be hard on you to be around a mute kid in this house. I bet it stirs up all kinds of crap from your own childhood."

"Of course I need therapy," I wrote, feeling rather annoyed that she wouldn't let it go. "I've needed therapy my whole life."

"Look at me. I'm backing off," Kitty said, laughing good-naturedly, palms forward, as she backpedaled across the room. She paused beside Mom's and Heidi's paintings, studying them quietly. Turning to face me again, she added, "I just worry about you sometimes, Annie. There's only so much a person can carry around without snapping. I know it's a horrible thing to say to a friend, but I'm afraid of what you might do. I'm afraid of what might happen to Heidi."

If only she knew the big snap had already occurred. I lowered my eyes, afraid that they would betray me.

"Aw, Annie, I didn't mean to hurt your feelings. I just want you to take care of yourself, to be gentle with yourself. That's all."

She walked over and gave me a hug.

"Still friends?" she asked, trying to read my body language.

I made an "of course we are" face. She smiled and gave me another quick hug.

"I'm here for you, Annie. You know that, don't you? Good. Listen, why don't you ask the Swiss Miss if she'd like to go ice skating with me this weekend so you can have a break. Tell her I'm taking her home to the Alps. She'll love that. It can even be a sleep over if she can stand to be apart from that four-star bedroom of hers. Talk about a kid in hog heaven. Well, let me know, okay? And please walk me to the fire escape so I don't fall off this roof and break my neck."

I obliged Kitty her escort. But before returning to my attic, I went over and sat outside Heidi's glass door, watching her sleep, her arm around the teddy bear I'd given her for Christmas. The sketch pad we used to play Pictionary was still

perched on Mom's—no, Heidi's—easel. She'd
drawn the Tin Man and his oil can from *The Wiz-
ard of Oz*. Kitty had gotten the word "oil" right away
and Heidi was so pleased she spontaneously threw
her arms around Kitty's neck. Heidi didn't make a
sound, but her body language said she was squeal-
ing with delight inside.

It had been a nice finale to a fun evening. The
two of them got along better than I had hoped. I
think I started feeling a tad melodramatic after
watching them goof around for a while. I kept flashing to scenes from the movie *Beaches* after Hillary
realizes she's dying and wants her best friend C.C.
to take care of her little girl once she's gone. Hillary
kind of manipulated C.C. into becoming pals with
her daughter, too. But I think she had to work harder
at it with those two than I will with Kitty and Heidi.

How pitiful can I get? Heidi's been here a little
over a week and already I'm thinking in terms of
her tragic loss when I'm carted away. I mean, how
much of a loss could it be if Roberto pulled a slick
one and got enough evidence together to help the
FBI nab me?

Maybe it would even be better if she lost me
right away before it would really be a loss at all.
It's not like she's deeply attached to me or anything. I'm little more than a Santa Claus type who
offered to help her out once a long time ago. And
failed miserably. I'm not even sure how good it is
for her to have a mute role model anyway. It may
discourage her from working at finding her own
voice again.

She came so close to actually letting a squeal
escape tonight with Kitty there to remind her how
fun, how harmless making noise can be. Maybe I
should just turn myself in, get myself out of the
way now before any damage is done.

If only I were noble enough to seriously consider that. Alas. Any confessions from me will be strictly coerced. I'm just not your basic martyr type. Roberto will have to set me up tomorrow with this "package from Juanita" front to assist me in such euthanasia. I can't bring myself to pull the plug on my own. At least not yet.

# Chapter-Fifty-Six

Tuesday,
Jan. 5, 1993

I drove to the cemetery after meeting with Roberto today. I don't know how long I've been sitting here shivering in the cold, staring at that big bronze hand on his tombstone, clutching Juanita's bequest.

"Well, aren't you even going to open it?" Roberto had asked impatiently after handing me the package at the school parking lot. He was waiting for me there this morning when I dropped Heidi off at school. I guess he wanted to show off his P.I. skills by anticipating my movements like that. It was a little spooky, reminding me more of dear ol' Dad than the Roberto I used to know.

"For Annie's Eyes Only," the package read in Juanita's sprawling handwriting. I pointed that out to Roberto in response to his urging to open it as he looked on. I knew to take such dictates seriously even if Roberto didn't, so I tucked the package under my arm. It felt like a book.

"I could have just opened it myself and not even told you about it," he reminded me poutily. That was more like the Roberto I knew. It made me smile.

"But you did what your mother asked, because you loved her," I wrote. "Now, I'm going to do what she asked, because I loved her too."

I could see the anger on his face as he looked at what I had written. Lips tight. Jaw muscles flexing. Pupils constricted. Nostrils flared. Who says you need words to talk?

He shifted glaring eyes from the piece of paper to my face and raised a hand as if to strike me. I tried not to flinch but I probably did. Hesitating a moment, he struck the notepad in my still out-stretched hand, sending it skidding across the parking lot.

"Don't give me that 'I'm one of the good guys' shit!," he yelled, waving a finger in my face. "I got my fill of that crap from your old man. I know what he really was and I know what you really are, too. Don't think I don't, Annie. I know *exactly* what you are. I just can't prove it, yet. You may have fooled my mother but not me. I'm gonna see to it that you get yours. I'm gonna see to it personally."

He wheeled around, stalked back to his rental car and peeled out of the parking lot before I could retrieve my notepad to reply. It's just as well. I don't know how I would have responded. He's right about me, after all. I must admit, though, that I'm somewhat comforted by his admission that he has more hunch than hard evidence.

I climbed back aboard Gypsy, relieved that the Roberto encounter had been relatively harmless. Taking a deep breath and locking my doors, I opened the package before leaving the parking lot. My diary from 1984, of all things. It detailed my second resolution to kill him. I was feeling rather bold that year. Or was it suicidal?

Dear Diary,

Here is my New Year's resolution. I, Annie, do hereby solemnly swear on my mother's and sister's graves to accidentally kill him before this year is through. I'll accidentally pour Liquid Plumber in his booze or I'll accidentally put rat killer in his salt shaker or accidentally put acid in his lemons. And when they come tell me he's dead, I'll cry from being so happy, but they'll think it's 'cause I'm so sad, and they'll say, "Poor little Orphan Annie. Hasn't life been cruel to her?" Get it? I'll be Orphan Annie, waiting for the sun to come out tomorrow. But it'll already be out inside of me. Hee. Hee.

Oh, boo-hoo! Boo-hoo! Woe is me. Isn't it sad—that he isn't already dead? Hee. Hee.

That brought back memories. Of course, I never went through with that plan. Or any other plan. I just wrote it for him to read and that was as far as I went. The diaries always disappeared after the resolution entries, so what more was there to write? I never dreamed Juanita would run across any of the diaries, much less keep one.

I never dreamed a lot of things about Juanita, it seems. The letter she enclosed with the diary said that she.... Well, I should just copy down the whole thing:

My Dearest Annie,

Oh, where to begin a letter such as this. I know you read it now only because death is mine. You must feel strange, yes? Imagine me then. It is a mystery to me even how I died. Tell me. Was mine a passing to your father's liking or to mine? What silliness. I am a dead woman. Why do I ask such? Perhaps I do the silly so the hard comes not so quickly. You understand this thing I do? Ah, but you have the diary book in your hands. Yes, you understand, I think.

Always in my life I have done the bad thing for what is good. The quick way to good is through the bad, not around. That is what I thought always. Such thinking is troublesome. It brings me no shame but it sometimes brings grief to those my heart has no wish to harm. I feared my heart would stop beating if I told you what I will and saw in your eyes that I pained you. So, I wait until the heart beats no more to tell you this thing. I hope it brings you no ache, sweet Annie, but I am the coward who cannot bear to test my hope outside the grave.

I know diary books are meant for no eyes but your own, but for many years my eyes watched your father take the books from the hiding drawer beside your bed and steal your quiet thoughts. I tell you nothing new in this, I think. You found him out somehow and wrote for his eyes each year. I did not know this right way. I did not know until the very diary in your hand lay open on your bed the year after I found the first in accident. Then I knew why you never seemed lost when the first book disappeared. You thought he took it from you after reading your message to him.

It was I who took them all, Annie. After the second diary book appeared, I watched for others like frogs watch for flies. Every year's beginning, I snatched a new book off your bed. Once I had them to safety in my home, I burned your writings so he would never know. I feared for you, Annie. I feared he would use your youth courage to heap horror on you. These bad things I did only for want to save you, though. I hope this thing you know.

This single diary book I kept. It gave me good humor, the accidents you planned. So, I kept your diary book as my secret treasure piece of you. It warmed my heart to have a piece of you with me when your father gave me much coldness.

His coldness was greater after your leaving. This was not your doing. It was my wish to take leave of him for Roberto's sake that brought your father's ice. He made it so I could not do as I would. Those few years seemed longer than the many years before. I saw much bitterness in Roberto grow, until I feared he might try things you only wrote.

When I had the accident of hearing your father speak on the phone one day about changing his after-death wishes, I had great interest. He spoke of much goodness for you and for me and Roberto. I did not think he could do such. It gave me surprise in my heart that clouded my mind. I had thinking that he wished to make right what he wronged.

I know now he had want only of sealing private evils in his tomb. But my knowing came only with the letters we together watched burn. Maybe if my knowing had come sooner, your diary book would not have so quickly captured my mind. I had only surprise and fear that later phone calls might take back the goodness. For this cause, I took your diary book from its hiding place in my house and read once more your words. They helped me be clear in my mind. The fault is not yours that I used your words so.

From that day I searched with care for a potion that could cause secret harm to a man with such pressure in his blood. It took months of time but at last what I sought was mine. Day after day I drew needles full from the vial and tainted the lemons of his basket.

At last the morning came when I found him in bed, hands pressed to head, eyes wide, body curled in memory of great pain, lemon skins scattered. Forgive me if I tell you I smiled at the sight. The death was fresh, his body barely cool. I untwisted his limbs and closed his eyes, so he looked to slumber. I gathered the lemon skins for grinding in the sink place and set about peeling untainted lemons to give them replacement.

I felt freedom like when America soil I first touched. It was a day of such happiness. Regret came only when to me and then to you the secret letters came. I knew grief had been brought to you by my doings. It sorrowed me. I wished to tell you right away what I tell you now, but I felt much weakness and could not bear it.

I have no want of pardon in telling you, Annie. Feel no need to make offer of such to my departed soul. I know I took from you a deed you may have had need of. Such loss cannot be restored. I have hope only that the loss is eased by knowing your wishes for him came true.

Beyond this hope, only my fondest farewell can I offer you, sweet Annie.

Juanita

I'm not sure what I felt after reading that. I must have felt something, though, to have headed straight for the cemetery, straight to his grave.

The one thought that keeps doing a broken-record routine in my head as I sit here is that I didn't have to kill anyone. The peaceful death in his sleep that drove me over the brink of manageable rage. It never happened. He very much got his due. Justice was served. I didn't have to kill him again and again. He was already dead. Exterminated.

My future, my life, Heidi's future—they're all in jeopardy now and all because of a flashpoint that was merely an illusion. Incredulous. Maybe that's the thing I'm feeling. If that's even a feeling. I see Roberto closing in, playing out some vendetta against me that's based on an illusion too. I see that look of near realization on Sally's face; I hear Kitty speaking the unspeakable about him. And suddenly my sense of invincibility, invisibility, is all crumbling. I guess I just can't believe I started this tumble toward my own demise without cause.

It's not like I can just say, "Oops! Pardon me. My mistake."

The crazy thing is that I like my life now. I couldn't say that before I started killing. I was like the sun: a self-contained, burning, churning ball of rage, waiting in silence until the day I either consumed myself or went super nova. I had no sense of purpose, satisfaction, hope. I was alive only in the most basic biological sense. Mine was a miserable, pain-filled, anger-fueled existence.

I'm not like that anymore. The killing has been like a birthing for me, letting me escape the rule-bound womb of the society that created me. It let me escape to a place where I can grow, develop, write my own life script apart from restrictive paradigms. Shooting one's way out of the womb is not the only way to be born, I know. Now. But it's one way. And it's been a particularly freeing way for me.

I haven't had to sit by helplessly taking whatever crap the justice system handed out. I've been able to shout fifteen times—well, sixteen if you count the copy cat—that there is a penalty for hurting the children. So, if you're going to get your jollies at a kid's expense, you better hope the justice system puts you away for good, because this little kid grew up and she's big enough to come after you.

Yes, I like my life now. I like the fund and the shelter. I like being surrounded by people of hope and courage. I like what killing has done for me.

No wonder it's hard to know how to react to Juanita's little bombshell, besides to burn it along with my diary. If I'd known how he really died, I wouldn't have spent the last year on such a murderous rampage. If I hadn't spent the last year on such a murderous rampage, my life wouldn't be what I like about it today. On the other hand, as the consequences of killing loom closer, I'm bummed out. I feel like I'm on such a fast track to prison. Or to the grave.

It's funny how things change. When I started I was prepared to pay for the killing, no matter what the price. Of course, my life wasn't worth shit then, so even the highest price seemed like a bargain. I never expected the value of my life to appreciate so rapidly along the way. Now suddenly the price seems extreme. This may actually cost me dearly. Who knew?

# Chapter Fifty-Seven

It's funny. I've been trying to work up the nerve to step into a therapist's office for a good chunk of my life, always stopping just short of actually doing it. But now that Heidi is in my life, I suddenly find myself sitting here in the waiting room while the shrink is meeting with Heidi. Once she's finished, I'm supposed to go back into that office. Then Heidi and I go back together. Yikes!

Heidi was in therapy before she moved here, so this is old hat. I hadn't really considered what that might mean to her, so I was solemn, apologetic even, when I approached her last week about resuming therapy. Sally had suggested an office and gave me the names of a man and a woman there who are particularly good, so Heidi could have a choice of gender. Between what her stepfather did to her and what her mother did to her, I couldn't imagine her feeling particularly safe with either gender.

"Of course, you don't have to do this," I was prepared to respond if—no, when—Heidi showed the slightest apprehension. "It's just that you've been through so much that some friends of mine thought it might be helpful. I've still got the final say on it, though, so just say the word and we'll forget it."

I already had it written down. I'd even flipped to that page in my notepad. But I never showed it to Heidi. Her face lit up at the first mention of therapy and she pointed right away to the woman's name: Daisy.

"Daisies are my favorite flower," she wrote.

"They were my sister's favorite flower, too," I wrote in reply. "I'll have someone call for an appointment today."

She smiled and threw her arms around my neck with such enthusiasm that she almost strangled me with my own scarf.

So much for my plans to save her from the horrors of therapy. I didn't even manage to save myself it seems. Oh, well. I guess if a nine-year-old can take it, I can take it, too. I hope. Besides, It's not like I'm going to discuss my little shooting problem or anything about life with him. This is just about giving Heidi what she needs.

Oh, yeah. I almost forgot. I was flipping through this month's *Psychology Today* as I sat here earlier and I ran across a little blurb about that False Memory Syndrome. That's the thing Sissy said her brother's defense had used to discredit her testimony at the trial. Turns out it's not a syndrome at all. The magazine said it's just a foundation that has been set up—by a woman of all people—to "help" those who have "imagined" they've been sexually abused. I don't know. Sounds scary to me, especially having met someone against whom it was wrongly used.

Sounds like just another ploy to shame survivors into keeping the secret. And just as Marilyn was starting to get people to take sexual abuse seriously. Damn.

* * * *

Well, therapy wasn't so bad. I think I had imagined some hocus-pocus exploration of the mysteries of the psyche. Instead, Daisy is pleasant, gentle, laid back. Her voice is like a soothing salve. She normalized the awkwardness Heidi and I are experiencing as we adjust to one another. We all came up with some goals to work toward and strategized on ways to overcome the obvious communication hurdles for future therapy sessions. Then we made an appointment for next week. That was that.

There, there. That didn't hurt, did it?

Well, just a tad. Journaling during the week was something Heidi and I agreed to do. Parts or all of which will be shared with Daisy as a way of communicating with her. So, it looks like I'll be locking this journal away in The Crucifier trunk for a while. Maybe for good.

That really feels strange. Losing Jurisprudence so unexpectedly was one thing, but now this, too? This feels like the last thing keeping my Crucifier self a part of me. As strange as it feels, though, I'm very much willing to put this away so I can move on to something different. Better? I sure hope so.

But if not, I've always got the key to that trunk.

# Chapter Fifty-Eight

I keep sitting here staring at this blank page, vainly trying to come up with words for what I feel. Is it betrayal? Disappointment? Fear? Those seem like such understated words. I guess the only word that really fits is the one I'm fighting most against uttering: murderous.

I feel like an alcoholic struggling against taking a sip of the drink that's suddenly been thrust upon me; yet I can feel in my deepest inner vacuum that I won't be able to resist. Not only am I going to take a sip, I'm going to knock back the whole glass in one greedy gulp. What frightens me most about this is not knowing if I'll slam the glass down on the bar and demand another, ruining everything just as I'm starting to build a fresh life for myself—for Heidi.

These past several months have been like getting another shot at life. Sheesh. I can't believe I said "shot" at a time like this. Anyway, therapy has really helped. I'm actually tackling a lifetime of grief head on. I didn't know I had the courage. But it turns out I do, with someone to face it with me. Who knew?

I know I've got a lot more rancid garbage yet to sift through. Heck, I'm carrying around my own private landfill. But at least I'm making progress on the part that's safe for me to talk about. At least I have a sense of hope.

Well, until today I had a sense of hope. Now all I have is a rerun of the old familiar murderous rage. I know it's good that my first response was picking up this pen instead of unpacking a doll and the SIG, but as I sit here scratching away furiously at this paper target, I already know this "healthy release" isn't going to extinguish the fire. I know that as soon as I put the paper and pen away I'm going to resurrect The Crucifier. I won't be satisfied until that therapist is dead.

Oh, I'm not talking about Daisy. She's great. It's one of the other therapists in the office, the man Sally recommended, the one Heidi could have picked. I opened up the newspaper this morning and buried in the Metro section was the whole story of how he was cleared in a professional inquiry of charges that he made sexual advances toward a young client. He didn't even get so much as an official reprimand. He's completely free to continue his practice.

In my mind, I keep seeing him making a move on Heidi. After everything else she's been through....If she'd chosen him as her therapist, she'd be fucked up even more right now instead of moving beyond the crap she's been handed. How many other unsuspecting children, adults, has he screwed with? How many others' vulnerability will he take advantage of in the future?

I swear. Here he's got people with the potential to reclaim their lives, to go a completely different route from the one I've gone. And what does he do? He gives them another push in my direction. I can't allow that. I won't. Not when I've got the means to permanently stop it.

It's scary to think about making a hit in my own city, even so. I guess it feels riskier than doing a hit-and-run routine in some faraway place. I mean, where am I going to run and hide?

It's riskier because the stakes are higher, too. My life is worth more to me than it was fifteen hits ago. I no longer feel so ambivalent toward a lifetime of incarceration. I don't even have a clue how long a life sentence would be for me, now that I know he didn't die of natural causes. No one in my family seems to die of natural causes. Who knows what our natural life span is? We could be talking fifty, sixty, seventy years behind bars. Unless I get the death penalty. Doing this could cost me. One little slip and it's over.

I wish I could just weigh the costs of this hit like a reasonable person and decide it just doesn't fit my budget. The only problem is that after putting fifteen other hits on my tab, I'm already so deeply in debt the bill collectors will be knocking on my door any time now. I might as well enjoy one last spending spree while I still can. It's not really going to be any more costly than it would have been anyway.

Besides, there's Ellie Nesler out there giving me hope. Her bail was reduced yesterday from $400,000 to $100,000. I could afford bail like that. Either one.

Last month she shot her son's molester right there in court. Five bullets to the back of the head. Bam! He's dead. Now all kinds of people are rallying to her support.

The creep she shot had been convicted of molestation before, but the justice system let him back out there to do the same thing again. This time he was on trial for molesting several boys, one of whom was Ellie's son. I guess she knew it wouldn't matter if he was convicted again. He'd eventually get out and molest someone else's son.

The he-deserved-what-he-got public opinion out there gives me hope that people will think my targets deserved what they got, too. Most of them were even more slimy than Ellie's man.

But then again, sexual abuse seems to be falling out of vogue these days. I keep running across more and more articles and TV programs inspired by the False Memory Syndrome Foundation and fewer and fewer about Marilyn's crusade. I've read that Marilyn's memories were repressed until adulthood, after all. Now that the False Memory Syndrome is all the rage, I suppose Marilyn's truth is now in question. Never mind that she has people to corroborate what happened to her.

I'm just amazed by the whole False Memory Syndrome phenomenon. In a horrified sort of way. I was already disgusted when I learned that this organization had been started by a woman. But now I find out it was started by a mother who chose not to believe her adult daughter's revelation that dear ol' Dad had molested her as a child. Mom knew hubby better than that, after all. What's a mom with a Ph.D. to do but start a foundation that discredits survivors everywhere, that tells America what it's dying to hear: incest doesn't really happen in your family or mine. Therapists just get poor, impressionable women to imagine stuff like that happened.

Fits right in with America's view of women as downright stupid, over emotional, weak willed, little helpless things that need to be rescued from the baddies. This time it's from the evil, money-grubbing therapists. No wonder the media has eaten up this whole false memory thing.

I feel bad for women like Sissy and Kitty when I hear about it all. And for Winnie. She forgot her life as fast as she lived it. I guess it was the only way to keep him from stealing away that life spark that made her Winnie. If she had lived instead of me, she wouldn't have remembered shit about him. I bet his death would have triggered all sorts of memories, though. And right at the same time this foundation comes along to tell her she's crazy.

At least Kitty had witnesses to remember for her. At least she has a transcript of her uncle's trial and his conviction to corroborate her truth. Back when we were in college, Kitty showed me a study on delayed memories of sexual abuse. It said that most people who recover memories are like Kitty. They're able to go back and verify what they remember through photographs, medical records, other family members, perpetrator confessions and other evidence. Winnie would have been one of the twenty or so percent with no proof. She probably wouldn't have even had a "for your eyes only" note to hint at the truth. She was never any threat to him.

I guess it's people like Winnie that this foundation hurts most. That makes me sad.

Of course, sometimes I have to laugh inside when I see reports on news magazines refuting the validity of repressed memories in general. Like those reporters remember every damn second of their lives, like they've never suddenly remembered something long tucked away. Yeah, right. It's not even the traumatic stuff that they've lost. And found.

I've come up with my own one-liner on repressed memories: "Well, I don't remember my throat getting slit, so I guess I can talk." Bam-ba-da-ding! Thank yew! Thank yew!

But seriously folks, I hate seeing adult survivors shamed back into silence, all because one mother out there wanted to feel more comfortable about not believing her daughter's truth. And it does seem to be the adult survivors this has hurt most. America is still willing to believe sexual abuse happens to kids like Ellie Nesler's son. It's just when adults speak of it that we roll our eyes, roll our videos, roll our presses in disbelief.

Uh, excuse me, America. I don't want to be

rude or speak out of turn or anything. But don't you know we grow up? Yoo-hoo! Knock, knock! Helllllllooo! Is anybody there? Sheesh. The state of education in this country is worse than we thought.

# Chapter Fifty-Nine

Friday,
May 28, 1993

The newspaper article on this local target noted he only lives a couple of miles from me. Heidi and I have been taking evening bike rides together since early spring when I got her a bike for her birthday. So I just altered our route a bit and have been casing the area ever since. Not to mention making myself a familiar sight to neighbors.

I've seen him out in the yard several times, painting the trim, watering the lawn, sweeping the driveway. He's got a "for sale" sign up, so I guess he's grooming the house for that. I can only speculate on why he's trying to sell it. Business is bad because of what he did? He's been ostracized by his neighbors? Guilt has driven him to become a Tibetan monk? Of course, it could just be that he's moving somewhere for a fresh start professionally so he can screw up a new set of unsuspecting clients. Asshole.

I was surprised that I didn't recognize him from therapy. Even though I can't put many names with faces, I know what a lot of the other therapists in the office look like just from sitting around in the waiting room. I tend to be early. Daisy tends to be late. I guess I shouldn't be surprised that he's kept a low profile, though. Considering the circumstances, I think I'd be prone to hiding my face around the office, too.

I haven't noticed a wedding ring on his finger, an extra car, toys in the driveway—anything to indicate he has a family. I hope he lives alone, since I plan to break into his house this evening after dark and make the hit.

Heidi and I are supposed to spend Memorial Day week with Kitty at her dad's cabin on the lake. Kitty is dying to teach Heidi to water-ski, so they left for the lake this morning while I hung around reading letters to the fund, writing checks, getting other things squared away at the house before leaving on vacation. Gypsy and I pulled through the gate of the house around six as planned, turning north toward the lake instead of south toward his neighborhood. All for the benefit of the security camera, of course.

I haven't backtracked yet. I've paused at this secluded little rest stop just outside of town for a quiet picnic dinner and the staging of my alibi. Weak though it may be, I plan to call Kitty through a TTD operator just before going to his house, tell her I'm at a town a couple of hours into the trip and that I had a flat tire. I'll tell her I plan to continue my trip tomorrow after getting the tire fixed, since I don't want to travel that far on a spare.

I want this alibi to be as authentic as possible, so I've already propped a nail up against a back tire and run over it to give myself a flat. No one seemed to notice me at all. Just the way I like it. American indifference has its advantages.

As soon as it gets dark, I'll head back into town, park a couple of blocks over (where Volvos are commonplace) and take a pleasant evening stroll to his house, everything from cowboy attire to china doll in my shoulder bag. I know I shouldn't have bothered with the clothes at all for this target but nostalgia got the best of me. I couldn't resist bringing them along. I figure I'll slip them on while I'm hiding in the shadows, just before breaking into his house.

This hit has stirred quite a bit of nostalgia for me today. Slipping bullets into the clip, choosing among the three remaining china dolls, breathing the aroma of leather from coat, boots, holster. It's all been tinged with the bittersweet feelings of a last hoorah. Whether that's really what tonight is, I don't know. But there's a sense of closure to it all the same.

Maybe it's just that I'm mourning the passing of an era of carefree killing, of reckless abandon, of an all-consuming quest. My loyalties are divided now, my focus more broad. This thing I do tonight is just a sidebar to the rest of my life, while once such deeds defined my life. Even if I'm free after tonight to kill again, it'll never be like it once was, when being free to kill again meant passionately exercising that freedom for fear it might slip away.

I hope I've really chosen something better for myself in these past several months and not just something more socially acceptable. I'm not sure how I'll know. Or what I'll do if I realize I've chosen badly, settled for too little. That's kind of a scary thought. I mean, what if I shoot this guy tonight and as the gunpowder flashes I "see the light" and realize killing is the life for me? What will I do? Just disappear into the night without a trace? I guess I could. I'd hate to do that—mostly because of Heidi—but it's certainly an option.

Sheesh. I can't believe what I'm writing here. This has gone from a too-risky-for-comfort, let's-just-hurry-up-and-get-this-over-with hit to some freaky, existential crossroads in my life. Suddenly you'd think I was Robert Frost on a snowy eve trying to decide whether to take the road less traveled; although I can't imagine that he had murder in mind when he wrote that poem. I just don't know what to think, anymore. Which is probably best. I've obviously thought far too much for one day. So, I'll switch from Robert Frost to Scarlett O'Hara and think about all this crap tomorrow. For now, I've got work to do.

# Chapter Sixty

Saturday,
May 29, 1993

Well, it's tomorrow. I'm sitting here on some bluffs overlooking the lake, keeping a sleepy eye peeled for Kitty and Heidi as the sun dips into the water. I found a note signed by Cat Woman and Swiss Miss when I arrived early this afternoon. It informed me they've gone off for a day of fishing, so I'm on my own until they bring back supper.

We had originally planned to spend the day skiing, so I guess the impromptu fishing trip was Kitty's way of giving me some time to myself to recuperate from the "flat tire" ordeal. She's a good friend. I wish I could say the same thing about myself. I shudder to think of the betrayal she may someday feel.

I needed to sleep today, so I was glad they were gone. I'm not used to this creature-of-the-night stuff anymore, so last night really wore me out. I finally woke up just in time to wander out here and enjoy the sunset. There's something to be said for the freedom to sit beside a lake, watching the sky romp through the color spectrum, listening to the water lap against the rocks in its own rhythm, while the crickets and locust sing backup in a rhythm of their own. I hope I haven't jeopardized the freedom to embrace such small wonders as this by not walking away from my life after last night's hit.

It's not that things went badly. He wasn't home when I broke into his house. So I got a pop out of the refrigerator and swiped a dorky little "ski nut" magnet for Kitty. It's made out of a walnut with glued-on eyes, sitting on a pair of water skis. That should be gaudy enough for her. Then I just sat in the darkened living room listening to *Fried Green Tomatoes* on tape until I heard him slam the car door outside. Fannie Flagg's voice is more versatile than I realized. I wouldn't mind having a voice with that nice Southern lilt.

Anyway, he was in the still-darkened kitchen, illuminated only by the light of an open refrigerator where he appeared to scrounge for a midnight snack. I wanted him to see me before I shot him, so I flipped on the kitchen light.

The look of utter bewilderment disappointed me. I guess I've grown accustomed to being recognized by my targets. Sounds like an ego thing to me. How embarrassing.

Anyway, he's dead now. And I made a pretty clean getaway, except that it put me checking into a hotel awfully late by the time I made it to the town I told Kitty I'd be staying. So after checking in, I made my rounds to movie theaters, all-night groceries and restaurants, hoping to find dated and time-coded tickets and receipts that had been discarded in parking lots. I came up with a ticket for the 10:15 showing of *Made in America*. I hope no one asks me about it, since I haven't even seen it. I tried to find a ticket stub from *Benny & Joon*, since I saw that last week, but I didn't have any luck. Oh, well. I also found a Shoney's receipt time coded for earlier in the evening. I've got them both safely tucked away in my car's ashtray where I hope I'll never need them to be found.

The whole time I was hunting for those pieces of my pitiful little alibi, I kept hearing this voice of opportunity in my head asking, "Why are you doing this? Why don't you just go away?" It had an appeal that frightened me. I suspect I'm here at the lake now only because I had an even louder responsibility voice hassling me about the prospect of abandoning Heidi.

"Oh, that's just great," Responsibility chided. "You want to become the roving savior of this country's children by walking away from the one kid in the country who's really counting on you."

"Don't give me that," Opportunity retorted. "Kitty and Heidi are crazy about each other. They'll be okay if you leave. No, *fantastic*."

"That's not the point. You already set this kid up for more abandonment and loss when you brought her to live with a wanted criminal. You sure as heck better not walk out on her just to save your own skin," Responsibility replied. "She deserves better than that."

"Yeah, like putting her through the trauma of watching you be arrested, tried and maybe even executed is something 'better.' Imagine the memories a trial will trigger for Heidi."

"What? You're going to 'hurt her for her own good' to avoid some future pain that may or may not happen? Come on, Annie, it was a clean hit. It was a *clean* hit. Maybe you were out of line risking Heidi's future over a mere 'might have been,' but leaving her won't make up for that."

That's as far as the inner debate got before I declared Responsibility the victor. So, this morning I took my flat tire to a nearby Chevron station, got yet another receipt and came to the lake.

I must not be completely convinced that I made the right choice, though. While I was napping this afternoon, I dreamed Heidi was with me in Jurisprudence while the police chased us all over town, bullets flying all around.

"Stay down! Stay down!" I kept yelling in Whoopi Goldberg's voice. Isn't that funny? I find a ticket stub to one of her movies and suddenly I'm borrowing her voice. At least it's a nice, distinctive voice.

Anyway, I woke up with the sinking feeling that I should have let Opportunity speak more about the danger I posed to Heidi's life before I sold out to the more noble-sounding arguments of Responsibility. Oh, well. It's done for now, so I might as well enjoy our week of fun in the sun. I'm no threat to Heidi here. At least I hope not.

"Ahoy, Annie!" Kitty just called out from the ski boat on the lake below. You'd think she was a swashbuckling pirate on the high seas. She always gets giddy this way when she's at the lake.

Heidi was beaming in her new daisy-print swimsuit, hoisting a largemouth bass into the air for me to see and motioning to the ice chest. It must be teeming with untold numbers of fish. I couldn't really see for sure from my perch on the bluffs, but her body language told enough. She's been taking weekend drama classes to help her communicate better minus the voice. I'd say she's getting the hang of it.

I stood and waved back, my spirits boosted by the mere sight of them. It reminded me that more than responsibility drew me to the lake today. These people make me happy. They enrich my life. Disappearing without them would be as much a loss to me as to them. Even if they survived such abandonment unscathed, I wouldn't.

Well, I better stop writing. I've got to go meet them down at the boathouse. Wait. "Got to" nothing. I can't wait to see them, hear about their day. And no doubt about the whopper that got away.

# Chapter Sixty-One

We had a great time at the lake. Heidi learned to ski. I learned how to clean a fish. Make that many fish. Kitty—well, she already knew everything. Something she immensely enjoyed rubbing in while we entertained her with our bumbling efforts. Even the rainy spell that hit in the middle of the week didn't put a damper on things. The cooler weather just gave us an excuse to lounge around in the warmth of the fireplace, working jigsaw puzzles, playing Scrabble and charades, and toasting—no, torching—marshmallows.

And it gave me a chance to think. There the three of us were—enjoying ourselves, each other, being alive—and it made me realize that every effort others have made to destroy each of us has failed miserably. The trauma we endured hasn't left us shadows of the human beings we could have been. We're still capable of reveling in the best life offers. Healing and growth are within our reach. We're a lot more than what's been done to us.

Well, I keep saying "us" and "we," but it's really "they" and "them."

As long as I've known Kitty, she's refused to let what her uncle did to her govern her life. She lives deliberately without making excuses or apologies. Her uncle has taken too much of her life, too many of her memories and she'll be damned if he's going to take anymore.

When I'm with Heidi, I get the feeling she'll live just as triumphantly as Kitty. I marvel that she's retained the ability to trust people, to connect with them. She has that same inner spark, that same spunk I remember so fondly—so jealously—about Winnie. Already Heidi openly tells on paper and in pictures what she's been through. She tells it with pain but not with shame.

Even if Heidi's mother didn't want to believe, the justice system believed Heidi. Daisy, Kitty and I believe her. It must make such a difference to be validated like that. To be able to tell the secret without any more fear of disbelief or reprisal.

Then there's me. Except for the pieces Kitty—and now Sally—know about him, my long-held secret is still intact. I haven't even told Daisy, even though she's astute enough to suspect. Instead of dancing on his grave to a Grateful Dead tape, like Kitty did when her uncle died of prostate cancer, I began a killing spree.

I could have been free. I mean, the bastard was dead. He'd done as much to me as he could do. Well, except for the little matter of his death threat. But instead of saying, "The end. You've done as much to me as you're ever going to do," I picked up where he left off. *So, you couldn't destroy me in your lifetime, huh? Well, here, let me help you out. Let me go around killing people who remind me of you until I either get locked up or killed or executed. Does that sound like a good plan to you?*

I'm sure he'd be thrilled. The dirty work continues while he rests in peace.

I've tried to frame the killing in terms of urgency. You know, the justice system isn't working, something's got to be done to stop people like him and it's got to be done now. Who cares if my life is sacrificed along the way? But at the lake I found myself thinking, *Wait a minute. That's my life you're sacrificing. It's just as valuable as the ones you're trying to save.*

In the wee hours of a sleepless, rainy night, I was thinking this. And it dawned on me that I really was The Crucifier. Only, the innocent one I'd been crucifying all this time was me. Enough! I'd had enough! I still wanted people like him stopped, but I knew I had to find a way that left my life, left me, intact. I was worth saving, too.

I felt the disjointed pieces of myself come together that night. No more locked doors inside. No more secrets from myself.

I slipped the keys to the boat off the peg by the cabin door, not really caring that I'd get drenched in the driving rain outside. Maybe I even wanted a good cleansing by that rain. I stopped by Gypsy en route to the boathouse, retrieving my shoulder bag from the locked trunk. Then I felt my way down the path to the lake.

By the time I got inside the boathouse, I was shivering from the unseasonably chilly rain, so the laundry basket full of beach towels that Kitty's dad keeps on hand was a welcome sight. Once I was dry, I scrounged up a slicker. I'd been cleansed quite enough by then, thank you. All I wanted was to stay warm and dry.

Then I tossed my bag aboard the boat and headed out across the lake toward a mountain island that's sprinkled with lights at night. Thank goodness I had Kitty teach me this week how to take the boat in and out of the boathouse

The whole point of this little late-night excursion was to ceremoniously see The Crucifier to her final resting place at the bottom of the lake. Except for the silver star. I wanted to keep that one memento to remember her by. Something to keep on the shelf with my shooting trophies and medals. But the rest had to go.

Only, it didn't occur to me to bring along some

rocks to weigh down the bag. There I was saying my final good-byes to that chapter of my life, only to have the bag bob on top of the lake instead of sinking. I guess the SIG wasn't weighty enough.

I fished the bag back out of the water and felt my way around the boat until I found a heavy box of tools to stuff inside. Then I zipped it back up and hoisted it over the side of the boat. As soon as I let go, it was gone. I hope the bottom of the lake is where it stays.

I felt like the issue was so thoroughly resolved for me afterwards that it kind of slipped my mind that I'm still a wanted woman. I know. That sounds utterly ridiculous. How does it slip one's mind that there's a penalty for killing sixteen people? Maybe it's just that after killing so many without getting caught, I forgot that my range of control in this is limited to deciding to kill or not to kill. As far as I was concerned, the saga was over when I tossed my gear off the boat. She lived happily ever after. The end. Period.

It caught me off guard, then, after I got back home and walked into the garage to find Sally and Kitty inspecting Gypsy's tires.

"Face it, Kitty," Sally said. "Annie lied about having a flat."

"Not necessarily. She said she got it fixed," Kitty replied in my defense. But haltingly, like a child offering up defense for the existence of Santa Claus after catching Mom or Dad in the act.

"You think I want to believe this?" Sally asked, her voice cracking as though she might cry. "I've been fighting these thoughts for months. Ever since Sissy's brother died. I just can't anymore. It's gone too far."

I closed the door to the garage loudly, so they'd know I was there. The hand-in-the-cookie-jar look they both shared at the moment would have amused me any other time, but at the moment it felt threatening. No doubt the quizzical look I gave them appeared just as forced as it really was. I started walking toward them.

"Annie, I—" Kitty began. "Look, did you have a flat tire or not?"

My gee-I'm-confused-about-what's-going-on nod must have infuriated Sally. Red-faced, she thrust the local newspapers she'd been carrying into my arms.

"Was that before or after you tried to kill Daniel?" she demanded.

Tried? I did kill him. I checked his pulse. The confused look was real this time.

"Sally! Not like this. Let me. Annie, Sally has some purely circumstantial evidence linking you to the last couple of Crucifier killings. Well, to some of the others, too. The most recent murder was the night you didn't show up at the lake. The wrong person was shot and Sally is good friends with the guy who police think was the intended target."

The wrong person? I had no difficulty looking appropriately shocked. Just not for the right reason.

"I know, Annie. This is a horrible thing for friends to insinuate. It would just help us feel better if you had some proof about the flat tire, that's all. But as a lawyer, I have to tell you it might be better if you just ask us to leave without showing us anything at all."

As *a* lawyer, not *my* lawyer. I caught that. I hadn't ever considered that Kitty might refuse to represent me. I should have. I know better than anyone else that she didn't go into law to help guilty people stay out of prison.

I walked over to Gypsy, put the newspapers on the trunk and reached into the glove compartment for the receipt from getting my tire patched. I felt like such a creep when I saw the relief on Kitty's face. Sally's observation felt much more deserved.

"That's not enough. A receipt from the next morning? Come on. Don't insult me like that."

"You're out of line, Sally," Kitty retorted. "We wanted an explanation about the flat and we got it. She didn't even have to give us that."

"Bullshit, Kitty! Bullshit! We're friends. I've known you my whole life, Annie. I shouldn't have to wonder if you're a murderer. How do you think that makes me feel? One of my *friends* may have killed another one of my friends' brother. Why? All because I invited you over for Thanksgiving dinner. And now you may have tried to kill another one of my friends. Why? Because he was one of the counselors I recommended for Heidi. You don't use friends like that, Annie. You don't use *me* like that."

"Sally—"

"No, Kitty! I didn't bring you with me to play diplomat. I brought you because I was afraid to come here alone. I was afraid I wouldn't leave here alive if I threw those newspapers in Annie's face like I wanted to and she realized I knew the truth. How do you like that, Annie? I'm scared of you."

I shook my head, trying to communicate that she had nothing to fear. I doubt I succeeded. Why should she believe anything I tell her?

"I just don't know what to think anymore, Annie. I'm confused. I'm scared. I'm angry. I hope so much that you're right, Kitty. You know? I hope I'm so far out of line that I'll come groveling for forgiveness someday for being so incredibly stupid. But right now I just feel like tearing you apart, Annie, to make you understand that you can't go around assuming people are guilty every time they're found innocent. Some people are, you know—innocent. Daniel is. It's all there."

She motioned toward the newspapers lying on Gypsy, angry tears choking away any other words. Then she raised her fist as though she really might hit me, but she whirled around and stalked out of the garage instead, hitting the door with her fist to punctuate her exit.

"Maybe I should go make sure she's okay," Kitty said somewhat apologetically.

I nodded in agreement. Before she left, she reached into her pocket and pulled out a business card. She seemed embarrassed to give it to me. I, in turn, was embarrassed to get it. It had the name of a lawyer from the firm he used. I knew I'd sunk pretty low if I needed to consult the kind of unscrupulous lawyers he'd retained.

"Look, I'll come over later this evening. Maybe after Heidi's gone to bed?"

I indicated that would be fine. After she left, I just stood there feeling stunned until the silence became too much to bear. Then I gathered the newspapers, walked rather numbly to the conference room and locked the door behind me.

I messed up. The newspaper accounts make that abundantly clear. No doubt to downplay their own contributing gaffe: They published Daniel's middle initial as "B" when it's really "P." They printed the address in the phone book for Daniel B., too. Apparently I missed the correction printed the next day. I never read those things.

The man I killed was an engineer who had just volunteered for a lengthy stint overseas with Habitat for Humanity. That's why he was selling his house. To support himself while he was there. Do I feel like a complete sleaze or what? Wouldn't you know the one time I royally screw up, I take out a real sweetheart of a guy. Why couldn't he have been a crooked politician, an unscrupulous businessman, even a rotten judge?

I would feel so much better about all this right now if my flub had at least eliminated someone remotely guilty of something—anything. Then I could minimize it, justify it all by feeding myself some lines about society being a better place without him. I could congratulate myself on an unintentional job well done. Now The Crucifier's swan song is the senseless murder of an innocent man. A decent man. Did I mention how rotten this feels?

I think it feels even worse than if I'd killed the right Daniel, only to later discover he was innocent. At least then I could try to convince myself that he was guilty of something, even if not this particular charge. Where there's smoke there's fire, after all. Right? What do I do now? Deny that I killed the wrong guy?

Wait. I know. I could do a paranoid number and convince myself that these newspaper articles aren't even real. They've been fabricated as part of an FBI sting operation in which Sally is participating. They figure if they make me feel guilty enough, they'll get me to confess to Sally or go to the police and turn myself in.

That'd be a swell twist. I almost wish it were true. As it is, I don't know what to do with the guilt. Maybe I really should turn myself in.

Whoa! Wait just a minute, young lady. Get that thought out of your brain right this second. I'm going to crack open that cranium and wash it out with soap if you don't watch yourself. This is no time to be noble. You can't undo anything by surrendering.

Yeah, yeah. I know. But dammit, this isn't the way I wanted to end this part of my life. I wanted to be like Juanita. Regrets, sure. But no shame. Now I feel nothing but.

I can't believe I was so careless. I could have avoided the whole thing if I'd just looked further into the case against the therapist. It was hardly a case at all. It's ridiculous that the newspaper even covered the story. With his accuser's full knowledge, he'd videotaped the session when the client threatened to fabricate the exact charge she later filed against him. After I killed the wrong guy, she even went public about her lie, because she was afraid I'd try again once I found out I missed. I guess I'm not alone in my feelings of guilt. It's not a very satisfying companionship, I'm afraid.

Okay, Annie. Time for a deep breath. This is the worst mistake of your entire life. Period. No excuses. No second chances. No plea bargains. It's done and that's the way it forever stands.

Chances are you'll get ample opportunity to pay for that error. Between Sally's suspicions and Roberto's misguided vendetta, things don't look good for you at all. There's no need to rush the process. The justice system will be coming for you soon enough. So let it do its job for once. It doesn't need any more help from you.

If the guilt gets too big before then, just remind yourself how absurd it is that you didn't run across a truly innocent target before now. If you hadn't stopped those fifteen others, maybe no one would have. It certainly wasn't anyone else's priority anyway. There's no shame in wanting kids to be able to grow up in safety. The shame is that killing was the best option you had for ensuring that. There should be something beyond not-guilty verdicts and early parole, something between the bang of a gavel and the bang of a gun.

You were bound to do something like this sooner or later, Annie. One of the hazards of the job.

There are things you need to do. You've got Heidi

to think about. You've still got two china dolls locked
away in the attic, not to mention all that loose cash
stashed in that trunk with the dolls. And this journal. You've got to do something with this.

You're just starting to take your life back from
him, Annie. Don't give up now. Don't blow it.

* * * *

"I hope you called that lawyer." Those were the
first words out of Kitty's mouth when she came
over tonight. Really encouraging, huh. I felt like
razzing her about that, but she looked so serious I
just wrote that an appointment was set for Friday.

"That may not be soon enough, Annie. Sally's
decided to go to the police with her suspicions tomorrow morning. All you'd had was opportunity
with her friend's brother. But when I told her about
your dad...." Kitty paused. "I feel like a stinking
Judas, Annie. I had no idea that she'd hear 'motive' when I mentioned your dad. When this latest
thing happened and she remembered suggesting
him to you as a possible therapist for Heidi, I guess
it was one coincidence too much.

"You should know she rifled through some of
your WJF Fund papers while we were at the lake
and found canceled checks to some of the people
affected by The Crucifier's killings. I know it's circumstantial but still...."

I picked up my pen to write. I didn't know what
to say, really. Something. But I was too stunned
at the thought of the fund being my one big slip. I
couldn't even think in words. Kitty reached over
and grabbed my hand before I had a chance to
write anything.

"I don't want to know, Annie. Understand?
Even if you're innocent, I can't defend you. I think

you understand that."

I nodded and mouthed, "It's okay."

"I don't want to have to testify against you either, though, so I don't want to know. Innocent. Guilty. It doesn't matter. Just promise not to tell me. Promise me that."

"Promise," I wrote.

"Thanks." She leaned back in the rocking chair, eyes closed, forefingers caressing her temples. She didn't speak for several minutes.

"So, what does Heidi know?" she finally asked.

I wrote that I'd taken Heidi to Toys R Us this evening to pick out a present for her new friend Amy's upcoming birthday party. Then we'd gone to Chuck E. Cheese's for dinner and a long "talk." What I didn't tell Kitty was that I'd disposed of a china doll in each of those establishment's bathroom trash cans. But then, that would have been breaking my promise to her, so it's just as well.

I really didn't know what to tell Heidi. I couldn't exactly say something like, *Guess what? I shoot people, just like your mom. So, the police will be coming to take me away soon.* I've set that kid up so badly. Me and my "mistakes." Sheesh.

I did tell Heidi that I was in trouble and might have to live in jail for a while. Since she couldn't stay with me if that happened, I wondered how she might feel about living with Kitty.

Heidi's biggest concern? "Where will I keep my desk?"

I was glad to see Kitty get a chuckle out of that one. Kitty and Heidi have a long-running joke about Heidi's room being bigger than Kitty's whole apartment and Heidi's desk being bigger than Kitty's guest room. Kitty's laughter was a relief for both of us tonight.

"Actually, I've been wondering how you'd feel if I

moved in here for a while—you know, if worse comes to worst and you're in jail by this time tomorrow."

"That would be great," I wrote, but I was really feeling rather horrified at the thought of being in jail so soon.

"Or, if you were planning to disappear tonight...."

That got my attention. But I was so dumfounded to hear such a suggestion coming out of Kitty's mouth that I didn't really know how to respond. So, I didn't. Beyond a wide-eyed look of shock.

"Now, I'm not implying you should, Annie. I'm not convinced Sally has as much cause to suspect you as she thinks she does. But I just keep thinking about all those refrigerator magnets you got me on those road trips of yours...."

She closed her eyes again and gave her head a hard shake, as though to toss that thought somewhere far, far away.

"I don't think it's an accident that Sally's waiting to talk to her agency lawyers tomorrow before going to the police," Kitty continued, only slower now, like it had become painful to speak. "She's a mess, isn't she? She feels this duty to take her suspicions to the police but deep down she'd like to see you pull a Thelma and Louise, minus the Grand Canyon."

"What about you?" I wrote.

"Me? Oh, man. Me. I'm going to be some kind of pissed if I ever find out you really did this, Annie. How dare you sacrifice me, Heidi, yourself for something so cheap as revenge. How dare you!"

"It was about more than revenge," I wrote in ferocious protest. Luckily I realized what I had written a split second before showing it to her. I wadded that one up.

"But that's hypothetical, now isn't it?" she continued deadpan, watching me wad the paper, not at all wanting to see what I had written. "I guess if you were to leave tonight, you'd come off looking kind of guilty. But then again, I could always hope you ran for fear of being railroaded for something you didn't do. If you go to trial and the evidence is particularly damning...."

"I may lose you either way; you may lose me. I don't even want to think about what Heidi may lose. I guess that's why I was thinking about moving in here for a while. I see Heidi on the verge of losing so much that I'd like to at least see her keep that awesome bedroom of hers."

"That would make me feel a lot better about things," I wrote. "I'm worried about Heidi, too."

"So, do you think she'd mind if I took the spare bunk bed tonight? I'd kind of like to be on hand in case anything ugly happens in the morning."

Actually, I did mind. I'd had a thought about Mom's old desk and Kitty's presence would get in the way of me acting on it. I was just about to suggest she stay in one of the spare bedrooms in the main house when Kitty responded to my hesitation.

"All right. I'll admit it. I have an ulterior motive here. There is a part of me that's afraid this is the last time I'll ever see you. And I'll be damned if I'm going to let you take Heidi with you when you go. You're not putting her through that, Annie. Got that? So, I'm not asking anymore. I'm telling you: I'm sleeping in Heidi's room tonight."

"Good!" I quickly wrote. "I'm glad you care so much about her."

"Oh, I know that, Annie. Deep down, anyway. This whole mess has just blindsided me so bad that I don't know which way is up."

"Me, too," I wrote, but I could tell in her face that she didn't quite know whether to believe me. Oh, well. I didn't know if I quite believed me, either.

We visited a while longer, mostly discussing logistical stuff like when Heidi has therapy, when Amy's birthday party is scheduled, where financial records are kept. I felt like we were planning my funeral minus the body. I was feeling pretty low by the time Kitty gave into her yawns and bid me goodnight with a "See you in the morning."

I don't think she realized what she'd said until she was climbing onto the roof. She suddenly froze, then turned around and came back down the steps.

"Could I have a hug just in case I don't—you know, see you in the morning?"

She had me convinced I'd never see her again before she finally left for good. I was in tears as I went over to the trunk and unlocked it. I have no idea how long I sat there on the floor in front of that trunk, emptying a box of Kleenex, counting the remaining cash, wondering what I should do.

I kept thinking of Thelma and Louise. What they could have done with the kind of cash I have. Forget trying to outrun the cops in a car. They could have flown to Mexico before anyone even knew enough to seriously suspect them.

"But how are we gonna get to Mexico from Arkansas without flyin' over Texas, Louise?" Thelma would ask.

"I can route you through Denver," the ticket agent would pipe in. "There's a flight leaving in thirty minutes at Gate 12."

"That's how we're gonna do it, Thelma," Louise would respond triumphantly.

"Can you tell me if they sell them little bottles of Wild Turkey on the airplane?" Thelma would ask the ticket agent.

"As many as you want, Thelma. As many as you want," Louise would promise as she led Thelma away by the arm.

Cut to the plane taking off into the sunrise, before it banks and heads west. Roll credits. The end.

Money. It's almost like there's no way to ensure a happy ending without it. Not in this country, anyway. And here I am with a hefty pile of that insurance stacked on the floor in front of me. How many other women have that available to them? None of the other women living in this house do, and they really need it. They deserve it.

Not me. But I'm the one who's got it. I really can disappear into the night without a trace. I guess the only question now is will I? I don't have the answer yet.

# Chapter Sixty-Two

Tuesday,
June 8, 1993

I guess I had a touch of his insomnia last night. Imagine that. I've had so little to lose sleep over. I kept thinking I should go to bed and try to get some rest, but I just watched the sunrise so I guess it's too late for that. It's too late for disappearing into the night, too. I took the cash down to the main house a couple of hours ago and stashed it in his secret cabinet with the Annie Oakley gun and Juanita's papers. That way I can always get to it if I change my mind.

I came up here on the roof afterwards and have been sitting here ever since trying to do exactly that: change my mind. I guess the sunrise has been a "time's up" bell for me. Like the prisoner scheduled to be executed at dawn, I'm just biding my time until someone comes to lead me away.

How pitiful can I get? I don't even have Annie Oakley's pistol here with me so I can make a last stand. I'm just waiting like a good little victim for the blue flashing lights to come down the drive and take me peaceably away. What a wimpy ending. If I'm going to roll over and die like this, I wish I could at least muster the courage for a dignified death. Something like a flying leap off this roof would suffice. Or better yet, I could arrange a punishment that fits my crimes: put a hand to my forehead, put the barrel of Annie Oakley's pistol against my hand and fire.

But oh, no. I couldn't bring myself to do something like that. I just sit here and wait.

I don't know. Maybe I'm being too hard on

myself. Maybe last night's sleeplessness is getting to me, not to mention the stress of waiting for the inevitable. I guess we criminals are prone to crankiness when we know we're caught. We don't mind the crime, just these annoying penalties for the crime. They come along at such inconvenient times. Namely, when we're so enjoying having gotten away with what we've done.

Being reduced to a common criminal puts such a crimp in one's lifestyle. At least before you get caught you can lie to yourself about how you're not like all the others. Not nearly so lacking in integrity, not nearly so deserving of consequences. Maybe that self-deception is just as easy after getting caught, considering the tales I've heard of how "innocent" everyone in prison claims to be.

Me? I know I did it. I don't agree with the laws governing what I did, so in that sense I'll probably claim I'm innocent. But I'm sure I'll pay all the same. So, why the heck am I still sitting here, waiting to pay for something I think should carry no penalty? I hope I'm not just being noble. That can be such a nice word for stupid.

I think I'm just taking a calculated risk. A risk that the justice system will move as slowly as it usually does. With any luck I could be out on bond, waiting a year or more for my case to come to trial. A year of freedom. That has more appeal than a lifetime on the run. I could do a lot of living in a year. And I could always jump bail before the trial ended—or even started for that matter. Besides, it'll give me a chance to get that new book I heard about in the news: *How to Disappear Completely and Never Be Found.*

It could probably tell me how to take on Juanita's identity. With the cash I have stashed in his cabinet, I wouldn't draw any attention to myself with huge cash withdrawals. I could even slowly add to the money until I decided to run.

I guess what I'm trying to give myself in staying is more options. And more time to consider which option I prefer. Maybe I'll prefer prison in the end. Maybe I can be like that prisoner in Phoenix who wrote for the *San Francisco Chronicle*. Only, I'll give women prisoners a voice for a change. Wouldn't that be something? Me giving the voiceless a voice. Me asking that America question why it puts women in jail for protecting themselves, why it doesn't offer them more protection, better options, long before they're driven to break its laws. I always wanted to be a columnist. This could be my big break.

Of course, I'm in no hurry to begin a prison career, but that's certainly the risk I'm taking by staying. There's no guarantee a judge would grant someone like me bail. I may have really blown it by staying. This may be the last sunrise I ever watch as a free woman.

I guess that realization is why I'm giving myself such a hard time about failing to run while I still can. But it's done. I'll be glad when I just accept that and forgo the self flagellation for "wimping out." I don't think I have wimped out. I haven't given up yet at all. I've just chosen a shaky route.

I really need to get this journal stashed away before shaky deteriorates to crumbling, though. There'll be no bail for Bonzo if a search warrant yields this little FBI agent's dream book. The hiding place I have in mind is behind that secret spring door in Heidi's desk, the one she's too little to open yet.

The trick will be getting Heidi and Kitty out of the bedroom long enough to hide this there. It's probably getting late enough in the morning to wake them without incurring the wrath of Heidi. The child is not a morning person. Then again, she is a coffee cake freak and that's what Shirley makes for breakfast on Tuesdays. So, maybe I can get them to rush downstairs before it's all gone.

I can bow out of eating breakfast myself by telling Kitty I'd like to make a trip to the cemetery while I still can. Which is the truth. I want to say good-bye to Mom and Winnie. And perhaps spit on his grave. This could be my last chance to visit until I'm buried alongside them. I figure I'll stash this, go pick up some flowers and stay at the cemetery as long as I can.

So, I guess this is it. The feeling in the pit of my stomach is like being at the very top of a roller coaster the instant before that free-fall plunge. It's a little scary not knowing what waits for me at the bottom. If there even is one. But I've come too far to get off now. I just wish I could scream on the ride down.

# Chapter Sixty-Three

Wednesday,
June 24, 1993

I remember feeling like someone was following me that morning as I drove to the florist and then on to the cemetery. But knowing the new heights my paranoia had reached over the preceding several hours, I ignored what I felt beyond an occasional glance in my rearview mirror. Still, I wasn't surprised when a voice interrupted my thoughts as I stood at the foot of Mom's and Winnie's graves. I was surprised only that I recognized the voice.

"What? No flowers for Daddy?" Roberto snidely asked. He was standing behind me. I'd been so intent on saying my good-byes that I hadn't even heard him walk up.

When I turned around to face him, I found he wasn't alone. A vaguely familiar man was standing beside him. Where had I seen that close crop hairdo before? His P.I. mentor from Hawaii maybe? Then it clicked: "Sarge." The marina. Duh, of course he was from the marina. It made perfect sense. Roberto hadn't been able to take me to the marina, so he'd brought the marina to me.

"Surprised to see us?" Roberto asked, grinning like he'd just pulled off the coup of the century. And maybe he had. I know visions of extradition certainly flashed through my mind, a possibility I'd forgotten to consider in my decision not to run. My only comfort was the fact that "Sarge" didn't share Roberto's I-gotcha-now grin.

"Is this one of your private investigator friends?" I wrote to Roberto, casually hooking my left thumb in the back pocket of my jeans as I handed my notepad to him. That was a little trick I'd learned as a kid to hide my birthmark whenever I wanted to make someone think I was Winnie. I wasn't sure if "Sarge" would remember seeing that mark at the marina or not but I definitely didn't want to trigger any repressed memories just then.

"Oh, you don't know each other? I was under the impression that you two had already met."

Roberto could be such a smart ass these days. Whatever happened to lovable little Bobby? As if I didn't know....

I looked at "Sarge" without the slightest hint of recognition in my face and shook my head no. The amazing thing was he didn't look as though we'd ever met before, either. He was studying me carefully. No doubt about that. He didn't try to hide it.

"My name's James. Nice to meet you," he finally said, shaking my hand. His manners had greatly improved since first we met. I was impressed.

I've never seen a smile slide off a face as fast as Roberto lost his. I think I even caught a glimpse of little Bobby wanting to cry.

"Nice to meet you?" Roberto asked, utterly astounded.

"That's what I said," James stated firmly. "I don't know this lady."

"She's the one. I'm telling you," Roberto insisted.

James gave me another hard look. Particularly my throat. I'd only recently stopped covering the scars. Part of some shame work I'd done in therapy. But I'd been particularly careful to keep those scars from sight at the marina, so no one would question my deafness.

"Nope," he finally said. "I'd of remembered throat cuts like that. She ain't the one. Sorry to bother you like this ma'am."

Roberto stood there dumbfounded as James walked away.

"I could have sworn," Roberto muttered more to himself than to me. "I could have sworn."

He finally just turned and followed James back to his car. He didn't even say good-bye. My legs felt like they might buckle after that, so I took a seat on my empty grave, never mind the dew soaking through my jeans. I couldn't believe what had happened.

I tried to picture the "me" that James saw standing before him. Besides the hair, glasses, artsy earrings and exposed scars on my throat, I was tanned from a week of play at the lake, instead of creature-of-the-night pale. I'd dropped some more weight since Heidi and I started bike riding together. And I bet my hazel eyes looked cemetery grass green today instead of water and sky blue. As vaguely familiar as he was to me after all these months, having changed so little in appearance himself, it was little wonder he didn't know me.

That boosted my spirits. It made my good-bye to Winnie and Mom feel less tragic, less final. If the closest thing to a witness available couldn't place me at the marina, mere graveside visits while out on bail certainly seemed within reach.

I was able to return home after that and actually enjoy joining Kitty and Heidi in a swim. I even taught them how to play underwater tea party.

Then Ruby came running into the gym. She was monitoring the security system that morning.

"Some police just ordered me to let them through the gates. They said they have a search warrant. I didn't know what to do, so I let them in. You don't think Misty's husband is trying to get her, do you? I didn't know what to do."

"You did the right thing, Ruby," Kitty assured

her. "Annie's expecting them. But you better go tell Misty to lock herself in her room for a while just to play it safe."

"Oh, good. Oh, good," Ruby said, her voice still tinged with panic. "I wish you'd tell me when you're expecting folks, Annie—well, you know, leave me a note or something. You forgot to tell me about that Charlie guy coming to fix the leaky spot on the roof while you were on vacation, too. That about scared me to death. I just know I'm gonna let someone bad in sometime. I just know I am."

"I'll go call your lawyer," Kitty said as soon as Ruby was gone. "It'd probably be better not to tell the authorities anything until he gets there. Heidi, they may take Annie away now. But I'll be right back as soon as I use the telephone. Wait for me."

Heidi nodded, but her eyes were fixed on me, wide with fright. I winked at her and smiled in a weak attempt to offer reassurance, but I don't think either of us felt the least bit comforted.

I had just started toweling off when the arrest was made. Somehow I never envisioned being carted off to jail in a soggy swimsuit. I guess I need to plan a little better for future arrests. I didn't even get to hug Heidi before the handcuffs were slapped on and I was read my rights.

My rights. Now that was a unique experience. Having the right to remain silent after all these years of involuntary, even coerced silence. Well, I accepted that right. And it turned out pretty good for me that I did, since my most excellent, letter-of-the-law, I-never-ask-if-my-clients-did-it, sleaze ball lawyer didn't have to trot along behind me wiping up spilled words.

That way, he's been able to concentrate on obliterating the truly pitiful handful of circumstantial evidence against me: my shooting medals and trophies, the hand on top of his monument, the canceled checks, the photograph of him holding a Baretta while posing with Roger Moore, my boot size, Misty's memory of me with the Browning the day Roberto showed up. Other than that, all they've got is Sally's and Roberto's suspicions.

Still, the judge ordered me held without bond. I had motive and opportunity, after all. I couldn't believe it. My worst nightmare come true all because he wanted to send a strong message to vigilante types everywhere. Especially female ones. Who cares if that meant a harmless woman had to rot in jail?

Listen to me. I think I'm starting to believe my own lawyer's lies. Sheesh.

Well, anyway, I was a week or so into the rest of my life in jail when I got taken out of my cell to see my lawyer. Only this time without the usual handcuffs and leg chains. Those things chaff like crazy, so I was glad for the small gesture of trust that I wouldn't try to escape. I had every intention of being a good girl in hopes that they'd skip future chains.

But when I met my lawyer, he was grinning like Roberto as he twirled my bathing suit 'round and 'round.

"Is this really all you came here with? A rich heiress like you?"

I still didn't understand what was going on, so I just nodded.

"Well, you're in luck, my dear. I happen to have had these freshly laundered sweats in my car trunk," he said holding out a gym bag, "and you can borrow them. But be forewarned. I'll add them to your bill if I don't get them back."

I indicated that I didn't understand what was going on.

"What? No one's told you? You're free. Insuffi-
cient evidence, my dear. They'll have a false arrest
lawsuit on their hands before the day's through. A
movie stub and restaurant receipt found in your
car puts you somewhere else at the time of one
killing. Your handwriting doesn't match The
Crucifier's. The hairs they found on that houseboat aren't yours. The Jenkins woman herself gives
you an alibi for the Texas murder. She says that
one happened the same evening she ran into you
at a mall on your birthday. And a P.I. wanna-be
who thought he had some dirt on you admitted
that someone he'd brought into town from the
marina killing couldn't ID you.

"But the real clincher came from The Crucifier
herself. The police got a package from her clearing
you, just like she did with some guy who got arrested a long time ago. Only, this time she enclosed a bullet from one of the guns she often used
and a typed letter saying she's retiring from killing. Can you believe it? She's tired of innocent
people like you getting blamed for things she does.
She claims to have acquired some sophisticated
surveillance equipment and says she's going into
the hard evidence business. She enclosed video
and audio taped evidence that pretty much nails
a child molester who lives a few hours from here.

"With some hard work on my part—for which
you will pay dearly, I assure you—I got all charges
dropped. So change clothes and go home. Here's
some money for a cab; I'll call one for you on my
car phone when I leave. Sorry I can't drive you
home myself, but I've got to be in court in—oh,
shit—fifteen minutes ago. Just drop those clothes
off at the office sometime. Good luck! Oh, and the
press shouldn't bother you here. I told them you
were released early this morning and that you're

already home. You'll probably need to write up some kind of official 'poor me' statement for them tomorrow."

He dashed out of the room, leaving me standing there feeling rather lost. Even after I'd turned in my orange jail-wear and was sitting around waiting for my taxi to arrive, I felt lost. I just sat there void of emotion, staring blankly at a pile of newspapers.

I know I should have been ecstatic, but I couldn't even muster the slightest feeling of relief. I just kept thinking about Jurisprudence's theft as I sat there, knowing that I could have just as easily used his spy toys to gather evidence, too. I didn't have to kill anyone. I could have gotten every one of those people convicted on new charges. I could have gathered evidence so damning that they would have all gotten maximum sentences on every count against them. Yet going that route never even occurred to me. Talk about feeling stupid.

I don't know how long I sat there berating myself before I actually saw what my eyes were fixed upon. I felt like I'd been jolted back to life when the image reached my brain: his ugly, flat-lipped picture under the banner headline, "Deceased Philanthropist Accused of Incest." A subhead asked, "Was Suspect in Crucifier Killings Driven to Crime by Community Leader's Abuse?" A second photo depicted his newly vandalized monument at the cemetery. Someone had slapped a spot of red paint onto the palm of his hand. Wish I'd thought of doing that.

I snatched up the paper. I could tell from the tone of the article that Kitty and Sally were trying to help by explaining why I'd done what I'd done. Still, it took my breath away to see those things in print.

*I'm dead.* That's all I could think. I'd been freed

from jail only to be sent to my death. The irony was a little too macabre for me. I had the urge to go up to the desk and beg to be re-arrested, to confess everything. I could hardly believe that telling Kitty about him all those years ago had finally caught up with me. I couldn't believe that one slip was going to end up killing me.

Another one of those jolts hit me just about then. Kitty! I wasn't the dead one. She was. She was staying in my attic. And the media had no doubt already informed the hit man that I was home. I jumped up and went out to the street, pacing up and down the sidewalk until my taxi finally eased up to the curb. I gave the driver the address, adding that the quicker I got there the bigger his tip would be.

Unfortunately, he was a free spirit, unimpressed by the lures of money, so I was out of luck in buying a hair-raising taxi ride that would get me back home just in time to save the day.

It was just as well. That way I had more time to remember that I wasn't living out the climax of some action movie. Nothing was going to happen to Kitty before I got there. It had taken this guy a good three or four days to kill Juanita. Surely he'd take his time killing me, too.

I had pretty much composed myself by the time Ruby made me get out of the taxi so she could see me in the security cameras before opening the gates.

"Why didn't you tell me you were coming—well, you know what I mean. I heard on the news that they'd let you out, but I didn't believe it, since they said you'd been here since early this morning. You know, you didn't tell me Richard was coming to fumigate your apartment today, either. He said you'd been complaining to Charlie for months that you couldn't get rid of the roaches up there. But then, I guess you couldn't tell me, you still being in jail and all. Somebody should of told me, though."

I had never complained to Charlie about roaches. At first I was just puzzled, but then it hit me. Square in the stomach. The "lottery" money Richard had won. The car show he was supposedly attending when Juanita was killed. His reaction when I told Charlie about Juanita's death. Richard was the one. I didn't want to believe it—somehow more for Charlie's sake than for my own—but I knew it was true. And if Richard had heard the same news report that Ruby had, he thought I was here. He wasn't wasting any time.

"Where's Kitty?" I quickly wrote on the first writing surface available.

"Oh, I wish you hadn't written on that. That's a nice piece of stationery. I was thinking about writing a letter on that. I hadn't decided who to yet, but—"

"Where's Kitty?" I pointed to it again.

"Oh, I think her and Heidi are straightening up your attic. Those FBI people made a awful mess of it once they took you away. Hey! Where are you going in such a hurry, Annie?"

I was going to the cabinet to get Annie Oakley's pistol, but I didn't take time to explain that. I just went. Once I grabbed it, I sprinted down halls and up stairs to Heidi's room.

It's frustrating how running jars my head. By the time I got to Heidi's room, I was feeling pretty woozy. I kept focusing on the glass door leading to the roof, trying to make my body go in that direction. It took forever. Well, probably just seconds, but every added second felt like an eternity. Like the proverbial second too late.

Once I made it to the door, I knew I'd gone as far as I could go. Any step out onto that roof would be my last. I'd tumble over the eaves of the house without even being able to shout a warning to Kitty or identify myself as the one Richard wanted. So I just lay down half-in, half-out of the doorway. That way, at least I could see across the walkway to my doorway.

I wasn't too late. Richard was still on the roof, anyway. He had his blind side to me as he sprayed a fine mist of something onto the walkway from a pesticide canister. Yeah, like I'm so sure I have a problem with cockroaches on the roof.

As I watched him, I kept thinking of Juanita taking that plunge off the balcony. And I wondered for the first time whether the gardener's fall from the ladder and my grandparents' fall over the cliff were really accidents at all.

I wasn't sure what Richard was spraying, but I imagined the little "accident" he had planned involved a plunge off the roof. That stuff would have to be pretty slick for that.

I wanted to kill him. I'll admit that. I mean, he'd no doubt killed Juanita and now he was here threatening Kitty's life and maybe Heidi's too. Besides, he was the last ounce of life that stinking, rotting corpse had been able to buy and I rather relished the thought of snuffing that out once and for all.

I knew how bad it would look if I shot him in the back but that was just tough. The only thing really stopping me was I couldn't get the world to stop spinning long enough to take that shot.

There I was, holding the gun of the surest shot ever born but I couldn't be sure the bullet would fly true to its mark. I took my time, knowing I only had one shot. If that.

So much was at stake. More than I could really allow myself to think about at the time. I guess that's why I waited so very long before squeezing the trigger. Too long.

The attic door slid open and Heidi skipped out just ahead of Kitty.

"Ruby said she's around here somewhere looking like crazy for us," Kitty was saying to Heidi. "We'll see if we can find her first."

Richard just casually started walking up the slope of the roof toward the fire escape steps when he heard the door open. He didn't even bother to make sure I was the one walking out onto the roof, the bastard. It all happened so fast. Kitty and Heidi were about to step onto the walkway; he was about to walk away.

"No! Stop!" I could hear myself screaming in my head. The voice was amazingly grown up.

I don't remember adjusting my aim or squeezing the trigger. I just suddenly felt the gun kick and smelled gunpowder.

The bullet hit him in the right shoulder. His hand contracted around the trigger of his sprayer in reflex, coating the slope around his feet. He started slipping, sliding toward the walkway, unable to catch his balance. His feet went out from under him like he'd stepped onto a sheet of ice when he hit the walkway. He went crashing through the railing, tumbling out of control over the side of the roof.

A fresh pack of Camels fell out of his shirt pocket as he fell. That pack of cigarettes hugged the edge of the roof near the spot where he disap-' peared, spinning eerily.

I didn't see him hit the ground. I didn't have to. I just kept staring at those cigarettes, knowing Richard was dead. He was dead. I was so enamored by the thought of finally being beyond the reach of the grave, that at first I didn't even notice the shouts, the screams, from the opposite end of the walkway.

Screams *and* shouts? I turned my head toward

the sound—no, sounds—out of curiosity more than anything else. I'd jarred my head so badly that I thought I saw Heidi standing there screaming her heart out.

"Put the gun down, Annie! Put down the gun!" Kitty was shouting herself hoarse above the screams. *Above* the screams. Heidi was screaming.

I lay down the gun and raised my hands, waving them for Heidi to see. I know I should have felt terrible at that point, having traumatized Heidi so. But all I felt was thrilled that she'd found her voice again. She needed to scream. And was she ever letting loose a mighty roar.

Leaving the pistol where it lay, I tried to make my way across the walkway to congratulate her. It was too slick. I was too dizzy.

"What have you done, Annie?" Kitty was yelling at me by then, holding a sobbing Heidi. "What have you done?"

I wanted to tell her. I wanted to shout it to her. No more secrets. No more! I could tell everything. I could tell anyone. It was over.

"Annie," Kitty called out to me. "I'm going to call the police. I don't understand what's going on. All I know is I saw you shoot Richard. And I've got to call the police. Do you understand?"

I understood, all right. I'd just had charges dropped for murders I really committed and now I was about to go back to jail for protecting myself, protecting my family. It was too much.

I guess that's why I went back into Heidi's room and got this journal from its hiding place. I guess that's why I went back to his den and got the money and Juanita's papers. I guess that's why I jumped into Kitty's jeep and drove away. Gypsy had been impounded. That'll teach Kitty to leave her keys in the ignition. And her purse in the floorboard.

I drove straight to the airport to try out that quick flight to Mexico in honor of Thelma and Louise. I even bought the ticket. But as I sat waiting for the plane—staring at Kitty's car keys in one hand and her purse in the other, wondering why I hadn't just left them in her jeep—I spotted the key to the cabin on the lake.

I didn't want to go to Mexico. I wanted to go to the cabin.

After a taxi ride to the next town, I used Kitty's driver's license and credit card to rent a car. As long as I had her signature down pat, no one seemed to care that I was too tall, too heavy, and too blonde to be the woman in the photo. They barely even looked at me. I guess having a hamburger meat throat has its advantages.

I've been here at the lake ever since. Just waiting. For what? That's been the million-dollar question, all right. Have I been waiting for some SWAT team to find me and take me out? Have I been waiting for Kitty and Heidi to conveniently show up so I can say my good-byes and explain what happened with Richard, send a farewell note back to Sally, an explanation to Roberto about who really killed Juanita and an apology to Charlie for killing his best friend? Tie up all the loose ends in my life?

When I sat on the bluffs and watched a particularly gorgeous sunset my second evening here, I thought, *Maybe that's what I've been waiting for.* When I lay in the hammock one clear night and counted three shooting stars, when I went swimming in the lake during that pelting rainstorm yesterday and then saw a double rainbow, when I said to hell with the vertigo and dashed through the woods with complete abandon, trusting the pine-needled forest floor to catch me when I fell— *maybe that's what I've been waiting for,* I thought.

Maybe there were just some final experiences I needed to have, some lasting memories I needed to make before.... Before what? Before whatever I was waiting for happened, I guess.

I think it finally happened yesterday. I heard on the radio that a woman in Virginia named Lorena Bobbit cut off her husband's penis, saying she'd done it because he'd repeatedly raped and beaten her during their marriage. Needless to say, she's the one in deep doo-doo today, not him.

Men across the country have apparently gone into collective shock over this one. They're not as accustomed to being mutilated as women are. Poor babies.

As I've thought about Lorena's "crime" since then, it has occurred to me that I may have been released so quickly for The Crucifier killings because serial killers are usually white males. Hard, irrefutable, without-a-shadow-of-a-doubt evidence is needed for crimes perpetrated by them. But a woman like Lorena—who endures abuse over a long period of time, denying her reality, trying to keep the relationship intact—when she finally lashes out in desperation, she's automatically pegged a danger to society. Case closed. Throw away the key.

Now that I've shot a man in the back, I know I'm in the same boat. That disgusts me. I mean, running like this for killing sixteen people is one thing. But to be on the lam because I killed someone who was staging my accidental death....

While I was in jail that week or so, I spent a lot of time pacing in front of the bars like a caged lioness, wishing I'd disappeared when I'd had the chance. I think that's why the automatic reflex to run kicked in after I shot Richard. I didn't think about what I was doing. I just went.

I'm thinking about it now, though. And that scares me some, especially since I keep thinking about how I didn't choose this. I just ran because I had to, like the sun shines in the sky because it has to. Like I kept silent about him all my life. Because I had to.

Now I find myself wondering what I've gained by killing Richard if I've just traded the threat of a hit man for the threat of a SWAT team. Ah, so that's what I'm afraid of: nothing. How like me.

I remember how I felt in the moments just after killing Richard. I need a descriptor so much more encompassing than "free" to contain that sense of release. Let a genie out of its bottle, let astronauts break free from earth's gravity, let a newborn eagle peck through its shell, let bats out of hell, and mix well. That's what I remember feeling. Yes, I remember....

I guess that's why I want to go back. To jail? Not particularly. But I want to go back to that feeling.

I keep seeing Mom's painting in my mind. The one of the woman with the prison bars in the background. That's the prison I've lived in all my life. The one in the background. The one you have to look really close to see. Going back may be my ticket out of that dungeon, may be my last chance to be free.

If I were merely trading one prison for another, I don't think I'd bother. The thing is, every time I take away the prison bars in the background, something happens to that painting in my mind. The chains in the hair, the anguish in the smile, the deep pits in the eyes, the specter of death in the shadows—they all just slip away. Nothing remains but the radiance of that woman's face. Even when I slam bars in front of her face, the radiance remains. The difference between the face of death and the face of life....

I'm going back.

As The Crucifier, as the one who shot Richard in self-defense, as Winston J. Fleming III's abused daughter—I'm going back. It doesn't matter what happens to me there. The important things have already been settled. Inside.

He's dead. I'm not.

## About the Author

The author lives in Louisville, Kentucky. She once owned a pellet pistol, but she never killed anyone with it. Hovever, she did ace a marksmanship class in college and can at times be found in video arcades pumping quarters into shoot-em-up games.

# WATCH FOR THESE NEW COMMONWEALTH BOOKS

|  | ISBN # | U.S. | Can |
|---|---|---|---|
| ❏ **RIBBONS AND ROSES,** D.B. Taylor | 1-55197-088-0 | $4.99 | $6.99 |
| ❏ **PRISON DREAMS,** John O. Powers | 1-55197-039-2 | $4.99 | $6.99 |
| ❏ **A VOW OF CHASTITY,** Marcia Jean Greenshields | 1-55197-106-2 | $4.99 | $6.99 |
| ❏ **LAVENDER'S BLUE,** Janet Tyers | 1-55197-058-9 | $4.99 | $6.99 |
| ❏ **HINTS AND ALLEGATIONS,** Kimberly A. Dascenzo | 1-55197-073-2 | $4.99 | $6.99 |
| ❏ **BROKEN BRIDGES,** Elizabeth Gorlay | 1-55197-119-4 | $4.99 | $6.99 |
| ❏ **PAINTING THE WHITE HOUSE,** Hal Marcovitz | 1-55197-095-3 | $4.99 | $6.99 |
| ❏ **THE KISS OF JUDAS,** J.R. Thompson | 1-55197-045-7 | $4.99 | $6.99 |
| ❏ **BALLARD'S WAR,** Tom Holzel | 1-55197-112-7 | $4.99 | $6.99 |
| ❏ **ROSES FOR SARAH,** Anne Philips | 1-55197-125-9 | $4.99 | $6.99 |
| ❏ **THE TASKMASTER,** Mary F. Murchison | 1-55197-113-5 | $4.99 | $6.99 |
| ❏ **SECOND TIME,** Thomas E. Sprain | 1-55197-135-6 | $4.99 | $6.99 |
| ❏ **MY BROTHER'S TOWN,** B.A. Stuart | 1-55197-138-0 | $4.99 | $6.99 |
| ❏ **MISSING PIECES,** Carole W. Holden | 1-55197-172-0 | $4.99 | $6.99 |
| ❏ **DIARY OF A GHOST,** Alice Richards Laule | 1-55197-132-1 | $4.99 | $6.99 |

*Available at your local bookstore or use this page to order.*

Send to:    COMMONWEALTH PUBLICATIONS INC.
9764 - 45th Avenue
Edmonton, Alberta, CANADA  T6E 5C5

Please send me the items I have checked above. I am enclosing $_____ (please add $2.50 per book to cover postage and handling). Send check or money order, no cash or C.O.D.'s, please.

Mr./Mrs./Ms._____

Address_____

City/State_____ Zip_____

*Please allow four to six weeks for delivery.*
*Prices and availability subject to change without notice.*

Annie has been vowing to kill her abusive father for years. This year's different. He's already dead. Now, more than ever, she's determined to go through with her murderous plans. If only she can decide who to kill.

# Our Little Secret

*by*
Edwina Dae